Because We Love

A Novel of Faith and Hope

And now faith, hope and love abide,
These three,
And the greatest of these is love.

1 Corinthians 13:13

Because We Love

A Novel of Faith and Hope

BY CAMALA HAYES

Published by Camala Hayes, Calgary, Canada

ISBN 0-978-1-77354-190-7 Print
         0-978-1-77354-191-4 eBook

For Mike,
My one-in-a-million man.

Introduction

This novel is a story about the power of love—between a woman and a man, between friends, between child and parent, between God and humanity.

It is also my response to the practices of ISIS, the Taliban, Al Qaida, Boka Haram and similar political systems as reported in the media. Although "*Because We Love*" is a work of fiction, I have put nothing in this book that has not actually happened under the above radical groups in the past or present time.

The descriptions of Christian spiritual experiences in this novel are based on the author's own experiences.

The description of what has come to be known as "The Man in White" is based on many Muslims' personal accounts.

Camala Hayes,
B.A., M.A. (Psychology and Philosophy of World Religions)
M.Div. (Master of Divinity)
www.camalakhayes.ca

CHAPTER ONE

Aishah

Palm Springs, California
In a Future Time

Aishah followed obediently behind her husband, keeping her head slightly bowed. Shrouded in black from head to toe, her small figure stood out in sharp relief against the high sun-bleached walls concealing the houses beyond. She raised her head for only a moment, and through the narrow slit above her veil her wide brown eyes scanned the sidewalk ahead. Tangles of red, orange and purple bougainvillea escaped over garden walls and cascaded wildly downward, as if defying the sombre religious laws which ruled her life. Forbidden female flesh flashed for only an instant as Aishah's hand darted from her long sleeve to capture a bright blossom.

Behind her veil, she smiled. And then her smile faded.

I've got to tell him. I can't put it off any longer. I've got to tell him this morning or it will be too late. As soon as we get there, I'll tell him.

Even though it was just past dawn, the air was warm. They had walked only a few blocks but already Aishah felt drops of sweat trickling down between her breasts. She picked her way around the debris which littered the sidewalk so often now. "Hard times", the government said. She knew better. Too many people had fled the country. Too many deserted houses lying behind those garden walls. Too few taxpayers left to pay for city upkeep. Among other things, this meant that fallen palm branches, rusted cans, paper cups—anything deposited during last month's sand storm would remain for days to come.

Was the treasure still there, then? Yes. She saw it again. Still trapped in the gutter, half-buried by sugar-sand. It had been there yesterday and the day before. A book—its cover missing and its pages yellowed by wind and sun. Aishah could not tell what kind of book it was. She had a sudden image of long ago. A childhood time. A time before books were banned. Her father, calling her into their back yard. *Look what I have for you.* She could see the scene clearly. A barrel of books. *From a garage sale. Only five dollars. They're yours.* Pure joy.

Aishah blinked back tears. She was getting nearer now. Her steps slowed. If she didn't risk taking the book, maybe someone else would. She glanced quickly up and down the street. In one fluid motion, she stooped as if to tie an errant shoelace, scooping the small book into her long sleeve to join the bougainvillea blossom. Carefully, she looked around again. Still no one in sight. *Good.*

She quickened her pace slightly to catch up to her husband as she heard the sound of a vehicle approaching from behind. Not daring to look back, Aishah held her breath as the morality squad's familiar black jeep slowed to a crawl beside them. Four scraggly-faced youth, struggling to grow the beards required by the government, peered at the couple. Aishah exhaled sharply when the jeep picked up speed and continued down the street.

At the end of the block the couple reached their destination. The sign on the building read, "Palm Springs Desert Delights"— their bistro. They made their way to the alley at the back. Aishah waited quietly as her husband unlocked the door and entered. Following him into the kitchen of the restaurant, she slammed the door behind her. Scarcely before the sound had abated, Aishah's head covering, veil and abaya lay in an untidy heap in the middle of the black and white tiled floor. She kicked at the pile.

"Mohammed Haddad," she chided, "You want to lose weight? Never mind the sauna. Try living in that thing." Freed from the constraints of her hijab, her long dark hair tumbled in an unruly mass, moist tendrils curling around her face.

Above his shaggy beard her husband's brown eyes smiled down at her. He traced his fingers along her damp forehead.

"But you are so fetching when you sweat."

"Oh, you!" she laughed, pushing him toward the bags of flour waiting to be turned into what Aishah called *Mo's delights*. "We've got no time for that now. I find you fetching, too. So go fetch me some flour and let's make some delights."

"Let's." Mo gathered her into his arms. "Do you know when you take off your abaya you remind me of a brightly coloured butterfly emerging from a dark cocoon?"

Aishah glanced down at her working attire. A lemon yellow peasant top over purple tights did little to hide the curves she considered a bit excessive for her five foot frame. At least she told everyone she was five feet tall. No harm in adding another inch, she reasoned to herself.

Standing on tiptoe to meet Mo's eyes, she whispered, "I am happy to be your butterfly, but right now we need to get to work."

Mo patted her well-rounded bottom. As he did every day, he retrieved her abaya from the middle of the floor. The book fell out, landing with a slight smack. The scarlet blossom floated down to rest softly on top of it.

"Oh, Aishah," he sighed. "Now what have you done?"

"It's just a book, that's all. I noticed it a few days ago. It's been lying in the gutter, almost buried in sand. Today I just couldn't resist. No one saw me take it. It's okay, Mo."

"It's not okay, and you know it. We are not allowed books." He picked up the small paperback. "What kind of book is it, anyway? Not that it matters." He turned the first page.

Aishah reached up, snatching the slim volume from his hand. "It's just a pocket book. I don't know what it's about. See? The cover is missing. Just something to read. I don't care what it is, really. I just need to read something again. It's been so long." She paused, flipping through the pages. "Oh, it looks like a romance." The word "Christmas" caught her eye. She snapped the book shut. "I'll just take it home. No one will ever know. I've got it now, so I may as well keep it, right?"

Mo remained silent, his eyes unsmiling.

"Mo, I may as well keep it. I already picked it up and brought it here. I haven't read a book in years. What harm can there possibly be in reading this little book? Please."

He sighed. "I never can refuse you anything, you know that. But I don't want you to get into trouble. The morality squad might consider this worth a whipping. Are you sure you want to take that chance?"

Aishah's hand went to the small scar above her left eyebrow. "I'm sure. You don't know what this means to me."

He gazed steadily at her.

"Besides, no one is ever going to find out. I'll hide it at home." Aishah made an effort to keep her voice light. "Thanks, sweetheart." She stood on tiptoe to kiss him again, giving his beard a gentle tug. She stuffed the book in the pocket of her abaya as she hung it on the hook at the back door. "Let's wash up."

Together they began the day's work. They had done this so often, rising before dawn for morning prayers, walking to their bistro, standing side by side at the kitchen sink as they washed their hands, Mo trying to avoid the gobs of suds Aishah always flung at his bushy beard. Still laughing, they would begin the day's baking. It was a team effort, requiring no instructions from the other. Mixing machines hummed smoothly as they prepared various cookies, muffins and cakes.

Aishah liked to chop the dried fruit and nuts by hand.

"My therapy," she had once explained to Mo. "Since I am no good at punching dough and sometimes I'd like to punch something."

"Not me, I hope." Mo laughed and jumped out of range.

"Of course not, silly. Especially not you. You are the one who keeps me sane in this crazy system."

Mo once said he could read Aishah's mood by how she handled the cutting knife: erratic whacks meant she was angry, regular-spaced whacks meant she was thinking seriously about something.

This morning, her knife whacked rhythmically, producing piles of chopped dates, raisins and nuts, as she silently rehearsed the words she planned to say to Mo.

When everything had been diced and added to the dough, the baking trays were slid into the ovens. The aroma of cinnamon, nutmeg and cloves filled the kitchen and a comfortable silence descended on the couple as they sat at the small table, sipping their first cup of coffee and keeping an eye on their baking.

Aishah smiled at Mo. *Now is a good time to tell him. I'll tell him now.*

Just then the timer for the cookies sounded. And then the muffins and then the date loaves. And then everything had to be stacked onto the bistro trolleys. An hour passed before they could sit down again.

As Aishah placed a hot muffin on Mo's plate, she marvelled aloud, "Look how high they've risen. It's like magic."

"It is," Mo agreed. "Like the dough is alive or something."

Aishah swallowed hard. She had been rehearsing her next words for the past two days and she didn't want to make any mistakes.

"Mo, I don't know where to begin, but that's what I want to talk to you about."

"About what? You want to talk to me about muffins?"

"No, about life. You said it was like they were alive, watching the muffins rise like that."

"Oh, that. Okay. Life. Let's talk about life." Mo spoke past a mouth full of muffin. "Go ahead. What do you have to say about life? That's a big topic. You talk, I'll eat."

"Good. This is serious. Please don't interrupt until I'm finished. Just hear me out." She took a deep breath and began. "I know you are disappointed in me—"

"I'm not disappoint—" Mo began.

"No, don't interrupt. I know you are disappointed in me. Almost twenty years of marriage and still Allah has not blessed me with a child. Any other man would have divorced me by now, or married more wives. But you didn't do that."

"Because I love—" Mo interrupted again.

"Hush," she said gently. "I know. I remember on our wedding day, just after the new government took control. I hadn't realized what it meant. I was shocked when I saw that I had to sign the marriage papers as wife number one…" Aishah paused as she felt her throat begin to tighten. She took a sip of her coffee and cleared her throat. "I will never forget how you took the pen from my hand and crossed out the spaces for a second, third, and fourth wife. I knew then how much you loved me."

"I still do. Even more than I did on that day."

"But, Mo, maybe it is possible that Allah is displeased with us. We haven't followed the law perfectly. Maybe that's why we have no children. We haven't kept the law."

"Aishah, we've done our best. We have no children because of physical problems, not because we're doing something displeasing to Allah."

"But people are talking, Mo. I overhear them in the bistro while I'm waiting on tables. Some of the women are saying maybe they shouldn't come here. Allah is not blessing us with a baby, so something must be wrong, they think. But then others say, yes, but look how they leave food out for the hungry every night. Look how faithfully Mo attends prayers at the mosque." Aishah spoke rapidly. "But then someone else pipes up with the fact that you never report anyone to the morality squad. They say if you are a faithful follower of the Prophet (peace be upon him) you would have accused someone of something in all these years."

"Well, how do they know I've seen anything I should report? They just like to gossip, honey. Ignore them."

"And the discussion always ends with the fact that you have taken only one wife—so surely Allah is displeased. And that's why we don't have a child." Tears coursed down Aishah's cheeks. "That's what they are saying."

Mo sat back stiffly in his chair. "You aren't suggesting I take another wife, are you? I just can't do that."

"No… but Allah has provided a way for us. I truly believe He has heard our prayers and has provided an answer." Aishah swiped at her wet cheeks with the back of her hand. "Yesterday while I was waiting on tables in the women's section a woman asked if she could speak privately with me. I'd never seen her before, so I thought she was probably just another person looking for food. I said 'okay' and I talked with her in the back store room."

Mo leaned forward. "And?"

"And as soon as I closed the door, the woman told me…" Aishah's voice trailed off.

"Told you what?"

"That she and her husband are Christians. Secretly, of course."

Mo jerked back. "What? There was a Christian in your bistro? And you spoke with her? That could mean big trouble for us."

"Well, how was I to know? She was wearing a veil like all the other women, so I didn't know at first." Aishah hurried on. "Which makes me wonder, how are we supposed to tell the infidels from the rest of us if we all dress the same?"

Mo ignored her question. "We can't get involved—"

Aishah raised her hand. "No, just hear me out."

Mo sighed and settled back into his chair.

"Anyway, to make a long story short, she and her husband have come under suspicion. He was arrested, and now he's disappeared—so you know what that means—and she expects to be arrested in the next couple of months. She says the morality squad is watching her every move, just waiting to find more witnesses against her. They took her travel permit away, so there's no way she can get out of the valley. She has no one to help her."

Mo's eyes never left Aishah's face. She swallowed hard as she continued. "Their crime is talking to people about Jesus. Her husband has probably already been executed and if she is arrested, she will be executed, too. Or she will just disappear as so many others have and be buried somewhere out in the desert. I know we cannot save her—"

"No, we cannot." Mo's voice was firm.

"I know we cannot save her," Aishah repeated, speaking more slowly. "But here's the thing. She is pregnant, expecting in a few months. She asks, will we take the child when it is born?" Aishah saw Mo's eyes widen. She felt her face flush as she rushed on. "She says we can raise it in our faith. She says she trusts her God in this. Can you believe it? She is convinced her God wants her to give the child to us. A child for us, Mo!"

As Aishah's words tumbled out, Mo sat motionless, his lips pressed into a thin line.

"I said we will have to seek Allah's will. She said we can take a few days to think it over, but time is short. If we won't take the baby, she'll look for someone else. She says I will need to pretend to be pregnant so the baby comes as no surprise to anyone when I get it."

"That's crazy, Aishah. And you know it." Aishah heard the note of finality in Mo's voice. It was the response she had dreaded, but she had expected it and continued on with the words she had rehearsed.

"Mo, I lay awake all last night praying about this."

"Surely you're not seriously considering such a wild idea! My answer is, no. Not that you've asked me," he added.

"I'm asking you now," Aishah persisted. "We wouldn't need to lie to people. If they say it looks like you are expecting a baby, we can say, yes, we are expecting a baby to arrive. Allah be praised. After all these years Allah has blessed us. If they ask me why we didn't say something sooner, I can just remind them of the many times I have miscarried and that I didn't want to say anything until my pregnancy was well on the way."

"Do you really think they are going to believe that?"

"Sure." Aishah raced on. "And then we'll all celebrate the news. Praise Allah—and hand out free donuts, or something. What do you think would be appropriate for the celebration?"

Mo stood up. His face was red. "There will be no celebration because we are not going to do this."

Aishah bit her lip to stop the tears from coming. *Keep calm, keep calm. This is no time to lose control.*

Mo paced the floor of the kitchen. "As usual, you are getting carried away with a hare-brained idea. This is unbelievable. What do you think we are getting ourselves in for? We can't jump into something like this. Definitely not. You know the risks. If we were found out, we would be the next to die. We've adjusted to how things are for us. We have each other. We've carved out a good life in spite of the new government and all their laws. That should be enough for you. We are happy together just the way we are."

"Mo, I am not happy." Aishah fought unsuccessfully to hold back her tears. "It's not your fault. I love you very much, but I need a child. I have prayed every day of our married life—for almost twenty years—every day, that Allah would bless us with a child. Each time I got pregnant I begged Allah that this time I would be able to carry the baby to term. And every time, my prayer went unanswered. You don't know what that was like for me, Mo. A piece of me died each time."

Aishah struggled to keep the memories from flooding back. "I cry when you are asleep at night. And then I get angry." She saw Mo's disapproving look. "I know, I know, I shouldn't question Allah's will, but I do. I am desperate, Mo. I've even considered praying to the Christian God, to Jesus."

Aishah took a step backward as Mo shouted at her, "Don't ever speak that name again. Do you hear me? Christians believe in more than one God—that's shirk—unforgivable sin. You know that, Aishah. Don't ever say that name again."

Staring into Mo's angry face, Aishah recalled that only a few nights ago she had actually begun her desperate prayer with the words, *"Whoever is up there…"* She knew she could never tell Mo that. Instead, she said, "I'm just trying to tell you how badly I want a child. Well, now we have an opportunity to get one. Who's to say it is not Allah's will?"

Mo was calmer now. "You know a baby would change our lives, sweetheart. How could you continue working dawn till dark with a baby? You know we don't have any extra money to hire help. We barely make ends meet now, and if we—"

"Babies are no trouble, Mo, they just eat and sleep."

"Eat and sleep?" A look of amazement crossed his face. "You haven't been around babies much, have you? I come from a big family and let me tell you, babies are a lot of work."

"But ours won't be. I know it won't. Allah will see to that. I see this baby as a gift from Allah, Mo. I want to take it. I want to save a life. Don't you want to save a life?" Aishah struggled to speak slowly. "You know the patrol will kill the baby with the mother. Probably a public execution, just to make an example of it. I hear they kill the baby first, in front of the mother. I can't let that happen. You can't let that happen."

Aishah's eyes pleaded with Mo as she waited for him to speak.

"But Aishah," he finally said, "What if the morality squad finds out that we didn't report the infidel, and worse than that, we have taken an infidel's baby as our own? Are you willing to risk our lives for this baby? They will kill us, too. That is the law. I have never gone against the law. Sure, I didn't take more wives, but that was still a legal option especially with my small income. I don't report people to the morality squad, but Aishah, I keep the laws, at least as best as I can. We simply cannot do this."

"But," Aishah drew a ragged breath, "Surely you cannot believe Allah would have a tiny baby killed?"

"It is an infidel's baby and so it is an infidel," Mo replied.

"The Koran says we are not to take an innocent life," argued Aishah, surprised that she could draw that piece of information from her scanty knowledge of the Koran.

Mo looked surprised, too. Taking Aishah's small hand in his, he said softly, " The Unity government enforces the law now, and they follow the example of terrorist groups in other countries. We have to go along with Unity's decisions, honey."

Aishah could control her anger no longer. "Don't you "*honey*" me in that condescending tone! We don't have to go along with their decisions! Will you go to the public beheading then? Will you go to see a baby torn apart in front of its mother?" she shouted, tears streaming unheeded down her cheeks.

"You know I couldn't do that."

"Why not?" Aishah choked out her words. "It is the law. If you don't go, people will notice. They'll be watching to see who is there."

"Sweetheart," her husband spoke gently as he gathered her into his arms. "Calm down. We need to open up the cafe now." He paused, looking at her tear-stained face. "Look, I will think about this, okay?"

His question was met with Aishah's loud sobs.

"Okay, sweetheart?" he asked again. "I can't believe I am saying this, but I promise you I will definitely think about it."

"Don't just think about it, you pray!" Aishah hiccupped as she always did when she had a crying jag.

"I'll pray, of course. I promise. Just give me a few days to let this all sink in. I don't see how you can even consider this."

"Two days, Mo. We need to decide soon."

He nodded. "Okay. Two days. I can't say the answer will be yes, but I won't say no right now. Okay? It's time to open up the cafe. We can talk more tonight after closing. Dry your tears." He ran his hand gently over Aishah's red cheeks. "I know you don't need to wear your veil in the women's section, but maybe you should put it on today."

Aishah hiccupped and sniffed for a few minutes before finally responding.

"Okay," she said, taking her street garments from the hook at the back door. "I've never been one of those women who look pretty when they cry. My nose runs and my eyes swell up." A sudden thought came to her. She turned to face Mo. "Don't you dare ask the imam's advice on this."

"Of course not," Mo said. "Although I'd like to—but I know I can't. This is something we have to decide for ourselves—figure it out for ourselves. I'm not saying I will agree to take the baby. I would definitely need to know this is Allah's will. We'll be breaking the law."

"But we will be saving a life, isn't that more important?" Aishah fastened her veil over her face. She waited for an answer. "Isn't it?"

Mo sighed.

Aishah looked into her husband's eyes. With a sinking feeling she realized what his decision would be. *He's not going to agree.* Turning away to avoid their usual kiss, she backed through the kitchen's swinging doors, pulling the cart piled high with still-warm baking.

"See you at closing time," she managed to whisper past the lump in her throat.

CHAPTER TWO

Aishah

Once inside the women's section of the bistro, Aishah paused for a moment as her eyes adjusted to the darkness. She remembered the day she and Mo had hung the thick black drapery covering the entire wall of floor-to-ceiling windows.

"It's a shame we have to do this," Mo had said, as they stood back to admire their efforts.

"I agree," she replied. "No one likes sunlight more than I do. But I want the women to have a place where they are free to remove their veils—so we have to make sure that no one can see in from the street. This is the best we can do for now. Maybe when we get some extra money we can install nice blinds."

There never was any extra money, but no one seemed to mind the black curtains. The women—Aishah called them *my women*— soon felt comfortable removing their veils in the all-female setting protected from any outsiders' gaze. She told Mo it was easy to spot the newcomers.

"They always leave their outside clothes on at first. But after a couple of visits they hang their abayas and veils at the front entrance like everyone else. I love to see them in their *at home* clothes, laughing and talking with each other." Aishah had heard that many people called her section of the Desert Delights Bistro simply, "The Women's Place".

"That makes me really happy," she told Mo.

"It makes me happy, too," he had replied. "Good for you, Aishah. You've worked hard to make a place for them."

Now, as she remembered how Mo had encouraged her, she smiled. She was about to turn on the rows of ceiling lights when she noticed that a ray of sunlight had somehow found its way into the bistro. One brilliant shaft pierced the darkness. Reaching across the width of the floor, it bounced gaily off the polished black and white tiles, landed on a row of sparkling glass tabletops, and didn't stop until it hit the opposite wall.

"We can't have that." Aishah followed the path of light to its source. The heavy curtains had been pushed aside by a customer's chair the previous day. She moved the chair and straightened the offending curtain. Immediately the bistro was plunged into darkness once more. Aishah's legs suddenly buckled beneath her.

"Oh, no. Not again." She spoke out loud as she plunked down on the closest chair. She felt the familiar light-headedness and the heavy thump of her heart in her chest. She never knew what triggered what she described to Mo as her "waking nightmares." They didn't come as often as they used to. Still, they came. At unexpected times. Like now.

"Post-traumatic stress disorder," someone had once whispered to her. "Lots of us have it."

Aishah's mind went back to what she talked about only in whispers—and only to Mo—the time before the takeover. Before veils, before public executions, before books were banned. Before so many laws.

Everyone had been familiar with the terms "ISIS" or "Taliban" or "al Qaeda". On their television screens they had witnessed what life was like in places taken over by those political systems. Still, that was far away. It was happening to other people. It could never happen here.

But it had.

After years of political turmoil, followed by a global pandemic, a majority of Americans had voted for a President and a new third party called simply: "Unity." The new government promised to heal the country's divisions and bring back the political and economic stability everyone longed for. At first everything seemed okay. Then it all fell apart.

The President was assassinated. The Vice President fired all high-ranking officials in every department, replacing them with people no one had ever heard of. On every street corner, in every coffee shop and around every dining room table one question dominated the conversation: *Where did these people come from?*

When the Constitution was abolished, the truth was revealed: The entire project had been planned for years by an over-seas terrorist group whose roots could be traced back to ISIS and other foreign entities. All Americans took comfort in knowing that the take-over had come from outside, and not from within. But it was cold comfort, because by then it was too late.

America reeled in the ensuing bloodbath as all resistance was brutally put down. In the end, a black flag flew over the land.

Two decades had now passed. A whole generation had reached adulthood never knowing any other way of life, but all those over the age of twenty remembered only too well what it was like before the Unity Party seized power. For Aishah, it seemed like it had happened only yesterday. No matter how hard she tried, she could not erase the images from those early years: public beheadings at football stadiums—amputations of hands or feet—televised coverage of the violence used to discourage anyone from resisting the new laws. And then, suddenly no television at all. Or newspapers. Or radio. Or internet. Even cell phone reception was sketchy. Some said all conversations were being secretly recorded. In hushed tones people discussed reports that millions of Americans had simply disappeared. Had they escaped to freedom in Mexico or Canada, or were they dead—buried in mass graves somewhere in the desert?

Rumours flourished. But nobody knew.

"We never will know," Aishah whispered into the darkness of the empty bistro. She tried to force her thoughts back to the present, but she couldn't stop her mind from racing.

Mo said we would be okay. And then we found out even we were not safe. Not the right kind of Muslim, they said. Not observant enough. We lost so many good people, even our imam. She shook her head, as if to dispel her unpleasant thoughts. *Mo says it's no good thinking about it now. It's over and done.*

She rose from her chair. She punched the light switches in rapid order, blinking as the bistro was flooded with light. She filled the glass display case with stacks of muffins and cookies. She readied the coffee makers. Then, zig-zagging her way around the tables to the front entrance, she unlocked the door, flipping the sign from "Closed" to "Open". Pausing to look at the rows of brass hooks waiting for the women's abayas and veils, she hesitated. Then she removed her veil and head covering and hung them on one of the hooks.

I've seen them when they've been crying. It's only fair they see me. I'll tell them I'm having my moody time of the month. Or just a bad day. They won't ask for a reason.

She made her way to the back of the bistro. She studied the assortment of vividly-coloured aprons hanging behind the counter and chose her favourite: a wild geometric pattern of turquoise, orange and green. She tied it snugly around her waist, then decided to loosen it. *I should start making it baggy, just in case.* She poured herself a cup of coffee and sat by the back counter to wait for her first customer. She was glad when the silence was broken by the sound of the front door opening and two women talking excitedly to each other. No more time to dwell on the past.

Aishah called out the mandatory greeting: "Peace be upon you."

The women answered, "And upon you, peace."

Aishah joined them at the front entrance. "Let me help you hang up your things."

Although it was a busy day at the bistro, time passed slowly for Aishah. She couldn't get the image of Mo's angry face out of her mind. Several times she had to apologize when she made mistakes—pouring coffee instead of tea and bringing muffins to the wrong table.

He's going to say "no", I'm sure of it. But maybe not, if I pray hard. How am I going to stand two days of not knowing?

She forced back her tears, hoping the women wouldn't notice. But they did, always asking if they could do anything to help. When she said she was just having a blue day, they said they understood—they had days like that, too. Finally it was four-thirty and the door closed behind the last lingering customer.

Aishah began her closing time chores, mopping the tiled floor, polishing the glass tables. As she re-arranged the chairs for the fourth time, she realized she was stalling. *I'm not ready to face Mo just yet.*

She glanced at the row of coffee cups on the back wall—large mismatched mugs of brilliant yellow, purple, lime green and orange. She smiled as she remembered the look on Mo's face when he had watched her unpacking those mugs the day before they had opened the women's section.

"I'm trying to make up for the lack of colour in their lives," she had explained.

"Wow!" was his only comment.

He's always been so good about everything. He's always encouraged me, even though he probably thought some of my ideas were crazy.

She stood behind the back counter, surveying the empty and now immaculate bistro: the round glass tables, each with its own small bouquet of bright blossoms, the intricately patterned white wrought iron chairs with the red cushions.

Aishah still found it hard to believe the women's bistro belonged to her. She had never imagined she would own anything.

She remembered every detail of the day they discovered the cafe. They had driven from L.A. to Palm Springs for a weekend get-away, and there it was—sitting abandoned on what had once been a busy corner of downtown Palm Springs—a faded "For Sale" sign hanging crookedly on the front door. Aishah said she just knew it was meant for them.

"You could run your own place, Mo, instead of working at your Dad's restaurants."

"I don't just work in one of my Dad's restaurants, Aishah. You know that. I'm the manager of the largest one."

"Yeah, I know. But we could live in our own home, instead of living with your parents." Aishah had been saying those same words to Mo for eight years.

They picked up the keys from the real estate office. When they reached the bistro, Mo sneezed as soon as he stepped through the front door. Years of dust had settled on the tables and chairs strewn haphazardly across the spacious dining room.

Aishah frowned. "It looks like the owners left in a hurry. You know what that means."

Neither of them spoke as they made their way through the clutter to the kitchen in the back.

Mo's eyes lit up when he saw the wall of ovens. He began opening cupboard doors. "Everything we need is here. See, honey—even the mixers and bowls—everything. It's not the latest, it's pretty old, but I could use this stuff." He looked at the grime in the sink and turned to Aishah. "It sure needs a lot of work, though."

"But we could do it together. We could do it, Mo. I know we could. You can do the repairs, I can clean and paint. There's space upstairs where we could live if we can't afford a house right away." Her face glowed. "And it would be just you and me, together. Just you and me, at last. We've scrimped and saved for years. Let's go see the realtor. I'll bet you can make a deal."

They were surprised when their offer was accepted.

"Guess things are getting worse," Mo said as they drove away from the real estate office.

"Remember when Palm Springs was such a busy place, with the tourists and music festivals and everything? My parents brought me here a few times when I was little." Aishah turned to gaze out the car window as they passed a golf course now grown over with wild desert shrubs and weeds.

"Well, at least at these prices we'll be able to find a house we can afford."

They had driven out of the city in silence. Once on the highway, Aishah told Mo of her dream of running a cafe just for women.

"A private place. Where they don't need to wear their veils—unless they want to," she added. "You men get together for coffee and just to talk. But we women have only our families and our walled yards. Even at your folks' big house, Mo, I feel caged in. Women need to get out of the house and see other people."

Mo nodded. "Yeah, I know *you* do, honey."

Encouraged, Aishah spoke more rapidly. "Let me have half of the cafe for women only. It's too large for just one bistro, anyway. I could take those glass tables that were probably used on the sidewalk patio. And the fancy chairs. They're too feminine for you guys. We could build a wall down the middle to separate the women's part from the men's and no one will even know we are there. I'll work really hard. And any profit will be yours, of course. Just let me use part of the cafe."

Aishah had never forgotten Mo's next words: "I can do better than that, sweetheart. I'll put your name on the title as owner along with me. We are a team, you and I. All that I have is yours, too."

The memory brought tears to Aishah's eyes. "He gave everything up for me. Because he loves me." Her words echoed in the empty bistro. "Living in that big house by the ocean—managing a high-end restaurant—being close to his family and friends." She blinked back her tears. "And now… and now this is how I am treating him."

She jumped from her chair and pushed open the kitchen door. Mo's back was to her as he stood at the sink. He had rolled up his sleeves and begun rinsing the day's dirty dishes. Aishah felt the same warm rush of affection she always did when she saw him. She ran to him.

"Mo, I'm sorry I'm so much trouble. Let's not talk about it anymore today. If you say you will be praying to know Allah's will, then I believe you. Let's just leave it there for now."

Soapy water dripped down to his elbows as Mo turned to gather her into his arms. "Okay, honey. I'm glad you trust me in this. I know it is hard for you. You're right. Let's give it a rest for now."

"Well, maybe just one more thing..." Aishah spoke into his chest. "Remember the time I told you that I felt guilty we didn't try to help anyone when the Unity Party first took over? Remember what you said? You said that what is past, is past. That all we can do is be kind to anyone who needs us right now. Well, maybe this is our chance to make up for not doing anything back then."

Mo was silent.

"I'm just saying..." Aishah whispered.

Mo smiled as he bent to kiss his wife.

CHAPTER THREE

Aishah

Although she knew it was forbidden, Aishah could barely keep from dancing as she walked behind Mo the next morning. Her sturdy black shoes, mandatory for all women, bounced across the pavement. The sidewalk was still littered with debris and the curb remained sifted full of sand, but even if there had been another book visible, Aishah would not have noticed. Her eyes sparkled, betraying the smile beneath her veil.

I can't believe it. A dream, Allah sent Mo a dream and it's all okay.

Mo had told her about it as soon as she woke that morning. After a restless night, she had trouble coming fully awake. She sat up in bed, her tousled hair tumbling down over her breasts. She always slept nude. "My Lady Godiva" Mo once called her.

"Your Lady who?" she had asked.

Mo told her the ancient story about the wife of an English Lord who made a deal with her husband that she would ride naked on horseback through the town of Canterbury if he would reduce taxes for the poor.

"Did she really do that?" Aishah asked.

"According to the legend, yes. She used her long hair to cover her breasts. Her husband kept his end of the bargain and the people had an easier life."

"We could use a woman like her around here," Aishah replied. "But women aren't even allowed to ride bikes now. A horse? And in the nude? Guess that won't be happening." They had laughed together.

This morning, though, Aishah could see Mo was serious. He looked confused, or perhaps bewildered, she decided, as she propped herself up on her pillows and prepared to listen to him.

"I was walking on a desert path with many other people," Mo began, "when I heard a child crying, off in the distance somewhere. No one else seemed to hear it. I had to make a decision on whether to leave the group to find the child, or stay with the group and ignore the crying. I agonized over the decision and the baby's crying kept following me. It was like a nightmare, Aishah. Finally I decided to leave the group. I found a baby laying under the shade of a bush and beside the bush a spring of water gurgled out of the ground. I held the baby and I dipped my fingers into the water and the baby sucked my fingers. It seemed to be hungry. I wondered what to do. And then I woke up."

Aishah held her breath. The meaning of the dream seemed clear to her. But would Mo interpret it as she did? She felt her chest tighten. "So… what do you think your dream means?" She struggled to keep her voice steady.

Mo said each word slowly: "I believe Allah wants us to take the baby and care for it."

Aishah could contain her joy no longer. She threw her arms around him. "Oh, sweetheart, thank you, thank you."

"Don't thank me. Thank Allah. I'd never have agreed to this without that dream."

"Thank you, Allah. Thank you," breathed Aishah. Then a sobering thought came to her. Leaning back, she looked up into

Mo's eyes. "It took me a couple of days to get up the courage to ask you and another day passed yesterday. The Christian woman hasn't returned. What if she doesn't come back? What if she found someone else who made up their mind right away? What if we missed our chance?"

"She'll be back. I'm certain of it. The dream means we were meant to have this baby. She'll be back. Don't worry."

But Aishah definitely *did* worry. Each day she watched for the woman to return to the café, and at the close of each day she had to report to Mo that she hadn't shown up. Again. After a week, Aishah was convinced the woman would not return.

But then, one afternoon, there she was—sitting alone at the same corner table as before. Even though her face was veiled, Aishah recognized the slender figure in the shabby black abaya. Aishah's heart thumped loudly in her ears as she approached the table. The woman looked up. Above her veil, her startling green eyes met Aishah's gaze.

"Meet me in the store room in five minutes," Aishah whispered as she bent down to place a brightly coloured mug of coffee in front of the stranger. The woman nodded almost imperceptibly.

When Aishah pushed open the storeroom door a few minutes later, the woman was already there. She was pacing what little space was available between the sacks of flour stacked against the walls. She stopped abruptly, turning to Aishah. "What have you decided?" Her voice trembled.

"We will take the baby." Aishah spoke softly, aware that anyone in the hallway to the restroom might hear their voices. She paused for a moment. "You are certain you want to give your baby to us? We will raise the child as a faithful Muslim. Do you understand that?" Aishah studied the woman's eyes, looking for any sign of disagreement.

"I do…" The stranger faltered, then continued in a steadier voice, "God will take care of things for us. I am sure of it. I have absolute trust in the Lord."

"Well, I wouldn't give my baby to a Christian couple to be raised as an infidel. It would be better if it were killed."

As soon as the words were out of her mouth, Aishah regretted saying them. *What are you doing? Don't say that! She might change her mind.*

The woman opened her mouth as if to say something, and then hesitated a moment before answering.

"That is your belief and your choice to believe that. I trust my Lord in this. Besides, you may feel differently once you hold this baby in your arms. I love this child already as it moves inside of me. Here…" She took Aishah's hands in hers, placing them on either side of her rounded belly. "Feel life. This is the life you will care for."

Aishah's eyes widened as she felt the woman's abdomen ripple with sporadic movements. Then she felt a sudden thrust against her palm.

"Was that a kick?" she asked, forgetting to whisper.

"It was."

The two women stood close together, the stranger's slender hands cupping Aishah's hands, emerald eyes and brown eyes meeting in the shared wonder of unborn life. For several moments neither woman moved or spoke. Aishah's uncovered face registered her joy and surprise at the activity beneath her hands.

For the first time, the Christian woman removed her veil. Aishah was shocked to see how thin she was. Her skin seemed stretched over high cheek bones. Her face was colourless except for the dark circles under her unusual green eyes. A few dark curls had escaped from under her hijab—curls very similar to Aishah's own. The woman's eyes met Aishah's gaze.

An unbidden thought raced through Aishah's mind: *Are we so different?* Immediately another voice inside of her insisted, *But she is an infidel.*

The two women stood face to face, mere inches separating them. In that moment, it seemed to Aishah that an unspoken bond was formed between them—Muslim and infidel.

"I will love this baby more than my own life," Aishah said, as if taking a solemn vow.

"I know you will. Let me hug my baby's mother."

Before Aishah could resist, she was enveloped in a close embrace. Had she ever hugged another woman? She couldn't remember. And then a flash of memory—her mother's arms wrapped around her. Aishah's knees went weak. *So long ago. What had happened to her?* She inhaled sharply.

As if sensing her confusion, the stranger stepped back.

"We need to discuss the details," she said, moving to sit on the rickety wooden chair in the corner of the room. "I know you don't have much time to talk."

"Wait," interrupted Aishah. "I'd like to know your name."

"It's safer for you if I don't tell you. It's not important. What is important is that you know this baby is a child of love—my husband's and my love. We never planned to have this baby. I have prayed about it, trying to sort it all out, wondering where God is in all of this. As I have struggled, I have come to believe that God will bring good out of this. Somehow. Perhaps my baby can be a gift of love that I can leave for others—for you and Mo."

Aishah nodded. "It *is* a gift," she said softly. "I have miscarried five times and I have wanted a baby so badly. This baby will be a child of our love, too, my husband's and my love, I promise."

"I know that. That's the reason we chose you. We started asking around about a month ago, right after we discovered the "N" splashed in red paint on our garage door."

Before she could stop herself, Aishah gasped. Her eyes widened as she whispered the forbidden name: "Jesus of Nazareth. *The Nazarene.* The morality squad paints that on Christian houses."

The woman nodded. "We knew then that someone had found out we were Christians. We knew we didn't have much time to make a plan. But we wanted to save our unborn child—somehow. My husband started asking around and heard about you and Mo."

Aishah flinched.

"Oh, don't worry, we were very careful who we spoke to. My husband," she began, then paused for a moment as her eyes filled with tears. "My husband," she began again in a steadier voice, "visited the men's bistro—listened and watched—and asked a few questions. People said you leave baking outside the backdoor of the bistro each night. We learned your husband never took another wife. That was really important to us, if you were going to be the parents of our child."

"Mo says I am worth four wives and besides he can hardly handle me." Aishah giggled nervously, swiping at the tears of relief trickling down her cheeks. *She is going to give us the baby!*

There was an awkward pause, as the stranger remained silent. Aishah searched for something to say.

Finally, she said. "So now what? How are we going to work this out?"

"Well, first of all, you need to rig up some sort of padding that can grow with you in the next few months. You need a 'baby bump.' It needs to get larger gradually. Start wearing maternity clothes tomorrow. Or your abaya. It can hide anything."

Aishah made a face.

The woman smiled. "Well, whatever you want to wear, but make sure a little bump shows right away so everyone notices. I think I'm almost six months pregnant, so you only have three months or so until your due date."

"I'm not sure I can act like I'm pregnant," Aishah said.

"Just imitate the pregnant women around you here. There's plenty of them these days. You can do it. I know you can."

Aishah bit her bottom lip. "I don't know… This isn't going to be easy."

"I know that, but Mo will help you. Together you two can carry it off. In a way, you and Mo are like me and my husband were, a team that works together, in good times and in bad."

"You think we are like you?" Aishah was unable to hide her surprise.

"Sure you are. You are trusting Allah about taking this baby, aren't you? Well, I am trusting Jesus to arrange that the baby is born before I am arrested." Aishah heard the catch in the woman's voice. "Anyway," she said a few heartbeats later, "I've been staying in deserted houses and I have to move around a lot—so I don't know where I will be, but as soon as the baby is born I will send you a message."

"How?"

"Either a phone call or a note left under your door at home. Whichever I can manage at the time. I'll just say something like, 'Your parcel has arrived. Pick it up at two o'clock', or whatever."

"Where?"

"I need to give you the baby where no one can see us. I have prayed about where this might be. This is a sacred event for me. I would have preferred a church, but of course they've all been destroyed or converted into mosques. I've thought of a spot, though. There is only one Christian site that hasn't been altered at all. It would be perfect. If all goes well, I will give you my baby there."

"Where is that?" asked Aishah again. *Were there any Christian buildings left standing in Palm Springs?*

"I was thinking of The Date Farm. You know, the amusement park, with the rides and stuff that used to be there? The Christian part of it? There were statues and scenes that told the story of Jesus—"

"Those statues have all been smashed and the park is now just a playground for children," interrupted Aishah.

"I know. But the tomb is still there. Exactly the same as it was before. Nobody has destroyed it. I guess your people call it a cave now, but at one time it was the highlight of the faith walk."

"I thought the cross was your special thing," Aishah said, unable to hide her curiosity about the forbidden religion.

"Well, yes and no. The cross symbolizes God in Christ sacrificing His life for us, but the empty tomb reminds us of Jesus' resurrection."

Aishah noticed that although the woman's face was haggard, her eyes lit up as she talked. She found herself unable to look away from her gaze.

"Anyway," the woman continued, "We don't have time to talk about that right now. The point is that The Date Farm is now a place with lots of moms and kids milling around. The kids like to play hide and seek in the ruins, especially in the tomb. And the moms like to visit at the outdoor café—have a date shake with their friends and just keep an eye on the kids from there. It isn't strictly a women's café like your bistro. Men *could* come in. They seldom do. Still, it means the women have to keep their veils on, just in case—which is great for you and me because no one will be able to recognize us. It will be safe for us both to go there."

Aishah's mind raced. *What a place to* go! *The tomb! Can I do this?*

"I'm not sure I can— " she began.

"So I am thinking," the woman continued, "I can send you the message that the parcel has arrived. I'll tell you what time to meet me, but I won't have to tell you where, because I am telling you now that it will be the tomb at The Date Farm. That way you'd be safe if anyone intercepted the message somehow. They would just think it was a parcel you are picking up."

Aishah bit her bottom lip again, but said nothing.

"I will wait for you in the tomb with the baby. You come in and we will just exchange the baby. One thing about these veils and abayas, no one knows who we are or what we might be hiding. My husband says—said," she corrected herself, "that the women here carry their prisons around with them." For the first time Aishah caught a hint of bitterness in the woman's voice. "I may as well laugh as cry."

"I know the feeling," Aishah said softly.

"We will leave separately a few moments apart and no one will be the wiser. Just two more black-covered women strolling in the garden. I have made a list of things you will need."

She produced a crumpled scrap of paper from her pocket and handed it to Aishah. "I have no money to buy clothes and things for the baby. In fact, I am one of the people picking up the left-over baking you leave behind the restaurant every night."

Aishah tried to hide her shock as the reality of the woman's situation dawned on her. *No food… no place to live. That's why she's so thin and pale.*

She felt her face redden as she mumbled, "I'm so sorry. Mo and I feel awful about so many things, but there's nothing we can do, except leave out a bit of food."

"I know. I pray for all of you, and for the government."

Aishah was astonished. "You pray for them? Why would you do that? Most of you have been driven out or killed. After all they've done, you still pray for them?"

"Yes, because Jesus said we are to love our enemies and be kind to those who persecute us. God doesn't just love the Christians, Aishah. He loves you, too."

Aishah clapped her hands over her ears. "That's enough. I don't want to hear any more about your Jesus. It's against the law to talk about Him to us. And it's against the law for me to listen, so stop right now."

She expected the woman to keep talking, but to her surprise, she didn't. Instead, she sat silently with her head bowed.

Oh, no! Now she's praying!

The stranger looked up. "Okay," she said, rising from her chair and fastening her veil across her face once again. She opened the storeroom door and turned back to face Aishah.

"Never forget that God loves you, Aishah."

The door clicked shut behind her.

Aishah stood in the centre of the small room for a few more moments, staring at the wall in front of her. It had all happened too fast. *Why didn't I ask her more questions? Why didn't I offer to help her?* She couldn't get the image of the woman's green eyes out of her mind. *Those eyes held a light...*

Finally, shaking her head as if to waken herself from a trance, she left the store room.

Standing behind the back counter, she surveyed the crowded cafe. The soft sound of women's voices punctuated by occasional bursts of laughter filled her ears. Everything looked and sounded the same, but somehow Aishah felt different. Only a few moments had passed, but she felt somehow her world had shifted. She thought again of the glow in the Christian woman's eyes. *It's hope—that's what I saw. I saw hope in her eyes. And I feel like there is hope for me, too. I haven't felt like this in a long time.*

She glanced over at the table where the stranger had been seated. It was empty.

The afternoon limped along as Aishah waited on tables and tried to chat with the women in her usual carefree manner, but finally the front door closed behind the last two customers. Ignoring the messy tables and dirty coffee cups, Aishah rushed back to the kitchen to tell Mo the news. He looked tired, sprawled out on the old easy chair they had found at a flea market. Seeing him, Aishah suddenly realized how exhausted she was, also. She plunked down into her comfortable rocking chair.

It's bad enough we are on our feet all day—now we're awake all night, worrying about the baby. He's tired. This isn't a good time to tell him. Maybe I should wait.

Mo used his foot to push an empty wooden fruit crate over to Aishah.

"Here, put your feet up. You look tired."

Aishah gratefully accepted the makeshift footstool, basking in the spicy aroma of the morning's baking and the comforting quietness of the kitchen. She had been so eager to tell Mo her news, but now that the time had come, she didn't know how to begin.

After a few moments of silence, she suddenly blurted out, "She was here today."

"You mean…" Mo's voice trailed off.

Aishah nodded.

"And?"

"And I told her we would take the baby." Aishah rushed on with her account of the meeting. "I need to look pregnant, right now, well, tomorrow anyway. We're lucky I've been wearing baggy tops in this heat—and I need to look more pregnant as time goes on. About three months, she says, until the baby is born. So that's near the end of December. She says my stomach has to get bigger gradually, just like a real pregnancy."

"How're you going to make that happens?" Mo squinted his eyes the way he did when he was having trouble working out the cafe's monthly budget.

"She says we should make some kind of a cushion—or a 'baby bump' she called it. I figure you could rig up something and I could wear it like an apron under my abaya and we will enlarge it gradually over the next three months."

Aishah was not prepared for Mo's sudden outburst.

"That's insane, Aishah." He raised his voice. "Is she crazy? Are you crazy? We can't do this. Call the whole thing off."

I should have waited. He's tired, and worried and he's having second thoughts about it. In spite of his dream, he's scared. He probably didn't realize how complicated it would be. And I didn't, either.

"We can't call the whole thing off, Mo." She spoke softly, pushing her footstool away and leaning toward him. "This is just like getting pregnant, once it's done, it's done. No going back now. You promised me. And besides, I don't even know her name or where she lives. I only know where to meet her to get the baby when it is born."

"And where is that?"

Aishah swallowed hard. She knew Mo was not going to like her answer. Her voice shook as she said, "That old amusement park. You know—The Date Farm."

Mo jumped from his chair. He stood looking down at Aishah.

"The Date Farm!" He was almost shouting. "You've got to be kidding me. Of all the places to meet. That's almost as bad as meeting in the ruins of a church somewhere. You can't go there. Don't you know the history of that place? Part of it used to be what they called a 'Biblical Journey', or something like that."

"Faith Walk," corrected Aishah, forcing herself to meet the anger in Mo's eyes.

He ignored her. "It was full of statues of Jesus and the disciples. Statues, Aishah! Totally forbidden! And people wore headsets that told them about Jesus' life! Definitely against our law."

"Honey, calm down." Aishah stood up and placed her hand on Mo's arm. She spoke with a confidence she did not feel. "There are no statues there now. Everything has been smashed to pieces. Definitely no headsets are being handed out. You aren't familiar with The Date Farm because we don't have children, but anyone with kids knows it's just a park now." She repeated the Christian woman's description. "Just a place for the kids to play hide and seek and climb around in the ruins. It's a place to relax, Mo. It's got nothing to do with Christianity".

In spite of her best efforts to speak calmly, Aishah found herself babbling as she sought to convince Mo of the Farm's respectability. "It's got nothing to do with Christianity now," she repeated. "That's all gone, years ago. Even the rides are gone. It's just ruins and weeds and places for the kids to play. It's harmless. I'll just go into the park and pick up the baby—in the tomb—so that nobody will see us."

"Not there! Not the tomb, where dead people are placed. A place of death." Mo groaned. "That's the worst place. You're not going there, Aishah."

"It's not a place of death to the Christians, though," Aishah spoke steadily. "Not to Christians. They believe the tomb was a place of resurrection—new life. They believe Jesus rose from the dead there."

"Well, we know better, don't we? That's just a crazy myth his followers invented. Jesus was a prophet, like other prophets before him. And that's all. Nobody rises from the dead."

"They say it was a miracle," Aishah said, wondering why she was arguing about this.

"And we say it is a myth. Passed down over the centuries. A tomb is a place of death, and that's that. You're not going there. I've heard that the tomb at The Date Farm is haunted, or something... I've heard that some people feel funny when they go in there."

"What do you mean—'funny'?" How do they feel?" Aishah remembered how she had felt in the store room with the Christian woman.

"I don't know. Just odd, they say… kind of like there are ghosts there."

"Well, I don't believe in ghosts and neither should you." Aishah spoke with a steady, firm voice. She took a deep breath. "Where's your faith, Mo? You're always preaching to me about mine. I'm not afraid of some Christian ghosts lurking around in an old ruined amusement park. Next you'll be telling me it's the Holy Ghost."

"Stop that right now, Aishah. You're going too far. I don't want to hear any more of that kind of talk. Ever again." Mo's face had turned white.

"Okay, okay," Aishah apologized. *Why does Mo always get so angry in any discussion about religion? Does he have doubts?* "I'm sorry," she said. "I know I've overstepped the bounds, once again." She sighed. "Again… but what is done is done. We have to take the baby. I know it's scary. I'm scared, too."

Mo sat down again. His shoulders slumped. "Aishah, we're risking our lives for this child."

"Every mother risks her life to have a child. It's always been this way. Maybe more so now than before—not many doctors are left, and the midwives aren't qualified…" Her voice trailed off. "But that's not the point. The point is: the baby is coming and we have promised to take it. We cannot go back on our word now."

Mo looked down at the floor. "You could just not show up."

Aishah stared at his bowed head. Finally she spoke. "I could not do that. I promised her I would be there."

Mo lifted his head to meet Aishah's eyes. "But she's an infidel, so it's okay if you don't keep your promise. You know that."

Aishah levelled a cold stare at him. "I can't believe you said that. Maybe some people would do that. I would never do that to her." Then her expression softened. "Mo, I told her we would raise the child as a Muslim. She's willing to give us her child even under those conditions. How can we be unwilling to take this baby?"

"And risk our life for it?" asked Mo.

"And risk our life for it." Aishah repeated. Her voice carried a note of finality. After no response from Mo, she added, "What about your dream? You and I both know it was a sign from Allah. Don't we?"

Mo didn't respond.

"You believe that, don't you?"

Mo sat without speaking. He looked down at his hands for several moments, not meeting Aishah's tear-filled eyes.

Finally, she broke the silence. "What are you doing?"

"I'm praying," Mo spat out his words, "that no one will ever find out about this and that Allah will keep us safe."

"Good. Pray hard. But I know that He will." She heard again the Christian woman's parting words: *"Never forget that God loves you."*

"Oh, Aishah…" Mo rose from his chair to kneel at Aishah's knees. Putting his arms around her waist he gazed steadily into her eyes. "Sometimes I think in spite of all your lack of respect, you have more faith than I do."

"Probably." She leaned forward to kiss him firmly on the lips. "Probably, I do. So that's that, then." They stood up together. "I haven't done the cleaning in my bistro." She heard the tiredness in her own voice.

"I'll help you," Mo said.

As they walked through the swinging doors into the women's section, Aishah giggled.

"I feel pregnant already. Exhausted and weepy."

Mo smiled at her. "I do, too."

Aishah squeezed his hand hard. "Don't worry, Mo. Nothing is going to go wrong. No one will ever know our secret."

CHAPTER FOUR

Natalie

Calgary, Alberta, Canada
In the foothills of the Canadian Rocky Mountains
Hallowe'en Night

Natalie watched as feathery snowflakes swirled wildly in the greyness outside her living room window. The temperature had dipped to below freezing that afternoon as an early storm swept in from the Rocky Mountains, covering the city in a thick blanket of snow. In spite of the weather, she knew that "trick or treaters" would soon be arriving at her front door to collect their Hallowe'en candy. And that was good, because late afternoon was always her blue time of day—her lonely time.

She sipped her tea slowly. *The house is too big for me. I knew that when Greg passed away, and now with Karyn married and living in California... I really should move into a condo.*

She hadn't planned to leave the house today. *Why would anyone go out on such a day?* But still... something had been niggling at the edges of her consciousness all afternoon: *You should go pick up the mail.* It seemed silly. There was never anything interesting, anyway. Just ads and bills. She argued with her inner voice for a few more minutes, but the thought persisted: *You should go.*

Finally, Natalie set down her unfinished cup of tea. She would go out, after all, just to get out of the gloomy house—fill in the time until the kids started coming. And get rid of the voice in her head. She retrieved her snow boots, jacket, toque and red maple leaf mittens from the downstairs closet where she'd stashed them last spring. She knew that after a few days of freezing weather she'd be used to the cold and wouldn't be bundling up quite so warmly. *But tonight everything goes on.*

Natalie struggled through the deep snow, feeling icy wetness as it spilled over the top of her boots and melted on her ankles. There were no tire tracks on the street and no footprints ahead of her.

I'm probably the first person out since the storm began.

The thickly falling snowflakes swallowed the big city sounds she was accustomed to hearing and she suddenly felt very alone in her silent white world. She tried to shake off a vague feeling that something bad was about to happen.

It's just a snowstorm, silly. Nothing's wrong.

Still, she was glad when she caught a glimpse of red mailboxes through the veil of white in front of her. Reaching her destination, she fumbled for the key in her pocket. Finally, she removed her mitten which promptly landed in the snow at her feet. Ignoring it, Natalie's fingers closed on the key and she opened her mailbox.

There was only one piece of mail—just a crumpled scrap of brown paper, taped together to form an envelope. Her heart stopped. In the early darkness she couldn't see any return address, but she didn't need to. She knew it was from Karyn. And she knew it must be bad news—*or else why would she risk mailing a letter from Palm Springs to Canada?*

Please God, please God…

She dropped the piece of paper in the soft snow and quickly stooped to pick it up. Leaving her red mitten lying where it had fallen, Natalie started for home, clutching the letter in her cold hand. As she felt patches of ice beneath her boots, she realized she was risking a fall, but she couldn't force herself to slow down.

Once her front door had closed behind her, she sank into the chair in the entranceway, her jacket and toque still on, the snow on her boots melting to form puddles on the floor.

When had Karyn written this?

She turned the letter over. The postmark was almost a month ago.

Why had it taken so long to get here?

She answered her own question out loud. "Because communication is not a priority with that Unity government they've got down there. Especially if it's mail to Canada. It's a miracle the letter arrived at all."

When she peeled off the tape holding the paper together and read her daughter's familiar handwriting, a cold feeling not unlike the weather outside washed over her. She stared down at the paper in her hand.

Oh, no. They've been found out. Stephen is dead. Karyn is pregnant. Please God, show me what to do.

"Hallowe'en apples! Trick or treat!" The next door neighbour's kids called loudly as they ran up the driveway. Natalie couldn't move. When she heard the chime of the doorbell, she forced herself to stand up. Setting the crumpled note beside the large bowl of candy, she opened the door to find two small tigers and one lion holding out orange plastic pumpkins. Forcing a smile to her lips, she dumped handfuls of miniature chocolate bars into the outstretched buckets.

"Hi, Natalie," It was the kids' mom, Linda, waiting at the bottom of the steps. "Isn't this terrible weather for Hallowe'en night? And it was so nice yesterday."

"It will probably be warmer tomorrow. I hear a Chinook is on the way." Natalie's voice sounded strange even to her own ears. "You know what they say about Calgary: if you don't like the weather, just wait ten minutes and it will change."

"For sure," Linda agreed. "Have a happy Hallowe'en."

"You, too." Natalie closed the front door.

She walked across the carpet, leaving a trail of wet footprints. She picked up the phone. Karyn had given her this number almost a year ago and she had used it several times, just to talk to somebody there and reassure herself that things were probably alright. Her call was answered on the second ring.

"Hello, you have reached Calgary Missions to Muslims in America. This is John speaking. How may I help you?"

"John, this is Natalie, Karyn's mom. This is an emergency. Now, don't tell me what I'm asking is impossible. How soon can you get me down to Palm Springs?"

CHAPTER FIVE

Aishah

Aishah couldn't believe how smoothly everything was going. In just two days Mo had come up with his creation of a baby bump: a large round pocket sewn onto the front of an old apron. He stood watching as Aishah paraded back and forth in front of him that evening, a small round bulge plainly visible under her abaya.

"See, honey, it can grow with your pregnancy," he said. "We'll just stuff more padding into it as time goes on, maybe change the shape a bit." She was nervous wearing her 'baby bump' the next morning, but as she told Mo at the end of the day, "It couldn't have gone better. At first everyone seemed surprised that I'd left it until almost my sixth month to say anything. But then, some of the women who have had miscarriages like I have, said they understood why I'd waited. They would have done the same thing."

"That's great, honey." Mo sounded as relieved as she was.

"And some of them said they'd be bringing in some maternity clothes. Just a loan, in case they need them again."

"Guess they didn't want to see you wearing black all the time."

"Guess not. And another thing…"

"There's more?" Mo teased.

"The women are going to have a baby shower for me."

"A what?"

"You know—a shower—a party, lots of food, silly games, and gifts for the baby. So, we will have lots of nice things when it arrives." Aishah paused as she remembered all of the baby clothes she had bought the first time she had been pregnant. They had closed the door to the nursery when she lost the baby, but Mo had said he was sure they would have another, not to give things away—their next baby could use them. But with the next pregnancy it happened again. And then again—and again—and again. When the doctor told them it was unlikely Aishah would be able to conceive again, they finally gave up hoping for a child.

"Don't tell anyone," Aishah had sobbed in Mo's arms.

"I won't, sweetheart." He rocked her gently. "Maybe we could adopt a baby, somehow..." His voice had trailed off as Aishah shook her head.

"I don't know if I could do that, Mo. Under Shariah law we couldn't give the child our last name. It would have to keep the name of its birth father. If it was a girl, she'd have to wear a veil in front of you—her dad, for goodness sake! And if it was a boy, I'd have to wear a veil in front of him. In our own home! You and I—and the child itself—would be reminded every day that we weren't really a family."

Mo nodded silently.

"Besides, where would we ever find a baby? There's always some family member willing to take in an orphaned child related to them. And adopting from an unwed mother—well, you and I both know what happens to them long before the baby is born."

So Aishah and Mo gave everything away, even the crib he had built. As Aishah pushed the memories from her mind, she wondered if Mo was remembering also. She managed to smile at him. "So, they've asked if they could have the shower some afternoon at the bistro. Naturally I said yes."

"Are you sure we should be doing that?" Mo frowned. "We don't want to do anything out of the ordinary—anything that will attract attention to us. That sounds like something from before Unity took over. We have to make sure we keep only our own traditions. Of course we'll be having the Aqiqah with my family when the baby is a week old."

"Of course, we'll do the religious ceremony. We can't have too many celebrations, as far as I'm concerned. My women want to have this party for me at the bistro, though, because they won't be coming to L.A."

"I guess that makes sense." Mo said. "Okay. I'm really looking forward to spending that week with all my family. It will be a huge event, for sure. Mom and Dad haven't changed one bit since they got older—they still look for any excuse to hold a party. And their oldest son finally having a child? That's big for them."

"Even if the baby is a girl?" teased Aishah. "They'll all be hoping for a boy."

"Well, I'm hoping for a boy, too. Aren't you?"

"Boy or girl, I don't care." Aishah shrugged. "Everybody seems to prefer sons. But not me. A girl would be great. If it's Allah's will that we have a girl, then we should rejoice in Allah's will being fulfilled, shouldn't we? Doesn't the Koran say somewhere that Allah creates only perfection? So, a girl is His perfect creation."

"Aishah, you are quite the theologian." Mo smiled. "I can't argue with that."

"Don't make fun of me! I don't pretend to understand Allah's word on this—and that's not my fault. Maybe if they let us females learn to read—"

Mo interrupted her. "You grew up when girls were still allowed to go to school, Aishah. So that's no excuse. You could read the Koran in English if you wanted to."

"But that's not really reading Allah's words, is it?"

"Well… no. But learning Arabic is hard. I'm struggling with it. You could read the Koran in English, though. That's better than nothing."

"I've tried. I know it must be my fault, but I have trouble understanding it."

"You could make more of an effort. Just read it, anyway. I do." Aishah made a face. "By the way," Mo continued, "how are you doing with that book you found?"

Aishah looked away. "Okay… It's just a romantic novel." *I can't tell him that the whole thing takes place at Christmas time and there's a wedding in a church and everything.* She turned back to Mo. "But getting back to what we were talking about, I know that a boy would have an easier life. If our baby is a girl, I think I might feel sorry for her, the way things are now."

She frowned, then shrugged. "Well, not to worry! We don't get to choose. We'll take what we get, like all the other parents do. So that's that. We can have the shower in a couple of weeks. I know! We'll call it a 'Thanks Be To Allah' celebration, with special prayers and everything. You ask the imam about this, Mo. We'll play down the fun part. Although what makes you guys think you will ever know what really went on, anyway?" She grinned. "Is that good enough?"

"I guess it will have to be," Mo sighed. "We want to be sure we don't provide ammunition for the morality squad. Those young punks are always sniffing around, trying to find something wrong with what folks are doing—or not doing. Lately they seem to be looking for any excuse to accuse people of being too modern, not observing the old ways."

"Isn't that a twist?" Aishah said. "Before Unity took over, it was the older folks who criticized the young people for trying new things. Now it's just the reverse: the young people who have never known anything except strict religious laws insist we go back to the old ways, and by that they mean centuries ago."

"Yeah, this is different." Mo said slowly. "Anyway, our imam preached last Friday about Allah's followers in America not following our laws as closely as we should. Especially the converts, he said, and there are plenty of them—"

"Yeah, more of them than us," Aishah interrupted. "Well, they didn't have much of a choice—convert to Islam or die. We can hardly expect them to be enthusiastic believers. Sometimes in the bistro I try to figure out who's who. I can't tell who was born Muslim, who converted by choice, or who was forced to convert and is just pretending to believe. And you know what? I don't care. I like them all."

Mo ignored her comment. "Anyway, the imam says we aren't sombre enough, serious enough. And we always want to change things. His sermon last Friday was about Americans always wanting to find new ways of doing things—"

"Where's he from, anyway?" interrupted Aishah again. "Pakistan? Iran? Afghanistan? Saudi Arabia?"

"I don't know. But his sermon was about innovation. He says that's the main problem we have. He said we are always trying to invent new ways. He even used the term 'Good old American know-how'."

"He didn't!" Aishah raised her eyebrows. "And you're always scolding me for saying things like that!"

"He wasn't saying it was a good thing, Aishah. Just the opposite. He said that's why the country is doing so poorly. Instead of keeping the laws and traditions of the past we introduce changes. He said when a society isn't doing well, it's a sure sign we are not keeping the law as strictly as we should. We should tighten up, he says."

"Tighten up? What's that mean?" Aishah began unloading cups from the dishwasher.

"It means enforcing the laws more strictly. And he said we ask too many questions. Allah's will for humanity was revealed to the Prophet (peace be upon him) and who are we to try to improve on that? There should be no questioning."

Aishah slammed a cupboard door. "Good grief! That was back in the Seventh Century. Surely things should have changed! Remember when we had that young American imam? He was in favour of change. I liked him."

"But he didn't last long here did he? He wasn't popular with some of the government officials."

"Yeah, but I'll bet he's somewhere now, preaching change. I wouldn't be surprised if 'Good Old American Know How' reared its ugly head again, someday." Aishah saw the frown on Mo's face deepen as she spoke. *Those Friday afternoon sermons at the mosque are changing him. And I don't think I like the changes.* She moved closer to him, looking up into his eyes.

"Mo, I know I don't take my religion as seriously as you do. I know I'm probably one of the people the imam was preaching about last Friday. Maybe if women were welcome at the mosque I would go and then I would understand some of these things better." She waved away his denial. "We used to have a nice space, but now we have to sit in that dirty side room and we can't see or hear what is going on. That's why the women don't go. We know when we are not wanted. You can't deny that."

Mo remained silent.

After a moment, Aishah continued, "I know you worry about me when I talk like this, but you don't need to, Mo. I would never, never criticize the law or complain about things to anyone except you. Ever. I know the cost. Okay?"

Mo didn't respond.

"Okay?" Aishah asked more softly.

Mo gazed down at her. His stern expression melted.

"Okay." He hugged her. "Oh, Aishah," he whispered into her dark curls, "You are a handful, but I don't know what I'd do without you. What if something terrible happened to you? I couldn't live without you."

"Of course you could. Besides, nothing's going to happen to me." She tilted her head to look up at him. "But, just in case it did, will you promise me that you would love our child and care for it, girl, or boy? Because you love me. Will you promise me that?"

"I promise, girl or boy." Mo smiled down at her. "Because I love you." He turned to begin reloading the dishwasher. "But I'm still praying for a boy."

Aishah gave his back a light punch. She began scrubbing the stainless steel counters.

"I'm learning to knit," she said a few moments later. "My ladies…" she paused for a moment as she realized that she always thought of her bistro customers as *her* ladies. "My ladies," she continued, "are teaching me to knit."

Mo raised his eyebrows. "And how's that going?"

"About the same as my cooking lessons went," Aishah giggled. "But there's an upside to it all. The women have just about given up on me as a knitter, or a crochetter, or whatever it is we're supposed to be doing. They're taking things into their own hands—literally—so we'll soon have lots of sweaters and booties for our baby. I'm knitting a blanket though. So far it looks more like a scarf, but it's the thought that counts, right?"

"Right." Mo turned away, but not before Aishah saw the broad grin spreading beneath his beard.

"One thing, though," Aishah's voice suddenly grew strained. "I'm worried about something."

"What?" asked Mo. "Something other than this whole baby project?"

"Well, I guess it's part of this whole project. You know how Meanie occasionally comes to the cafe?"

"Meanie?"

"Well, that's what we call her, not to her face of course. Her name is Veeda."

"Oh, you mean Brian's wife."

"Yeah. Every time she comes through that front door the women just clam up. They've been talking and laughing, but when Veeda comes in, you could hear a pin drop. It's weird. Everyone acts like they're afraid they'll say something wrong and Veeda will report back to the "M" squad."

"The morality squad? And will she report to them?"

"Maybe. They say she has done that before. Her sons are very involved in the Squad. So the women watch what they say. They even speak more softly with their heads down."

"I hope you watch what you say, too," Mo said. "You're inclined to blurt things out, you know."

"I know. I should think before I speak, for sure. But even *I* shut up when she comes through the door. Today Veeda was the only one who wanted to know every little detail about my pregnancy."

"Like what?"

"Like how come I haven't had any morning sickness—how do I feel—am I gaining weight—how come I don't look like I am gaining weight except on my stomach? That's not normal, she says. Stuff like that. She asked for my exact due date—how long have I known I was pregnant. On and on."

"Maybe she's sincerely interested," Mo said.

"Maybe, but she has a look on her face that I just can't quite figure out, like she doesn't believe me."

"Veeda is an unhappy woman, Aishah. She was Brian's first wife for quite a few years, but then he did so well in real estate—"

"I guess so!" Aishah interrupted. "All those people abandoning their homes."

"Anyway, he made lots of money and can afford four wives. He treats them all badly but I hear he treats Veeda the worst. His other wives are young, some of them just teenagers. They're all having babies and she's not. So it's probably hard for her to see you pregnant now, too."

"I know all that," Aishah said. "The women talk about it. Veeda often leaves her veil on in the bistro. We all think it's to hide bruises. Once I noticed she had a black eye."

Mo winced. "I didn't know that. Has she spoken to the imam?"

"I don't know. But I *do* know that a few others of my ladies are in the same situation, although not as bad. They told me they've gone to the imam and his advice is they must try harder to please their husband."

"Really?" Mo sounded surprised.

"Really." Aishah pressed her lips into a thin line. "You men know nothing about what goes on in a woman's world now. You and I are so lucky to have grown up in the time before. Maybe our parents didn't follow the law as carefully as we do now, but they were kind to each other."

"I know," Mo said. "But I don't believe the law says we should be cruel to our wife, Aishah. It all depends on how you choose to understand the Koran. Brian obviously prefers to believe it's okay to hit Veeda, so he'll go along with that kind of interpretation. Brian had a rough childhood. His parents died when he was barely a teenager and he grew up on the streets. Not that I'm excusing his actions, but he's a damaged person, you could say. One thing he does do, though. He takes boys off the street, gives them a room and food in one of his apartments—teaches them the law."

"I know all about what he does, Mo. All of those boys are trained to work in the morality squad. They're as mean as he is."

Mo sighed. "Well anyway, back to the wife-beating thing, The Prophet (peace be upon him) according to one of his wives, Aishah, your namesake—"

Aishah interrupted, "Yeah. I'd like to know what she had to say."

"She said that he never once hit his wives or his maidservants."

"That's good to know," Aishah said. "Why doesn't somebody remind Brian of that? Oh, I forgot. He's too rich and powerful." Aishah felt hot anger rising in her chest. "And another thing, I think taking three younger wives is cruel. And that definitely is part of our law. Imagine how Veeda feels? She's pushing fifty and has ruined her health by having all those babies."

"We can't argue with the law," Mo said wearily. "So let's not get into that again. It's not like all husbands beat their wives, and it's not like this never happened before the take-over. Not that I am defending a husband beating his wife," he added quickly.

"I agree it happened before," Aishah said, "And it happened with all groups, not just with Muslims, but at least there were laws against it back then, and shelters for the women to go to for help. Now, they have nowhere to go. They just have to stay in a horrible situation all of their lives. Some commit suicide."

"We can't do anything about that," Mo sighed. "I am very sorry about it, but I can't do anything. It's just one more thing that I can't do anything about."

"Okay, I know that." Aishah remembered the time Mo had said he felt powerless to protect his own wife, let alone anyone else's. She heard the same defeated tone in his voice now. *I've got to quit letting this bother me. I'm just making Mo feel badly.* "I'm not blaming you, honey," she said gently, "But what should I do about Veeda?"

"Just be extra nice to her, if you can. You should still be careful what you say around her, though."

Aishah stood on tiptoe to kiss him on the tip of his nose. "You are a good man, Mohammed Haddad. I'll try harder."

Aishah made a special effort to show kindness to Veeda, often joining her as she sat alone at a table. Aishah encouraged the other women to do the same. No one noticed any softening of Veeda's bad temper. Her loud criticism of everything and everyone continued. But they did notice she put her hand over her mouth to muffle a laugh one day when Aishah told one of her funny stories, and they looked at each other in surprise. Aishah decided she would pray for Veeda in her daily prayers.

* * *

As the weeks passed, Aishah's "baby bump" grew. She kept a close watch on the pregnant women at the bistro and as their stomach size increased, so did her "baby bump". She paid special attention to how the women walked as their bodies changed shape.

Mo laughed out loud when she practised walking in front of him one evening, but quit laughing when she scolded him: "Don't laugh. They have to place their feet slightly apart to keep their balance—all that extra weight in front of them."

"Want me to add some more weight to your apron?"

"No, thanks." It was Aishah's turn to laugh.

The women in the bistro regularly complimented her on how well she looked and how little weight she had gained. Veeda, however, always found something negative to say. In fact, Aishah felt that Veeda took special delight in saying unkind things.

One afternoon she motioned Aishah over to where she was sitting—alone, as usual. Aishah noticed Veeda hadn't bothered to tie back her thinning gray hair as she usually did. It hung in greasy strands around her narrow face. Her lips were swollen— the top one was slightly split.

Aishah hoped her smile conveyed her sympathy as she said, "Yes, Veeda? What can I bring you?"

"More coffee."

Veeda's voice always reminded Aishah of the cartoons she watched on T.V. as a child.

"You know the one, Mo," she had told him one night. "Where the villain scraped his fingernails down the chalkboard to torture his victim?"

Mo had laughed. "It can't be that bad, honey."

"Well, almost."

Now, as Aishah returned with her coffee, Veeda narrowed her eyes to scan Aishah's body from head to toe.

"You don't look good to me," she said, her loud voice more raspy than usual.

The women at the nearby tables stopped talking and a hush spread across the bistro.

"You're too skinny. Skinny all over except for that stomach bulge." Veeda poked Aishah's stomach. Aishah inhaled sharply. "You should be more careful about what you eat. Looks like you're are not putting on enough weight. You will have a skinny baby. Probably a sickly baby, too. It will be too small. Make sure you are eating the right food, or you'll be sorry. But maybe it's too late now, anyway. When is your due date again?"

"A little more than a month," Aishah said, forcing a smile as she refilled Veeda's coffee cup. *How many times has she asked me that?*

"Probably too late now, then. The damage is already done." Veeda smirked. Aishah moved on to chat with the women at the next table.

Although she tried to hide any outward expression of anxiety, Veeda's comments fueled the fears that were always on Aishah's mind. *Does the Christian woman have enough to eat? Where is she? What if they've already found her and she's dead? Why didn't I insist she tell me where she was?*

When she shared these thoughts with Mo one evening he had reminded her, "She wouldn't even give you her name. So she would never have told you where she is hiding out. Besides, she'll be moving around a lot. Quit beating up on yourself. You did the best you could at the time."

"She's living in deserted houses," Aishah moaned. "Moving from house to house. All I can do is pray for her." In that instant Aishah realized what she hadn't acknowledged before, even to herself. *I am praying for an infidel. Mo won't like that.* One glance at Mo's face told her she was right.

He had frowned and turned away.

Aishah's thoughts were interrupted by a question from one of the younger women. "We are all wondering where you are going to have the baby, at home or at a birthing house?"

Everyone turned to see what Aishah would say.

Aishah had expected this question sooner or later. Everyone knew Unity preferred home births, so she chose her words carefully. "Mo and I will be driving to L.A. a few days before the birth, so that my friend there can deliver the baby. A childhood friend," she added, avoiding the women's gaze by bending her head to scrub at a smudge on the glass tabletop. She felt a hot flush spread across her face.

Mo says I shouldn't feel guilty about lying to my friends. But I do. Would they support me in this decision if they knew? Mo says they would.

"Your friend! Lucky you!" several women commented. All of the women agreed it was good to know someone who was a midwife instead of relying on the midwives the imam recommended. Aishah tried to close her ears to the lurid details of childbirth the women seemed eager to share. She nodded and made an effort to appear to be listening, but her thoughts were on the Christian woman.

Please, Allah, give her an easy time. Please don't let her be all alone when the baby is born.

Aishah noticed that for once Veeda did not dominate the conversation. Instead, she sat staring down at her coffee cup in silence.

Veeda must have had some bad experiences. Nine babies! Aishah walked over to Veeda's table.

"Have another muffin with your coffee, Veeda. It's on the house." She placed the largest muffin on her serving tray on Veeda's plate. Not looking up, Veeda nodded. Aishah thought she heard a muffled *thank you.*

"I was in hard labour twenty-four hours," one woman volunteered, speaking above the general hubbub of conversation, "And the midwife wouldn't give me anything to ease the pain."

Aishah grimaced. *Please, won't somebody change the topic of conversation?* Finally, she decided to take matters into her own hands.

"So, tell me about how you felt when you first saw your baby's face?" she asked, interrupting one woman's description of a forceps delivery.

Everyone laughed. "We know what you're doing," Marg said, "And we don't blame you."

The conversation switched to happier memories and Aishah breathed a sigh of relief. Veeda caught her eye and gave a tight-lipped grin. Aishah smiled back.

We're kindred spirits on this topic, at least.

Aishah was pouring what she estimated was her hundredth cup of coffee when the phone on the back counter rang. Adopting her late pregnancy walk, she waddled to the back of the bistro.

"Hello. This is Desert Delights, Aishah speaking. How may I help you?"

"Your package has arrived early. Please pick it up at three o'clock Saturday afternoon."

It was the voice of the Christian woman. The phone fell from Aishah's hand, clattering noisily on the glass countertop. She snatched it up again. The woman was repeating her message.

Aishah wasn't sure she heard correctly. "It's too soon. We're not ready," she began to protest, but the woman had ended the call.

Aishah stood at the counter clutching the phone. All colour drained from her face.

CHAPTER SIX

Aishah

"Is something wrong?" Ronda had come to stand beside her. "You look really pale. I'm sorry if we scared you with all that crazy birthing talk. Most babies are born just fine with very little pain. Look at how the population of Palm Springs is exploding— babies everywhere. It's not so bad. Don't worry. You probably won't feel any pain at all."

Aishah hesitated a moment before meeting Ronda's eyes. She couldn't stop the thought that raced unbidden through her mind. *No, I won't feel any pain. Someone else has felt the pain for me.*

Struggling to answer in her normal voice, she sat down at the closest table. "You didn't scare me," she finally said. I'm just feeling a bit tired. I'll be fine." A wild jumble of thoughts stampeded through her mind.

At least a month early! How are we going to explain it to everyone? Well, babies come early, obviously, so mine can, too. We'll work this out somehow.

She desperately wanted to talk to Mo. *I can't go in there, but maybe I should phone him? No, then he'll be as upset as I am. I'll just have to wait until closing time.* Aishah drummed her fingers impatiently on the polished glass. It seemed to her that every woman in the bistro wanted to bring her coffee or a doughnut or apologize for scaring her. She finally decided to resume waiting on tables rather than be the object of so much attention.

As she worked, she kept listening for the cuckoo clock to signal the hour. Its merry sound always comforted her. Her father had brought her a cuckoo clock from Germany when she was four years old. When she and Mo were furnishing the bistro, Aishah had spied a similar clock in a pile of junk at a used furniture store. When she showed it to Mo, he hesitated, saying it didn't fit into her bistro décor—and he wasn't sure if images of a bird would be allowed—but he understood why she wanted it.

Okay," he finally said, but if anyone objects, we'll have to get rid of it."

Aishah nodded, clutching the clock to her chest.

"And," Mo continued, "As long as it brings back only good memories, not bad ones. We want to forget those, don't we?"

Aishah's brown eyes filled with tears. "I'll never forget that my parents were taken, Mo. You know that."

"Okay, okay," Mo had glanced around the store to see if anyone was listening to their conversation.

Aishah's thoughts were jolted back to the present by the sound of the cuckoo chiming its merry song. She sighed. *Three o'clock, Dad. Just an hour and a half to go.* The afternoon seemed to be stretching on forever, but finally it was four-thirty. She managed a smile and a hurried "Peace" to the last women leaving. Flipping the sign on the front door to "Closed", Aishah abandoned her late-pregnancy waddle as she ran through the empty cafe. In the kitchen, Mo was already filling the sink with hot water. He looked up as she entered.

"Those women of yours sure like to stay until the very last minute, don't they?" He stopped speaking when he saw Aishah's pale face. "What's wrong? You don't look well."

Out of breath, Aishah blurted out, "The baby is born."

"The baby is born? Are you sure? It's too soon."

"The package has arrived early," Aishah almost screamed at him. It felt good to be able to express her excitement—or fear. She wasn't sure which feeling dominated. "We have to go pick it up on Saturday afternoon."

Mo stared at her.

"At three o'clock," she added, wondering why she felt that detail was important right now.

Leaving the tap running, Mo turned to face Aishah. His hands dripped soapy water onto the floor. "That's only two days from now. This isn't what we'd planned."

"I know. But I've figured it out. Tomorrow's Friday, we're closed anyway. We'll put a note on the bistro door saying we're closed for the next week or so due to a family emergency and explain later." Aishah rushed on. "I'll say I could tell the baby was coming early and we had to leave for L.A unexpectedly. I've been out there waiting on tables for two hours, Mo, figuring this all out." She collapsed into her rocker, still out of breath. "I can't believe it! It's finally happened!"

Mo turned off the tap just as sudsy water began running down the front of the cupboard. He sat in his easy chair opposite Aishah. "Boy or girl?"

"Boy or girl? Is that all you care about? I don't know whether it's a boy or girl. I didn't ask. Who cares? Our baby is born."

"I'm sorry. I'm just surprised and that's the first thing that popped into my head."

"I'm sorry, too, honey. I didn't mean to snap at you. I always do that when I'm stressed out. You know I don't mean it. I'm as surprised as you are, but I guess I've had more time to think about it than you have. I've kept this bottled up all afternoon. I'm feeling a little crazy." She reached over to take Mo's hand.

"It's okay, as long as we go crazy together," he smiled.

"So we have to get ready, Mo. All our stuff has to be ready for L.A. The baby's stuff. We have to let your folks know we are coming early—figure out what to tell them."

"Well, they knew we would be coming to visit as soon as the baby was born," Mo said.

"But a month early, Mo! They won't be expecting us for another month. You'll have to call them as soon as we get the baby. But you can't call them until I actually have the baby so that we can tell them it's a girl or a boy."

Mo nodded, repeating after her: "As soon as we get the baby, I'll phone and tell them about it and we'll drive to L.A."

"I'm not ready for this." Aishah bit her bottom lip. "I haven't even bought baby formula yet. I don't even know what to buy."

"Didn't you ask the women about that?"

"No, I couldn't. Everyone just assumed I'd be nursing the baby, so I just went along with it. How could I say anything?"

Mo nodded.

"I know," Aishah's face brightened. "I'll just buy several kinds. Surely something will be okay. How fussy can a baby be, anyway?"

"Don't ask me," Mo shrugged. "I don't know much more about newborns than you do."

"I don't know anything," Aishah said with a nervous giggle. She thought she saw Mo grin, but sometimes it was hard to read his expression behind his shaggy beard.

After a moment, he said, "Anyway, let's do the cleanup and go home. We need to make a list. You always do better when you make a list, honey. I'll be at Friday prayers most of tomorrow. I'll hint to the men I see at the mosque that you are not feeling quite right."

"That's a good way of putting it," Aishah said.

"Well, I'm being honest, aren't I?"

Aishah nodded. "You are always honest, sweetheart."

"I am," he said. "Well, usually I am. Not now, I guess. But it can't be helped. So, here's the plan: we'll pack up the car Saturday morning and then in the afternoon we pick up the baby at The Date Farm and head straight from there to L.A."

Aishah nodded. "You'll have to wait in the car in the parking lot. Somebody might recognize you if you go inside."

"I hate to see you going in there alone." Mo frowned. "What if something goes wrong? What if someone recognizes you?"

"Nobody's going to recognize me. One blessing of the veil. All women look the same. I'll go into the cave, get the baby and come straight back to the car, and we'll leave for L.A. Nobody will notice me, Mo. Just another veiled mom carrying a baby." Aishah stood up, grabbed Mo's hands and forced him to follow her in a few forbidden twirls around the kitchen.

"Your eyes are dancing, too," Mo leaned back to look at her.

"I'm just so excited. It's finally happening."

"I don't know that I would call my feelings excitement exactly," Mo said. "I'm worried. But it's too late to turn back now.

There's the call to prayer. Pray that everything goes okay. We need all the help we can get."

"I will, I will," Aishah answered solemnly. "Harder than I've ever prayed before. Maybe I should throw in a prayer to the Christian God or whomever, just to cover all our bases—just to make sure."

"Don't you dare," Mo warned. "That's inviting disaster."

But Aishah had already started praying.

That night they went to bed shortly after dinner, both of them exhausted from the day's events. Once again they went over all the details of picking up the baby and driving to L.A. Finally, it seemed that neither of them had anything more to say. They kissed goodnight and Mo cuddled Aishah in his arms as he always did. He fell asleep in mere minutes.

Aishah was just dozing off when she heard Mo suddenly groan, "Oh, no."

"What is it?" she asked, immediately wide awake. "Have we forgotten something?" Turning on the bedside light, she saw the look of anguish on Mo's face.

"I've had a nightmare—snakes and stuff. Maybe it's a message. Maybe I should have asked the imam. What if this isn't right? What if it is not Allah's will? How do we know for sure? Taking this baby is a big thing, Aishah. It's not like breaking the law by reading that book you found. This is huge. I'm really worried. Maybe we shouldn't go. So you don't show up? So what? She can't do anything about it."

Aishah thought carefully before answering. *It's been two months now. He's been worrying all this time! I should have known he'd have second thoughts. He always has doubts when he makes a decision. That's how he is. I just need to reassure him.*

She leaned over him, holding back her long hair with one hand, and placing her other hand gently on the side of his face.

"No, she can't do anything about it if we don't show up. But her death and the death of the baby will be on our conscience. I refuse to believe Allah would want that little one to die—infidel or not. This is our gift from Allah. We've been over this so many times before. Why can't you just accept it? You had your dream about the baby, sweetheart, remember? You know that it meant Allah was saying we should take the baby. So we are taking the baby."

Aishah took a deep breath and exhaled slowly as she studied the look of anguish in Mo's eyes.

He began pacing the bedroom. Neither of them spoke. Finally he sat down on the edge of the bed, his face in his hands.

Aishah spoke more gently. "It's too late to turn back now, anyway. I've looked pregnant for the last two months. How do we explain it if we have no baby to show for it?"

From behind his fingers Mo's voice was faint. "Maybe say the baby died?"

Aishah couldn't believe her ears. "What? What did you just say? I mustn't have heard you correctly."

"We could just say the baby died at birth."

Aishah stared at him for several moments, then, crouching down beside him, she gently pulled his hands from his face.

"Look at me, sweetheart. I love you. You know that. It will be okay. I know it will be okay."

"You can't know that," Mo said.

Aishah thought of the ring of certainty she had heard in the Christian woman's voice that day in the store room. *Remember God loves you.*

"I do know that," she said. "But just to be sure, let's pray together right now. Maybe just silently if you're more comfortable with that. Just ask Allah to help you. Allah is merciful, you are always telling me. Just ask Allah to help you know you are doing the right thing."

Both were silent for what seemed to Aishah a long time.

"Well?" she finally said.

"Nothing." Mo looked at her. "I felt nothing."

"Then we are going," Aishah said, "Because I definitely felt a warm feeling. Allah, the Compassionate, the Merciful wants us to take this child. I am sure of it." Aishah saw the tears in Mo's eyes.

He breathed a heavy sigh. "What can I do? I'm doing this because I love you, Aishah."

"I know that, sweetheart. And together we're going to love this baby and raise it as our own, and we're going to be thankful to Allah for the rest of our days. So there," she concluded. "That's the situation."

"That's the situation," Mo repeated. His voice did not carry the certainty Aishah longed to hear.

Aishah saw the worry etched on Mo's face. *Well, I have enough confidence for both of us. I think I do… maybe I do…* She dismissed her doubts by chattering to Mo about all the details of the baby's wardrobe and what they needed to pack. Mo fell asleep somewhere in the middle of the one-sided conversation.

Aishah tossed and turned until finally she fell into a fitful sleep. She dreamed that she was in a dark cave with the Christian woman. The woman was holding out the baby for her to take, but every time Aishah stepped forward and reached for the child, the woman snatched it back. The scene was repeated over and over and over again. When Aishah woke to the sound of the pre-dawn call to prayer, her forehead was beaded with sweat.

Did my dream mean the Christian woman has changed her mind? What if she won't give the baby to me, after all? Then what kind of a mess will I be in?

Aishah climbed quickly out of bed, glad to escape the dream and begin a new day. Mo was already in their prayer room, preparing for his morning prayers. He looked up as she joined him.

"Good morning, sweetheart," she said brightly.

CHAPTER SEVEN

Aishah

After Mo left for the mosque, Aishah started packing. She tried not to think of her dream but she couldn't banish the image of the Christian woman snatching the baby back from her outstretched arms. *She wouldn't do that to me. I know she wouldn't. But what if she did? I need a plan. Maybe just say the baby died, like Mo suggested? Would anyone believe that?*

She sorted through all the things she had collected for the baby, many of them gifts from the women at the bistro. Mo had promised to pick up several kinds of formula on his way home.

So that should be everything we need. She snapped the suitcase shut.

"It will all be okay. I know it will be okay. Please, Allah, make everything work out for us," she prayed aloud.

When Mo finally returned, Aishah had prepared his favourite meal from the *old days,* as she sometimes called the time before the takeover.

"Is that turkey I smell?" Mo's face registered surprise as he walked through the kitchen door.

Aishah gave him a hug. "Yes, it's turkey. And sweet potatoes and stuffing and cranberry sauce—the whole thing. I remembered that this weekend is when everyone used to celebrate Thanksgiving. We should have had this last night, I'm a day late, but I've made a Thanksgiving dinner because I am so thankful. Not just for the baby, sweetheart, but for you. You are my one in a million man. No, make that one in two million."

Mo smiled as he hugged her.

"Okay. I don't believe that's true, but I'm willing to accept your opinion." He sniffed the air. Mmmm... A turkey dinner! And you're always saying you can't cook."

"I don't say that I *can't* cook. I say that I *don't* cook. That way if I ever do actually produce something great, everyone is overwhelmed and amazed at my effort—like you are now. Anyway, most of this was in the freezer, I was just waiting for a turkey dinner occasion. And this is certainly it. Our last night together, just the two of us. Tomorrow we will be a family. A new life begins for us tomorrow."

"I know it does, honey, and I love that you made my favourite dinner. But let's keep the Thanksgiving celebration part a secret, okay? It might sound like we are going back to the old ways... we wouldn't be popular with the M squad, if they heard about it. We'd probably get a visit and we don't want to attract any attention, especially now."

"Of course," Aishah said quickly. "Our little secret. You carve, I'll light the candles. Save room for pumpkin pie."

They went to bed early that night.

"Our last night as a childless couple," Aishah murmured as she snuggled into Mo's arms. "Will you still want to make love to me when I smell like baby powder and formula and maybe even baby throw-up?"

Mo laughed. "I'm pretty sure I will. But just in case...

Aishah giggled.

* * *

Saturday morning they packed the car for the trip. Mo put the baby's car seat in the back, along with the diaper bag and formula. They both tried to keep busy in an effort to keep their minds off what would be happening at three o'clock. Mo decided to clean out the garage. Aishah rearranged her kitchen cupboards.

"I'm nervous," she said as they lingered over a lunch they had scarcely touched. Mo said that was an understatement. They puttered around the house and yard, until finally Mo announced it was time to leave.

Aishah adjusted her large baby bump underneath her abaya. "For the last time," she muttered. "I can't say I'll be sorry to see the last of this thing. I have new sympathy for pregnant women. I guess I shouldn't complain. I can imagine how real moms feel when they gain weight—watching their figure change into a blob of baby."

"Don't think of yourself as not a real Mom," Mo said. "You're a real Mom, too. When you look after a child and love it, you are a real Mom."

"You're right, as usual."

Aishah made one final adjustment to the baby's car seat before climbing into the front seat.

"Open the glove compartment, honey," Mo said, as he backed out of the driveway.

A large "Baby on Board" sign fell into what remained of Aishah's lap.

"See, I'm ready for this." Mo grinned.

Aishah laughed. "I'm so glad to hear that, sweetheart, because there's no going back now."

Mo turned onto the main street. "Not as much traffic as there used to be," he said. "Not many people can afford a car."

"Thank goodness we can, even if it does have a lot of miles on it. It still gets us around," Aishah was staring straight ahead, drumming her fingers on the Baby on Board sign on her lap.

"Let's hope it gets us safely to L.A.," Mo said. "I was planning to take it in for a tune-up next week."

"We'll be fine," Aishah assured him, drumming her fingers even more loudly. "I know that everything will work out fine for us."

When she noticed Mo glance over at her hands, she put the sign in the door compartment beside her and clasped her hands together tightly on her rounded tummy.

They drove on in silence until they reached the entrance to The Date Farm. They were surprised to see so many cars in the parking lot.

"At least one place is still busy," Mo said. "The building looks kind of run-down though. Needs a paint job, that's for sure."

Aishah nodded, her eyes searching for an empty spot. "We need to park near the front door so that when I come out we can leave really quickly."

"I know, I know." He drove around the lot several times. A place finally opened up right next to the disabled parking spot in front of the main entrance.

"See?" Aishah said. "I told you so. Allah is with us."

Before she climbed out of the car, Aishah adjusted her baby bump one more time.

"Well, here I go. Pray for me." Her dark eyes implored him above her veil.

"I will, I will." Aishah could hear the tension in his voice and felt his eyes on her as she waddled to the door. She looked back. He waved. She pushed the weathered door open.

Inside, chaos reigned. Aishah instinctively took a step back. She hadn't been alone in a crowd like this in years. The store was jam-packed with moms and kids milling around. The occasional man stood out among the black-clad, veiled women. *Probably looking for their wives and kids.* She was immediately amazed that she could even register the thought—her head was spinning. Her heart thumped so loudly she was sure others could hear it as she wove her way toward the back of the store.

Several times she had to hold her baby bump in place with both hands as she stepped aside to avoid children darting wildly around the high shelves. Every shelf was loaded to capacity with cups and plates, aprons, and an assortment of Palm Springs souvenirs. The tallest shelves near the back were stacked high with date products: cakes, cookies, plastic packages of dates of all varieties, jars of jam, honey and The Date Farm's famous dried date shake mix. The sweet smell of dates pervaded the air.

Above the noise and confusion, the whine of several blenders preparing date shakes at the side counter almost obliterated even the loudest of the children's excited squeals.

"Get back here right now or we're leaving without you."

Aishah jumped. She turned as the woman next to her shouted at two children who were enjoying a wild game of hide and seek among the high shelves. Aishah stood on tip toe, trying to find the Exit sign which would lead her to the outdoor restaurant.

Now is one of those times I would like to be taller. Ah, there it is.

It seemed to Aishah that it was a long way through the crowded store, but finally she reached her destination. She pushed open the back door marked *Patio Restaurant.* It was quieter out here. Aishah forced herself to walk slowly as she wended her way around the crowded tables. Women chatted with each other, lifting their veils for a forkful of food while they jiggled babies on their lap and kept a close eye on their toddlers who were running around.

Aishah remembered the Christian woman's comment: "No one will notice you. Just one more veiled woman with a baby." *She was right about that.*

A little girl suddenly darted in front of Aishah, almost tripping her. The child's mother jumped up and apologized.

"It's okay, it's okay," Aishah assured her, anxious to continue on.

She breathed a sigh of relief when she finally made it through the crowded restaurant and out onto the short path leading to the gate and the derelict garden area beyond. But then she hesitated.

From behind her veil she studied the scene before her. Children ran happily amongst the ruins—older kids who didn't need to be supervised. They chased each other through the over-grown garden, screaming and laughing as they jumped over broken statues and dodged patches of cacti spreading unrestrained after many years of neglect. Aishah took a deep breath. She pushed open the iron gate. It squeaked in protest.

Off to her right, the black skeleton of what had once been the amusement park's roller coaster loomed against the cloudless sky. She glanced up at it and for a fleeting instant felt again the thrill of fear she had experienced as a child riding a roller coaster in Los Angeles—before such pleasures were banned.

Shaking off her memories, Aishah placed her feet firmly on the gravel path winding through the park. The sound of boisterous children soon faded.

Several iron benches still lined the walkway, although they were rusted and needed paint. It was obvious that at one time this had been a carefully groomed area, dotted with flowering shrubs and waterfalls. The crumbling remnants of a fountain were still visible, with small trickles of water making their way to a stagnant, algae-covered pool.

Aishah encountered only a few other women on the path. Sometimes they were sitting on the benches. Sometimes they were wandering a short way off the walk, searching for their children and calling out their names. "Liam and Addie, it's time to go home. Come here, right now."

Aishah carefully placed one foot in front of the other. As she walked, a hush seemed to fall over the park. Even the birds' songs ceased. The only sound she could hear was the crunch of gravel beneath her feet. She realized she was now deep in the heart of the park—and alone. Very alone. She tried to remember the last time she had walked outdoors without a male chaperone, but couldn't. She straightened her shoulders.

I told Mo I wasn't afraid to be here. I have to do this.

Aishah brushed at the beads of sweat forming on her forehead above her veil. She looked up as a dry, raspy sound filled her ears. Although there was no breeze, the palm fronds high above her head tossed restlessly. *It's almost like they are singing. But what a mournful tune!* Aishah quickened her pace.

Further on, her feet came to an abrupt halt. Huge rough-hewn lengths of wood lay scattered beside the path. Two pieces of timber had fallen over each other, accidently forming the shape of a cross.

This must be where the three crosses once stood. I can't be far from the tomb now.

Rounding a corner, she stopped once more. There it was— just as the Christian woman had said it would be—a large gray mound on the crest of a small hill.

Aishah shivered. "The Tomb of Jesus Christ," she whispered. Fighting down a sudden rush of fear threatening to engulf her, she scolded herself. *Don't be silly. It's not really Jesus' tomb. You've got to go in.*

Forgetting her late pregnancy walk, she drew closer. She could see now that the cave had been constructed of grey concrete, with markings to make it look like natural stone. The yawning entrance to the tomb stared back at her—as black as her abaya. Aishah bent down to look inside. Although the sun was shining brilliantly, deep shadow hid the interior from sight. She took a deep breath, trying to calm her wildly pounding heart before she stepped through the opening.

Inside it was cool and damp. The air smelled musty. It took a few moments for her eyes to adjust to the darkness.

And then she saw her.

A lone beam of sunlight penetrated the gloom, coming to rest on a tall black-clad woman leaning against the stone slab in the centre of the cave. She was gazing down at the small white bundle she held in her arms. Aishah took a step closer. She could see the tiny pale oval of the baby's face peeking from its wrappings.

Aishah's sharp intake of breath alerted the woman to her presence. She looked up, but didn't speak. Hesitating, Aishah drew nearer. No words were spoken as the woman silently stood and held out the baby. As Aishah's arms reached out to receive the child, the image of her nightmare flashed in front of her once more—*the mother stepping away with the baby.* Thick fear rose in her chest. She was almost surprised when she felt the slight weight of the warm bundle placed in her arms.

Through the narrow slits above their veils the two women's eyes met for what Aishah knew would be the last time. No words passed between them as Aishah looked deeply into the emerald eyes of the child's mother. The unknown woman abruptly gestured at the cloth bag on the floor at her feet.

When she spoke, her voice was hoarse. "Don't follow me out. Wait a few moments before you leave."

Aishah nodded. She watched wordlessly as the woman left the cave, walking with slow and deliberate steps. Aishah's eyes followed the tall black figure until it disappeared from view around the bend in the path. Then she looked down at the sleeping infant's face. She listened for the sound of the baby's breathing, but heard nothing. Alarmed, she leaned down, putting her ear close to its mouth. She exhaled a sigh of relief when she felt a slight whisper of breath.

A sudden movement at the entrance to the cave caught Aishah's attention. She glanced toward the opening. *Had someone been standing there?* She decided it was only her imagination playing tricks on her. *Maybe just sunlight reflecting off the dust particles and forming the shape of a person,* she reassured herself. *And yet… it looked like a man. In white clothes.*

She turned her gaze once again to the sleeping baby in her arms and as she did, she was suddenly engulfed by a feeling she had never before experienced. It flowed throughout her entire body, beginning at the top of her head and ending at her feet. In the days to come, when she had time to think about it, she decided it felt something like being held in her mother's arms. *Maybe I just had a flashback to when I was little and my mother held me,* she would later tell herself. But at the time, no thought was possible. She leaned, dream-like, against the stone platform in the centre of the tomb.

The baby's soft whimper jolted Aishah back to an awareness of her surroundings.

How long had she been there? Five minutes, twenty-five minutes, an hour? She had no idea. The baby was sleeping again with its head lying on her left wrist, covering her watch. *I can't risk waking it to check the time. Anyway, what does it matter? I've got to get out of here.* She grabbed the small bag at her feet and hurried to the mouth of the cave.

Brilliant sunlight blinded her. Pausing to give her eyes time to adjust to the glare, she glanced down at the baby one more time. Then she began to retrace her steps down the path, past the remains of the crosses and on toward the outdoor restaurant. It took an effort not to break into a run, but she knew she could not risk arousing suspicion.

Aishah marvelled that life in the park could carry on as usual around her. Somehow she thought things should be different now. But nothing had changed. Children continued their wild game of hide and seek. The woman Aishah had encountered before was still looking for her youngsters. She nodded to Aishah, not noticing that this petit veiled woman now carried a baby in her arms. Aishah nodded back.

She reached the gate to the patio area and pushed it open. She heard the same squeak as when she had entered. *Was it only a few minutes ago?*

She picked her way carefully through the crowded restaurant, dodging small children and excusing herself as she tried to avoid bumping into strollers and randomly placed tables and chairs. Carefully cradling the baby in one arm, she reached out to push open the door leading into the back of store. *Not far to go now.* She began to make her way through the noisy crush of people.

Standing on tiptoe, she tried to see over the high shelves blocking her way to the front exit and safety.

Please, Allah. Just get me through that door.

The familiar raucous voice of Veeda rose above the hubbub, breaking the spell Aishah was under.

"AISHAH, IS THAT YOU?"

CHAPTER EIGHT

Aishah

Aishah froze at the sound—but only for a second—before ducking behind an island of shelves stacked high with merchandise. For once in her life she was glad of her diminutive height. She felt the baby squirm in her arms. *Don't cry, please don't cry.* She looked down. Two greenish-blue eyes blinked up at her.

Suddenly, the shelves shielding Aishah from Veeda's sight collapsed. Aishah watched in stunned surprise as glass jars of coffee, jam and honey, bags of dried date shake mix—all toppled with a crash, knocking Veeda to the floor and almost burying her. Customers from all corners of the store converged on the scene. Veeda lay covered by a gummy blanket of jam and honey mixed with coffee grounds, date shake powder and broken glass.

Aishah heard calls of "Are you alright? Are you hurt?" as two men lifted the shelves and several women tried to help Veeda get up from the sticky mess.

Ignoring the chaos behind her, Aishah headed straight for the front exit. She pushed the door open and forced herself to walk at a normal pace past the disabled parking space and on to their car.

Plunking herself unceremoniously in the front seat, she commanded in a loud whisper, "Go!"

Mo leaned toward her. "What happened?"

"Don't ask, just drive."

He backed carefully out of the parking stall and pulled onto the highway.

The atmosphere in the car was tense. Several times Mo glanced sideways at Aishah. Her eyes never left the face of the sleeping baby on her lap. They were several miles down the road before Mo ventured his question again.

"Could you tell me what happened, exactly?"

"A miracle," Aishah answered. "It was a miracle." And she told him about Veeda shouting her name and the collapse of the shelves.

"Well," he said, "If it was a miracle, it was a weird miracle—involving jam and coffee grounds."

"It was the timing, Mo. Perfect timing. That was the miracle. Everyone ran to help Veeda so the way to the front door was cleared for me. Nobody even noticed me. I got out without Veeda recognizing me. I think I did, anyway," she added in a less confident tone. "I'm not sure… Anyway, it's a sign Allah wanted us to have this baby." She looked down at the baby in her arms. "You think so, too, don't you, my little sweetheart?"

As if in response to her voice the bundle on her lap wiggled. The baby's eyes opened to focus unsteadily on Aishah's eyes above her veil.

"Oh…" Aishah said, "It's awake."

"It?" asked Mo. "Is the baby a boy or girl?"

"I don't know." Aishah giggled nervously. "I'll take a look." She carefully unwrapped the white blanket.

"Well?" asked Mo.

"I don't know yet. So far just a white onesie, so that doesn't tell us anything."

After unsnapping the domes of the sleepers, Aishah awkwardly undid the tiny diaper. She was silent for a moment.

"Well?" Mo asked again, keeping his eyes on the road ahead.

"A girl. Our baby is a girl, Mo."

Mo exhaled sharply and Aishah realized he had been holding his breath as he waited for her answer.

She turned to look at him. "Are you disappointed?" she asked softly. "I know you wanted a boy."

"You know what, Aishah? I'm not disappointed. I'm surprised that I'm not disappointed… I'm just thankful for the baby… for her… for you. That we got through it all safely so far." He was silent for a moment, before he said again, "I'm just thankful."

Aishah heard the catch in his voice and she realized how anxious Mo must have been as he waited in the car.

After a short silence, he said, "I have no words to describe how I feel."

"Let's pull over at the next rest stop," Aishah said. "I think it's safe to do that. We need a bathroom break. Besides our little girl should be in her car seat, not lying on my lap."

"Okay," Mo said.

At the next rest stop they found a shady spot at the far edge of the gas station parking lot. Mo put the car seat on a wooden picnic table. Very carefully Aishah placed the baby in it. Neither of them could take their eyes off the infant.

"She's so small," Mo said, as he leaned closer to stare at the baby, now kicking her tiny feet.

"You can touch her, you know. She won't break," Aishah teased.

Cautiously Mo stroked the baby's downy head. "Look at her dark hair, she'll look like us, honey."

Aishah nodded gazing into the baby's emerald eyes. *I was praying she'd have brown eyes and dark hair. Oh, well, at least she has dark hair and maybe her eyes will turn brown, like ours. Babies' eyes change colour, I've heard.* She glanced up at Mo. *Funny that he doesn't seem to notice her eyes.*

"I can see the pulse on her head… or something," he said in wonder.

"That's her fontanel. Where the bones of her skull haven't closed over yet—so that she could pass through the birth canal," explained Aishah, proud of her knowledge of newborns.

"Look at her miniature fingernails," Mo placed his finger on the tiny palm. Immediately the baby's fingers tightened, curling around his finger in a firm grasp.

"Look at that," he whispered. "Look at how she grabbed on to me."

"Just a reflex, honey." Aishah laughed. "All babies do that."

"No, I don't think so." Mo said slowly. "I think she wanted me to know she's hanging on to me. She needs me." Aishah could see that he was fighting back tears as he spoke to the baby. "I'll look after you always." He looked deeply into the baby's eyes. "I promise. Don't you worry, my little daughter." He turned to Aishah. "How could she give her up?"

"She gave her up because she loves her," Aishah said softly. "I saw it in her eyes." Now she was crying, too.

"We have to be worthy of this gift. All of our lives we have to remember someone we don't even know gave us our child. She trusted us with her baby." Mo's voice broke.

"I know," whispered Aishah. "We will never forget her, even if we don't know her name."

The couple stood for several moments, gazing down at the baby. Mo was the first to break the spell. As Aishah watched wordlessly, he bent close to the baby's tiny right ear. He whispered softly the *Adham*, the Call to Prayer: *God is Great. There is no god but God. Mohammed is the messenger of God.* Then he took a small envelope from his shirt pocket. Opening it, he shook the contents into the palm of his hand. Not wanting to break the spell by speaking, Aishah raised her eyebrows in a silent question.

"It's dried date powder." Mo pinched a small amount of the powder and with the tip of his finger placed it on the baby's tongue. The baby made small smacking sounds with her lips.

"Look at that. She likes it," he said. "The Prophet, (peace be upon him), did this for all of his grandsons and other newborns brought to him."

"And you did it for your daughter." Aishah's voice held a tone of wonder. "Not quite the tradition, Mo." She couldn't resist teasing.

"Well, I wish I would have been able to do it immediately after she was born." Aishah heard the concern in his voice. "The Prophet (peace be upon him) believed that the first words a newborn should hear is the *Adham*. We weren't able to do that." Mo's frown deepened. "And I've heard that Christian mothers often take scented oil and make the sign of the cross on their newborn's forehead."

Aishah nodded. "I've heard that, too. They say something about marking the baby with the sign of the cross to show that the baby belongs to Christ."

They stared at each other in silence. Then they shifted their gaze to the baby. *Was that a glint of oil on the baby's forehead? Or was it just the sun shining through the leaves of the trees?*

Aishah broke the spell, saying lightly, "Our poor little girl—doesn't know whose she is."

"Yes, she does." Mo said firmly. "She's ours, yours and mine. She is part of the *Umma*, the world-wide Household of Faith. And I said the *Adham* last, so that cancels out any Christian hocus pocus."

"Our hocus pocus cancels out their—" Aishah stopped short when she saw the offended look on Mo's face. "Don't worry, Mo. We will raise her to be a faithful Muslim. She will be as loving and caring and generous as you are. *Inshallah*. We will be such good examples, how could she possibly go wrong?"

"Not a chance," Mo agreed smiling. "Look, she's sleeping. I'm hungry. We didn't eat much lunch. Did you bring any sandwiches?"

"Yes, I did." Aishah leaned over and whispered in his ear, "Traditional American Thanksgiving left-over turkey sandwiches. Don't tell anyone. We'll eat them in thanksgiving for our baby."

"I give up. You are impossible." Mo laughed as he reached into the lunch bag.

Aishah and Mo sat side by side at the picnic table, never taking their eyes off the baby even as they fumbled with the plastic wrap on their sandwiches.

A veiled woman and her husband paused as they passed the table.

"What a beautiful baby. Girl or boy?" the man asked, as they bent for a closer look.

"A girl," Mo responded.

After the couple had left, Aishah teased Mo. "You stuck your chest out when you said that."

"I did not."

"Yes, you did. It's okay to be proud of her. Allah's perfect creation of a girl for us. I'd better change her and we'll get going."

"What skinny legs." Mo watched as the baby's thin legs flailed. "And flabby skin. She's not very fat. She's really tiny."

"She'll fatten up," Aishah reassured him. "Actually, it's good she's a tiny baby. We're going to have to say she came a bit early, you know."

"Well, she did," Mo said. "That's the truth."

Aishah laughed. "You're getting to be as bad as me—or as good as me—at telling the truth."

"I'll never be as good as you are at stretching things, Aishah."

"I know. It's my special talent." She laughed. The baby had begun sucking on her fist. Aishah rummaged in the bag she had brought out of the tomb. "Look," she held up a baby bottle. "Lots of formula, already prepared." She wondered for a moment. *Somebody must have been there to help her.* She turned to Mo, "I'll warm this in the mothers' room in the store and be right back. You watch her."

"What? Me? What if she cries or something? I don't know what to do."

"Oh for goodness sake! She's not going to cry. Look, she's happy sucking on her fist. I'll be right back."

It took only a few moments for Aishah to warm the bottle, but as she walked back across the parking lot, she heard the baby's piercing thin wail long before she was even close to their picnic table. Mo was gently jiggling the car seat. Aishah laughed when she saw the look of embarrassment on his face.

"What took you so long?" he asked. "People are staring at us."

Ignoring Mo's question, Aishah lifted the tiny infant from the car seat. "Shh, it's okay, little girl. Mommy has your bottle for you," she crooned. Laying the baby in the crook of her arm, she guided the nipple into the baby's open mouth. Abruptly the crying ceased.

"How did you know how to do that?" Mo asked in awe.

"Just my maternal instinct," Aishah said. "Well, not really. I've been watching the women in the bistro feed their babies."

Again, the baby's bright eyes focussed on Aisha's eyes above her veil. The infant sucked noisily. After only a few moments she was asleep again.

Aishah looked at the half-full bottle. "I guess that's all she wanted. Now I have to burp her."

"Don't wake her up," Mo said. "She's really loud for such a tiny baby. I called Mom and Dad while you were gone and they said they could hear her, she sounded healthy, my Mom said. They said not to bother trying to talk—they'd see us tomorrow."

Aishah rolled her eyes.

The burping accomplished, Aishah placed the baby once more in the car seat. She fastened it securely in the back seat and climbed in beside it.

"I'll ride back here with her. See, I told you things would be different once we had a baby."

Mo agreed. "Yeah. I sure feel different, anyway."

* * *

They stopped once for Mo to say his prayers, then they carried on to their hotel on the outskirts of Los Angeles, arriving as the sun was setting. Aishah lifted the car seat from the car as Mo retrieved their overnight bags from the trunk. They lingered for a few moments, marvelling at the radiant red and gold bands of colour splashed across the western sky.

"I think everything will be okay," Mo finally said. "I think we've done it, honey." He put his arm around Aishah. "I need to apologize to you. Big time. I'm sorry I gave you so much trouble when we were deciding about this. I'd take it all back, if I could. I hope you can forgive me, sweetheart."

"Of course I can. Look at all the stuff you've forgiven me for!" Aishah stood on tip-toe to kiss him. The car seat bumped between them. "Whoops, the baby is coming between us already. I forgive you on the condition that you never mention it again. Deal?"

"It's a deal," Mo said. He picked up their bags. "We can stay here and just unwind tonight—take our time getting to the folks tomorrow afternoon. We need a breather. Let's check in, say our evening prayers and then find a place to eat."

"Let's order in," Aishah said. "I need to take this thing off." She tugged at her veil. "My baby hasn't even seen my face."

Once in their hotel room, Aishah unfastened her veil. "See. It's me. Your Mom," she smiled down at the squirming infant in her arms. The baby grew quiet, struggling to focus her eyes on Aishah's face. After another feeding, the baby once again fell asleep. Aishah placed her carefully in the car-seat.

"Well, that was easy. I don't know why people make such a fuss about caring for newborns."

"Yeah, so far so good." Mo looked down at the tiny bundle. "Maybe Allah blessed us with an extra good baby." He glanced at Aishah's stomach. "Where's your baby bump?"

"I wondered when you'd notice. I left it in the trash can at the picnic spot. The recycle one." She snickered. "Just in case someone else wanted to use it."

They were still laughing together as their pizza arrived along with a large bottle of cola.

"If we were really good Muslims maybe we wouldn't be able to have this—all the caffeine." Aishah filled their glasses.

"Lucky there's no hard and fast rule on that or we wouldn't be able to run a coffee shop, either."

"Do you ever feel guilty about drinking coffee and cola?" Aishah asked. She took a long drink, and burped.

"Well, maybe sometimes I do. And sometimes I don't. Tonight is one of the times I don't."

"I never feel guilty about it," Aishah said.

Mo smiled. "Now why doesn't that surprise me?"

When only the empty pizza box remained and the last of the cola was poured into their glasses, Mo said, "Okay, her name." He leaned back in his chair. "We'll announce it formally at the Aqiqah, but we should decide now so we can tell my folks tomorrow."

"We promised your mom we'd name the baby after her if it was a girl," Aishah said. "So, let's call her 'Fathima' after your mom. Maybe she'll like me better if we do that. She once called me an uppity woman."

"She likes you fine, sweetheart. I think she's just overwhelmed by your energy. But I know she will love it if we name the baby after her."

"Okay, Fathima it is. And Caroline, after my Mom," Aishah added.

"Fathima Caroline," Mo repeated. "That's a big name for such a little baby."

"She'll grow into it. Besides she'll probably get some sort of nickname later on, like you did." Aishah began rummaging in the canvas bag she had brought from the cave. "I'm going to get a couple of bottles ready, just in case Fathima Caroline wakes up in the night."

Mo leaned over the baby's car seat. "Oh, she won't. Look how peacefully she's sleeping. Good night again, my little sweetheart—and you, too, honey." He kissed Aishah and got into bed.

When Aishah crawled in beside him only a few minutes later, she marvelled at how quickly Mo always fell sleep. She usually lay awake for some time, thinking over the past day and planning for the next one. Tonight was no exception. Finally, she felt herself drifting off. Once again, she dreamt of the Christian woman. She was sinking in some kind of quicksand and reaching out to Aishah, begging her to pull her to safety. But Aishah's arms were shackled by chains and she could not help the woman, no matter how hard she struggled to free herself. Aishah woke up to the sound of her own sobs. Mo was holding her.

"What's wrong, sweetheart," he asked softly. "Has something happened to the baby?"

"No," Aishah managed to say between her sobs, "Nothing's wrong with the baby."

"What's the problem, then, honey? How can I help?"

"You can't help. That's the problem. Nobody can."

"Try me."

"It's this whole mess we're in… This whole life we're living. It's abayas and veils and not being able to look a man in the eye, and I can't even take a picture of our baby on our cell phone—unless I want to risk a whipping if they check my phone. It's all of that. And I'm not even allowed to drive a car," Aishah wailed. Mo was silent. "And another thing, being afraid all the time that we're displeasing Allah. You were even worried about having a

Thanksgiving dinner." Aishah's voice had become angry. "And beatings, and the morality squad patrols, and beheadings... It's all of that."

"That doesn't happen as much as it used to, though," Mo said.

"That's because there's nobody left to execute. Well, not many people. What about her mother?" She inclined her head toward the sleeping baby. "They killed her father and they're going to kill her mother. And I couldn't do anything about it. Nothing." She started crying again.

"Is that what this is all about? We did what we could. Why bring this all up now? We've been living under these laws for twenty years now. There's no way out of it. This is our life, Aishah. You're just tired and that's why you're so upset."

"Yes, I'm tired." Aishah retorted. "Sick and tired of the whole mess. You don't need to tell me how many years it's been. I don't care—I still can't get used to it. I've tried. But it's not right, Mo. I know that now." The soft glow of the nightlight illuminated her tear-stained face.

Aishah's voice grew calmer. "Something happened to me in the tomb today. When I looked into that woman's eyes something changed me. I saw her anguish and yet love, and yes, hope for the baby and me. I can't explain it."

Aishah paused for a moment, remembering what she thought she had seen at the mouth of the tomb: the *Man in White*. She looked away from Mo. *I will never be able to tell him that.*

She turned to meet his gaze again. "I know I'll never be the same after today. I will never ever believe that it is Allah's will for people—men and women and even infants—to be killed in Allah's name. I don't care if they are infidels. I don't care what they are. It isn't right. I know it, I know it." Her voice rose.

"Shh, shh," warned Mo, taking Aishah in his arms as choking sobs began again. "You'll wake the baby. I'm not saying it's right, honey. But this is how it is now. I know you remember better times… I remember better times, too. But we have each other, and now the baby. We have our life together and that is the most important thing. We have to do the best we can. Can you do that? For me and the baby? You are a good person, sweetheart. You're kind and compassionate, and you make people feel better. Everyone says so. Focus on those things. The things you *can* do, not the things you *can't* do. Be a good example of a caring Muslim woman."

Aishah's sobs were quieter now as Mo cradled her in his arms. He looked down at her tear-stained face. "I tell you what. I will always listen to you and I won't ask you to stop questioning things, if you promise me that you will confide only in me, if you'll talk about these things only with me. Can you do that? Can we keep this just between the two of us?"

"I know what you're trying to say," sniffled Aishah. "And you're right. We have to do the best we can within our laws. It's too dangerous not to. But, Mo, maybe someday things will change? Especially for our little girl. I want a better life for her. Can't things change someday?"

"Maybe they will," he said." There's always hope."

"That's it! "Aishah sat bolt upright, excitement in her voice. "Hope. You said there's always Hope. Let's call our baby 'Hope', because that's what she is for us. And every time I say her name, I will be reminded that there is always hope. I can hope for better times to return. Could we call her that, Mo? Maybe as her second name? Keep the first name Fathima, after your Mom, but we'll call her Hope."

"I'm okay with that," he said slowly. "Hope… A good name to have in our family. I need to be reminded, too, honey. We can always hope."

"And we can pray," Aishah reminded him. "You know sometimes I don't know who I am praying to. I'm just praying. But whoever I'm praying to doesn't ask us to murder women and babies."

"Okay, okay, sweetheart. We'll just keep that to ourselves, won't we? I think you've had a lot of this bottled up for a long time. I guess I've made a big mistake in telling you not to talk about it. So, let it all out with me. But only me. Promise?"

She nodded.

"I promise I'll always be here for you," Mo said solemnly. "I love you."

"I love you, too, and I'll always be here for you." Aishah blew her nose loudly. "Oh, no. I woke the baby. I mean, Hope. You go back to sleep. I'm okay. You're right. I just needed to get it out of my system. But I'll be taking you up on your offer to hear me rant now and then."

"Okay," Mo said, as he rolled over in bed. A few minutes later as Aishah fed the baby, she could hear Mo snoring gently.

"You have such a good daddy, Hope," she said as she placed the sleeping infant in her car seat once again. "Thank you, Allah, for Hope," she whispered, "and for some sleep."

The baby woke up three more times before sunrise. As the thin wail pierced Aishah's sleep yet again, she glanced at the bedside clock.

"Six o'clock," she muttered groggily. "She can't be hungry again."

Aishah could hear the faint sound of the early call to prayer, but decided not to wake Mo. *He needs his sleep, these next few days are not going to be easy for us. Those green eyes! Can we carry it off? What if something happens and they find out the baby isn't ours?* "But she *is* ours, now," she spoke out loud, in an effort to convince herself. "Nothing is going to go wrong."

In the semi-darkness Aishah slipped into her robe and warmed another bottle. As the baby sucked vigorously, Aishah said gently, "That's four times for you last night. How can you be so hungry?"

Hope's blue-green eyes blinked up at her.

Once fed, burped and changed, the baby resumed sleeping. Aishah figured out the hotel's coffee maker and made herself a cup of coffee, sipping it slowly as she gazed at the infant's tiny face.

Mo greeted her an hour later. "Good morning, sweetheart. Sleep well?" he asked.

Aishah threw a cushion at him.

"Have a cup of coffee and watch the baby." She said. "I'm taking a shower. I need to make myself look presentable for your folks."

"It's okay," Mo said. "If you look tired, you'll just look like any woman who has just had a baby. We'll go to a pancake house for breakfast. Strawberries and waffles, how's that sound?"

"Great. I always love trying to poke a fork full of waffle and strawberries and whipped cream up under my veil and into my mouth." She saw Mo's shoulders slump. "Sorry about that, honey—and the pillow. I've had a rough night. Sure, let's go for waffles."

The baby slept through their breakfast and on through the rest of the trip. They arrived at Mo's parent's sprawling cliff-side home before lunch.

Mo got out of the car and took a deep breath. "Ahhh... sea air. That's what I've been missing. Remember when we lived here how we would go outside to say our prayers just so we could breathe in the salt air?"

"I do. Do you wish we hadn't left?"

"Nah," Mo put his arm around her. "You were right. We needed to have a life of our own. Besides, I love what we have built together—the bistro—our home—and now that we're a family..."

Mo's mother hurried down the front steps to greet them. She patted Aishah's arm and asked if she could hold her namesake. Mo winked at Aishah, in a silent *"See? I told you."* Aishah smiled back at him as she handed the baby to his mother. By nightfall all of Mo's brothers and sisters had arrived for the evening meal and their first glimpse of the baby—seven sets of parents, each with at least three children in tow. Aishah never could keep track of which kids belonged to which parents, but Mo said he couldn't, either, so not to worry.

Aishah watched from the living room window as two catering trucks from one of the family's restaurants pulled into the driveway.

"No wonder your Mom likes entertaining," she whispered to Mo. "She doesn't have to do any of the cooking."

The men and older boys ate in one large dining room, the women and children ate in the other, so there was no need for the women to wear their abayas and veils. As Aishah had expected, the women were dressed in "fancy clothes" as she described them to Mo later. Even the little girls wore party dresses. Aishah had chosen a loose-fitting dress she thought was appropriate for a mother who had just given birth. It was bright red, but even so, she felt somewhat drab in comparison to the sparkling gowns surrounding her.

Mo's sisters and his brothers' wives complimented Aishah on the baby. "She's very tiny, though," one younger woman said.

"Well, she came early," Mo's mom volunteered. "Aishah will soon fatten her up, won't you, dear?"

"Of course," murmured Aishah. After a moment, she added, "I'm having a bit of trouble nursing her, so I have to supplement her feeds with a bottle." *Now why did I say that?*

"It's hard with your first one," Mo's mother said. "I remember I had problems. You'll be okay. Just give it time."

Aishah nodded.

"I guess you'll be hoping the next one is a boy, won't you?" asked Mo's youngest sister, jiggling her own baby boy on her knee.

Aishah looked down at Hope cradled in her lap. "Inshallah. I love my baby girl very much. I couldn't love a boy any more than I do Fathima Hope. If it is Allah's will I have a boy, then of course I will love a boy, too."

There was an awkward pause in the conversation. Finally, Mo's Mom broke the silence. "Let's just celebrate Fathima's birth, for now. A beautiful little girl to add to our family. Dessert is served." Everyone resumed their lighthearted conversation and laughter. Later that night Mo joined Aishah and the baby in Mo's childhood bedroom, next to his parent's room. The couple sat on the edge of the bed, sharing their accounts of their separate dinner conversations.

"My brothers said they supposed I was praying our next one was a boy," Mo said.

"The women said the same thing to me." Aishah grinned. "What did you say to them?"

"I didn't know what to say so I just said, *Inshallah*. What did you say?"

"I didn't know what to say, either, so I said the same thing, *Inshallah*."

"Well, no one can argue with that," Mo said.

They looked at each other and together they collapsed on the bed in a fit of uncontrollable laughter.

"Shush. We'll wake the baby," Mo warned. "And these walls are thin. Mom and Dad will hear us."

"Yeah, women aren't supposed to laugh this loud," giggled Aishah. "I hope your Mom didn't hear me. We must be incredibly tired or something. It's really not that funny."

"It is to me," Mo said. "We both came up with such a brilliant answer."

"Well, I think we're tired and stressed out over this whole thing. The sooner we get home, the better. Saturday night can't come too soon for me. Pretending I'm breast-feeding isn't easy. I don't know why I said that. I'm wishing now we had said the baby was born on Wednesday—then we wouldn't have had to stay so long."

"We have to stay until she's a week old, Aishah. That's the tradition. Besides, at least we can honestly say she came on Saturday. I know it's not when she was born, but at least it's a partial truth. I don't like deceiving my family."

"I know you don't, honey." Aishah glanced at the infant beginning to stir restlessly in the family crib Mo's mother had placed at the foot of their bed. "Maybe the baby will sleep better tonight when she's not in her car seat."

The baby began its piercing cry.

"Feeding time, again," groaned Aishah.

Mo slept soundly all night. Aishah and the baby did not. Monday night was the same.

They went to bed, but had barely fallen asleep when the baby woke up, crying loudly. Aishah tried feeding her, changing her, and pacing the small bedroom but nothing would stop her loud wail.

Mo whispered anxiously, "Mom and Dad are probably awake now, too."

"Maybe they'd like to take the baby for a while," suggested Aishah.

"You must be joking," Mo replied.

Hope finally fell asleep, only to wake in less than a couple of hours, again crying loudly. The scene repeated itself all that night. When Mo and Aishah joined the family for breakfast the next morning, they were met with icy stares. Aishah groaned inwardly. *Just another five days.* The following nights she slept on the couch in the downstairs den with Hope in her car seat once again.

"Your folks will be able to get some sleep if I'm down there with her," she said to Mo.

Mo nodded. "I'll take a turn, too."

Aishah's eyes filled with tears. "I'm just so tired, but I'm afraid you won't wake up when she cries."

"I could try, sweetheart."

"No. I guess I'll just have to do this. But thanks, my one in a million man."

The days—and nights—passed slowly for Aishah, but Saturday evening finally arrived. Mo was right—it was one of the biggest celebrations Aishah had ever attended. Mo's father had closed one of his restaurants for the event. Mo said even he had never seen so much food.

"And look how many friends they have," Aishah whispered to Mo from behind her veil. After the Imam read from the Koran and everyone had seen the baby, Mo's dad said a few words, and Mo said even fewer before the women and children went to their separate dining room. Aishah was glad to be able to remove her veil and be more relaxed. She'd given up trying to compete with the dresses the other women were wearing and had told Mo she didn't care how she looked anymore, either.

He said she was beautiful. She rolled her bloodshot eyes at him.

After the Aqiqah the baby followed her usual pattern of keeping everyone awake all night. Mo was up well before dawn, packing the car with the gifts they had received. During breakfast he announced they'd be leaving right away. No one offered any objections.

As they backed out of the driveway, waving goodbye, Aishah settled into the backseat beside the baby. "I think your Mom's glad to see the last of us. She said to come again, maybe when the baby is a bit older."

Mo laughed.

Aishah turned to look at the sleeping baby beside her. "Oh, yeah. Now you sleep. Why couldn't you do that last night?" Above her veil, Aishah's red-rimmed eyes smiled at the baby, and then at Mo. "She'll settle down once we're home. I'm sure of it."

He nodded.

A comfortable silence filled the car as Mo concentrated on his driving. Aishah felt too tired to talk. She wondered what was going through Mo's mind, but decided not to ask. They both needed some quiet time to plan for the days to come. People would naturally have questions about the baby's early arrival. They had to be convincing with their story. Aishah stared, unseeing, out the side window.

I can't deny I am worried about Veeda. What if she did recognize me? What if she saw the baby in my arms? If she did, she's not going to believe our story that the baby was born in L.A." Aishah envisioned the scene—Veeda confronting her in the bistro in front of all the other women. In her mind she rehearsed all the possible stories she could come up with.

Perhaps just a flat denial would work best. Just tell her it wasn't me. She glanced at Mo. *Should I tell him about my fears? Maybe he'd have an idea of what I should say. But he looks so content as if everything is fine now. I don't want to ruin his day.*

She gnawed on her bottom lip.

I won't say anything. Anyway, maybe that old saying is true— Ninety-five per cent of the things you worry about never actually happen. She looked down at the baby and settled herself more comfortably.

I'll just take a nap. Rest up for tonight. I sure need the sleep. I won't think about it anymore.

But she thought about it throughout the long drive home.

CHAPTER NINE

Aishah

Aishah had assured Mo that the baby would "settle down" once they were back in their own home, but almost a week had passed with no sign of that happening. Hope woke every two hours, crying lustily until she was fed.

"It's just that she's so tiny," Aishah explained to Mo as she crawled out of bed for the third time that night. "Her stomach is too small to hold enough milk to last more than a couple of hours."

"I'll get this feeding," he said. "You go back to sleep."

Aishah took him up on his offer.

Just before dawn the Call to Prayer sounded and the baby's cry began immediately afterward.

"Don't even think of complaining that the Call to Prayer is too loud," Mo said to Aishah. "Remember what happened to Tammy."

"Yeah, eighteen months in prison. She's never been the same since. Don't worry—I won't be saying anything to anyone. We can try covering Hope's window with a blanket to muffle the sound."

Mo nodded and headed for their small prayer room at one end of the hallway while Aishah went to the baby's room at the opposite end. Usually she could hear Mo praying, but not this morning. The baby's cries drowned out all other sound. Aishah jiggled the baby in one arm while she prepared a bottle with the other. She caught a glimpse of her reflection in the door of the microwave oven. Her dark hair hung in limp strands around her face, emphasizing the circles under her eyes. White splatters of formula stuck to the front of her navy housecoat.

"Yikes! I'm a mess. This is all your fault," she said to Hope, who was now sucking on her bottle.

When Mo came into the kitchen, Aishah handed him the drowsy baby.

"Coffee?" she asked.

"Yeah, I need it."

They sipped silently, both gazing at Hope's serene face.

"About the miracle thing at The Date Farm," Mo finally said. "You think it was a miracle the shelf fell on Veeda at just the right moment. I think the miracle was that Hope didn't cry. She's certainly cried ever since."

Aishah glared at him. "She's just a little baby. She can't help it. I think maybe she's got colic."

"What's that?"

"Well, something like stomach cramps. She'll grow out of it."

"When?"

"I don't know," Aishah snapped. "A few months maybe. It's not like I could get a book on this or look it up on the internet. I'll have to ask my ladies for advice when I open the bistro again. I promised I'd be back on Monday morning."

Mo wrinkled his brow. "That's just two days from now. How will you be able to wait on tables with Hope needing all of your attention?"

"They'll help," Aishah assured him. "They'll hold her, I think. They've all had babies. They know how it is. The bistro's been closed now almost two weeks. Holding a baby for a while will seem like a small price to pay for a little outing with their friends. Besides, we can't afford to keep the women's section closed any longer. It'll be fine, don't worry."

"I guess you're right." Mo sighed. "We definitely need the money. But let me go early and do the baking on my own. I'll take the car and come back for you later so we can both open up at ten."

Hope managed a tired smile. "Oh, that would be great. That'll give me more time to shower and get myself together a bit. I know I look terrible."

Mo got up and planted a kiss on her forehead. "You're even more gorgeous now that you're a mother."

"With these black circles under my eyes? I look like a raccoon."

Mo gave her a long lingering kiss. "You're one gorgeous raccoon, then, sweetheart."

* * *

Monday morning came all too soon. Hope had continued her pattern of sleeping only two hours at a time, day and night. When she wasn't sleeping, she was crying. The only time she was quiet was when she was sucking on her bottle.

"But I'm going back to work this morning," Aishah insisted.

That first morning was hectic, with Aishah grabbing only a muffin and coffee for breakfast just seconds before her first customer arrived. Hope had been fed and was sleeping. The women gathered around the baby's cradle near the back counter.

"She's a tiny angel," one of them said.

"Look at that dark hair!" another crooned. "It'll probably be curly like yours, Aishah."

A large black-clad frame abruptly pushed into the circle of women. As if on cue, everyone stepped out of Veeda's way.

"She's really scrawny, isn't she?" Veeda said loudly. The other women exchanged glances, avoiding Aishah's eyes.

Aishah took a deep breath.

"Well, she came sooner than we expected, so, yes, she's small," she said. And then, hoping to change the subject, added, "Veeda, you must know all about babies. I need some advice here. Hope only sleeps for a couple of hours and then needs to eat again. She cries a lot. Is that normal?"

"There's no such thing as normal when it comes to babies." Veeda gave Aishah a small tight smile. Aishah could tell she was pleased she had been singled out for advice. "You could try a soother. Look how she's sucking her fist. Give her a soother to suck on and you may be able to stretch feeding times out a bit."

"But she cries like she has pain—and doubles her knees up to her chin," Aishah said.

"Oh, that's colic, all right," Veeda nodded knowingly. "Driving babies around the block a few times sometimes calms them down. Too bad you can't do that." Veeda's voice had returned to its usual harshness. The smug smirk on her face was firmly in place. "You'll survive. We all do. You're not the first woman to have a colicky baby, you know."

"Well, thanks, Veeda. I really appreciate your helpful advice." Aishah made a mental note to tell Mo he could take Hope for a drive to stop the crying.

Veeda suddenly stuck out her foot, kicking the baby's cradle. Hope woke up and began her ear-piercing cry.

"Oh, sorry," Veeda said. "Guess I don't know my own strength. I'll have coffee and a blueberry muffin at my usual table, Aishah."

Aishah bent over the crying baby, fighting back an angry response. *Mo says to try kindness, but he doesn't have to deal with her.*

"I'll take the baby," one of the women volunteered.

Aishah handed Hope to her. "Thanks. I'll get everyone's coffee."

"I'll serve the muffins for you," another woman offered.

"Aishah!" Veeda bellowed from her table at the front of the bistro. "What day did you say Hope was born?"

Aishah swallowed hard. "Saturday."

"Well, that's odd. I was at The Date Farm Saturday and I'm sure I saw you there."

Aishah's grip on the coffee pot tightened. "Must have been someone who looked like me, I guess."

"Yeah. It sure did look like you," Veeda insisted. "I even called your name—but just then a whole row of shelves fell on me. Knocked me to the floor. By the time I crawled out of the mess—"

"Oh, tell us about that." Aishah spoke rapidly. "A whole shelf? Were you hurt? Did the store manager apologize? Did they give you any free stuff? They should have, you know. I tripped in a cheese cake restaurant once and they gave me a whole cheese cake to take home."

"You may trip, but I never trip. I have perfect balance. I definitely did not trip. Something weird happened. That whole shelf collapsed for absolutely no reason at all." Veeda's voice had grown even louder.

"That *is* weird." Aishah looked around at the other women who were hanging on Veeda's every word. She begged them silently: *Say something, say anything. Just this once, help me out with Veeda, instead of just sitting there.* She waited, but no one spoke up. Finally she said, "Veeda, it must have been some neglect on their part. Maybe stacking too much stuff on the shelves. They should give you a free date shake."

"They did better than that." Veeda looked at the listening faces surrounding her. Her thin lips twisted into a smug smile. "I have free date shakes there for a year—as many times as I want to go. So, you won't be seeing me here very much."

The women glanced quickly at each other. No one spoke.

After an awkward pause, Aishah said, "Well, we will all miss you." She glanced around at the silent gathering. "Won't we, ladies?"

"Oh, yes, of course we will. We will for sure," everyone agreed. Someone snickered and Aishah shot a warning glance in her direction.

"Time for Hope's bottle," she said, glad that Hope's whimpering was rapidly turning into a lusty cry.

As Aishah hurried toward the back of the store, Veeda called out to her, "Aren't you nursing that baby? Shame on you, Aishah."

Several women turned to see what Aishah would say.

"Oh, I tried the first week. I just didn't have enough milk for her. I would have loved to nurse her."

Veeda sniffed and tossed her head. "Well, I had plenty of milk for my babies."

"Good for you. I guess it must be Allah's will that my baby has the bottle. I'm just thankful that I have her." Hope's wails threatened to drown out even Veeda's loud voice.

"Well, she sure is noisy," complained Veeda. "It's not nearly as peaceful here with her crying like that."

"I know, I know." Aishah said, "I'm sure she'll settle down in the next few days."

* * *

But Hope didn't "settle down" as Aishah had anticipated. In fact, as the days passed, things went from bad to worse. Aishah had never heard of the term *projectile vomiting*, but several women in the bistro told her that was the baby's problem.

"Projectile" the first part means *expelled with force*," she explained to Mo after dinner one night as he cleaned up yet another milky mess spattered across their kitchen floor.

"Okay," he said. "I get that first part. Don't bother explaining the second part, I get the vomit part."

"Well, it could be worse. At least it isn't sour milk," Aishah said. "It's always just after she's fed, so it's just formula after all."

"Yeah, that's some consolation, Aishah." Mo continued scrubbing the floor on his hands and knees. As he glanced up at Aishah holding the baby, she noticed the laughter crinkling at the corners of his eyes. "Remember how you said babies were no trouble?"

"I love you, Mo," she said. "Nice bum." She pushed him gently with her foot.

"I love you back," Mo laughed. "I'll show you how much if we ever get this baby to sleep."

Aishah giggled. She beamed down at the baby. "You're a little sweetheart, even if you do make a mess. Now you go to sleep. You wouldn't want to come between your mommy and daddy, would you?"

The baby burped.

Aishah and Mo laughed again.

Hope's eyelids fluttered a few times before closing. Aishah carried her to her room and gently laid her in her crib.

"Now…" she said, and smiled.

* * *

Aishah was still smiling the next morning even when the baby's loud wail woke her just after the Call to Prayer echoed across the city. Aishah and Mo got out of bed simultaneously and a new day began.

It was a particularly noisy and messy day in the bistro, thanks to the baby. Aishah noticed fewer women volunteered to hold Hope.

"I can't blame them," she said as she and Mo lingered over dessert and coffee that evening. "They come to the bistro to relax. They don't want to have Hope throw up on them. And she cries so loudly. I've put her cradle behind the back counter, away from the tables—but that doesn't help much, noise-wise. I'm running back and forth between Hope and the ladies all day long." Aishah dark eyes filled with tears. "It's really wearing me out."

"Maybe we should close the women's section after all," Mo said.

"You know we can't," wailed Aishah. "We need the money. Although, that's another thing—some of the women have quit coming. I'm losing customers."

Mo pushed his chair away from the table and patted his knee. "Come over here, sweetheart."

Aishah snuggled into his arms and sniffed, blinking away her tears.

"We'll figure this out. We always do," Mo said gently. He gave her a little squeeze.

After a few moments of comfortable silence, Aishah announced. "What we need is a nanny."

"A nanny? Good idea, honey, but we can't afford something like that. That's for rich people like Brian. And even he didn't hire a nanny for Veeda with all those kids."

"No, he just took more wives and got more babies," sneered Aishah. "Don't get me started on Brian and Veeda."

"I thought you didn't see as much of her now that she gets free date shakes?"

"I'm not that lucky. Seems no one will drive her to The Date Farm."

"None of her sons will take her?" Mo asked. "Teenagers are usually happy to drive anyone—anywhere—anytime."

Aishah rolled her eyes. "They're following their dad's example of being mean to their mom."

"Well, I guess it is a long way. Not that I'm defending them," he added hastily.

"Anyway, I'm still stuck with her and she keeps making snide comments about Hope. Like today." Aishah imitated Veeda's harsh voice: "Where'd those green eyes come from? You and Mo both have brown eyes—it's really odd that your baby has those eyes."

Mo looked startled. "What did you say to that?"

"I told her we were surprised, too, but my mother's eyes were that same colour."

Mo raised his eyebrows. "Were they?"

"Of course not, silly. But it was the first thing that popped into my head."

Mo grinned. "What am I going to do with you?"

Aishah grinned back at him. "Well, anyway, it worked. There's the evening call to prayer." They both looked toward the baby's bedroom. "And there's the baby, right on schedule. I'll feed her. You go pray that Allah sends us a nanny."

"I'll be praying for a miracle, then," Mo tossed over his shoulder as he walked down the hall to the prayer room.

"I'm praying, too," Aishah called after him. As she picked up the crying baby, she murmured, "Allah, The Compassionate and Merciful, please hear my prayer and send us a nanny." Then she added, "And soon. Thank you."

Baby Hope stopped crying and blinked up at her mother.

"Oh you," Aishah smiled down at the baby. "I love you, you little handful. We'll get through this somehow."

* * *

About mid-morning the following day, Aishah noticed a black-clad, veiled woman sitting alone at a table close to the front door. The few women who had shown up for coffee that morning, glanced at the newcomer briefly, then continued their conversation. Hope was crying in her crib behind the back counter. Ignoring the baby, Aishah brought the stranger a cup of coffee.

"Peace be upon you. The first cup is on the house for new-comers." She smiled as she inclined her head toward the loud wails. "That's my baby, I'll feed her now and she'll quieten down."

"Don't worry about it," the stranger replied. "I know what it's like to have a crying baby."

Aishah smiled a polite smile. *Not like this, you don't.* A few moments later as she was giving Hope her bottle, Aishah felt a light touch on her shoulder.

"Let me hold her for a while."

Aishah looked up into the kindly gray eyes above the black veil and as she told Mo over dinner that night, "I don't know what came over me. It was like I was hypnotized or something. I handed Hope over to her. Just like that."

"How'd that work out?" Mo helped himself to another lamb chop.

"Great. Hope quit crying right away and stared up at her. That woman held her all morning and I kept taking her coffee and muffins. She sat behind the counter. She said she'd just sit back there and enjoy the baby."

"Wow. No throw up episodes, then, I gather?"

"Well, yeah, it was a bad morning for that, but it didn't seem to faze Natalie. That's her name—Natalie. She just mopped up the floor and kept a towel over her shoulder for any dribbles. She said when she was a young mom, her baby girl had colic and she grew out of it in a few months. She seems to know all about babies. I was sorry to see her go at noon. She said she'd maybe come by tomorrow, though. Sure hope she does. Maybe our prayers have been answered—for a nanny," she explained as she saw the questioning look on Mo's face. "You did pray for a nanny, didn't you?"

Mo nodded. "But honey, you can't expect Allah to answer prayers just like that—" He snapped his fingers.

"I can, too, and I do, so there. Where's your faith, Mo? That's not such a big thing to ask for. We asked for a baby and we got one, didn't we? That's a big thing. A nanny would be small potatoes." Aishah stabbed a potato with her fork and waved it at him.

"Oh, you," Mo grinned at her. "You're more of a believer than you let on. Even with all of your jokes."

"Well, wait and see. You should see how Natalie looked at Hope—she even had tears in her eyes. She told me she has a soft spot in her heart for babies. I have a good feeling about this."

"And do you have a good feeling about how we would pay her?"

"I'll pray about it." Aishah's eyes twinkled. "And you will, too, won't you?" When Mo didn't respond quickly enough, she asked again, "Won't you?"

"Sure, I will. Just don't get your hopes up."

"Hope's up." Aishah giggled as the baby began to wail.

Mo closed his eyes and groaned. "Oh, Aishah. I give up on you."

"No, you don't," Aishah said as she picked up the crying baby. "Daddy doesn't give up on us, does he?" she crooned as she rocked the baby in her arms. "Look, he's getting your bottle."

Mo responded to the prompt and got the baby's bottle ready.

CHAPTER TEN   *Aishah*

The next morning, Natalie was one of the first to show up
at the bistro. She hung her abaya and veil at the front door.
As she had the previous day, she looked after Hope, feeding her,
changing her diaper and cleaning up after her each time she
vomited. She volunteered to stay over the lunch time.

"Well, your lunch is on the house," Aishah said, placing a
sandwich and a glass of milk on the table in front of her. As they
ate lunch together, Aishah learned that Natalie was new to Palm
Springs, arriving only a few days earlier, and was living with her
brother.

"I don't know anyone here. The days are really long for me.
Mike's gone all day, looking for work. He doesn't mind dropping
me off here in the morning and picking me up on his way home
in the afternoon. Would you mind terribly if I just hung out here
at the bistro? I'll watch the baby. Otherwise I'm stuck in that
little condo, alone all day. Nothing to read— " She stopped in
mid-sentence. "Nothing to do," she finally said.

"Mind?" Aishah's eyes twinkled. "I'd love it. Come as often
as you'd like. I'm sorry that we can't afford to pay you for looking
after Hope, but at least I can give you food, no charge."

"Oh, you don't need to pay me. It would be great just to be
around other people."

Over the next few weeks they settled into a routine—Natalie arriving each morning and staying until closing time. Aishah told Natalie she had a magic touch with Hope. Natalie smiled and said that the baby just liked to be held.

"Well, whatever it is, my regular customers are starting to come back now that they don't have to listen to her crying. I can't begin to thank you enough."

That night as Aishah and Mo engaged in their usual pillow talk, Aishah raised the subject of a nanny again.

"Natalie's the answer to our prayers. If we could only afford her as a full-time nanny, she'd be perfect. Today she even cleaned the empty suite above the bistro so that she could take Hope up there when she is having an especially bad day."

"What's she like?" Mo asked.

"Kind of ordinary, I would say. I'm guessing she's around fifty. Just average height. Nice grey eyes. Light brown hair. She doesn't smile very often. In fact, she looks kind of sad. She never wears jeans like the other women—just long skirts and loose tops. Not very colourful."

"That sounds like a picture of a perfect nanny to me," Mo said. "Something like Mary Poppins."

Aishah laughed. "You still remember that old movie? I do, too. I'd give anything to see a movie again. Even that one. Anyway, the women like her, Hope likes her, and I like her. So you'd better be praying hard that somehow we can hire her."

"I *am* praying hard," Mo said.

"Good. After all, I'm a mere woman. I'm sure your prayers count for more than mine with Allah."

"And I'm sure you don't really believe that, but I know better than go down that road with you, sweetheart. And no arguments in bed, remember our rule?"

"Right. Just don't forget to pray about this."

"I won't. Mmmm… you smell nice."

"That's baby powder, silly." Aishah snuggled closer.

* * *

Almost two months had passed when Natalie told Aishah her bad news. They were wiping tables together after another busy afternoon at the bistro.

"My brother still hasn't been able to find work here." Natalie kept her head down as she scrubbed vigorously at the glass. "He's planning to try L.A. next. I don't want to leave here, but as you know, if he goes, I have to go with him. I can't live here alone."

Aishah's hand stopped in mid-swipe. She had always known that Natalie might not be staying on forever, but she had avoided thinking about it. She felt like she'd been punched in the stomach. Then she got angry.

"Here we go again," she said. "Can't have an unattached female wandering around on her own, can we?"

Natalie looked up, but didn't speak.

Aishah realized she'd begun to say things to Natalie that she knew should only be said to Mo. *Things like criticizing the law.*

"Sorry," she hastily apologized. "I'm afraid I'm a bit out of line there. I just feel so badly that you have to leave."

"That's okay, Aishah. Sometimes it's really hard for us, isn't it? I'm not looking forward to bouncing around the country with Mike, but he's the only male family member I have. I'd stay here if I could. I love Palm Springs. And the women here have been really nice to me. Especially you. So, thanks for that."

"I should be thanking you," Aishah said. "I wish you could stay, too. I don't know what I'll do without you. I've been praying for someone to help with Hope. Frankly, I thought you were Allah's answer to my prayers. But I guess not…"

"Have you been praying about that? So have I!" Aishah was surprised at the excitement in Natalie's usually calm voice. "I want so badly to be here with you and the baby, instead of moving every few weeks. Maybe we could work something out."

"I'm sorry, Natalie, but we can't afford a nanny." Aishah bit her bottom lip. "I really wish we could hire you, but we can't."

"Oh, money isn't that much of an issue with me. My husband left me enough to live on. Mike looks after my bank account and he says I'll always be okay if I watch my P's and Q's."

"P's and Q's?"

"That means I have to be careful how I spend my money," Natalie explained.

"Oh." Aishah grinned. *Natalie's always using expressions I've never heard before—probably because she comes from one of the northern states.*

"The big problem is the male authority thing," Natalie said. "Even if I could afford to rent a place here, I can't live—"

"Alone." Aishah finished Natalie's sentence for her. Her face lit up. "I have the answer to that. I'll have Mo ask our imam about it. Maybe you could live with us."

"Maybe as a servant? That might be allowed…" Natalie said slowly.

Aishah wrinkled her nose. "Well, not exactly as our servant. You could be our nanny for Hope. We have a casita in our front yard that we never use. You could stay in it. It would be like you were living with us because it's totally enclosed by our garden walls, so you wouldn't be breaking any laws about a woman living alone. It's tiny, but everything's there—small kitchenette, dining area and bedroom all in one, nice bathroom. You might find it a little cramped."

"It sounds perfect," Natalie said.

"You'd be looking after Hope in our house most of the time, anyway. We have a nice back yard—big pool and everything. You could spend a lot of time outside with Hope. Let me talk it over with Mo tonight. He can ask the imam after Friday prayers tomorrow. What about your brother? Do you think he will agree to this?"

"Oh, I'm certain he will."

As Natalie left to get into the car waiting at the curb, Aishah called after her, "Don't forget to pray for a miracle. I do that all the time."

Natalie turned back and waved at Aishah. "I do that all the time, too. Peace."

Aishah locked the front door and flipped the sign to "Closed" as she whispered her prayer. "Please Allah, or whoever is listening, it's me, Aishah, asking for just one more miracle. Please let the imam and Mo agree to this. If it's Your will, of course," she added.

Silently she scolded herself. *You are really getting cheeky with Allah. Cheeky? I'm beginning to sound like Natalie. Well, that's not all bad. She does have a nice soft accent. And she's very polite. She'll make a great nanny for Hope.*

When she discussed the plan with Mo over dinner that night, she was surprised to see how readily he agreed.

"If the imam says it's okay," he added. "I know you need help—*we* need help," he corrected himself.

Friday afternoon Aishah waited anxiously for Mo's return from the mosque. When she finally heard the back door close, she ran to meet him in the kitchen.

"What did he say?"

"Well..."

Aishah's eager smile faded.

Mo hastily added, "He said, yes."

"Yes, to the nanny? For sure?"

"For sure." Mo said. "Did you know Natalie's brother speaks Arabic? He's helping teach at the mosque. The imam is really impressed with him."

"Wow! Natalie never mentioned that. Actually, she doesn't talk about him very much. But if the imam likes him that's all we need to know."

Mo nodded. "He says he's sure that any sister of Mike's would make a wonderful nanny. So we'll do it. One thing though—the imam reminded me that I am responsible for all females under my roof: wife, child and servant. He said it about three times."

"No worries. We'll be good. All of us," Aishah said. "I can hardly wait to tell Natalie tomorrow morning." She tap-danced sideways across the kitchen floor.

Mo laughed. "Where'd you learn that? Maybe it's just as well dancing is forbidden, sweetheart."

"From a childhood friend. I wasn't very good at it back then, either." Her face sobered. "You know, this is another answer to our prayers. Allah is merciful. First a baby, then a nanny we can afford. I can hardly believe things are working out so well."

Mo agreed. "I know. We don't deserve all these good things."

"Maybe I don't, but you do. You're the best person I know. And you certainly keep the law better than I do."

"Yeah, I guess you're right there," Mo said. Aishah noticed his eyes were crinkling up at the corners—a sure sign he was struggling to suppress a laugh.

"Don't worry, Mo. I am going to raise our little girl to be the best Muslim woman you ever saw." Aishah stood on tiptoe to kiss him, but as she did, an unbidden thought raced through her mind.

What about the baby's mother? That day in the storeroom… What was it she said? Something about she was confident her God would make everything work out. She couldn't have meant she wanted her baby to be a Muslim, could she? She would want her to be a Christian. She said she trusted her God.

"Well, I trust Allah."

Aishah realized she had spoken her last thought out loud when she heard Mo say, "So do I."

"I'll tell Natalie in the morning," she said. "She'll be as happy as I am." As she noticed Mo's grin, she added, "Well, maybe not quite."

* * *

The next morning Aishah paced back and forth in the front entrance of the bistro as she waited for Natalie to arrive. When she heard the familiar knock, she flung the door open.

Ignoring Natalie's "Peace be upon you," Aishah blurted out her news.

"It's okay. The imam says it's okay to have you live with us as a nanny."

Natalie surprised Aishah by giving her a big hug. "I'm so happy," she said. Aishah laughed, but pulled away quickly from Natalie's embrace. It reminded her of that day in the storeroom and she was trying to put all of that out of her mind.

Stepping back, she said, "Well, we have to be good. Mo says the imam told him three times he is responsible for both of us now—and Hope, of course."

"I'll try to behave," Natalie teased, as the front door opened and the first customers of the day entered.

Aishah couldn't resist sharing her good news with everyone who came that day.

"Even Veeda seems glad you are staying," she whispered to Natalie. "She likes you."

"I'm trying to like her, too," Natalie said. When Aishah made a face, Natalie added, "I said I'm *trying*. I didn't say I was succeeding." Aishah giggled and to her surprise, Natalie joined her.

When closing time finally came, the two women celebrated with a cappuccino before cleaning up for the day. Natalie said she was happy to move into the casita immediately.

"You can come for me first thing tomorrow morning if you like."

As they chatted about how they would work out a schedule, Natalie agreed with all of Aishah's suggestions.

"You're being too agreeable," Aishah said.

Natalie laughed. "I'm just happy I can stay here. Mike's not sure where he will be going next. It can't possibly be as nice as Palm Springs, though. I have such good memories of this place. My folks used to bring me here to watch tennis..." Her voice trailed off. "Anyway, about my duties, I'm sure we can work everything out."

"Sure. Nothing's carved in stone. Except for Ramadan, of course. That's definitely carved in stone." Aishah grinned. "We always take that month as our annual holiday, no matter what time of year it falls in. Everybody's fasting all day, so there's no business for us. Are you good at fasting, Natalie?"

Natalie grimaced.

"That's how I feel, too. But around here the morality squad enforces it—anyone caught eating or drinking during the day gets a whipping. It wasn't like that before, remember? I feel sorry for the converts. I don't think they believe in Ramadan—or a lot of things. It must be hard for them. Oh, well, Mo always tells me not to think about it, we can't do anything about it. Anyway, thanks to Mo, I'm good at fasting—wasn't so good when we first got married."

Natalie smiled, but said nothing.

"We usually spend most of the month with Mo's family in L.A., especially if Ramadan falls in the hot season." Aishah's eyes lit up. "They live on the ocean. It's way better than spending the month here in the heat. You'll have to come too—since we can't leave you here alone. Or maybe you'd like to spend that time with your brother?"

"I'm not sure. I never know where he might be."

"Well, you would like it at Mo's folks, I think. No cooking, just huge meals after sundown for the whole family, and a big buffet breakfast prepared for us before sunrise. But if you don't want that month to be your holidays, we can work something else out."

Aishah looked around the empty bistro and dropped her voice to a whisper. "Do you remember before Unity took over—all the holidays we had? Thanksgiving, then Christmas, Valentine's Day—that would be coming up soon, wouldn't it?"

"It's tomorrow," Natalie said.

"Oh, is it? Well, that wasn't a holiday, but it was fun. And Easter holidays. Remember all the fun we had?"

"Sure do." Natalie was rocking the baby in her arms and smiling down at her. Without looking up, she said, "How did you feel about all that? Did you feel you were missing out on something, or what?"

Aishah glanced around the empty bistro again before answering. "Don't tell anyone, Natalie, but I actually got involved in some of it."

Natalie looked up quickly. "You did?"

"My parents were university professors and so they mixed with all kinds of people from different backgrounds. We had some Christian friends. It was okay back then. I played with kids who were Christians when I was a little girl. Did you?"

Natalie nodded. "Yes, I did."

Aishah smiled. "In fact, my best friend was a Christian girl. Sybil Thompson. She lived next door. We played with her Barbie dolls at her house. I wasn't allowed to have a Barbie, but I never told Sybil's mom that. She had sewn all kinds of clothes for those dolls. We had such fun, dressing our Barbies in little fur coats and bikinis. It's hard to believe that now, isn't it?" Aishah smile faded. "I wonder what happened to Sybil and her family."

Natalie didn't respond. She continued looking down at the baby in her arms.

After a few moments of silence, Aishah whispered softly, "I guess not anything good."

Natalie looked up. Aishah thought she saw tears in her eyes.

"You never know," Natalie said. "Maybe they survived. Maybe they escaped somehow. They say millions of people made it to safety in that first year. Maybe she's living in Mexico—or Canada, right now."

"Canada, probably, if they made it." Aishah was biting her lip. "North lies freedom, they said back then—same as when the slaves fled from the south. I hope she's there, but I guess I'll never know. I was just a teenager when the take-over happened."

Neither woman spoke. Silence surrounded them as they gazed at the sleeping baby's face, avoiding each other's eyes.

"I think of her especially in the spring." Aishah finally said. "I can't remember exactly when Easter was, but in April, I think. I remember all the church bells ringing. Do you remember the sound of bells, Natalie?"

"I do."

Aishah hurried on as a flood of warm memories engulfed her. "Sybil's mom made a big deal of Easter. I'd go over to her house and we would boil eggs and dye them and decorate them. Then her mom would hide all the coloured eggs in their yard under bushes, in the grass, just everywhere. Easter Sunday morning I'd go over and Sybil and I would have such fun—an Easter egg hunt. My folks didn't mind. Mom said it was a crazy custom. Sometimes I even stayed for Easter dinner. Always a big ham on the table."

Natalie raised her eyebrows.

Aishah laughed. "Of course, I didn't eat any. Sybil's mom knew I couldn't eat pork. She always had something else special for me—sometimes pineapple chicken. My favourite. She even bought Halal food for me. I have good memories of Easter Sunday. Odd, isn't it?"

"What do you think of the Easter story?" Natalie asked. "Or did you ever hear it?"

"Oh, yes. I know it. Couldn't avoid knowing it back then with so many Christians around. Hot cross buns—we couldn't have those now, for sure . But chocolate eggs, Easter bunnies—that stuff was okay. I think Sybil's mom said the eggs represented new life, or something. It all confused me at first, but she said not to worry about that and she told me the story from the Bible."

"What do you think of their claim that Jesus was crucified and rose from the dead, Aishah?"

"Well, that's just a myth. Everyone knows that. It didn't really happen. I know Jesus was a prophet and a good man. But Mohammed (peace be upon him) is the last and greatest, of course. I certainly don't believe Jesus was God's son. That's like believing there is more than one God. That's shirk, as you know, Natalie." Aishah spoke more loudly and rapidly. "Really serious sin to believe that. Mo says that's what caused all the executions back then, and even today. If Christians could just get over this Jesus stuff, they'd be okay. They wouldn't be in so much trouble with the authorities."

Natalie continued to look down at the baby in her arms. "Yes, if they could just get over their belief in Jesus," she repeated slowly. "But they can't seem to do that, can they?"

"No, they can't. I don't see why they are so stubborn." Aishah took a quick sip of her coffee. "I don't hate them, though. Even though our imam says we shouldn't have anything to do with infidels. I don't hate them. I know there are verses in the

Koran that says we should hunt them down. Jews, too. But then, somewhere else it says people can choose their religion."

"So what do you make of that?" Natalie looked directly at Aishah.

"I don't know what to make of it. Mo says it's complicated, depends which verse was revealed last or something. If there are verses that contradict each other, the verse Allah revealed last cancels Allah's previous instructions."

"That's called the law of abrogation." Natalie bit her lip and stopped speaking.

Aishah raised her eyebrows. "How come you know that?"

"Oh, I guess Mike must have explained it to me sometime."

"I don't think Mo knows about it." Aishah sighed loudly. "In the old days we could do an internet search on something like this. But not anymore."

"What would you do if you found that Allah's last instructions were to kill the Christians and Jews?"

Aishah shifted in her chair. "We're not supposed to question the Koran, so I don't. Allah knows best. I try not to think about it. I'm just glad I don't have to even think about it at all. I don't know any Christians. There aren't any around here." She paused a moment. "Well, maybe a few, but they're hiding."

"How do you know that?" Natalie asked.

Aishah swallowed hard. She felt her face growing hot as she realized the conversation had wandered into dangerous territory. "Oh, I just hear things. Mo hears stuff in the men's bistro, sometimes the morality squad says something. News gets around."

"Would you help them if they came to you—for food or anything?"

Aishah's cuckoo clock sounded five times and she stood up quickly. "My goodness! Mo must be almost finished cleaning the men's section and we've barely started. I'll vacuum, you wipe the tables."

She turned on the vacuum cleaner, drowning out any further conversation.

She could feel Natalie's calm gray eyes following her as she worked. Her mind raced. *Don't talk about Christian friends ever again. That's all past—over and done with. Will you ever learn to let it go?* She pushed the vacuum more vigorously. *It's all Natalie's fault. She always draws stuff out of me.*

A sudden wave of fear froze all movement. *What if she tells her brother what we talked about? He's friends with the imam. If she tells him, and he reports me, I would have to go for questioning. Mo's always saying we don't want the morality squad investigating us for anything, big or small. What if they found out about the baby?* A torrent of thoughts ran through her mind.

She shoved the vacuum into the cleaning closet. When she turned around, she was surprised to find a veiled Natalie at her side.

"I'm leaving now. See you tomorrow."

Following her to the entrance, Aishah managed a strangled "Peace," as she locked the door behind her.

She knows more than she lets on. "Abrogation." How come she knows stuff like that? What if she is an informer? If she reports me... It's all over. For me. For Mo. For the baby.

She sat down heavily on the foyer bench, her face in her hands.

"Allah, please help me," she whispered.

CHAPTER ELEVEN

Natalie

Why did I say anything about abrogation? And Christians? Now she'll tell Mo. Will they report me for talking about Christianity? Lord, help me.

Natalie prayed silently as she climbed into the back seat of the waiting car. She didn't realize the driver had been speaking to her until after they had pulled away from the curb.

"Sorry, Mike. What were you saying?"

"I said, how did things go today, Natalie?"

Natalie made a quick decision not to tell Mike about her conversation with Aishah. He might say it was too risky for her to stay, now. She took a deep breath before answering, "Great! Everything worked out as we planned. They're going to hire me as their nanny. Mo checked it out with the imam and he couldn't say enough good things about you. Your Arabic really impressed him. He told Mo that any sister of yours must be a devout Muslim—or words to that effect."

Mike smiled. "Well, I've certainly spent a lot of time at the mosque."

"Sorry you had to do that," Natalie said. "I know how I feel these days—like I'm living a lie."

"Well, we are, aren't we? We wouldn't last long if we were truthful."

Natalie nodded. They drove several blocks in silence.

Finally, Mike said, "I remember when I first started smuggling Christians in and out of the States. Lying became part of my life. I wrestled with my conscience a lot those first years. That's when I got all these grey hairs." He gave a short laugh. "But now I think of all the lives I've saved and I've come to believe that this is my calling."

He stopped at a red light and they watched as a young teenage boy led three heavily-veiled women across the street.

"I guess that will be *my* calling," Natalie said, staring at the women.

"You'll be okay, Natalie. Look how well you've done so far."

Natalie didn't answer.

"So... how soon do you move in with them?" Mike asked.

"Right away." She told him about the casita. "Mo and Aishah will be coming for me in the morning. If all of this is okay with you, that is." Natalie leaned forward and placed her hand on Mike's shoulder. She struggled to keep her voice from breaking. It was just beginning to sink in: her prayers had been answered, she would be living with her grandchild. It was enough for now.

"Mike," she said, "I can't begin to thank you—"

"No thanks necessary," he interrupted. "I'll always remember you in my prayers. We all will."

"And I'll always remember that day in the Missions to Muslims office—how they said they didn't have anyone who could get me down here right away and you said you'd do it. You risked your life for me."

"You're my sister in Christ, Natalie. We're family. Besides, you sounded like you might try it on your own. I couldn't let that happen." He glanced at her in the rear-view mirror. "But I'm not the only one risking my life. You'll be living in danger every day. And there's no one to get you out when I leave. I know we've gone over this before, but I have to ask just one more time. Are you positive you won't come with me without the baby?"

Natalie nodded. "I just can't do it. She's my granddaughter. I won't leave unless I can take her with me."

"I'm sorry we can't get her out. Too many checkpoints. Fake passports worked okay for you and me, but without papers for the baby... If we got caught with her... Well, you know what would happen to all of us, Mo and Aishah, as well, when the whole story came out."

Natalie fought back her tears. "I guess you could say that my calling is to be with Hope, just like it's your calling to be with the underground church."

Mike nodded. "I understand that. I just hate to leave you down here all alone. I'm confident that someday there will be a secret group of Christians in Palm Springs and then you will have some support. The Lord willing."

"As Aishah would say, *Inshallah.* But for now, I guess it will be just me." Natalie managed a tremulous smile. "You have been the answer to my prayers, bringing me down here, overstaying our agreed time. I know others need you, too. So, where do you go next?"

"Los Angeles. I'm meeting up with a friend. We don't know where we'll go from there—maybe the East coast—maybe more trips like this one. I really shouldn't be telling you this—for everyone's safety, you understand?"

Natalie nodded. "Of course."

"You have my phone number, but don't use it unless it is a dire emergency. We change phones often, anyway, for security reasons. So that number won't work for long. I'll call you when I think it's safe. We never know when our phones are being monitored so always be careful what you say. I have a little code I use. I talk about the weather a lot. Basically *cool* means things are good and if I say it's getting *hot* then you'll know things are not good. Of course, if I'm back in Canada, I won't call you at all. Too risky. So don't worry when you don't hear from me for a long time." He glanced at Natalie in the rear view mirror. "Okay?"

"Okay." Natalie blinked back her tears as they pulled into the condo parking lot.

Over their farewell dinner Natalie tried to ignore the fist of fear slowly tightening around her heart. Talking seemed to help—as long as it wasn't about the future. She found herself chatting on about her sense of disbelief as they had driven through ghost towns and sparsely populated cities. She told Mike she felt like she had stepped back twenty years in time—old cars, crumbling roads, decrepit buildings. She knew she had told Mike the same things several times over the last two months, but each time he listened patiently.

"My husband and I used to spend winter breaks down here—we drove on that same highway. I just can't believe it—not a church—or library—or even one public monument left standing. And all those abandoned houses—it doesn't seem real."

"My first trip down, I was as shocked as you are," Mike said. "I guess I've gotten used to it over the years—a little bit, anyway. Now I'm just aghast at all the overgrown parks and untrimmed palm trees. Everything here needs a haircut, including the people. Look at me in this shaggy beard! I get some weird looks back in Canada."

Natalie ignored his attempt at humour. "There's no life—no enthusiasm. Half the women at the bistro look like they're still in shock—after all this time. Everybody worries about keeping the law."

"Yeah, they sure watch what they say," Mike agreed.

"Except for Aishah." Natalie told Mike how Aishah had talked about Unity one afternoon after all their customers had left. "She told me that everyone had thought Unity stood for uniting the people and instead it meant we all have to be the same: look the same, worship the same, talk the same, think the same. I was surprised that she would say that to me. But I'm flattered, too. I'm sure she'd never feel free to say that to the women at the bistro."

Mike nodded. "I don't think so, either. They never know who may report them. It's scary for everyone. You're very brave, Natalie—willing to live down here with them. I admire you for your faith."

"You admire my faith?" Natalie took a deep breath. *I have to tell him.*

All during their trip down from Canada and the two months they had shared their life together in the condo she had hidden her true feelings from Mike: her doubts and fears and especially the hatred she felt toward all Muslims. She tasted the now-familiar bitterness rising in her throat once again. *I was too late to save her.*

Natalie's voice broke as she said, "Mike, you wouldn't admire me if you knew what I'm really like inside."

Ever since that snowy night when her daughter's letter had arrived, she had carefully suppressed her anger. Everyone told her she was handling her grief so well—her husband's death and now only a year later, losing her daughter.

They said I was such a good example for those around me! If they only knew what I was really thinking.

Now, to her horror, her rage bubbled to the surface, erupting in a torrent of words.

"You know what, Mike? I hate these people. Yes, you heard right. I hate them. The sooner I can get out of here with the baby, the better. I don't care what happens to anyone else down here."

"Really?" Mike raised his eyebrows.

"Yes, really. I know as a Christian I should forgive them, but I'm having trouble doing that. Everybody I see. Even Mo and Aishah—well, at least they took the baby. I'll give them that much. But here I am, about to live with them, and I hate them for killing my daughter. I know I'm supposed to forgive them, but I can't."

Mike said nothing.

"Are you shocked? I'm a Christian and yet I have so much hatred in my heart."

Mike reached across the table and took her hand. "God understands that, Natalie. And so do I. Maybe I'd feel that way too, if I were in your shoes. But this forgiving thing will come. God will give you the gift of forgiveness, I'm sure of it. If that's what you really want."

"I do. I pray for it all the time, but nothing happens. I'm hoping the women in the bistro don't see the hatred in my eyes when I look at them."

"Well, they're not the ones responsible for much around here," Mike said. "Besides, they may look like dutiful Muslim women—with their veils and all, but most of them were forced to convert. And the men, too. The number of actual believing Muslims is pretty small. They're as trapped as you are, you know?"

"Yes, I know all that. But still, they're the ones I see every day and for me they represent the whole system. I know I'm being unreasonable. Maybe it's just part of my grief process, but I can't help it."

"Natalie, you know what I think you should do?"

"What?" Natalie heard hostility ringing in her voice. *Why does he always think he has the answer to everything? He doesn't know what it's like. He hasn't lost a daughter like I have. If he quotes one more Bible verse to me, I'll scream!*

"I think you should just give up on praying to God about forgiveness," Mike said. "Don't nag. Just believe that God has heard your prayer and will answer it. Act like you have already forgiven them, and I'll bet you'll find that sometime in the future you will have. Just accept that God will give you that gift, maybe not right now, but it will come. Do you think you can do that?"

Natalie took a deep breath before trusting herself to answer in a calm voice. "Yes, I can do that. It will take a miracle though."

"Well, then, that's no problem for God, is it?" Mike smiled.

"You're right." Natalie's tone softened. "I made it down here and I'm looking after the baby. So… no. Miracles are no problem for God."

They drank their tea in silence. She and Mike had become close friends in the last couple of months—sharing breakfast and dinner every day, enjoying long conversations sometimes into the wee hours of the morning. Still, Natalie was embarrassed at her outburst.

This was not how her British-born parents had raised her. Along with how to enjoy afternoon tea, Natalie had been taught to control her emotions: no angry outbursts, no crying and always be polite. Natalie could still hear her mother's voice: "Keep a stiff upper lip, no matter what happens to you."

She fought the urge to lay her head on the table and simply sob out all her fears and feelings of despair. *Never wear your emotions on your sleeve, Mother said. She would be aghast at my behaviour tonight.*

Mike glanced over at her. He rose from the table.

"You look tired, Natalie. And we both have to pack. I'll be leaving early tomorrow morning."

She stood up, also. "Thanks for being so understanding. I know I'm not very good company tonight."

"That's okay. I'll be out of here before Mo and Aishah come for you. If that's alright with you? One less acting job for me."

"That's fine," Natalie spoke past the lump in her throat. "I thank the Lord for you and your organization. Please tell them that when you return to Canada."

"I will." His eyes studied her face. "I'm not sure when that will be. I'd like to stay in America. I'm grateful Canada took us all in, but America is my country. I never in my wildest dreams thought I would be a refugee. I still have trouble believing what happened."

"Me, too," Natalie said. "Remember in the old days, when we used to ask each other, 'If you were arrested for being a Christian, would there be enough evidence to convict you?' We never thought it would one day become a reality, did we?"

Mike shook his head. "No. But after I got involved with Missions to Muslims in Calgary, I learned about America's new reality pretty fast. I knew right from the start that this was my life's work. I didn't take on some of the riskier jobs in the early years because I saw how hard it was on my parents—worrying about me all the time." He looked steadily at Natalie before continuing on. "That's why I've never gotten involved with anyone—just didn't want to lay that burden on a wife. Now that my folks have passed on, I'm going to be taking more risks."

"What's more risky than smuggling people across the border?" Natalie wanted to hear more so she sat down again, and so did Mike.

"Not much," he laughed. "Staying in America to set up secret Christian groups is probably more risky, though, because I'll be in one place for a while, and living among the people instead of just passing through. But if we truly love as Christ did, then we are to resist evil as he did. He didn't just stand by and do nothing, and neither can we. Unity is evil. So I can't just go on helping a few of the people escape, I've got to do something to defeat the whole system."

"So you're going to do that with Christ's love?"

Mike nodded. "I'm in this for the long haul. I may never see the change in my lifetime, but I believe it will come.

"And you said you admired *my* faith!"

"Well, I do. You're in an entirely different situation. You'll be alone. I'll have at least one other Christian working with me. You'll be stuck down here, whereas I might go back to Canada every once in a while to bring others down. So I'll get a break from all of this. You won't be getting any breaks."

Natalie grimaced. "Maybe a miracle will happen. Remember how quickly things changed when Unity took over? A change back to a free America can happen just as quickly."

"I believe it can. That's what many of us are working toward, and that's my prayer—a free America."

"Mine, too. So we'll work hard and pray even harder."

They joined hands across the table and bowed their heads as they asked God to shield them from harm. Mike finished their prayer, "We come to you in the Name of Jesus, Who loved us and gave His life for us." When they stood up, Mike gave Natalie a close hug. She broke away with a strangled, "Goodbye."

She climbed the stairs to her bedroom, clenching her jaw to stop her chin from trembling. Only after she was safely in her room, with the door closed behind her, did she allow her pent-up emotions to surface. She sat on the edge of her bed, burying her face in her hands as the tears coursed down her cheeks. She sobbed quietly.

"Lord, I am so afraid," she whispered. "There's no going back now. I'm all alone. Please protect me." She wondered how many times she had prayed for protection in the last few weeks.

AND HAVEN'T I ALWAYS ANSWERED YOU?

Natalie couldn't tell if the voice came from within herself or from somewhere in the room. She turned to see who had spoken, and as she did so, a feeling of peace descended on her.

"Yes, Lord. You have always answered me," she spoke into the empty room.

Natalie didn't know how long she remained wrapped in a comforting blanket of silence, but she knew time had passed as she heard the late night call to prayer echo across the city.

"From now on, Lord, every time I hear that call I'm going to pray that the people here will come to know You as the God of love," she said softly. "I want to tell them but I sure don't know how that's possible right now." She took a deep breath. "And besides, Lord, You know that I don't love them. You know the hate in my heart. How can I show them Your love when I have these feelings? So, it's all up to You. I always say that, don't I? Please work this all out somehow."

Lost in thought, Natalie gently caressed the quilt covering her bed. She felt the coolness of a slippery satin patch beneath her fingertips and looked down.

"Karyn's graduation dress… I am so glad I sewed all of her clothes," she murmured. She ran her fingers over another patch. "Her polka-dot sundress." As Natalie's hand moved across the quilt, she smiled. When she had delivered the patches to her church women's group back home they hadn't hesitated. *You need it in a week? No problem. We can do it.* And they had.

Natalie leaned across the bed and pulled firmly on the edge of a blue and white gingham patch. The Velcro strip attaching the fabric to the quilt lifted away, revealing a pocket. She reached inside and withdrew several tissue-paper pages. Smoothing the thin paper, she began to read her favourite verse from the Bible: Deuteronomy 32:11. *As an eagle stirs up its nest, and hovers over its young; as it spreads its wings, takes them up and bears them aloft on its pinions, the Lord alone guided him.*

She sat quietly for a few moments before tucking the page back into its pocket and pressing the Velcro seam closed.

She whispered a short prayer: "Loving God, thank You for showing us what You are like in Your Word. I am like one of those baby eagles. I need to learn to fly in this strange new world. Please pick me up when I falter, and carry me on your strong wings, just like that eagle. Amen."

Her eyes followed methodically from the top row of patches, across the next row and the next, as if reading lines of print on a page. She patted the quilt. *My Bible is with me here.*

Natalie switched off the light and climbed into bed. She expected to have a restless night but was surprised when she woke to the dawn Call to Prayer echoing across the city. Smelling the aroma of freshly brewed coffee, she dressed quickly and went down to the kitchen, hoping Mike was still there. But he had left.

She looked for a note on the kitchen table, but found only a plate of toast and beside it a new cell phone. She smiled. *Thanks, Mike. Even if I can't use it to call you.* The toast was still warm. Mike had decorated the top slice with a peanut butter heart and a cross inside of it.

Mike remembered it was Valentine's Day. A good day to begin my new life. Natalie took a huge bite of the forbidden symbol. She realized that she was looking forward to the day with a mix of emotions—confidence tinged with fear.

She hummed a little tune and then stopped short. *No singing allowed now, Natalie. Ever. Remember.*

She packed her few belongings, donned her abaya and veil, and was waiting inside the front door when Mo's car pulled up to the curb.

CHAPTER TWELVE

Natalie

"Hi, Natalie," Mo said, when she opened the front door for him. "Glad to finally meet you."

In an instant Natalie's new-found confidence melted away. She wasn't quite sure how to respond. She had studied Islam years ago at university and Mike had coached her on Shariah law and social customs all the way down to Palm Springs. *What did he say about meeting a man? Why am I forgetting this now?* She knew it was forbidden for men to touch a woman, so she knew she definitely should not reach out to shake his hand. But should she look at him when he spoke to her or should she keep her eyes downcast? She decided the safest route was to avoid any eye contact.

"Is this all you have?" Mo asked as he picked up her small suitcase.

Natalie nodded. Still focusing her eyes on the floor at her feet, she picked up her quilt from the chair in the hallway.

"I'll carry that for you." Mo reached out to take it from her.

Natalie clutched her bundle to her chest.

"Oh, no thanks. I can manage this. Could you bring my sewing machine from the den, though, please?"

"Sure."

Natalie waited at the front door.

As they were leaving, she turned to look back at the living room of the small condo.

"You know, I've liked it here," she said. It's been cozy."

"It'll be even cozier in the casita," Mo grinned. "Aishah says it reminds her of her doll house." He stopped. "She had a doll in the before time... I guess she's probably told you that. Of course we wouldn't have one now..."

Natalie nodded. "Of course not."

"Anyway, we expect you will be spending most of your time in our house with the baby."

Natalie stood looking at the dining room table, remembering all the evenings she and Mike had talked and even laughed over a cup of tea. "I've felt safe here," she said.

"Safe?" Mo asked. "Why wouldn't you feel safe, here or anywhere?" When Natalie didn't answer, he added, "I guess I don't understand what it's like to be a woman these days. Since all the changes, I mean. I guess it's harder for you, even than it is for Aishah. You've lived more of your life in the before time, haven't you? I mean you're older. . ." he stammered.

Even though she was wearing her veil, Natalie tried to suppress her smile, worried that her eyes might betray her amusement.

Mo hurried on. "But you are safe under my roof, Natalie. At our house, you'll be part of our family."

When Mo opened the car door for her, she was surprised. "Thanks, Mo. I mean, Mohammed," she said. Then, in her confusion, she glanced up and looked directly into his eyes.

Now it was her turn to feel embarrassed. Not only had she met his gaze, she had used Aishah's shortened form of his name. *I must be more careful. So much to remember! It was easy in the bistro with only women, but I haven't had any practice being around men. What will he think of me?*

Mo simply grinned. "Don't mention it."

Natalie climbed into the back seat. Hope was in her car seat in the middle, Aishah on the far side.

"Good morning," Aishah said, leaning across the baby.

"Hi," Natalie said, with a casualness she did not feel. Seeing Aishah reminded her of the previous day's conversation. *Did I say too much? She doesn't look like she suspects me. But still…*

"Is that your security blanket?" Aishah teased. "You're sure hanging on to it!"

Natalie looked down and realized she was holding the quilt with tight fists.

"Something like that," she replied, attempting to match Aishah's light tone. "My quilt always reminds me of home, makes me feel good. I guess you're right. It *is* my security blanket."

"Wish I had one." Aishah stroked the blue satin patch.

Natalie quickly lifted Aishah's hand and held it. "Maybe I could teach you how to quilt and you could make one."

"Hah!" snorted Aishah. "You haven't seen my sewing."

Mo glanced in the rear view mirror as he joined in his wife's laughter.

"That's okay, honey," he said. "I didn't marry you for your quilting ability."

Natalie was surprised at the easy banter the couple enjoyed. *Maybe living with them will be easier than I thought.*

When they reached the bistro, Natalie put the quilt in the trunk on top of her suitcase and sewing machine.

"I've locked it. So don't worry about your quilt," Mo assured her, his eyes crinkling up at the corners.

"Okay," Natalie said, but she was quite sure she would be doing just that all day long. *And, Mo, would be worrying, too, if he knew what was in there.* She half-smiled.

When they entered the bistro kitchen, Mo told her that their imam had given permission for her to remove her veil in his presence. "Since—and I'm sorry to have to say this—but the imam says he would be classifying you as our servant."

She tried to look hesitant but inwardly she was relieved that she would be allowed to have her face uncovered when the family was alone.

"I hope you're not offended," Aishah said. "I think it's from the old days where people had slaves—the imam isn't sure of the rules—he says Americans do things differently. Mo says our system is a mish-mash of various customs and laws—but anyway it's because you work for Mo now. One of the many perks, I'm sure." She giggled as she hung up her things and held out her hand to take Natalie's outer garments from her. When Natalie removed her veil, Mo studied her face for only a moment before demonstrating how to operate the large mixers and set the oven timers.

"There you go," he said, a few minutes later as she slid her first tray of muffins into the wall oven. "Congratulations. Your first batch. Well done, Natalie. You are a natural born baker."

"Well, I have done a lot of baking in my time," she smiled up at him forgetting again to avert her eyes.

"Glad to hear that," Aishah joined in the conversation. "Guess that means I can do less from now on."

All three of them laughed.

They sat around the kitchen table, talking about their favourite recipes as they enjoyed a cup of coffee and the first of the muffins.

When it came time to open up the women's bistro, Natalie was almost relaxed as she carried a sleeping Hope into the bistro and placed her in her cradle behind the back counter.

She poured Aishah another cup of coffee and they sat down to await the arrival of the first customer. Natalie had expected they would continue their easy banter, but instead Aishah said nothing, staring down at the table in front of her and stirring her coffee.

For several moments Natalie listened to the clank of Aishah's spoon as it traveled round and round in her cup. She wondered why Aishah had suddenly gone silent. *Things were fine in the kitchen. What's different now?* And then she remembered: *We're sitting at the same table we sat at yesterday—when we had the conversation about Christianity. She's as worried as I am that we said too much. She thinks maybe I'll report her."*

A feeling of relief washed over Natalie. She leaned across the table and touched Aishah's hand. The stirring stopped as Aishah looked up to meet Natalie's eyes.

"Can we make a pact together?" Natalie said. "Like sisters, maybe. Whatever you say to me in private stays private. And whatever I say to you in private stays private?"

"You mean yesterday's conversation, don't you?"

"Exactly."

"Okay," Aishah hesitated, and then in a louder voice said, "Okay. Let's always do that. You and me. Like sisters."

"Like sisters," repeated Natalie. "That's great. I'll be the older sister, obviously, so I'll always be right, of course."

Aishah grinned.

Natalie continued, "We can talk about anything to each other and never tell our secrets to another living soul."

Aishah's lips began to twitch into a smile. "I know," she giggled, "Like, what happens in Las Vegas stays in Las Vegas."

"Exactly!" Natalie jumped up to give Aishah a hug, spilling her coffee.

They laughed together as they mopped up the table.

Natalie always looked back on their conversation that morning as the moment when they had turned a corner in their relationship. During the next few weeks, she noticed Aishah's cautious attitude softening and they talked and joked together. She wished she could be as carefree in her own speech and manners. *But... one wrong word...*

"We really are like sisters, aren't we?" asked Aishah one day. "I never had a sister."

"I never had a sister, either," Natalie said. "But I'm glad I've got you now. Besides, I know sisters who don't get along at all, so maybe we are better than normal sisters."

"There's nothing normal about me," Aishah giggled. "I've never fit the mold in my family, you know. Not serious enough, not humble enough for a woman."

"I've never fit the mold in my family, either," Natalie replied. "Too serious, too quiet."

Aishah's expression suddenly turned solemn. "When Hope was born, I never would have thought it would turn out like this—that along with a baby, I would get a sister, too."

"I never would have thought that, either," Natalie said, matching Aishah's expression.

"You never know how things will turn out, do you?" Aishah beamed.

Natalie looked down at the black and white tiles at her feet. "You never do," she said softly. And then, lifting her head, she smiled directly into Aishah's eyes as she repeated more loudly, "You never do."

* * *

The sun-filled weeks passed rapidly. After Aishah and Mo left for the bistro each morning, Natalie lifted Hope from her crib, cuddled her closely, and swaying gently back and forth, she sang to her.

She knew that music of any kind was forbidden. But she also knew she had only these first few months before the baby would learn to talk and perhaps repeat forbidden words, so she sang the songs she had sung to her own daughter many years before. Leaning in close to the baby's ear, she sang softly—sometimes a lullaby, sometime a hymn, often choosing "Jesus Loves Me."

She wondered if there could be any Christian mothers in Palm Springs doing the same thing. *After all, nobody knows what really goes on behind those heavily-draped windows and walled yards.*

Occasionally Natalie accompanied Aishah and Mo to the bistro, helping out with the baking and customers while the baby slept. She sometimes volunteered to work at the restaurant so that Aishah could spend the day at home. When Aishah reminded her that their agreement covered childcare only, Natalie explained that a baby needed to see lots of her mom.

"Besides, I enjoy getting to know the women—" She stopped short. "I enjoy getting to know the women," she repeated, a note of astonishment ringing in her voice. "I really do. I like them."

"They like you, too," Aishah said. "They say you're a good listener."

But this time Natalie *wasn't* listening. She was staring at the opposite wall, a rare smile on her face.

* * *

Natalie felt almost happy as the days went by, but her nights were another story. She sometimes felt she could actually taste the loneliness rising thick and bittersweet in the back of her throat.

She couldn't sleep. She tried everything—reading the Bible hidden in her quilt, praying and meditating, even drinking warm milk before bedtime. "And I hate warm milk," she spoke out loud in the darkness of the casita.

Mike had called her from L.A. a few days after she had moved into the casita. He had wanted her to know he was relocating to the East coast. He didn't know where, exactly, but promised to get in touch with her "when it was cooler." It was now the end of May and no phone call had come.

She worried.

Three months! Perhaps he has returned to Canada? Or maybe something has happened to him?

Every sleepless night she thought of him, reliving their last goodbye hug in the condo. She had pulled away abruptly because… *Because what I felt in his arms scared me. He has become more than a friend to me.* She scolded herself out loud: "You're being silly. You're just feeling attracted to him because you know he's the only Christian you will ever talk to. He doesn't even call, for goodness sake! If he cared, he'd call, wouldn't he?"

Mo and Aishah quit asking her if she had heard from her brother. Natalie realized everyone was used to people mysteriously disappearing. No one dug too deeply into the circumstances. It was better not to know.

There's nothing I can do, no one I can talk to about my fears. Natalie's worst nights came when she opened the blue velvet patch containing her daughter's last letter. Just a folded scrap of brown paper. She had read the note so many times—by now she couldn't tell whether the tear stains blotting out some of the words were her own or Karyn's. Somehow, when she held the crumpled paper in her hand and read the familiar handwriting she felt closer to her daughter. She knew it was risky to keep the note. Still. . . she just couldn't part with it.

Dear Mom

They have executed Stephen. By the time you receive this I, too, will be with the Lord. But I think I can save my baby if I can hide out until it is born. A nice Muslim couple who run a bistro here have agreed to take the child and tell no one. Do what you can. I am trusting God.

In Christ Alone, Karyn

Holding the note gently in her hand, Natalie whispered, "I'm here, honey and I'm with your baby. I don't know what to do next. There's no way to get her out. Like you, I'm trusting God to show me what to do."

On one particularly agonizing night of tossing and turning, half-awake and half-asleep, Natalie whispered her prayer, "Dear God, what should I do? If I'm to take Hope away from here, please let me know how." She paused. "And give me peace, Lord. Please give me peace. This is too heavy a burden for me to bear. I'm placing it in Your hands."

She waited in the darkness for some feeling that her prayer had been answered, but felt nothing. She slept fitfully, as usual.

CHAPTER THIRTEEN

Natalie

It was mid-summer when Natalie realized that her prayer had been answered. The tension had lifted. *I'm calmer. Almost like I used to be before all this happened. Almost...*

She grew accustomed to wearing her black garments, walking out in public only when accompanied by Mo and generally leading an isolated life between the bistro and the high walls enclosing her tiny casita and the family house.

She weighed her words carefully before speaking. As far as she knew, she had never slipped up in betraying her Christian faith. She had referred to Allah as "God" a couple of times, but then, so did Mo and Aishah. She avoided starting any conversations with any of the women in the bistro, preferring that they introduce a subject. She learned by listening. She paid even closer attention to the conversations in the bistro as Ramadan approached. She wished she could remember more of what she had learned about it back home.

"Did your family keep strict Ramadan rules when you were a kid?" Aishah asked, as they prepared for their trip to L.A.

"No, we didn't," Natalie said. "I'd like to just fit in with Mo's family customs now, if that's okay with you."

"Of course. Actually, I had to learn a lot of stuff, too, when I married Mo. About all I knew was that Ramadan was the time when the Prophet, (peace be upon him), received The Koran from Allah. But Mo explained a lot to me, and now I'm as good at fasting and keeping the laws as the rest of them. The women don't do all the prayers at the mosque like the men do, though. Did you used to go the mosque more often during Ramadan?"

"No, I didn't."

"Maybe you're like me. I like to pray by myself, at the beach in front of Mo's parents' place."

"I would like that, too."

"Everyone eats a big breakfast before dawn prayers and then the men go to work as usual and you and I can join the other women and take long walks on the beach. We can always find some male member of the family to chaperone us. The kids play in the sand all morning, and the day goes by quite quickly. It's hard to feed the younger ones at noon, and not be able to eat anything ourselves, though. And we get really thirsty, but we all sleep in the afternoons, as long as we can, and before you know it, the sun has gone down and we can break the fast."

"That sounds really nice, Aishah."

"Yes, but the best part is the dinners each evening, after sundown, at one of Mo's dad's restaurants. Or sometimes they have the food brought in. So, no cooking for the entire month! It's always a party. The women eat separately, with the children, of course, but that's good—no veils and we can wear what we like— although the women in Mo's family like to dress up for dinner. I'm the only dowdy one. On our budget... Oh, well..."

"I'll sew some fancy dresses for you, Aishah, and for Hope, too. Sounds like I'll have lots of time on my hands. I'll take my sewing machine with us. Los Angeles probably has more fabric stores than Palm Springs. It'll be fun to go shopping."

"That'll be great! But the Eid celebration at the end of the month is when they really dress up. One new dress for that would be fine. What about you, though?"

"What will I wear? Something demure and nanny-like, for sure. Don't worry."

Aishah laughed. "I never worry about you, Natalie. I'll guide you through the way Mo's family does things. You'll be fine."

And she was.

Her favourite part of the day was the early morning walk on the beach when she was not yet feeling the pangs of hunger. Sometimes she would sit alone, a little way off from the group of women and children and watch the waves roll in. Every morning she prayed for each member of Mo's large family. She had memorized all of their names.

Aishah said Mo was impressed. "Neither of us can remember them all."

During the long afternoons, Natalie tried to forget about her hunger as she sewed several formal dresses for Aishah. She used the left-over pieces of fabric to make a dress for the baby. In the evening she stood back as Aishah entered the women's dining room carrying Hope in her arms. She smiled as Aishah tossed her dark hair over her shoulder and did a pirouette in front of the group of women. Hope's emerald eyes widened as she looked up at her mother and she smiled a toothless smile. Everyone laughed, including Natalie.

"Fathima Hope is lucky she has your dark curls, Aishah. And Mohammed tells me she inherited your mother's green eyes. How lovely," Mo's mother said.

Aishah smiled down at the baby.

"You must have a private seamstress," Mo's sister said. "I've never seen a dress like that. Is it an original?"

"Yes, it is." Aishah walked over to Natalie who was standing just inside the doorway. "This is my artistic, gifted nanny and friend, she can do pretty well anything— "

"I can't model clothes quite like you can, Aishah."

Everyone laughed again, and they sat down for dinner.

Aishah sat next to Natalie who held Hope on her lap. "Thank you," she whispered.

* * *

After their break for Ramadan, it was back to business as usual at the bistro.

Natalie settled into a comfortable routine. Daytime was filled with caring for the baby, either at home or at the bistro. Evenings were often spent around the pool, enjoying BBQ meals with Aishah and Mo.

Natalie sewed clothes for the baby and for Aishah—even creating swimsuits with sleeves, legs and high necklines that met modesty standards. At least, Mo said that they met his standards and after all, they were in their private walled yard. She noticed, though, that he added an additional two feet to the top of the walls.

Natalie loved her cozy casita and her quiet times alone at night. *Just me and my quilt.* She smiled. Mike had finally called and said it was quite cool where he was, and that he remembered her in his prayers. He said nothing that would ignite suspicion if their conversation was being monitored. A small spark of happiness glowed in Natalie's heart.

All in all, except for the loneliness and her continuing worries about Mike's infrequent phone calls, it was a better life than she had anticipated.

There had been only two unsettling events in the past few months. The first happened at the bistro one afternoon when Aishah was explaining to Natalie about the cuckoo clock.

"It's all I have left to remind me of my Dad," she said as they stood together admiring the clock. They hadn't noticed Veeda standing closely behind them. She moved away quickly, but not before they both saw the wide smirk on her face.

"She'll report this to Brian," Aishah whispered to Natalie. "I know it."

Sure enough, at closing time the next day Mo told them he'd received a call from the morality squad. They wanted him to hand over the clock.

"I'm sorry, honey, but I'll have to give it to them." Mo looked downcast.

Aishah cried and then ranted angrily. "I'm never serving that woman coffee again."

"You don't know for sure it was Veeda," Natalie pointed out.

"Well, who else could it be? And right away like this! If I could ban her from the bistro I would."

"You can't do that," Natalie said. "I'll serve her when she comes to the bistro."

A few weeks passed before Aishah spoke to Veeda again. By then something more terrifying had invaded their life and grieving the loss of a cuckoo clock seemed trivial in comparison.

It happened late one Friday afternoon when Mo returned from Friday prayers at the mosque. Aishah and Natalie were enjoying a cup of tea and watching Hope as she played with her blocks on the kitchen floor.

"Mo's late today," Aishah said as they heard the back door open.

Mo didn't speak as he walked into the kitchen and sat down at the table. His face was pale.

"Tea, honey?" Aishah asked.

"No… not now. Maybe a glass of water would help." Mo buried his face in his hands. "They made us watch them crucify a Christian today."

Aishah put her hand over her mouth as she gasped, "Oh, no."

Natalie simply stared at Mo's bowed head.

He abruptly pushed back his chair and headed down the hallway to the bathroom A few seconds later the women could hear retching sounds even though he had slammed the bathroom door closed.

"You go to him," Natalie said. "I'll take Hope for the night."

Aishah nodded and ran down the hallway as Natalie lifted the toddler into her arms.

"Come on, sweetheart, you can spend the night with me." She heard Mo throwing up again—dry, rasping heaves and then muffled sobs. Cold rage filled her heart. She looked down at the baby. "I've got to get you out of this barbaric country."

The next day Aishah and Mo didn't speak of the incident, nor did Natalie. No one at the bistro mentioned the crucifixion. The conversation was muted. Natalie studied the women's sombre faces. *I shouldn't be surprised. I'm as scared as they are.*

Life went on as usual at home and at the bistro. But it was at least two months before Natalie heard Mo laugh again.

* * *

Natalie realized she had been in Palm Springs almost a year as the end of November arrived and with it, Hope's first birthday. It was a warm day so they celebrated around the pool. Natalie and Aishah sat on their lounge chairs while Mo watched his chubby toddler splashing in the shallow end of the pool.

Aishah turned to Natalie. "I never thought Hope would grow out of her colic and vomiting, but look at her, she's fine now."

"Well, miracles do happen, you know," Natalie said. "Maybe this is just a small miracle. We both prayed, didn't we?"

"And Mo, too," Aishah said. "Don't forget him. He cleaned up a lot of messes and drove around the block a lot of nights to get her to sleep. I'll bet he outdid us in our prayers." She laughed. "And besides, he's a man, so his prayers count for more than ours."

"Do you really think so?"

"No, of course I don't. But you need twice as many witnesses in court if they're female, so maybe it's the same with prayer. Don't tell anyone I said that, though. Mo says I've got to quit joking about things like that. And he says that no matter what I might think about something, I should always remember that Allah knows best."

They watched Mo and the baby in silence. Aishah suddenly turned to Natalie. "I wish my mom and dad were alive to see her."

"They died when you were quite young, didn't they?"

"Yes." Aishah's voice had dropped to a whisper. "I was only ten."

"Oh, I'm so sorry," Natalie said, taking Aishah's small hand in hers. "Do you have any other family?"

"I had a brother," Aishah responded, still whispering. "Ahmed. He was taken, too."

"Taken?"

Aishah bit her lip. "Can I tell you something? Will you promise not to tell anyone?"

"Of course."

"They didn't die."

"Your parents didn't die? They're alive?" Natalie's words hung in the air for several seconds before Aishah responded.

"No... I don't know. They just disappeared. And my brother, too." Aishah's gaze was focused on a hummingbird as it hovered over the backyard feeder.

"That's terrible," Natalie said softly, leaning closer. "Can you tell me how it happened?"

"I've had to piece together what I *think* happened. Back then, I was too young to figure it all out. It was a few years before Unity completely took over, but the rules in our community were starting to tighten up. My parents taught at the university. They had Christians, Jews, and other infidels for friends. They must have known there are verses in the Koran against that. don't you think?"

"Yes, probably."

"Anyway, they invited all sorts of people to our house and visited in their homes, too. In fact, they went to a church occasionally for friends' weddings and funerals. I think what really caused the problem, though, is they belonged to a group of people who were trying to stop honour killings. You know—like when a teen aged girl disgraces the family by dressing immodestly or dating boys or, worst of all, converts to another religion. There weren't a lot of honour killings back then, but it did happen."

Natalie nodded again. She was afraid to say anything that might discourage Aishah from continuing.

"Well, my parents actually held some meetings in our house. They put ads in the newspapers and inside the city buses, saying: *If you are afraid of being the target of an honour killing, call this number.*"

"I saw that in Can—" Natalie began. "I saw that where I lived, too."

"Or it could have been the spoon thing."

Natalie wrinkled her brow. "The spoon thing?"

"Yeah, you know… when people started a movement requiring that young girls who were boarding a plane for certain countries could be taken aside for questioning if a spoon showed up on their security x-rays."

"What? A spoon? Why?"

"Didn't you hear about that? Sometimes parents took their girls back to their home country so they could marry them off when they were too young to be married under American law. Or sometimes for 'vacation cutting'—"

Natalie interrupted. "Vacation cutting?"

"It was called that because it happened during school vacation time during the summer. If they took the girls away for genital cutting early in the summer, the girls' wounds would be healed up by time school started again. In an effort to stop that, someone thought up the idea of letting the little girls know that if that was happening to them, they were supposed to hide a spoon in their panties and it would show up on the airports security screening. And then they'd get pulled aside and could tell security officials."

"I never heard about that," Natalie said slowly.

"Well, I think it was Sweden, or maybe it was Denmark, started it first, and there was a movement to start it in America, too. I think my parents probably got involved with that."

Natalie couldn't hold back. "You should be very proud of your parents. They gave their lives for those little girls."

Aishah took a deep breath. "As far as I can figure out, there must have been some sort of morality squad even back then, before the takeover, because one night, just after dinner my mom and me were in the kitchen loading the dishwasher and my dad and my brother were in the living room when we heard the doorbell and then loud voices when dad opened the front door. My mom must have known what was going to happen, because she told me to run over to Sybil's house—my Christian friend next door I told you about?"

Natalie nodded.

"Mom shoved me out of the back door and told me to run as fast as I could." Tears were streaming down Aishah's cheeks. "Those were the last words I heard my mother say. I took one look at her face and I just went."

"And then what happened?" Natalie asked gently.

"Nobody was home at Sybil's, so I sat on their back step until it got dark. I waited and waited, but nobody came for me. Finally, I went back home. I called for mom and dad and Ahmed, but no one was there. I went upstairs to my bedroom and crawled under the covers, but mom and dad and Ahmed never came back. I cried myself to sleep."

Putting her arms around Aishah, Natalie held her close. "I'm so sorry. I'm so sorry."

Between sobs, Aishah continued her story. "I thought my parents would come back for me the next morning, but they didn't. I never saw or heard from any of my family again. It must have been Unity or people who thought like them. Looking back now, it seems everyone but me knew what had happened, I guess, because Uncle Faisal, my dad's brother, came to our house early the next morning. I was still in my room, hiding under the covers, afraid of the noises I heard downstairs, when my uncle came into my room. He seemed surprised I was there. The worst part is, I think my uncle knew what was going to happen that night, or else how come he was at our house so early the next day... Or maybe he just heard about it? I don't know... He probably couldn't have done anything anyway. No one has ever spoken to me about it. I suppose they were afraid. So I guess I'll never know for sure. I've wondered all these years. Are they alive or dead?"

"Some people escaped, you know, Aishah. Some people made it to Mexico or Canada. Maybe your family got away, somehow," Natalie said gently.

"Maybe. But I doubt it. Anyway, my uncle took me to their house and I lived with them. I didn't talk about it to anyone. I guess everyone thought I'd forgotten about it and life went on as normal. But I've never really gotten over my family being taken away like that. I think that's why I'm so afraid of losing Hope. It would just kill me if I lost anyone else I loved. The first few months after she was born I used to dream almost every night about losing her. I used to dream that someone came and took her away from me." She sighed. "Thank goodness I don't have those nightmares anymore."

"I'm glad, Aishah." Natalie was staring hard at the crimson bougainvillea blossoms tumbling down the garden wall. *How could I ever take Hope away from her?*

She turned to face Aishah. "Were your uncle and aunt kind to you?"

"I guess my uncle and aunt did the best they could for me. They were older, they'd raised their own kids and really didn't want another one. I didn't get much affection, but I certainly had all the clothes and material things anyone could wish for." She laughed a dry laugh. "Guess that's why I never learned how to cook or keep house—just never had to do those things."

"You're fine, Aishah. Your house and your cooking are just fine." Natalie handed her a tissue.

Aishah sniffed. "My uncle sent me to a private boarding school. I liked it there—made some girlfriends." She smiled. "You know, Natalie, the funny thing about it was that I was just a normal kid when they sent me off to that school, but I learned a lot of things I probably shouldn't have, pretty fast. You see, the school was full of girls who were considered wild, so their parents had sent them there. And I think some of their attitudes rubbed off on me. I guess maybe that's why I question things so much, even in the Koran. Mo says I shouldn't. Maybe that's why I'm kind of weird, though."

"You're not weird, Aishah."

"Anyway, I was taken out of school when my uncle decided I was old enough to get married, so there went my dream of being like my mom and going to university. And, of course, that's the last I saw of any of my friends. Our community in L.A. was becoming more observant of Shariah law and my uncle and his family were very traditional. I tried to fit in as best I could—wore the abaya and hijab. Veils weren't required at that time."

Natalie could think of nothing to say, so she simply handed Aishah another tissue.

Aishah dabbed at her tears. "I met Mo the same year Unity took over. I was fifteen and we were married when I was sixteen, so we were married under Shariah law. Mo and I loved each other right from the start. Did I ever tell you he crossed out the spaces for more wives when we signed the legal documents? He's the best thing that came out of the whole mess."

"You've done really well," Natalie said. "Your Mom and Dad would be very proud of you. Who knows? Maybe they've been watching over you all this time." Natalie glanced up at the sky and then looked at Aishah. "From above."

"Do you think that could be true?" Aishah blinked back her tears, a note of hope in her voice. "They were taken for not keeping the law, you know. Do you think they could be in Paradise if they broke the law like that?"

"Well, I'm just a mere woman." Natalie winked, "But I believe God is a God of surprises. Only God knows for sure."

Aishah smiled. "Everyone thinks I'm an airhead—that I never have a serious thought or care. But I keep things inside me."

Natalie raised her eyebrows.

"Well, the important things, anyway. But I've never forgotten that day. I was angry and bitter those first years. I kept thinking about what happened. How I could get even. The more I thought about it, the worse I felt. It was like picking the scab off a wound, you know? It never got a chance to heal. Then one day I decided I wasn't going to live back in that dark part of my life anymore. I don't support Unity, and I think what those people did was wrong. But I don't hate them anymore. I've gone on with my life. And now I have Mo, and Hope... and you, too, Natalie." She smiled. "So now you know all my secrets."

"Your secrets are safe with me."

"Oh, Mo knows. I think that's when I fell in love with him. He helped me heal. We were talking before we were married and he just came out with it one night. He said he knew about my folks. He thought it was terrible and he promised to always protect me and love me. Right then I knew he was the one for me—not that I had any other choice. I wasn't considered a good catch. I had the reputation of being a rebellious female. My school background didn't help. Anyone who knew my parents didn't want me and I didn't have any money to bring into a marriage. Mo said he didn't care about any of that."

"You were lucky to find each other. God is love." Natalie gave Aishah's hand a little squeeze.

"Oh." Aishah sounded surprised. She looked up at Natalie and slowly repeated, "*God is Love.*"

Just then Mo dumped a dripping wet Hope onto Aishah's lap.

"Here you go, sweetheart. She's all yours."

"She's yours and mine." Aishah smiled up at Mo. "God is love."

Mo glanced at Aishah and raised his eyebrows. Natalie thought he was about to ask a question, but instead he simply nodded and jumped into the deep end of the pool.

"You go swim with your husband. I'll look after Hope," Natalie said.

"Okay." Aishah handed Hope to Natalie. "Look out, Mo!" she yelled as she did a cannonball into the pool, almost landing on top of him.

Natalie smiled as she wrapped the squirming toddler in a large towel.

"See, what nice parents you have, sweetheart?" She kissed the top of Hope's head.

"Do you know what, Baby Girl? Your mom just taught me something about forgiving. Not forgetting, but forgiving, in spite of everything. If she can do it, I can do it." *Thank you, God, for Aishah.*

Natalie took a deep breath and smiled into the baby's emerald eyes. "Today I begin to forgive."

CHAPTER FOURTEEN

Natalie

Natalie couldn't remember exactly when Mike had become something more than a friend to her. She decided it must have been somewhere after Hope's "terrible two's", or was it the "trying three's"? She wasn't sure. But here she was—a grandmother, for goodness sake—feeling like a teenager again—looking forward to Mike's calls with excitement and then afterward analyzing every word he said.

She told herself she was being silly. *At my age! And besides, he made it plain to me that he had never considered marriage because of his dangerous mission. Maybe he sensed something between us way back then, in the beginning. But that means maybe he felt something, too… No, it's just this crazy world I'm living in—he's my life-line to reality. That's all.*

Mike's calls were few and far between, their conversations mostly in their own invented code: *It's too hot to travel these days, especially with small children. We'll have to wait for cooler weather.* And so it had gone, for almost five years now.

But Natalie allowed herself to dream. Aishah and Mo didn't question her about her brother and she understood why. Over a casual cup of coffee she had slipped up and mentioned that sometimes Mike couldn't call her because he was out of the country. Aishah and Mo had looked quickly at her and then at each other. Mo cleared his throat and changed the subject. Only people closely connected to the government were allowed in or out of America. Everyone knew that.

Natalie decided that her blunder was perhaps a blessing in disguise. If Mo and Aishah thought Mike worked for Unity, they wouldn't want anything to do with him. She decided to leave them with their false opinion—no more questions for her to answer, no more lies to tell. Fortunately, their interest and time was occupied with a new problem that involved the entire family.

The day before Hope's fifth birthday, Natalie and Aishah embarked on their campaign to convince Mo that Hope should learn to read, even though under the Unity government's law only boys were educated.

"And she should learn some math, too," Aishah argued. "Even if she's a girl, Mo, it will be an advantage if she can help out with bills and things at the bistro."

"We'll have to teach her to read from the Koran," Natalie said, "It's the only book we have."

Mo flashed a glance at Aishah. "It's the only book we're *supposed* to have."

Aishah's face turned red. "We can teach her a lot without books, too," she raced on, "about nature and stuff and we can explain how things work"."

"Maybe I should teach her some mechanical stuff, too?" Mo smiled.

"Why not?" Natalie asked.

"I'm only joking, Natalie. Women aren't allowed to drive, so what's the point in teaching them how to change a tire?"

"I know how to change a tire," Natalie said.

"I don't, but I drove a car once," Aishah said. "Back in my wild teenage days. For about two blocks in L.A.—until I hit a tree."

"I drove a car, too," said Natalie. "A lot."

Mo grimaced. "Don't get started reminiscing about that, you two. If it was up to me, you'd be driving, but it's not up to me. It's against our law. And that's that. We were talking about reading, before we got side-tracked. I'm going to agree we teach Hope to read. I'm not absolutely certain we should be doing this, but I can't imagine going through life not knowing how to read. Just don't tell anyone about it."

"We won't," Aishah and Natalie said simultaneously.

Natalie wondered why Mo hadn't suggested asking the imam.

He has started getting permission for almost everything lately. Why not this? Maybe he is afraid the imam wouldn't allow it. Does Mo realize he's putting his little girl ahead of the law? Well, I'm certainly not going to point that out to him.

Instead, she said, "Mo, I know you are concerned, but we'll do our best to educate Hope without breaking any laws. We promise, don't we?" She turned to Aishah.

"Definitely. You have our solemn promise." Aishah grinned.

"For what that's worth," Mo said, the corners of his eyes crinkling with his smile as he looked at his wife. "But, seriously, I'm holding you to your promise. We do not want to break the law."

"We won't, we won't," Aishah promised again. "Besides, what possible harm could come from teaching our little girl to read?"

Mo shrugged.

Natalie smiled.

In the following days Natalie used every opportunity to begin the young child's education. She left the reading lessons to Aishah and sometimes Mo joined in, as together they pointed out letters, and then words, in their English translation of the Koran. Math was Mo's responsibility. Natalie was to teach everything else. She used everyday experiences and objects and was surprised at how much could be taught without using books. Hope's favourite word was "Why?"

"Why is it dark?"

"Why is it light?"

"Why is it cold?"

"Why is it hot?"

One afternoon, as Natalie and Hope lounged around their back yard pool, Hope observed, "Too hot today. Why is it so hot? I like the cool nights, Nana."

"Me, too," Natalie agreed. "I know of a country far away from here that has days that are as cool as our nights. And the nights there can get really cold."

"How cold could the night be, Nana?"

"As cold as this ice cube."

Hope's emerald eyes widened in surprise. "Can we go there, Nana, and get cool?"

"No, not right now. Maybe someday you will go there. In that country there is snow and ice in the winter time."

"Snow. I've never seen snow, have I?"

"Remember when we cleaned out your mom's freezer? All the white frost we took out? Snow is something like that, only very soft and it falls from the sky like feathers, in big white flakes. And you can stick out your tongue and catch a big snow flake on it and it will melt because your tongue is warm. And the snowflakes make it so that you can hardly hear any of the noise around you, cars and things."

Natalie was gazing at the far garden wall, a dreamy smile on her face. "And you can use your hands to form the snow into a ball—like an orange—and throw it at somebody and have a snowball fight."

"That would hurt," Hope interrupted her. "That's bad. Throwing an orange at someone would hurt them, Nana."

"The snowball just breaks up into snow again when it hits someone, Hope. It doesn't hurt them." Natalie decided not to tell Hope that you could make hard, icy snowballs and that they definitely *did* hurt. Instead, she continued, "And in this other country, you can slide down a snow-covered hill on a sleigh, and the ponds freeze over and you can wear skates and play tag— chase each other around," she explained to the little girl.

With an effort, Natalie broke into her own reverie. "See, over there?" she pointed to Mount San Jacinto. "That mountaintop has snow on it, see that?"

Hope followed her gaze. "Could we go there, Nana? I want to go there and make snow balls."

"We can go there someday. We have to save our money for the ride up the mountain."

"But I don't want to be as cold as this *ithe* cube," Hope lisped, dipping her chubby finger into her glass of lemonade and trying unsuccessfully to grasp a cube. "So maybe I don't want to go to that cold country you're talking about."

"Oh, it's not that cold all of the time," Natalie answered. "Just in the winter time. We have winter here, don't we, Hope? Well, when we have winter here, they have winter there, only just a lot colder. Our swimming pool would freeze in the winter there."

"Like my *ithe* cube. One big *ithe* cube. But what about the animals, Nana? Do the animals freeze? I wouldn't want my desert bunny to freeze." She looked toward the corner of their walled yard where a small fawn rabbit was nibbling at a piece of lettuce.

Natalie laughed. "Your bunny is meant to live here where it is warm. The bunnies in cold countries are used to the cold. They even get ready for winter. Do you know what they do?"

Hope shook her head.

"They grow extra fur and that fur is white, the same colour as the snow, so the coyotes can't see them. And then when spring comes they turn brown or grey again."

"We have coyotes here and sometimes they catch our bunnies," Hope frowned. "But, Nana, do the coyotes turn white, too?"

"No, just the bunnies. But they are a lot bigger than your bunny, and they can jump really long jumps and run really fast."

Hope looked up as a bird started singing in their jacaranda tree.

"What about the birds, Nana? Do the birds freeze, sitting in the trees?"

"No, they don't. They fluff out all their feathers and keep warm just like you do when you cuddle under my quilt on a chilly night. Some of the birds from the cold country fly down here where we live to spend the winter. Actually, some of the people up north used to fly down here in airplanes, too, and live here until spring when their country warmed up. Everyone used to call them *snowbirds* because they flew in and out like the birds, to escape the snow."

"Snowbirds, I like that. Will they be coming here this winter?"

"No, they don't come here anymore," Natalie said slowly.

Why not?"

"Oh, I guess they just decided they like their own country better. But maybe someday they will come back. So we just have their birds in the winter, now."

Natalie looked up as a V-shaped flock of Canada geese flew overhead, honking loudly.

"See, Hope? Those birds are from Canada. Canada geese, they are called. See the black and white markings? And see how they fly in a V shape?" Natalie traced a V on Hope's arm. "They have a leader at the point of the V and that leader has a harder time to fly because it's the first, but if you watch carefully, sometimes you will see the leader drop back into the end position in the V and then another goose will take a turn being leader. They help each other and no one gets too tired. We should all be like those geese, Hope—help another person if they are in trouble."

Hope nodded, she was watching the geese carefully. "Look, Nana! One of them is the new leader now! They're taking turns being the leader, just like when we play follow the leader with Mommy and Daddy." They watched until the geese disappeared from view. "I wonder if they are flying to their home in Canada. I've never heard of that place before—Canada."

"It's named after the first people who ever lived there. Do you know the name of the country we live in?" asked Natalie.

"Palm Springs," Hope answered confidently.

"That's right, we do live in Palm Springs, in an area or a state called California, but this is just a city in a much larger country."

"Bigger than Canada?" asked Hope.

Natalie smiled. *Hope always wants to be the biggest and the best. She is one spoiled little girl.* She gave her a hug as she said, "No. But America is almost as big as Canada. Here, let me show you on this watermelon." Natalie picked up a black felt pen Hope had been using to practise her letters.

"See, the earth is round, like this watermelon. Most of the earth is covered in water—with patches of land on it. This big piece of land here is called North America. Mexico is this country at the bottom, that's south, and then in the middle is your country, The United States of America. People living here just call it America and in Canada they call it 'The States' or 'The U.S.' Canada is here at the top, that's north. The Canada geese fly from up here," Natalie drew a line down, "to down here, to Palm Springs for the winter."

"Is it a long way, Nana?"

"It's a very long way. Some Canada Geese have decided they'll just stay here for the summer because they don't like the long trip back north. Lots of birds live here all year long, Hope. One very important bird lives here. I've pointed it out to you before. Remember that very big bird that flew away so high we couldn't see it any longer?"

"An eagle," Hope said proudly.

That's right. Probably a golden eagle. They live here in the desert. Some eagles can fly as high as an airplane, maybe higher. Some other eagles have white feathers on their head and they are called bald eagles."

"But they're not bald if they have feathers on their head, Nana."

"I know, but they are still called bald eagles. They are really, really large," Natalie got up and walked about seven or eight feet from Hope. "From one tip of their wing to the other tip of their wing, this is how large an eagle can grow. The mother eagle is even bigger and stronger than the father eagle, so she's the one that gives her little chicks a ride on her wings if they're just learning to fly and they get tired."

"Like Daddy sometimes picks me up when I get tired walking?"

"Just like that. But here's the really important thing about the eagle, Hope. The bald eagle is the symbol for America, your country. Because it is free to fly as high as it likes and wherever it likes. Would you like to do that?"

The little girl nodded, "I would for sure, Nana."

"Why don't we pretend we are eagles, Hope? Let's just fly around the pool and flap our wings." Natalie stood up and Hope joined her in a wild race around the pool. As they flapped their arms, Hope squealing with delight, Mo came out into the back yard.

"Look, Daddy. I'm an American eagle. I'm free, I'm free," yelled Hope.

Mo scooped her up into his arms on her next circuit around the pool. "What have you been teaching her, Natalie? Don't fill her head with silly ideas." He walked back into the kitchen, slamming the door behind him.

Natalie stared at the closed door. Anger mixed with despair churned in her chest. *I will never stop teaching her what it means to be free. Silly ideas, he said. There was a day when he wouldn't have thought freedom was a silly idea.*

She returned to her chair beside the pool. She dreaded these times when she felt powerless, unable to change anything. She lectured herself.

"I'm no closer to… To what? To taking her away? You know you can't do that. Even if there was a way out of here, you couldn't do that to Aishah and Mo. Closer to telling her about Jesus? You can't do

that either. She's too young. She'd say something to others, and I'd be caught out in my lies. Well, what do You expect me to do, Lord? Just tell me, and I'll do it. I can't stand this waiting any longer.

As Natalie sat staring down at the pool deck in front of her, she felt a slight rush of air and the coolness of a shadow crossing over her. She looked up as an eagle landed soundlessly on the high wall at the back of the yard.

She stared at it. *What is an eagle doing here? This has never happened before.* The eagle's tawny eyes stared boldly back at her.

Several moments passed. At least Natalie believed it had been several moments. It might have been more. The sun was setting over the misty mountains to the west when the eagle spread its wings and, just as silently as it had arrived, soared effortlessly into the sky. Natalie watched until it was just a dark speck against the crimson sunset.

I wish I could spread my wings and fly away, too, but I can't.

From somewhere in the recesses of her mind a forgotten hymn came to her. She could almost hear the choir singing the ancient words from Isaiah 40:31: *Those who wait for the Lord shall renew their strength. They shall mount up with wings like eagles. They shall run and not be weary, they shall walk and not faint…* The early evening call to prayer echoed across the valley. With renewed strength Natalie rose and went into her casita to pray—for Hope, for Aishah, for Mo, for everyone living in the Coachella Valley, for the country… *Because, in spite of it all, I love them, Lord, as You do. So I'll wait.*"

She went to bed early that night.

Only two more days before Ramadan begins. I should be packing for L.A. She sighed. *I'll do it tomorrow.* She had just turned off the light and crawled under her quilt when the phone rang.

"That must be Mike." Her heart skipped a few beats as she scrambled out of bed to pick up the phone she'd left on the kitchen table. "Hello?"

"Hi, it's me. Look, Natalie, it's time we stopped all this nonsense. I need to talk to you."

"Okay." She didn't know what else to say. *All this nonsense? What does he mean?*

"I'll be by in the morning."

"At my casita? You're here?"

"Yes."

"Okay."

"Around eight."

"Okay."

"So… See you then."

"Okay."

Natalie didn't sleep at all that night.

CHAPTER FIFTEEN

Natalie

Early the next morning, Natalie called Aishah to tell her that Mike had arrived in Palm Springs unexpectedly and she would like to take the day off to spend it with him.

"Oh," Aishah paused for a moment. "Well, be sure to invite him for dinner tonight."

Natalie heard the coolness in Aishah's voice. She grinned. *Poor Aishah. She'll worry all day that she'll do or say something wrong in front of the dreaded government informer.* "It's okay, Aishah. I think we'll be going out for dinner."

And they had, but not in a Palm Springs restaurant as Natalie had expected.

Mike had arrived promptly at eight that morning. Natalie opened the door before the doorbell rang. Everything that happened next was so surreal, Natalie wondered if perhaps she had finally gone to sleep after all and was dreaming.

Mike stomped around the tiny casita, pulling all the heavy curtains closed. Then he stood facing Natalie.

"Do you feel how I feel?"

Natalie gazed at him as a wide grin spread across her face.

"I do," she said.

And then she was in his arms and they were kissing—*We're like teenagers*—was the only thought that raced through her mind. Eventually Mike stepped back from her.

"Will you marry me? I've reserved a condo for us on the beach in San Diego and we'll have to leave this morning to get married in L.A. this afternoon and I've arranged all the papers for us and then we can drive down to San Diego and spend Ramadan as our honeymoon. How does that sound?" Mike was out of breath.

Natalie laughed. "That sounds like the best Ramadan I've ever had. But, Mike, why now? I mean, it's been five years."

"Because someone gave me a T-shirt when I was back in Canada last week that said: *When you're over the hill, you pick up speed.* I figured it was a message for me."

Natalie didn't know whether to laugh or cry. *Lord, You answered my prayers with a crazy T shirt?* She managed to say to Mike, "Over the hill? We're only in our fifties. That's not 'over the hill'. We've got lots of living to do."

"You're right. Anyway, if you're willing to share my risky life, I'm willing to share yours."

"You know that I'll want to live here with Hope, don't you? We'll have a strange marriage."

Mike nodded. "I know that. And I'll be away from you a lot. But mostly on the west coast now, so we can spend more time together. We're mature people, Natalie. We can do this."

"I'll pack," Natalie said. "Have some coffee and a muffin."

Aishah sounded relieved when Natalie called to tell her Mike would not be staying in Palm Springs. She agreed that Natalie should spend the month of Ramadan with her brother in San Diego.

"Finally, you're able to spend some time with him," she said. "Tell him I'm very sorry we didn't get a chance to visit."

"Okay, I will." Natalie smiled at Aishah's fib. "So I'll see you back here in a month. Oh, one more piece of good news. Mike says he'll be living a lot closer now. The San Francisco area, maybe. So he can pop in to see us now and then."

There was a pause, then Aishah said, "That's great."

Natalie smiled. "Well, see you in a month then. Say 'goodbye' to Hope and Mo for me."

"I will."

Before ending the call, Natalie heard Aishah say to Mo, "Well, that's odd."

"It *is* odd," Natalie said as she set her own phone down.

"What's odd?" Mike asked.

"We're odd, Mike. We are going to have a very strange life."

"We are going to have a very *happy* life," Mike said. "I'm finally learning to trust God totally. All my life I've been telling other people they should do that." He laughed as Natalie nodded in agreement. "I know. Sorry, but now it's my turn to take my own advice. It will all work out."

She smiled as she put on her street clothes and fastened her veil. "Never thought I'd have a Muslim wedding."

"We can exchange Christian vows afterward with a friend of mine in San Diego. Let's go."

Natalie locked the door of the casita behind them.

* * *

The month in San Diego flew by and Natalie was right: it was the best Ramadan she had ever had. Mike attended the required prayers and readings at the mosque each day, but the rest of the time was theirs to spend as they wanted. They walked the beaches, ate late night dinners and simply spent the time getting to know each other better.

"It's funny—we learned so much about each other in that first two months together in Palm Springs," Natalie said as they sat around their beach campfire late one night. "Then we had nothing but those weird phone conversations where we had to speak in code all the time. We really couldn't talk about anything that was important to us."

"Never mind, sweetheart. It was enough to keep us together and that's all that counts. We'll have to go back to that soon enough. So tell me all your secrets now."

Natalie shared with Mike how depressed she felt about getting Hope out of the country. "I couldn't take her away even if we could manage to do it somehow. Five years old is too young to separate her from her parents. It might damage her permanently. And I don't think I could do that to Aishah. She used to have nightmares about someone taking Hope from her."

She paused as she saw Mike grinning at her. "I know what that look is about," she said. "You're remembering that last conversation in the condo when I said I hated them all and didn't care what happened to any of them."

"So how long did it take to have a change of heart, so to speak?"

"About a year," Natalie said.

"Well, that's not so bad. It's taken the Lord a lot longer than that to get some things through my thick skull."

"Like five years, maybe? Plus a T shirt?"

"Yeah." They snuggled closer together and thanked God for each other as the flames flickered and the sparks ascended into the black sky.

* * *

Once she was back in Palm Springs and alone again in her casita, Natalie picked up her life where it had been interrupted. Except for Aishah's remark that Natalie seemed very happy after spending time with her brother, no further mention was made of Mike. Natalie refrained from talking about him. She was afraid she might reveal their true relationship. Phone calls were again sporadic and their conversations unsatisfactory.

Mike visited Palm Springs twice that year, though, and they spent a couple of weekends in L.A. before the next Ramadan rolled around and another month-long stay in San Diego.

As the years passed, the routine of Natalie's life remained unchanged except for her trips with her "brother".

She waited.

She sewed the required clothing for her growing grand-daughter—dark coloured garments she had never known existed—to cover the young child's knees and as much as possible of her arms and legs when in public. Then, as Hope grew taller, a light-weight black overcoat with the head and neck and chest covering, and finally, at Hope's insistence, the veil—*Because all of the other girls are wearing them, Nana.*

Aishah had tried to convince Hope she could wait a while longer.

"You're only eleven. You don't need to wear the veil until puberty—you know?"

"Sure, I know," Hope argued, "but all my friends are veiled and they're not any more mature than I am. I want to be grown up like you and Nana, Mom. Please can I wear it?"

"Ask your Dad. He's the one who makes those kinds of decisions. But just remember, once you start wearing it, there's no going back—you will always have to cover your face outside of our house and yard."

Mo said it was fine with him.

"Awesome! Thanks, Dad. I'll make some iced tea and we can all celebrate."

The next morning as Hope walked to the bistro wearing her veil, she held her head high and looked around to see if anyone was watching. Finally Natalie told her not to look so bold—the morality squad might drive by.

That evening after Hope had gone to bed, the three adults lingered at the kitchen table over a cup of tea.

"I hate to see her wear the veil, but she wanted to," Aishah said. "She's used to always getting her own way. I hope she doesn't regret it this time."

"She'll be okay," Mo said. "Actually, honey, it may be a good thing she's so eager to have her face covered. Brian won't be ogling her all the time, now."

"Let's count our blessings, then," Natalie said. "I know you think of the abaya and veil as a prison, Aishah, but I've heard some of the women say they like the feeling of no one being able to really see them. They enjoy the anonymity."

"Is that what they said to you?" asked Aishah.

"Well, maybe not exactly in those words, but I think that's what they meant."

"I can agree with that... I suppose," Aishah said slowly. "My problem is that I want to *choose* what I wear. Like before. If they want to have their faces covered and be covered from head to toe, that's fine with me. But what if I don't want that? Mo says the Koran doesn't say we have to be veiled. But under this government law I have no choice. And besides—what if a woman's husband is telling her what to wear and she doesn't really agree?"

Mo spoke up. "But, Aishah, as my wife who loves me wouldn't you wear the veil if I wanted you to?"

"As my husband who loves me, would you want me to wear the veil if you knew I hated it?"

"Well, no."

"So there you are, then," Aishah said.

"You two!" Natalie said, "You're arguing in circles."

"So what do you think, Natalie?" Mo asked.

"Well, I always find the hijab is helpful on a bad hair day and the niqab hides my wrinkles."

Mo and Aishah laughed and Mo changed the subject.

As Natalie climbed under her quilt that night, she felt confident that God would work things out, in spite of everything. "Like veils," she murmured into the darkness.

The presence of Mike in her life lifted her spirits, even if she didn't see him as often as she would have liked.

Family life with Aishah and Mo and Hope was good. It was as if they had created their own little oasis of love in the midst of all that went on around them: the violence, the spying, the limitations on their speech and actions.

As she did every night, Natalie breathed a prayer of thanksgiving for the sense of calm that enveloped them all.

She never could have imagined that something as simple as an invitation to a birthday party would shatter that peace forever.

CHAPTER SIXTEEN

Natalie

Hope burst through the kitchen's swinging doors and into the women's bistro.

"Can I go, Mom? Can I? Miriam called and invited me to her birthday party. All the other kids are going and Mrs. Martin says she needs me to help with the younger kids. It's at The Date Farm—"

Aishah's head jerked up. She stopped wiping the table for a moment, then looked back down, resuming the circular motion of her cloth.

"I've never been there. Dad doesn't have to take me, they'll pick me up. So can I go?"

Aishah didn't answer.

Natalie continued wiping a table a few feet away. She had been scrubbing the same spot for several moments. *The Date Farm! That used to be a Christian place!*

"Can I go?" Hope repeated. "I've always wanted to go there."

"I'll have to talk to your father," Aishah said.

"Mommmm," Hope wailed. "Puh – leese! It's only a birthday party. Dad won't care whether I go or not."

"I'll have to talk to your Dad," Aishah said even more firmly.

Natalie moved on to the next table, clearing coffee cups and plates. *Please let them say she can go.*

That night at dinner Hope brought the subject up again. "Can I go, Dad? It's at The Date Farm."

Mo and Aishah exchanged a quick glance before they both looked down at their dinner plates.

"Can I go, please? Mom says it's okay if you say I can go."

Mo sighed heavily. "If your Mom says okay, then you can go. What do you think, Aishah?"

Aishah sighed also. "I didn't say you could go, Hope. I said I had to talk to your father."

"Mom, it's only a birthday party. Why shouldn't I go?"

"I guess you can go," Aishah said. "But I need you to promise me one thing."

"Okay, okay, whatever you want."

"Promise me you will stay with the other kids at all times. That you won't go wandering off by yourself. Promise me you'll never go anywhere alone in the park."

"Sure, I promise. No problem." Hope gave Aishah a quick hug. "Thanks, Mom. Thanks, Dad. I'll do the dishes."

Natalie breathed a silent *Thank You*. Then she rose, saying, "I'll help her." She noticed Aishah and Mo were still looking at each other. Aishah was chewing on her bottom lip.

"Okay," Natalie said to Hope. "Let's get started. Power's off—again—so we have to do dishes by hand. I'll wash, you dry. Bet I can wash faster than you can dry."

"You're on," Hope said happily.

* * *

The morning of the birthday party arrived—sunny with a clear blue sky, as usual. Natalie and Aishah waited with Hope for her ride to the party. They stood on the sidewalk, just outside their front gate, their three black figures contrasting sharply against the high beige wall enclosing their yard. Aishah kept telling Hope to stay closer to their open gate just in case the squad drove by, but Hope insisted on stepping out a little further, anxiously looking up the street for the Martin's car. When it finally pulled up to the curb, the voices of excited children could be heard even through the closed windows of the air-conditioned SUV.

"Bye, Mom. Bye, Nana." Hope climbed into the back seat, slamming the door behind her.

"Remember your promise," Aishah called out as the car drove off.

Aishah and Natalie stood in the bright sunlight for a moment, looking after the departing vehicle before returning to their enclosure.

As they removed their veils, Natalie saw that Aishah was gnawing on her bottom lip again. "She'll be fine, Aishah," she said. "There's nothing to worry about."

"I don't know..." Aishah hesitated. "That place . . . I just don't know. I was only there once, but..."

"Want to talk about it?'

"No, I don't." Aishah turned and walked away.

"Okay," Natalie spoke to Aishah's retreating back. As she followed her into the house she wondered what could possibly have happened to Aishah at The Date Farm.

Mo arrived back from his early morning baking duties shortly after Hope had left. Aishah donned her veil and outer garments once again as she prepared to walk to the bistro behind Mo.

"Saturday's usually a quiet day at the cafe," she said to Natalie. "Stay home if you like. Take a break. You deserve it."

Natalie readily agreed. "I'll do some housework and have dinner ready when you two get back."

As soon as Aishah and Mo had left, Natalie returned to her casita. She stood beside the bed, surveying her quilt. She spoke softly into the empty room.

"A chance to read. Let's see... What scripture would be good for today?" Her eyes fell on the blue paisley print patch. "Hmmm... First Corinthians 13, the Love Chapter." As she pulled out the pages, she noticed how tattered and worn they were. "Seems I'm reading that chapter a lot. Guess I need to be reminded."

Settling into her white wicker rocker, she read greedily. When she had come to the end of Paul's First Letter to the Corinthians, she sat quietly, looking down at the thin tissue pages resting in her open hands. As she often did with Scripture, she rephrased the words in her mind.

If I speak the languages of humans and angels, but I don't have love, I am like a noisy gong or a clanging cymbal... If I give away everything I have, and sacrifice my body, but don't have love—then I have gained nothing.

Natalie tucked the pages back into their pocket and sealed the Velcro edge of the patch. She thought about what she had read as she cleaned her casita and then moved on to the main house.

When Aishah and Mo returned for dinner, the promised meal was ready. The three of them were laughing and talking at the kitchen table when they heard a car door slam. A moment later, Hope appeared.

"Hi, everybody," she said, removing her veil as she entered the kitchen. She wasn't jumping around energetically as she usually did. She didn't even grab a snack from the table as she normally would have.

"What's wrong, honey?" Aishah asked. "Didn't you have a good time?"

"Yeah, I had a good time," Hope said. "Date shakes and all that."

"Well, what else? Tell us all about it." Mo pulled out the chair beside him and patted the seat.

"If you don't mind, Dad, I think I'll just go to bed. I'm really tired. I'll tell you about the party tomorrow… if that's okay?" Hope stood quietly in the doorway.

"Sure, honey. You go on. It's a work day tomorrow. I've saved some cleaning at the bistro just for you."

Hope wrinkled her nose at him. "See you in the morning, then," she said as she left the room.

"I hope she's not coming down with something," Mo said.

Natalie ventured a casual glance at Aishah. She was staring after her daughter, a worried look had replaced her smile.

"You two go sit around the pool and enjoy the evening," Natalie said. "I'll clean up in here." She watched as Mo put his arm around Aishah and they walked out to the patio.

When she went to bed later that night, Natalie couldn't fall asleep. She kept thinking of how quiet Hope had been. Something had happened at the party—she could feel it in her bones. But did it have anything to do with the park at one time being a Christian place? She addressed her questions out loud to God: "You know what's happening. I'm trusting You in this." But still, she tossed and turned all night, a million thoughts racing through her head.

The next morning the bistro was busy with what Aishah called "bistro bustle". Natalie had thought she might get a chance to talk privately with Hope, but that didn't happen. She felt that Hope was deliberately avoiding any conversation with her, or for that matter, anyone. Instead of being her usual bouncy self and chattering constantly with the customers, Hope avoided everyone, except when waiting on their table. She spent most of the day with the few small children and babies the women had brought with them. She seldom smiled as she usually did while playing with the kids.

Natalie wasn't the only one who noticed the change in Hope. One woman commented to her, "Hope's very quiet. Is she okay?"

Natalie looked over at Hope who was sitting in a corner, gently rocking a baby in her arms. "Oh, she's not quite herself today," she said. "Just worn out from a birthday party at The Date Farm."

"What?" Veeda bellowed. Her raspy voice rose above the hum of the women's conversation. "The Date Farm? You let her go *there*?" All heads turned in Veeda's direction as they usually did when she spoke. "That place should be closed. Blown up. It's an evil place."

Aishah over-filled a customer's coffee cup and apologized profusely.

Natalie noticed and moved quickly to stand in front of Veeda. With a calmness she did not feel, she smiled. "Why Veeda, I'm surprised to hear you say that. I thought you liked The Date Farm. I recall you mentioned once that they gave you free date shakes after you had an accident there."

"Oh, that," Veeda snorted. "That was a long time ago. I don't have time for such nonsense these days. Brian says nobody should go there. The morality squad is keeping an eye on that place. Too many strange things going on there."

"Like what?" Natalie sat in the chair next to Veeda.

"I'm not saying. I'm not at liberty to say," sniffed Veeda. "But I know things. My sons are in the squad and my husband is privy to information from higher up. I'm not at liberty to say," she repeated, "but I know that bad things have happened to people who go there."

"What things?" Natalie asked again.

Veeda looked around at the now quiet bistro with a satisfied smirk on her face.

Natalie asked once more, "What things, Veeda?"

"Things like beatings or jail, or worse. That's what happens to some of the people who go to The Date Farm."

Veeda definitely had everyone's attention now.

Natalie glanced over to where Hope was sitting. She had stopped rocking the baby. Her face had turned white.

Natalie stood up. "Well, Veeda, we all want to thank you for sharing your knowledge with us. It's nice of you to care about all of us. Isn't it, ladies?"

Murmurs of "Certainly" and "Of course," filled the bistro.

Veeda smiled, her lips tightly compressed. "You're welcome, I'm sure. I'm always happy to give you my advice."

"We know you are," Natalie placed her hand gently on Veeda's shoulder. "Thanks again. We really appreciate you."

The jovial mood of the bistro had evaporated. Several women reached for their phones to call for a ride home and within a few minutes everyone had left.

Aishah said she was going into the kitchen to help Mo.

Natalie walked over to Hope who was clearing a back table.

"What's wrong, honey?"

"Nothing is wrong, Nana. That's the third time today you've asked me. I'm going to help Mom and Dad clean up in the kitchen." She stomped off, leaving a surprised and hurt Natalie to tidy up the bistro.

"Maybe it's just pre-teen moodiness," mused Natalie aloud.

She sighed as she began clearing the tables. *Yeah, teenagers. I remember.* She fought to suppress the memories that came flooding back. *Don't go down that road. You can't afford to fall apart now. You taught me to keep a stiff upper lip, Mother. I've been doing that for so long, it must be paralyzed by now.* She scrubbed all the tables until the glass sparkled.

* * *

In the coming days Natalie continued to notice a change in Hope. Aishah and Mo noticed it also.

"Guess our little girl is turning into a moody teenager," Mo observed one evening as Hope retired early once again after dinner.

"Well, we survived the colic and the terrible two's so I guess we'll make it through the teen years, as well," Aishah said. "What do you think, Natalie? You helped us get through those tough first years. Will we make it?"

"Sure, we'll get through the teen years. More coffee, anyone?" She rose to fill their cups.

"Speaking of teen years," Mo persisted, "We have a problem with Brian."

"Still?" asked Aishah. "I thought he'd given up on that."

"He's hinting, well, more than hinting, to me quite regularly now at the bistro."

"Hinting?" Natalie asked. "About what?"

"About marrying Hope."

Mo's coffee slopped over the edge of his cup as Natalie set it in front of him. She fought to keep her voice calm. "She just turned twelve. He can't be serious."

"He is, Natalie. He has always asked me about her—ever since that day when she ran into the men's bistro and I had to bring her back to you, remember, Aishah?"

Aishah nodded. "She was only five years old, Mo."

"Yeah, but ever since then Brian mentions her, says he's never seen eyes that colour. Remember how he used to want to come to our house to visit? He just wanted to look at Hope."

"I've kept her out of his sight for years now," Aishah said. "I was hoping he'd forget about her. Anyway, she's too young."

"Not really. Brian's second wife was twelve when he married her and lately he's begun talking about how the Prophet, (peace be upon him), married your namesake, Aishah, when she was nine—something like that."

"That was a long time ago," Aishah said.

Natalie sighed. "Well, anyway, Hope can't marry without your permission, Mo. So she's safe."

"Safe," echoed Aishah. "But for how long? A couple more years, at best. She has to marry someone. Even if it's not Brian, she has to marry. All women do."

Natalie looked at Aishah and then Mo and then back to Aishah, seeing the worry reflected in their eyes.

"Aishah's right, Natalie," Mo said. "Brian won't let this go on for long if he's got his mind made up. And he'll want to get her before someone else speaks to us about her. He's already warning the young guys not to even consider Hope."

"But Mo," Natalie began, aware she was sounding desperate, but no longer able to control the anxiety in her voice, "He's a terrible person. He beats his wives. Do you know that?"

"Yeah, I know that," Mo's shoulders slumped. "I can't do anything about that. Brian owns most of Palm Springs. He's the most powerful man in the city. He always gets what he wants, one way or another."

"Like the time he—" began Aishah.

Natalie interrupted her. "Let's not waste our time talking about Brian. We need to come up with some way to keep Hope out of his clutches. Isn't there anything we can do?"

"Well, we're okay for now. Brian has his four wives. He can't marry anyone else unless he divorces one of them," Mo said.

"And that's easy for him to do. Just say the words three times," Aishah said. "But what if one of them dies? I wouldn't put it past him to arrange that. And then he can marry again."

Natalie struggled to suppress her rising anger. "There must be something we can do."

"The only thing I can think of is that we find someone suitable for Hope and get her married before Brian is free to marry again. It's possible—"

Natalie interrupted Mo, unable to contain her anger any longer. "Listen to us! Are we crazy? This is a child we're talking about! She's far too young to marry. She should at least get through her teens and then she should be the one to choose if and when she marries. That's how it's always— "

"But that was then, and this is now, Natalie." It was Aishah's turn to interrupt.

"Keep your voices down," Mo warned. "She'll hear you."

All eyes turned to look down the hallway leading to Hope's bedroom. After a moment they continued their conversation in hushed tones, talking long into the night. Several solutions were presented, but none of them were thought workable. They always came back to the "lesser of two evils" as Natalie called it: "Hope has to marry someone, anyone but Brian."

Their discussion finally ended with Mo saying he would speak to the imam about it. "He knows Brian and he'll understand our concerns. Maybe he can help us."

Natalie's loud sigh was almost a groan.

"We'll all pray about this, won't we?"

"Of course," Mo assured her. Aishah nodded, her eyes brimming with tears. Mo put his arm around her shoulder. "We'll get through this together, Aishah. We always do."

Aishah sniffed as a tear coursed down her cheek.

Mo pushed his chair away from the table and stood up. "Come on, honey. We're all exhausted. Something will turn up in the next few weeks, I'm sure of it."

Natalie stood also. She hoped her voice carried more conviction that she felt. "I'm sure something will turn up. See you in the morning."

As she walked slowly to her casita, she stopped to gaze up at the black desert sky pierced by brilliant stars. A familiar wave of loneliness washed over her.

"But I know You are with me," she whispered.

CHAPTER SEVENTEEN

Natalie

Several weeks passed but they were no closer to finding someone for Hope to marry. Hope seemed unaware of the anxious atmosphere which permeated the house.

"It's like she's in her own little world," Aishah said as she and Natalie watched Hope quietly waiting on tables, rarely smiling, only speaking when spoken to. "I hope she gets over this mood soon. I miss the feisty girl we used know."

"Me, too," Natalie agreed. "I'm sure this will pass."

Hope glanced over at them. "You two talking about me?"

"Of course, sweetheart. Who else would we be talking about?" Aishah smiled at her.

Hope said nothing as she turned to clear off the table next to them.

Aishah and Natalie exchanged glances.

Late that night Natalie was awakened by a soft rap on the casita door. She slipped on her robe and opened the door a crack. A pyjama-clad Hope stood shivering in the cold.

"Can I come in, Nana? I need to talk to you."

Natalie's grogginess immediately left her as she opened the door wider. "Of course, come on in." She glanced toward the main house before closing the door. No glimmer of light shone through the dark curtains.

"They're asleep. They don't know I'm here," Hope said.

"Oh." Natalie tried to conceal her surprise. "I'll make some hot chocolate. Here, put this on." Reaching into her small clothes closet, she handed Hope her winter-weight robe. "For these cold desert nights," she explained. "I brought this from up north when I first came here."

Hope snuggled into the robe. "When I was little I always liked sitting on your lap when you wore this fluffy robe. It made me feel cuddly and warm."

"Well, now you can wear it yourself," Natalie said. "In fact, you can keep it, if you like."

Hope burst into tears.

"Come on, honey, it's just an old worn-out robe. It's not that great a gift," Natalie teased.

"It's not that, Nana," Hope sobbed. "You wouldn't give me anything or even talk to me if you knew what I've done. Everything is ruined for me. Mom and Dad will hate me. You'll hate me."

Natalie said nothing as she guided Hope to the tiny kitchen table. *Finally – we're going to find out what's wrong.* She handed Hope the box of tissues and poured them each a cup of hot chocolate. Then she sat next to Hope, cradling her arm around Hope's heaving shoulders.

"Nothing's that bad, honey. You've just kept this thing, whatever it is, bottled up inside for too long. Sometimes when we do that, we imagine things to be worse than they are—making a mountain out of a molehill, my mother used to say. Why don't you just tell me about it? I'll bet you'll feel better."

Hope didn't answer.

"Did something happen at the birthday party, honey? You've been different ever since then."

Hope's head jerked up at the mention of the birthday party.

"Promise you won't tell Mom and Dad?" she pleaded.

Natalie looked into Hope's tear-filled eyes. "I promise."

"It's something that happened at The Date Farm."

"I thought so. But, Hope, that was two months ago. You've been worrying about something that happened way back then?"

"Yeah. Oh, Nana, you'll all hate me." Hope burst into great gulping sobs.

"We could never hate you. Nothing on earth could make us hate you."

"That's just the p-p-p-point, Nana," Hope stammered, "It's not on earth."

"I'm confused, honey. Why don't you just start at the beginning and tell me what happened. You were at The Date Farm, you said, at the party? And then?"

"It's shirk," wailed Hope, "The worst kind. I'm so scared. I could be killed for this. And maybe Mom and Dad and maybe you, too." Her eyes widened with fear.

Natalie moved her chair closer to Hope, wrapping her arms around her.

"There, there," she crooned, stroking Hope's hair as she had when Hope was a little girl. "It will be alright. Everything will be alright."

Gradually Hope's sobs subsided. Natalie handed her another tissue. "Blow your nose, honey. Take your time. We've got all night. Tell me what happened."

Hope began her story. They had arrived at the birthday party with the other kids. They had ordered date shakes and anything else they wanted. After their lunch Miriam's mom told them to go play in the park while she visited with her friends.

"We weren't supposed to go too far down the path and at first we didn't. But then we started playing hide and seek and the older kids said there were better places to hide if we went further in."

"Like the tomb—the cave, I mean," said Natalie.

"Yeah, the cave. Have you been there, Nana?"

"Yes, but it was a very long time ago."

"Well, then you know what a good place it is to hide."

Natalie nodded, her eyes fixed on Hope's face. Hope's tears had stopped. Her face was flushed. She spoke rapidly.

"I didn't go anywhere alone, Nana. I promised Mom I would stay with the others and I did. Even when we hid in the cave there were three of us. I never meant to break my promise to Mom. But after we got found in the cave and started back out of the park to go home, I remembered I'd left my loot bag there."

"Your loot bag?"

"The bag of treats, Nana. Candy, hair clips—you know. Each kid at the party got one."

Natalie nodded.

"Well, the other kids said they'd wait for me to go back and get it—we'd only gone a little way. So I ran back to the cave to grab my treat bag. Oh, Nana, I didn't mean to break my promise to Mom." Hope began sobbing again. "I didn't mean to go into the cave alone."

"But you did?"

"I did." Hope's red rimmed eyes met Natalie's calm gaze directly.

"And what happened in the tomb, Hope?"

"I found something."

"What did you find?"

"A small book was lying there on the floor. Right next to my loot bag. I'm sure it wasn't there when I set my bag down. But there it was when I came back, just a few minutes later."

"Oh." Natalie didn't know why she felt disappointed. *What was I expecting—a vision, for goodness sake?* She squeezed Hope's hand.

"So you found a book. That's not so bad, honey. That's what you've been worrying about all this time? I know we aren't allowed to have books, but it's not going to cost you your life."

"It wasn't just any book, Nana. It was red and it had a big gold cross on the cover and in gold letters it said *The New Testament.*"

"Oh." Natalie took a deep breath. "So then?"

"I took the book. I couldn't help it. There it was, right beside my treat bag. Like it was meant for me to take it. A book, Nana! I never dreamed I'd own my very own book. I've never seen a book before, except for the Koran, of course. Well, maybe I saw Mom's book, the one without the cover. Well, actually, I've read some of it. Well, maybe all of it—several times. You know the book—the one she hides under her shoe box?"

Natalie raised her eyebrows. "Under her shoe box? No, I haven't seen it—but let's talk about that another time. Tell me about this book you found in the tomb."

"It's such a beautiful little book, so small. It has gold letters stamped right into the red cover. I couldn't resist bringing it home. I popped it into my treat bag and ran to catch up with the others. I've been reading it every chance I get. Usually at night in bed, under the covers, with a flashlight."

Natalie exhaled loudly. "Well, your Mom and Dad are not going to hate you for reading the Christian book. But they will be very concerned." She paused. "You do know it is part of the Christian Bible, don't you?"

Hope nodded wordlessly.

"They'll be angry, honey, but they won't hate you."

"But here's the thing, Nana." Hope's eyes lit up. "I've been reading it, some parts over and over. And I believe it. I believe Jesus is God's Son." She spoke more slowly, carefully pronouncing every word. "That's shirk. They can kill me for believing that."

Natalie stared at her, her mouth opened to speak but no words came out.

"And we could all die because of me. But what can I do? Oh, Nana, I had to tell someone. I tried hinting about it to Mom… I wouldn't even think of telling Dad. But when I asked what happened to people who believed in Jesus, Mom got really mad, right away. She said when people find out, they paint a red N sign on their house, and their family disowns them and they're killed, and they deserve it, because that's shirk, believing in more than one God."

Natalie interrupted Hope's outburst as she anticipated another sobbing jag coming on. "Actually, honey, your mom doesn't really believe Christians should be killed."

"She doesn't?" sniffed Hope.

"No, she told me once that she had Christian friends when she was a little girl. She said how much she liked them."

"Then I can tell her?"

"No, I'm afraid you can't, sweetheart."

"Why not?"

"Because Unity enforces harsh laws now. So your Mom wouldn't know what to do. And she would be very sad."

"And mad?"

"Mad, for a while, but underneath there would be sadness. And she would worry about all of us, in case someone found out."

"And she'd probably tell Dad," Hope said.

"Probably," Natalie agreed. "It would be really, really hard for you, honey. And they would want you to stop believing in Jesus."

"I can't do that. I do believe in Him," Hope sat up straight. "And I feel good in a way I can't explain." She paused, studying Natalie's face. "But you're not mad at me, are you? How come?"

Natalie took Hope's hand in hers. "Because I believe in Him, too."

Hope stared at her for several moments.

"When did you start to believe in Jesus, Nana?"

"Many years ago, when I was a few years older than you are now."

"How did you hear about Him?"

"By reading the Bible, like you have. I came to believe it was true."

"I've read where Jesus promises to be with us always, to the end of the world, it said. Do you believe that, Nana?"

"I do. What do you believe?"

"I feel Him here inside." Hope put her hand over her heart. "So I know He is with me."

It was Natalie's turn for tears. "Oh, Hope, I've been praying for you for so long. I am so happy for you."

Hope giggled as Natalie gave her a long hug.

She's so much like Aishah. But how will Aishah ever understand what has happened?

"You know, Nana, when I first came back from the birthday party and I read the book I'd found in the cave, I was scared, but I kept reading every night, anyway." Hope's words came out in a rush. "I didn't know what to believe. Was Jesus really God? I had never thought of God loving me enough to die for me. I'd always thought I had to keep the law—try to be good enough, you know? The thing that made me finally make up my mind to choose Jesus was something that happened in the bistro a few weeks ago."

"Really? In the bistro? What happened?"

"Do you remember the day when everyone was talking about Layla being accused of having an affair? You know, the sin of adultery?"

"I do remember that," Natalie said slowly. "The women were talking about her punishment. Stoning to death. But they shouldn't have told you about it."

"They didn't. Everyone quit talking when I came to their table to wait on them, but I heard enough to know what had happened. Veeda said it was Allah's will. Everyone agreed it was the law, even though some of them were crying when they said it. I'll never forget it. Layla was just a few years older than me."

"That was a really bad day," Natalie said. "I'll never forget it, either."

"But here's the thing, Nana. That night I took my little book to read under the covers with my flashlight and guess what happened? It just opened to the story of Jesus and the woman accused of adultery."

"Oh," Natalie managed to say.

"I read that the men were going to kill the woman and Jesus stooped and wrote something in the sand and then he said that whoever was without sin could throw the first stone and everybody holding rocks ready to throw at her just dropped their rocks and left."

Natalie nodded. "And Jesus asked the woman where her accusers were and she said that she didn't have any. And then Jesus said he didn't condemn her, either and she was to go and not sin again."

"That's it! You know the story, too!" Hope's face radiated a bright smile. "When I read that, I knew. I just had to choose Jesus. He would love me no matter what. Even if I broke the law—any law—even a big one like adultery. That's when I made up my mind."

Natalie stood up to give Hope a hug. "Thanks for telling me about this. You are very brave, Hope."

"I still feel badly that I can't tell Mom and Dad, though." Hope's smile faded.

"Someday maybe you'll be able to do that. Just not right now, okay? That's something we will always be praying about. But we have to let God take care of that. Just remember that Jesus loves your mom and dad even more than you do."

"That makes me feel better. Jesus loves my mom and dad." Hope smiled, "So here we are, two Christians—like a secret club. But, Nana, I've read that it's not supposed to be a secret. We are supposed to tell others about Jesus. We can't do that, can we?"

"Not right now, sweetheart. But some day when you are older... I have the feeling you will be telling lots of people about Him. I think you are special. I once knew a girl who wasn't that much older than you, and she told others all the time."

"Where?" asked Hope. "Where could she talk about Jesus?"

"Right here in Palm Springs."

"Here? That's weird. So where is she now?" asked Hope.

"She's with Jesus now."

"You mean they killed her?" Hope's voice quavered.

"Yes, they did. But they could never really kill her, could they? Because she lives on with Jesus. You and I will die someday, but we will go to live with Jesus, too."

"I know," Hope answered confidently. "I read about that in The Gospel of John, in the third chapter and the sixteenth verse. The words were underlined in red, so I thought it must be important. Something like: God loved the world so much that He gave us His only Son so that whoever believed in Him would not die but live forever."

Natalie nodded. "God loves the world—that means everyone."

"But He loves the Christians the most," Hope said.

Natalie smiled. "No, He loves the world—everyone—equally."

"Oh." Hope thought for a moment. "So this other girl you knew, if she's in heaven, when we get there will we meet her? I'd like to talk with her."

"I believe we will meet her," Natalie said. "And I know she'll be really happy to talk with you."

"You think?" asked Hope. "She probably wouldn't want to talk to somebody like me. I'm not brave like she was. I'm scared now. I don't think I could talk about Jesus and then be killed like she was."

Nana smiled. "I'm scared, too. But I don't think you need to worry about that right now. I think God wants you and me to read the Bible and pray together and when the time is right, if we're supposed to tell others about Jesus, God will let us know."

Hope exhaled loudly. "Whew! That's a relief."

Natalie laughed. "Oh, Hope, we are going to have fun in our secret club."

"Our secret club," Hope repeated. "We need a secret sign. I know the cross is the Christian sign, but we can't carry one of those around with us—even a little one in our pocket. It's too dangerous."

"You know what, Hope? We definitely can carry our secret sign around with us. Like this." Natalie made the sign of the cross over her chest. "Touch your forehead. Now touch above your stomach. Now your left shoulder. Now your right shoulder. See? The sign of the cross. You can make it when you are alone or with me. We just can't do it when others are around. But still, it's always with us, isn't it?"

Hope nodded and practiced the sign several times, laughing excitedly. "I can carry it with me always and no one will ever know."

"For now, though," Natalie said, "I think you should let me keep your Bible in my casita, just in case your Mom is cleaning your room and finds it."

"It's in the bottom of my sock drawer."

Natalie winced. "Not a good place, honey. Can you get it to me sometime soon, like tomorrow? We can always get together here to read it."

"In our secret club meeting?" Hope asked.

"Yes, but no one should ever know about this, Hope. Absolutely no one. Will you promise you'll never tell anyone, ever? At least not without asking me first?"

"I promise."

"Okay, then. You'd better go back now."

"Oh, Nana. You're the best." Hope hugged Natalie.

"I love you, too, sweetheart." Natalie held her close for a few moments. "Be really quiet going back in."

Natalie watched as Hope returned to the house. She turned to give a small wave of her hand in Natalie's direction before quietly shutting the door.

Before climbing back into bed, Natalie surveyed her quilt. "So much to teach her," she said aloud. "Where to start? Maybe have her memorize the Ten Commandments, Twenty Third Psalm... She will never have heard any of the stories from the Old Testament... But I can't think about that tonight."

She fell asleep repeating one simple prayer: "Thank You, God."

At dawn she woke as the Call to Prayer echoed across the city. She rose, pulled the heavy curtains back from her kitchen window and watched as the first rays of the sun conquered the darkness.

"A new day. A whole new life," she breathed. "For me, for Hope. Now what? What's next, Lord?"

CHAPTER EIGHTEEN

Natalie

Natalie sat with Aishah and Mo around the pool, watching Hope swim. Three years had passed since Hope had come to her that night. She had prayed that everything would be alright, and it was. No one had discovered their secret and Hope's new-found faith had blossomed.

Hope climbed out of the pool and grabbed a towel. "Just going to the casita to have a little break from the heat," she said.

Natalie smiled. *Probably going to read some scripture, too.* Natalie leaned back in her chair. After years of practice, she had finally relaxed into her role as a Muslim woman living under Shariah law. She glanced over at Mo and Aishah.

"She's beautiful." Aishah's eyes followed Hope's tall slim figure.

Natalie nodded. She felt drowsy in the early spring sunshine. *Maybe I'll just have a little nap.*

She was jolted out of her pre-slumber state by Mo's next words.

"She will have to get married soon."

"No, she won't," Aishah sharply contradicted. "She's not sixteen yet. I wasn't married until I was sixteen."

"I know, I know," Mo hastily agreed, "But that was then and this is now, as you always say. I'm being reasonable about this,

Aishah. Unity wants girls to get married younger. In fact, we should have at least promised her to someone years ago."

"That's disgusting," Aishah sniffed.

Natalie sat up straight, fighting the urge to enter into the conversation. With a shaking hand, she reached for her iced tea, but promptly set it down again as she heard the ice cubes clanking noisily against the glass. Both Aishah and Mo glanced over at her. She attempted a smile. She hoped her large sunglasses hid the shock she knew must be visible in her eyes.

We've been through this before. I thought we'd decided to just put this off indefinitely.

Mo continued his argument with Aishah. "Look at Aliyah and Nora's daughters. They're married now and they're younger than Hope."

"I know that," she replied. "Hope says she's lost all of her friends. Once they're married they live in a totally different world from her. And some are expecting their first baby, so that will make even more of a difference."

Natalie plunked her sunhat on her head, pulling the floppy brim down to shield her face from the sun—and from Aishah and Mo. *I need Mike to call. It's been almost three months since I've heard from him... Where is he? Maybe he could help. Maybe now's the time to take her...*

"She still sees them at the bistro, though?" asked Mo.

"Occasionally. If they're the first wife, their husband sometimes brings them. If not, then it depends on how well they get along with the older wives. Sometimes they get stuck at home looking after all the kids. I feel sorry for them."

Mo sighed. "You know I've tried my best to put off this marriage thing. All I could do was talk to the imam."

"Yeah, I know, honey," Aishah said. "He's been good about discouraging Brian. I think he gave us these past few years because he wants to keep his only daughter at home as long as he can, too."

"We can't wait much longer, though. We'll have to do the best we can for her." Mo turned to Natalie. "What do you think of all this, Natalie? You're being very quiet."

"I agree with Aishah." Natalie tried not to reveal the anger churning inside of her. "I think it's a shame to marry so young. But I know we have to do the best we can under the circumstances."

Mo nodded. "The trouble is, Brian has scared off any eligible man from asking for Hope. He is still interested in her. It's gotten to be kind of a fetish with him. The older he gets and the older she gets, the more determined he seems to be. He keeps asking how she's doing, saying that she's going to be past marrying age soon, but he'll take her off my hands—stuff like that. The other day I wanted to punch him in the nose."

Aishah and Natalie both looked at him in surprise.

"You wouldn't! That would mean big trouble, " Aishah said.

"But Brian still has his four wives, doesn't he?" Natalie asked. "He can't be taking another one."

"That's what is holding him back from seriously pursuing Hope," Mo said. "I'm surprised he hasn't just divorced Veeda. For some reason he's hanging onto her."

"The gossip at the bistro is that she inherited some money from her father," Aishah said. "She's in poor health. Heart condition, or something. Maybe he's waiting for her to die and he can get at her money somehow. Guess we'd better keep Veeda healthy." She smiled.

Neither Mo nor Natalie returned her smile. Finally Natalie spoke.

"If we can possibly find a man who is younger, preferably with no other wives, it would be better for her than marrying Brian. Anyone would be better than Brian."

"But she doesn't want to marry at all," Aisha argued. "Can't we just put this off a while longer?"

"Not likely," Mo said, "Eventually Brian's going to be free to marry her and we can't say no if she is still single. He could make life pretty miserable for us."

"How?" asked Aishah.

"Start digging around—accuse us of all kinds of things, whether they're true or not. Start rumours. He's done that to other people."

Aishah shot Mo a startled glance.

Natalie noticed their eyes lock for a moment.

They're afraid of being found out, even after all these years.

"Okay, I agree." Aishah finally said, looking down at her hands. "The best thing we can do is find someone who will accept waiting a little longer for her, get her engaged now, which is as good as being married. If she's promised to someone else…"

"Yeah, that's the best we can do." Mo took Aishah's hand. "And we have to do it soon, sweetheart."

"Well, who then?" Aishah sniffed as a tear rolled down her cheek. "Who are we going to find for her? I can't think of one young man around here that I would choose for her. And I'm not just being a possessive mother. You know as well as I do that this generation of guys has been totally ruined by Unity. They can legally beat their wives, make them stay at home—and they think it's great to have their wives pop out a baby every year."

"Okay, okay," Mo said. "I can see you are getting all wound up."

"Let's not waste our energy on that," Natalie said. "We have to think about Hope's future. Do you have anyone suitable in mind, Mo?"

"No, I don't." He buried his face in his hands.

Aishah moved closer and put her arm around him. "Don't feel it's your fault. I know you've done your best and you will do all you can for her."

"I made a vow when I first held Hope in my arms, remember that day, Aishah? I said I would always take care of her and protect her—and now I can't. I'm useless. I feel like I've let her down, and you too."

Natalie couldn't think of anything to say that would console him. They sat in an uncomfortable silence, broken only by Aishah's occasional sniff and an intermittent bird call. They heard the sound of the casita door slam and a moment later Hope ran past them and dove into the pool.

"Wow, that felt good," she shouted. "Look, Dad, watch me. I can stand on my head." Aishah and Natalie laughed as Hope presented her feet out of the water.

"Good for you, sweetheart," Natalie called out.

Aishah's eyes filled with tears again. "See, she's still a little girl showing off for her dad."

"I've never thanked you for teaching her to swim," Mo turned to Natalie. "I always thought it was silly for a female to learn—when is she ever going to have an opportunity to do that once she leaves us?"

"Maybe she'll get a rich husband who will allow it," Natalie tried to encourage him.

"Well, anyway, I just want to say thank you now, Natalie," Mo continued, "because swimming makes Hope really happy. Even if there's no swimming in her future, she's enjoyed a good childhood."

"Let's all pray about this," Natalie said. "I know, I know, that's what I always say. But doesn't it always work out? Let's pray that God will send the right man into Hope's life. A good husband for her."

"And soon," added Mo.

"Okay," Aishah stood up. "I feel better if we are at least doing something. I know you two think I'm not very religious because I miss a few prayer times—but I do lots of praying when I'm baking or cleaning—or just relaxing out here. If there really is someone up there, He hears from me quite often." She laughed. "Don't look so shocked, you two. Time for dinner. You're barbequing tonight, Mo. Natalie, you've got time for another swim before dinner."

"Okay," Natalie welcomed the chance to dive into the water. *Hides my tears. Wouldn't Aishah be surprised to see me crying?*

After dinner, they sat around the pool until almost midnight enjoying the cool desert air. Aishah and Natalie talked about the *old days*. Hope leaned forward in her chair, occasionally interrupting to ask a question.

"Things were really different, weren't they, Mom?"

"They sure were," Aishah said.

Mo finally herded them all to bed, warning that morning would come soon enough. When Natalie had closed the door of the casita behind her, she immediately picked up her phone. She knew she was breaking the rules about calling Mike, but this was an emergency. She listened to the phone ring twelve times before she hung up.

He's probably changed phones again. Or maybe he's in Canada. There's no way I can get in touch with him. Please, God, help us.

CHAPTER NINETEEN

Natalie

The next morning, Natalie joined Mo and Aishah after prayers. They lingered over breakfast, waiting for Hope to join them. When it was almost time to leave for the bistro and Hope still hadn't shown up, Aishah peeked into her bedroom.

"She's still asleep," she informed Mo. "You can walk back for her later, Mo. Teenagers need their sleep."

"Maybe we should wake her anyway," he said. "What if she decides to walk over on her own?"

"She wouldn't. She knows it's too risky. Those young thugs in the morality squad are always on the prowl—just looking for some unchaperoned female to harass."

"Sure, she knows that. But you know how she is. She's like you that way." Mo rumpled Aishah's hair.

"An independent spirit, your mom always said. And I don't think she meant it as a compliment." Aishah giggled.

Natalie picked up the notepad from the corner of the cupboard. "We'll leave a note." She glanced over at Mo. "What time should I say you'll be back for her?"

"Around nine-thirty. By then the baking will be finished and I'll walk her back to the cafe by ten to help you open up."

Natalie scribbled in large letters, underlining each word: "Under no circumstances are you to walk out alone. Dad will be back for you around nine-thirty."

She taped the note to the bathroom door. "She can't miss this."

Mo waited patiently while Natalie and Aishah donned their outdoor garments. The trio departed for the walk to the bistro— Mo leading the way and the two black-clad women following a few steps behind. Mo glanced around. The streets were empty in the early morning sunlight. No sign of morality squad jeeps.

When they entered the bistro, Aishah, threw her outer clothes in a pile on the kitchen floor. "This niqab stinks," she said.

Natalie wrinkled her nose. "Yes. If we could only quit breathing it wouldn't get so smelly." She smiled as she calmly removed her own street clothes and veil, picked up Aishah's garments, placed everything in the washing machine at the back of the kitchen and turned it on.

"When are you going to quit complaining about your veil?" Mo asked.

"Never." Aishah slammed cookie sheets in a neat row on the counter.

"The day she quits complaining is the day I'll start worrying something's wrong with her," Natalie said, reaching for the mixing bowl on the top shelf.

"Me, too, I guess," Mo grinned as he handed Natalie the bowl. The trio began their morning tasks together: mixing and baking the cookies and muffins, readying the coffee machines in the separate bistros, preparing fillings for the sandwiches Natalie had insisted they add to the noon menu, and finally loading the warm baking onto serving trays. Aishah and Natalie each pushed a trolley into the women's section. Aishah began placing purple and orange napkins on the tables.

Shortly after nine, Mo called into the women's bistro, "I'm done out here. I'm going to get Hope. Give her a call to let her know I'm coming."

Before either women could answer, the kitchen door had closed behind him.

Aishah reached for the phone on the back counter. After a few moments, a worried look crossed her face. "There's no answer."

"She's probably asleep," Natalie reassured her. "Don't worry. She won't go out alone."

"I'm not so sure. We might have put ideas into her head last night—all that talk about the time before. Did you notice how interested she was and how many times she said she wished she could do those things, too?" Aishah fingered the tiny scar above her eyebrow. "I got caught once, you know. I should have told her about that. That would have discouraged her going out alone."

Natalie patted Aishah's arm. "She won't do that."

"I wish I could be sure . . ."

Sudden loud pounding at the front door of the women's section jolted both women into action.

"I'll go," Natalie volunteered, running through the empty bistro to the front door. She grabbed a head covering and veil hanging in the entrance. Aishah followed her, snatching a tea towel from the counter to cover her face. When Natalie unlocked the front door it was pushed open and Hope's black-clad figure tumbled into the cloakroom. She was clutching her veil and head covering in her hand. Her hair was wildly dishevelled.

Aishah dropped the tea towel and screamed. "What happened?"

Above Hope's gasping sobs, a male voice answered from just outside the door:

"The morality squad stopped her about half a block from here. I think she's okay. Bruised, probably, but she hasn't collapsed or anything and she's walking okay. Maybe some cuts from the beating. They used their canes on her... but I think she's okay."

Natalie held the door slightly ajar. "Thank you, thank you," she stammered. She heard Mo's voice outside the door. "What's going on here?"

And the stranger's answer, "Let me explain."

Natalie closed the door. Aishah was holding the sobbing girl, stroking her uncovered head and face. "It's over now. You're okay. You're safe. Let's have a look at you."

Hope turned a tear-stained face to the two women. There was a large red welt in the centre of her forehead, her nose was bleeding and her right cheek looked swollen, but no cuts were visible. Leading her back into the kitchen, Aishah and Natalie removed Hope's abaya and sat her on a chair. Clad in a T-shirt and jeans, not much skin was visible, but her arms were covered with swollen welts.

"Wiggle your fingers and move your arms for us," Natalie instructed.

Hope, sobbing quietly, obeyed.

"Everything appears okay, I think." Natalie felt her heart thudding heavily in her chest, but she managed to keep her voice steady. "You're okay, sweetheart." She turned to Aishah. "She's alright, Aishah."

Aishah fussed, bringing tea and a plate of warm cookies for Hope. "Did you eat any breakfast before you came?"

Hope silently shook her head. Her sobs had turned to hiccups. She reached for a cookie, sipped some tea and reached for another cookie.

"I'm okay," she said, "Really. I'm okay now. I feel better."

"Well, now I'm mad," Aishah said.

"You're mad at me, Mom? I guess I don't blame you. It was dumb of me to go out like that. I just wondered what it would feel like to walk all by myself, like you talked about last night."

Aishah turned to Natalie. "I told you. It's our fault. We put ideas into her head."

"No, Mom. It's my fault. I should have known better. I don't blame you for being mad at me."

"I'm not mad at you. Well, maybe a little. I'm mad at those young punks. Yes, that's what they are, Natalie. Don't give me that look. Imagine! They drive around every day, all day long—hoping they'll find someone to pick on."

"I just thought… a few blocks, I can make it alone, why bother Dad?" Hope said. "Then there they were, out of nowhere. But you know, the worst of it—one of them was Tobias. He's only a couple of years older than me. He played with me here at the bistro when we were little, for gosh sakes. How could he do this? He said something about I needed to learn a lesson."

"Maybe he didn't know who you were," Natalie said.

"He knew it was me. He yelled my name when the jeep pulled up beside me. He told me that his dad wouldn't want me for a wife if I didn't know my proper place."

Aishah said, "One of Brian's sons did this?"

"Yes, it was him. He enjoyed hitting me."

Aishah wiped Hope's tear-stained face with a cool facecloth. "I'm not mad at you," she said again. "I'm not blaming you, honey. It's this whole system. When I was your age I could walk out alone with my face uncovered."

Natalie rose quickly and closed the door to the bistro. "Shush, not so loud. I left the front door unlocked. Someone might come in. You know we can't talk like this."

Aishah continued in a quieter voice. "Well, I will never believe that it's right—young punks beating up on girls, just for walking alone."

"We might think that, but we can't say it," Natalie turned to Hope. "You stay here and have some breakfast, honey. Your mom and I have to open up now. People will be coming into the bistro soon."

Hope nodded and reached for a banana from the fruit bowl. "I don't want anyone to see me like this." Her eyes welled up with tears. "Don't tell anyone about it, okay?"

"We won't," Natalie and Aishah said in unison. As they entered the rear of the bistro, Veeda stormed in the front door.

"I heard all about it." Excitement rang in her raspy voice as she removed her veil and stuffed it into the oversized black bag she always carried with her. She pointed a boney finger at Aishah. "Your girl should know better. You haven't raised her properly if she doesn't know better by now. That's what happens to disobedient women."

Aishah looked steadily at the side of Veeda's face, saying nothing. Veeda slowly raised her hand to cover a dark bruise extending across her right cheekbone. Her eye was bloodshot. Aishah touched Veeda's's shoulder lightly.

"Nobody deserves to be beaten, Veeda," she said gently. "Coffee's on the house for you this morning."

"Well, thanks," Veeda muttered, then in an angry voice, "I can pay for it, you know. I have my own money."

"I know you do. But I like to give special people a treat and today you're my special person."

A ghost of a smile flickered across Veeda's face. "Okay, just this once."

Several other women entered the bistro and as Aishah waited on them they offered their sympathy. "Is she okay?"

"Tell Hope we're sorry it happened."

"Is there anything we can do?" Others just shook their heads silently and patted Aishah's hand as she served them.

"It doesn't happen very often anymore," one woman commented. "Not like it used to."

"That's because most girls have been educated into knowing their place," Veeda interjected loudly. "It shouldn't happen at all because the girls should know better. And their parents should teach them. Mo's lucky he lives in Palm Springs. In some cities the father receives a beating for things like this. He's responsible for making sure his household keeps the law. He's done a poor job."

Several of the women exchanged glances. Aishah eyes narrowed and she opened her mouth as if to say something, but before she could speak Natalie stepped in front of her.

Deliberately making eye contact with each woman staring at her, she spoke in a steady voice: "The important thing is that Hope is okay. We are all thankful to Allah for that, aren't we, ladies?"

"Right, of course, Thanks be to Allah," the women murmured and in a few moments the hum of conversation in the bistro returned to normal.

Natalie noticed that Veeda left earlier than she usually did only a few moments later.

Natalie whispered to Aishah, "Well that's over. You did really well with her. You go check on Hope if you like. I can take care of things here."

Natalie was surprised when Aishah returned a few moments later.

"She's sleeping in Mo's easy chair," she explained. "I thought I'd leave her to sleep it off."

Everyone left early that afternoon.

"Guess they know we want to be with Hope," Aishah said.

"They're a good bunch."

Hope was awake and sitting at the table sipping a cup of tea when Aishah and Natalie came into the kitchen.

Mo walked into the kitchen at the same time.

"I didn't get a chance to leave until now," he said. "How are you doing, honey?"

He exhaled sharply as he surveyed Hope's bruised face.

"I'm okay, Dad." Hope looked as if she was going to burst into tears again when she saw her father.

Mo patted her shoulder. "Sorry I took so long. It's really busy in there. But Adam said he'd cover for me for a few moments."

"Adam? Who's that?" Aishah wanted to know.

"That is the tall dark stranger who rescued our little girl this morning," Mo answered, his eyes crinkled into a smile as he glanced toward Hope.

"My knight in shining armour, Dad? I wasn't exactly rescued. They weren't going to kill me, you know." Hope said.

"Well, look who's feeling better and back to their feisty self," Aishah scolded. "Maybe they weren't going to kill you, but you sure needed someone to come along. Thank Allah for this Adam, whoever he is." She turned to Mo. "Who is he, anyway? Have you met him before?"

"No, I don't know him. It's a long story. We'll have to talk about this after work. But, little lady," Mo turned to Hope, "We may have solved the problem of finding a husband for you."

Natalie had said nothing throughout the conversation. With her back to Aishah and Hope, she continued loading cups into the dishwasher. *Could the answer to our prayers really come this quickly?*

"Problem?" Hope turned her swollen face to look at her dad. "There's no problem, Dad. Let's just have no marriage. I'm happy the way I am." She gathered her long dark hair into a pony tail, expertly securing it with a rubber band.

"We've spoiled you," Mo said. "We'll talk later. But let me leave this with you. You will have to marry someone and this escapade of yours today has narrowed your choices considerably. No one wants a disobedient wife. Brian was in the bistro this morning and he joked to everyone about how he'd take you anyway and whip you into shape. Do you want that? This young man today may be the only man who will have you." He glared at Hope. "I have to get back to work."

He stalked out of the kitchen, punching the swinging doors open with his fist.

Hope stared wide-eyed at her mother.

"Now Dad's mad at me, too," she wailed.

Aishah's eyes were on the still-swinging doors. "He's not mad at you, honey. He's just mad at everything. Punching the door is the only way he has of saying how mad he is. He'll be his old self by closing time."

"We all will." Natalie said in her usual calm manner. "We will all get over this and carry on as before."

Aishah nodded. "You're right, Natalie. It's just a speed bump in the road of life. Okay, Hope?"

"Okay, Mom. I'll help clean up the kitchen. Maybe we can get it done so Dad doesn't have to do anything more today at closing time."

"Great. I'm anxious to get home early and hear more about this Adam, aren't you?"

"No, I'm not." Hope stacked the clean baking trays with a noisy clatter.

Natalie sighed inwardly. *I'll be glad when this day is over. I don't think I could handle anything more today.*

The phone rang and Hope picked it up.

"Hello, Desert Delights Bistro. How may I help you?"

Aishah and Natalie leaned in to listen as Hope said, "Yes." Then, after a long pause, her voice wavering, "Yes, of course. As soon as possible. Goodbye." She turned to Natalie.

"That was Veeda. She's in the hospital. She says she's dying and she says you are to go there right away, Nana."

CHAPTER TWENTY

Natalie

"Veeda sounded really bad," Hope said. "Her voice was so soft I could barely hear her."

Aishah picked up the phone. "I'll call Mo. He'll just have to close early and drive Natalie to the hospital."

Natalie was fastening her veil when Mo rushed back to the kitchen. On the short drive to the medical centre Natalie told Mo all she knew of the situation.

"Just drop me off at the women's entrance. You can't come in anyway. I'll call for a ride home later. If this is as bad as Hope says it sounds, I might be here quite a while. "

"Whatever you think is best," Mo answered. "Just call when you need me."

"Thanks, Mo. This has been a bad day for everyone, it seems."

"You got that right, Natalie." She heard the weariness in Mo's voice. "Sorry I lost my temper," he said.

"That's okay. Normal reaction for a dad, I think."

Natalie closed the car door and entered the women's wing of the hospital. At the information desk she learned that Veeda was in the cardiac care ward on the third floor. She removed her veil in the elevator. When she reached Veeda's private room, she tapped gently on the door.

"Come in."

Natalie hardly recognized the frail voice. She pushed open the door and entered. Propped up on pillows in the high hospital bed, Veeda's large frame appeared small and fragile. From under her pale blue hospital gown an assortment of tubes and wires connected her to monitors at the side of the bed. Natalie took a deep breath as she approached her.

"Peace be upon you, Veeda." She spoke over the gentle beep of the monitors.

"And upon you, peace," Veeda responded in a raspy whisper.

Natalie put her hand on Veeda's shoulder, leery of disturbing any of the mysterious tubing.

"I came as soon as I could," she said.

"I didn't think you'd come."

"Of course I would come. Is there anything I can do for you?" Natalie wasn't sure what to say, but she knew Veeda always wanted to be in charge of the conversation, so she waited as Veeda took a ragged breath.

"There's nothing anyone can do for me. Just being here for me is good." Veeda spoke softly and slowly, pausing after every few words to take another breath. "Brian says he can't stand hospitals and not to expect him to come. Which is fine with me because they'd have to wheel my bed to some other ward where male visitors are allowed, and I'd have to be veiled, and I'm too tired for all of that."

Natalie nodded, noticing the bruises covering the right side of Veeda's face.

Veeda took a few more breaths. "My boys are all too busy tonight… they say. And my girls can only come if they can get a ride and permission from their husbands. So, I guess you're it, Natalie."

Natalie was surprised to see Veeda's eyes glistening with unshed tears. She pulled up a chair to sit close to the head of the bed.

"I've all the time in the world for you, Veeda." She risked taking Veeda's hand, tubes and all, lightly in hers. "I can stay all night, if you want."

"I'm not sure I'll make it through the night. But thanks. We'll see." She paused as she took several laboured breaths. "The doctor says maybe tonight or maybe tomorrow."

"I'm sorry, Veeda."

"No need. I just wanted to tell you something. Well, two things really."

Natalie leaned in closer to hear Veeda's weakening voice.

"First thing is—I know your secret. Aishah's and your secret."

Natalie felt the muscles in her stomach tighten.

"I've known for a long time," Veeda continued in halting breaths. "Right from the beginning when I saw Aishah at The Date Farm the weekend Hope was born. Just before the shelf collapsed on me. I saw that baby in Aishah's arms. And I figured it out later. Hope couldn't have been born in L.A. like they said. Aishah got her here in Palm Springs. Somehow. Probably at The Date Farm that day. It's always a crazy crowd there."

Natalie's heart thumped wildly

The Date Farm! Of course. Karyn would have chosen a Christian place. The Tomb. I'll bet she gave Aishah the baby in the Tomb. And that's why Aishah and Mo didn't want Hope to go there for that birthday party.

Natalie's mind raced. Veeda's eyes were fastened on her. Natalie brought her thoughts back to the bedside. "Why didn't you ever say anything?" she whispered.

"I don't know. I really don't. Aishah had always been so nice to me. The bistro was the only place where I felt safe. Maybe I didn't want to report her and lose my safe place." Her voice trailed off weakly.

"Or maybe you just cared what happened to Mo and Aishah and the baby," Natalie suggested softly.

"Maybe… Anyway, time passed and then it was too late. If I said anything I would be considered part of the whole scheme. And then I saw how happy Aishah was. She changed, you know. Didn't burst into tears all the time or have those odd spaced-out fits she used to have. And Hope was growing into such a beautiful little girl. Did you know even when she was a toddler she would come up to my table and take my hand and squeeze it and say *Peace be upon you* in that little lisp she had back then? I just thought . . . I thought, it's too late now. Let it go."

"But you've always been so strict about keeping the law, Veeda."

"I know. Weird, isn't it?" Veeda attempted a weak giggle Natalie had never heard before. "Kept all the smaller laws and let that big whopper pass."

"You did the right thing," Natalie said.

"Well, you would think that, for sure. I know who you are. You're Hope's grandmother. I thought it was odd when you showed up out of the blue the very first week Aishah brought the baby to the bistro. And then what clinched it for me was when Hope's permanent teeth came in. They're just like yours. Even that one side tooth that overlaps a little. One day Hope smiled at me and I saw your smile, Natalie—same dimples and everything. I can't believe Aishah and Mo haven't realized who you are. Or have they?"

Natalie's chest felt tight as she stammered, "No, they haven't. Will you be telling them?"

"Me? Never. Your secret will go to the grave with me, so to speak." Again, Veeda attempted a weak giggle, but ended up gasping for breath.

A nurse entered the room, glancing at Natalie. "If you don't mind, could you come back in fifteen minutes or so?"

"Of course." She rose to leave. "I'll be back in a little while."

"There's something else, even more important, that I have to tell you." Veeda tried to sit up, setting off several beeping monitors at her bedside. "Promise me you will come back."

"I promise. Definitely I will come back. You just rest."

Natalie bought a plastic wrapped sandwich and a bottle of water from the machine down the hall. She returned to sit in a chair outside Veeda's room. She couldn't eat the stale sandwich, but she sipped on the water. Her mind raced.

What could be more important than what Veeda has already told me?

The nurse came out of Veeda's room, interrupting her thoughts.

"She's asking for you," the nurse said.

"How's she doing?" Natalie asked.

The nurse shook her head.

"How long does she have?"

"Maybe a couple of hours, maybe a couple of days. Hard to tell. I think tonight will be her last night, though. I'm glad somebody came to be with her."

Natalie hesitated, and then said, "My daughter was a nurse. She said she always tried to be with people when they were dying. So I think I'll just stay, if you don't mind."

"Not at all. I'll bring you a blanket. Maybe you can catch some sleep in that easy chair in her room."

"Thank you." Natalie turned toward Veeda's door. "I'll just go see how she is doing."

When Natalie entered the room, Veeda was propped up by her pillows as before, but she appeared to be more comfortable.

"The nurse gave me a shot, so my pain isn't as bad," she said. "But I need to tell you something that happened this afternoon, just after the ambulance brought me here. Sit."

Natalie obeyed, moving her chair close to the head of the bed.

"I think you are the one I need to talk to about this. You see, when I figured out that Aishah hadn't given birth to the baby, I wondered where she would get a newborn in Palm Springs. There are no unwed mothers anymore. Brian had been bragging about how they were hunting down a few Christians around about that time. One in particular. They had arrested and executed the husband, but they couldn't find his wife."

Natalie swallowed hard a few times as she fought the urge to throw up. Veeda was looking intently at her.

"I figure she must have been pregnant and somehow she and Aishah hatched a plan to save the baby's life. It would just be like Aishah to do something crazy like that. I figure the woman is probably buried out in the desert somewhere."

Natalie cleared her throat. "Why are you telling me all this now, Veeda?"

"I need to know if you are a Christian. Like your daughter was. You can tell me. I'm dying. I won't tell anyone. I've kept the secret about Hope for, let's see, about fourteen years now, right?"

"Fifteen," Natalie said.

"So, are you a Christian or not, Natalie? Answer me right now." Even though her voice was weak, Natalie heard the commanding tone Veeda had always used with everyone at the bistro.

"I am." She felt a flood of relief as she spoke the words she had not been able to utter to a Muslim since arriving in Palm Spring so many years before. In a stronger voice, she repeated, "Yes, I am a Christian."

Veeda stared at her. Natalie's grey eyes stared back. In a feeble, but still recognizable raspy voice, Veeda said, "Good. I thought so. I need to talk to you, since you're the only Christian I know."

Natalie nodded. "Okay."

"Here's the thing. I came into the hospital right after lunch today, hadn't felt good all morning. Maybe you noticed at the bistro?"

Natalie shook her head, feeling guilty that she had not noticed.

"Lots of chest pain and I felt sick, so I called 911. After all the junk they did to me, they finally settled me here in this room and I fell asleep late in the afternoon. I woke up about an hour later, I think it was, doesn't matter. All the curtains were pulled so it was quite dark in here. Someone was standing at the foot of my bed. Right here," she gestured beyond her feet. "A man in white, and he kind of glowed—like light was around his head. I couldn't see his face because of the glow surrounding him…" Veeda's voice trailed into silence.

Natalie couldn't believe what she was hearing. *Could this have happened to Veeda, of all people!* Her voice was hushed as she said, "Did He say anything to you, this man in white?"

"He said my name. 'Veeda'. That's all, but I felt myself surrounded by warmth. I felt like I was a small child being held in my mother's arms. I felt…" Veeda hesitated as tears splashed down her cheeks, "I felt loved. I haven't felt like that since I was a little girl and my mother used to hold me. I never expected I would feel that again. I haven't felt loved for so long."

Natalie leaned over the bed to hold a now sobbing Veeda. "It's like something inside of me just melted away," Veeda said.

"And then what?" Natalie spoke softly.

"Then the vision ended, or the dream or whatever it was, and the brightness just slowly faded away and no one was there. But the feeling stayed, Natalie."

"I see. Who do you think the man in white was?"

"Well, of course I know who the man in white was," Veeda snapped. "We all know that. It's whispered around every once in a while, but nobody wants to talk about it. Who could we talk to? I remember once I heard that someone in the hospital claimed that he had seen the man in white and been cured of whatever it was he had."

"What happened?"

"He was charged with blasphemy and shot. But I'm dying anyway, so I don't mind saying I saw Jesus, that's who I saw. But what does He want with me? I'm an old woman. Just tell me what He could possibly want with me, Natalie." Veeda's voice grew louder. "I've kept our laws as best I could all my life. Except for not reporting Hope. I've tried not to question Allah's will for my life, even when it meant a husband who beat me. Still I've obeyed the law, so what more am I supposed to do?"

She was crying now, great gasping sobs, as she repeated her question over and over, "What more am I supposed to do?"

Natalie sent up what Hope called an "arrow prayer". *Please help me say the right thing.* Her next words came slowly and confidently, surprising not only Veeda, but herself. "He doesn't want anything more, Veeda. He never wanted all that you tried so hard to give. God just wants you. And He sent Jesus to you to tell you that. God loves you just the way you are. You felt that love here in this room. Jesus brings you God's love because Jesus *is* God. All He wants is for you to believe in Him."

Silence filled the room. From somewhere outside, Natalie heard the muffled ring of a phone. It seemed to Natalie that an eternity passed before Veeda spoke again.

"I do believe in Him," she whispered. "I saw Him, right here in this room. How could I not believe? So now what do I do?"

"Invite Him into your life, just like you would invite someone into your home if they knocked on your door."

"Out loud?"

"If you like. Or say it silently if you prefer. He'll hear you."

"Okay." Veeda closed her eyes and was quiet for a long moment. Then she said, "I did it. I asked Jesus to come into my life. I even said *please.*"

Natalie clasped Veeda's hand carefully. "So now you have the gift of eternal life, Veeda."

"I'm dying", Veeda said flatly. "So I don't have eternal life."

"Yes, we all die, Veeda, but everyone who believes in the Son of God does not die forever. They will be raised to new life, in the same way that Jesus was raised from the tomb. Your death will not be the end for you."

"You can't know that for sure." Veeda seemed to have gained more strength. "No one can know for sure if they've followed the law well enough to go to Paradise."

"But you will go to Paradise because God loves you, Veeda, not because you have kept all the laws. That's Jesus' promise to us."

"So I'll go to Paradise just because God loves me?"

"Just because God loves you. Do you remember how much you loved your children, even when they did bad things? They didn't need to earn your love, did they? You just loved them."

Veeda nodded.

"Well, that's how it is with God. You don't need to do anything to earn God's love."

"I don't need to do anything… I don't need to do anything." Veeda repeated the words slowly. She was silent for a moment. Then she smiled broadly, exposing the spaces in her mouth where her teeth had been knocked out.

"Oh, Veeda." Natalie was in tears. " I am so happy for you." She leaned over to hug Veeda's frail form once more. "May I pray with you to Jesus?"

Veeda nodded.

Natalie began, "Dear Lord Jesus, we are so thankful that You have come to Veeda in this way. Help her to feel safe in your love no matter what happens—"

"Too many words, Natalie. I'll pray," Veeda interrupted. "Thank You, thank You, thank You, Jesus. I'm not afraid any more. I want to be with You in Paradise. So take me soon." After a short pause she added, "The sooner, the better. In fact, tonight would be good."

Startled, Natalie closed the prayer. "Amen."

"You can go now. I want to be alone with Jesus."

Natalie smiled. *Still the same old Veeda. No, not quite!*

"Thank you, Natalie. I know you were scared to tell me your secret."

"Scared is putting it mildly," Natalie said, as she gently hugged Veeda goodbye. She was almost at the door when Veeda called out to her. She turned around.

"I've told Jesus I'm sorry. For a lot of things. Tell Aishah I'm sorry for all the mean things I said to her... and the cuckoo clock."

"I will, Veeda. Peace." Natalie closed the door softly.

CHAPTER TWENTY-ONE

Hope

They sat side by side on Hope's bed—Hope in her pyjamas, Aishah in her housecoat. Hope winced as her mother applied salve to the purple bruises on her face. Mo had left to give Natalie a ride home from the hospital. Hope braced herself for another safety lecture to go along with her mother's healing touch, but none came. Instead, her mother's next words surprised her.

"I once went through the same thing you're going through— bruises and all." Aishah dabbed gently at the welts on Hope's arm.

"Really, Mom? You? What for? Did you go out on the street alone?" Hope could hardly believe her ears. *No wonder she's not lecturing me. She's done it herself!*

"Hold out your arm, honey. Even worse than that," Aishah smiled. "I licked an ice cream cone in a public place. That was shortly before veils became the law—so my face wasn't covered. But it was considered lewd behaviour to show your tongue."

"Did the street patrol see you, or what?" Hope was having trouble picturing her mom doing such a thing. *I would never even think of doing something like that. Yikes! My mother licked an ice cream cone in public!* Hope regarded her mother with a new sense of respect, and even a little envy.

"Somebody reported me to our imam. He was very strict, that was in the beginning days of our new government and nobody really knew for sure what was allowed and what wasn't. But we soon found out. I was charged with violating general morals and caned. Publicly."

"In front of everybody? Where?" Hope's emerald eyes opened wider.

"In the center court of our largest shopping mall. They hit me lightly, except for this one guy." Aishah's hand went to the slight scar on her forehead. "This scar is the least of it, though. I can forget about it, but I've never forgotten how it felt to be beaten in front of everyone—people gathered around to watch. It was so humiliating. I guess that was the idea of it—to keep me from ever doing something like that again. And to show other females what could happen to them."

"Where was Dad in all of this?"

"Oh, that was before I met your dad. But in a way that incident was how we came to meet. I was kind of known as the brazen girl who stuck out her tongue in public after that. I was only fifteen but my uncle had been thinking about marriage for me. He was really angry because I had shamed the family. He said no man would ever want a woman like me. And he was right. Before the caning, young guys often looked at me and I knew they were interested. But after the caning every eligible man steered clear of me. To make a long story short, your dad was the only man who approached my uncle about marrying me."

"Did you love him, Mom?"

"Yes, I did."

"Right away, or did you grow to love him like everyone says a wife will when she marries?"

"Right away. The first time I met him. I looked at him and he looked at me and then he said something about me being very beautiful and that he'd heard I had a nice tongue, too."

"Oh, Mom, he didn't!"

"He did."

Hope couldn't believe her Dad would say such a thing. *Wow! My Mom and Dad talked like that! And that was the first time they had met—they weren't even engaged! Awesome!*

"What did you say?" asked Hope.

"I told him I did have a nice tongue and would he like to see it? And he said he would, but maybe later." Aishah's hand paused before reaching into the jar for more salve. She gazed at the opposite wall, a dreamy smile playing across her face. "It was love at first sight for both of us. And we have lived happily ever after."

Hope looked at her mother wistfully. *Love at first sight. That's just like in Mom's novel.* She felt happy and sad at the same time. "Oh, Mom," she took her mother's hand. "That's so romantic. That's what I would like. That is, if I ever do marry."

"Of course you will marry. You have to. Maybe this Adam is the man for you. Maybe he's like your dad—he said he liked a woman with spunk. That's what made him curious about me. Maybe Adam is like that, too. And I hear he's very good looking. That's a bonus, Hope."

Before she thought, Hope answered, "He *is* good looking, Mom, but…"

"But what?"

Hope stared at the floor, reliving the scene. She remembered his deep brown eyes burning in fury as he spoke firmly to the young patrol guys, "That's enough. Go on your business now."

When they had left and he turned toward her, Hope saw a look of astonishment flash across his face and then, just for a second, his eyes held an expression of tenderness. But as he pounded on the front door of the women's' bistro and they waited for someone to open the door, all that changed. His eyes grew cold.

"Don't you ever do this again," he said, "and straighten your niqab. I can see your face."

Hope struggled to adjust her veil, but the fastener was broken. Her feeling of gratitude melted away.

"Who are you to tell me what to do?"

"Someone much wiser than you, obviously." He shoved her through the open door into Natalie's arms.

With a start, Hope realized her mother was still waiting for an answer.

"But what? Hope?" Aishah said again.

"But he's bossy and I don't like his attitude."

"Attitude, schmattitude. Your dad's thinking about him maybe being the one for you, so maybe you'd better start thinking about that, too."

"Is that what you want for me, Mom?" Hope fought back her tears.

Aishah gathered her gently in her arms.

"I want only the best for you, honey. And so does your dad. We'll do the very best we can. But you know Brian has said he plans to marry you. He says he'd pay off any suitable young man who approaches us about you. We may have to offer someone more than he can and you know that we don't have— "

"Mom, that makes me feel like I'm a piece of property you and Dad are selling."

Aishah ignored Hope's comment. "And besides most of the men already have one wife. You don't want to be the second or third wife and have to get along with the previous wives and their children, do you, Hope? Some of their kids might be as old as you are now."

"Or even older, if I have to marry Brian." Hope's eyes were wide with fear. She stared at her mother. "Mom, I just don't want to get married at all."

"I know, I know, sweetheart. We'll do our very best. I promise you that. Try to get some sleep. It's been a long day. We'll talk more in the morning."

As Aishah tucked the covers up under Hope's chin, Hope turned her face away so that her mother couldn't see the tears coursing down her cheeks. She felt like a little girl again. *I thought they would always take care of me. And now they can't.* She heard her mother sigh as she turned off the light and closed the bedroom door.

Staring into the darkness, Hope whispered, "Please God, help me." She lay very still, waiting for an answer. But no answer came.

She lost touch of the hours as she tossed and turned, reliving the experience of the beating. She saw again the stranger's deep brown eyes and felt his strong arm around her as he waded into the group of boys.

He didn't even flinch from their sticks—he must have a few bruises, too.

She remembered his expression when her niqab came undone and he saw her face. He had a look of... what? Gentleness, mingled with surprise, maybe, she decided. But then the cold, hard look that followed. She couldn't quite figure it out.

And why did he suddenly turn angry and push me through the doorway like that? Who does he think he is? Bossing me around. Sure, he stopped the thugs, but that's no reason to order me around like that... shove me around like that.

She sat up in bed as she remembered. *He touched me! He put his hand on my arm and the other hand was in the centre of my back. And he saw my face, too. What does that mean? Will I have to marry him now? No, I won't. It's not my fault. But maybe that's why he looked so surprised when my veil came undone. Maybe he thinks now he has to marry me. I'll ask Dad in the morning. I'm not marrying him or anyone, and that's that.*

Hope finally fell asleep. She had been afraid that she would dream of the beating, but instead she dreamt of the stranger's smiling eyes.

When she awoke, the early morning call to prayer was sounding. She could hear her mom and dad as they prayed in their prayer room next to her bedroom. She knelt beside her bed.

"Oh God, hear my prayer, too," she whispered. "Please, please, send me a nice man to marry. I'll marry him even if I don't love him. Please Jesus, send me someone who will be kind to me. I'm not even asking that he love me. Although that would be nice." She paused. "Please. You can do miracles. I need a miracle. I am afraid of what is happening. I promise You I will be the best wife I can be. Please, just someone like Dad would be great. I'm not even asking for a Christian man. I know that's impossible. Just a nice kind man, please Jesus." Hope's desperate words echoed in the silence of her room.

She heard her Mom and Dad talking as they left the prayer room. And then the phone ringing. She pulled on her jeans and a sweatshirt and joined them in the kitchen. Natalie was already there, having breakfast with Aishah and Mo before they walked to the Bistro.

"Who called?" Hope asked.

"It was the hospital, honey," her dad answered. "Sorry to have to tell you bad news when you have enough on your plate right now, but Veeda died last night."

"She was such a terrible person," Aishah said, "I'm sure she won't be in Paradise, even though you told me she was sorry about the clock, Natalie. We all know what a hateful person she was."

"We don't know that she isn't in Paradise. We are not the ones who decide who is in Paradise and who isn't, are we?" Natalie's words were for Aishah, but her gaze was directed at Hope. "Allah is merciful, we all believe that, don't we?"

Aishah rolled her eyes. "You're too kind, Natalie. Hope, you and I are taking the day off. Do you think we can find some housework to do?"

Natalie and Mo left for the bistro. Hope sipped her orange juice and nibbled at the muffin Aishah had placed in front of her, but she really didn't feel like eating breakfast.

"Anything else I can get you, sweetheart?" Aishah asked.

"No, but I have to talk to Dad. As soon as he gets back tonight."

"That sounds urgent. Are you sure I can't help?"

"Well, maybe, Mom, but it has to do with the law." Hope told her mother about the stranger seeing her face and touching her. She became more agitated as she spoke. "So now I'm worried. Does that mean I have to marry him? It wasn't my fault." Hope burst into tears. "I need to talk with Dad."

"Listen, sweetheart, Dad will check it out with the imam, if you like. I'm sure you have nothing to worry about. As you say, it wasn't your fault."

"But you aren't positive, are you, Mom?"

"Well, no, not a hundred per cent. The law is complicated. I never heard of that, though. Anyway, we have something more important to talk about. Your Dad wants me to tell you what's happening with Adam. He called to see how you were last night and he and your dad had a long talk. He's a widower. He is looking for a wife, and he is interested in you."

Hope's eyes turned a glacial green. *Not in a million years.* "Oh, no," she said to her mother. "He's too bossy. I don't like the way he shoved me around. So, no. Definitely not. Don't even consider it."

"But we *are* considering it, honey. We have to. Now that Veeda has died, Brian is free to take another wife. He's wanted to marry you for a long time. He's mentioned it to your Dad several times, ever since you were about five years old."

"That's gross, Mom."

"I know. Don't get me started on child marriages. The point is, you know Brian gets what he wants, and he wants you."

"Well, he can't have me," Hope tried to speak firmly, but her bottom lip trembled.

"I'm afraid he can, unless you are engaged to marry someone else. So Dad is seriously considering the stranger."

Hope crossed her arms across her chest and stared at her mother. "Adam, you said his name was?" she sniffed.

"Yes. Adam Khoury."

"Well, I won't marry this Adam. So that's that."

"If you won't marry Adam, then you will almost certainly be marrying Brian, Hope. So that's that, too." Aishah sat back in her chair.

Hope stared at her mother. She felt trapped. Finally she put her head down on the table, burying her face in her hands. "Mom," she mumbled through her fingers, "This isn't fair. I don't want to marry anyone. Why can't things just stay the way they are? We're happy the way things are." Tears soaked the tablecloth.

"I know that," Aishah came over to Hope and put her arms around her. "I know that," she repeated. She was crying, too.

Hope dabbed at her tears, sniffing loudly. Abruptly, she said, "Well, what about Nana? What does Nana have to say about it?"

"Nana thinks you should marry Adam, under the circumstances," Aishah said. "But, Hope, it really doesn't matter what Nana thinks. Your Dad will make the decision." After a moment she added, "And me, of course. You know he'd always include me in anything like this, even though he doesn't have to. For us, this is a family decision."

"But Nana might— "

Aishah interrupted her. "She isn't family, Hope. She's just Nana. We love her, of course. But she really isn't family."

"She's family to me," Hope shouted. She pushed back her chair and stomped into the bathroom, slamming the door behind her. It was the first time she had heard her mother say anything about Nana not being part of their family. *Nana isn't pleased about this. I know it. And that's why Mom is cutting her out of the discussion. I'll talk to Nana about it tonight and she'll figure out some other way.*

But later that evening when she had tapped on the door of the casita and joined Natalie for their usual hot chocolate, Hope was surprised to hear Natalie echo her mother's words.

"I'm sorry, honey. I have to agree with your Mom and Dad. There's no other way. We don't have any other choice.

"Well, what about our prayers, Nana? Maybe God will answer our prayers and I won't have to marry anyone,"

"Maybe—you never know. But Hope, have you considered that maybe Adam *is* God's answer to our prayers? Maybe he's the right man for you."

"But he's not Christian, Nana. And besides I don't like him. He's too bossy."

"I know he's not Christian, honey. But he is kind and honest, according to what everyone tells your Dad. He's a very nice man. Under the circumstances, he may just be the answer we have been praying for."

"You mean, this Adam guy is the best God can do?"

Nana smiled. "Under the circumstances, yes, perhaps that's the best God can do."

Hope could feel her face turn red. "Sorry, Nana, I guess I shouldn't have put it that way."

"Put it any way you like. God knows your thoughts, so you may as well pour it all out to Him. He'll understand and love you anyway. I don't know what's ahead for you, honey, but I do know Jesus will be with you through it all. So even if things look dark and confusing to you now, just trust God. You won't be in this alone."

"But, how can I know for sure?" Hope could feel her chest tighten when she even thought of marriage and all that it meant.

"You can't know for sure, but let me share with you what has kept me going in the tough times of my life. Once, when I was feeling very alone and afraid, just like you are now, God told me I was never really on my own. I heard God's voice telling me that I was held within God, just like a baby in its mother's womb. But it was more than that—I actually *felt* in that moment that I was somehow *in* God, protected and safe. And God told me that no matter where I was in the future or what bad things might be happening to me, I should always remember that this is where I really was, *In God*."

Hope's eyes had grown wide through the account. "You heard God's voice?"

"I did."

"Oh, Nana. That's wonderful. I wish I could feel that."

"You can. That's why I'm telling you my very personal experience. I've told hardly anyone, but now I wish I had shared my story with more people because it's true for them, too, not just for me. We are in Christ, as St. Paul puts it. That's where we really live. No matter what terrible situation we may find ourselves in. Can you just trust God that this is true for you? See yourself where you really belong—where you really are?"

Natalie dipped her finger in her now cold chocolate drink and drew a circle on the polished tabletop. "This circle is God, Hope." She dipped her finger again, making a dot in the circle. "This is you. See yourself in the circle of God."

Hope stared at the circle on the table for several moments. Then she took a deep breath. She felt like a huge weight had just been lifted from her shoulders. Jumping up, she put her arms around Natalie.

"Thanks, Nana. I can do that for sure. I can do this marriage thing, too. I know that now. I know I'm not alone and I know where I really am."

"Good for you, sweetheart," Natalie said. "Just remember, we'll all be with you, too, your mom and dad, and me. We love you very much."

"I'm not saying I'm happy about this." Hope felt she had to make sure Nana understood. "I'm not happy at all. But I can do this. I *will* do this," she said, pressing her lips together firmly. "Even if I have to grit my teeth to get through it all."

"We all grit our teeth to get through a lot of things these days," Natalie said.

Hope was surprised at the bitterness she heard in Nana's voice. She had always thought Nana was happy and contented with her life.

"You, Nana? You're a tooth-gritter?" she teased, attempting to lighten Nana's mood.

"Yeah, big time," Natalie smiled back. "I think my back teeth are getting shorter all the time."

Hope laughed. "I love you, Nana," she said, giving her a hug. "I hope you don't have to grit your teeth too much because of me."

"Not too much," Natalie grinned. "You're the reason I can survive this daft system. I'll always be here for you, God willing."

Hope paused at the door, as she left. She looked back. "I'll always be here for you, too, Nana, God willing."

As she walked the short path back to the house, Hope wondered why she always felt better after talking with Nana.

Nothing has changed. I'll probably have to marry this Adam guy…
but I feel better now. I think it will be okay. Somehow.

When Hope walked into the kitchen, her mom and dad were sitting at the table talking. They stopped when she entered. Looking from one to the other, she said, "Talking about me again?"

"Yes, we were, sweetheart. Want a cup of tea?" Aishah asked.

Mo patted the chair beside him and Hope sat down.

"Guess you're talking about marrying me off." Hope made an attempt to sound lighthearted.

"Don't put it that way, honey," Aishah gave Hope's shoulder a little squeeze.

"I'm sorry, Mom… Dad… I know I'm being awful. Guess I'm just scared." To Hope's embarrassment her eyes filled with tears. She noticed that, as usual, when someone else cried, her mother followed right along. "Anyway," Hope continued as she swiped at a tear that had somehow escaped, "I've decided that you know what is best, under the circumstances."

Both Aishah and Mo looked surprised. "So I won't argue any more. I'm not happy, but that's how it goes, I guess."

"Honey, we're not happy about this, either," Mo said.

"But," Aishah added after a moment of silence, "We could not have found a better husband than Adam. He's only twenty-five—not too old for you. And, Hope, remember how I said my beating led to me meeting your Dad? Maybe it will be the same for you."

Hope lifted an eyebrow at her Mom. "Really, Mom? I doubt that very much."

Mo cleared his throat, "So, ask anything you like about Adam. I had a long talk with him and I think I know everything I need to know. I told him Brian would probably be offering him money to keep him from marrying you, and he said he would not accept it—no matter how much was offered. He owns a jeep—" Mo turned to Aishah, "Your favourite colour, honey—red—and runs private tours for tourists—trips into the desert. Likes to be outdoors and camp out."

Hope wrinkled her nose. "Camping out in the desert?"

"Well, maybe you will like it. Adam worked for a large tour company in Phoenix before coming here. He's been married before and his wife died of cancer only a couple of years after they were married. He moved here to start over again."

"Nana calls that *geographical therapy,*" Hope said. "She says it often works."

"Hmmm...," Mo said, "Maybe it's working for him. He seems to content here. He only has one jeep now, but he does plan to expand his business."

"That's not going to happen unless the tourists come back," Aishah said.

"Anyway," Mo continued, ignoring Aishah's comment, "He's not rich, but he makes enough to support a wife, and that's all that counts, isn't it?"

Hope didn't respond. Her eyes remained firmly focussed on her father.

"We've arranged for you two to meet and you can talk things over. You will have to show him your face and hands, Hope. It's customary for the prospective groom to see you unveiled."

"He's already seen my face," Hope said flatly. "Where will we meet?"

"Here. Your mom and I will stay in the dining room and you can sit with him in the living room."

"When?"

"Tomorrow night, if that's okay with you," Mo said. "The sooner, the better under the circumstances."

"Okay, Dad. Guess I'll go to bed now. I need my beauty sleep for tomorrow."

As Hope left the kitchen, she heard Mo say, "I wonder what Natalie said to her." And then she heard him comforting Aishah, "She agrees, honey. Don't cry. It's the best we can do."

Hope climbed into bed and whispered into the darkness, "You hold my future in Your hands, Lord. I know that, but still I'm scared. But thank you for Mom and Dad and Nana. They are trying their best." She paused, "And if Adam is to be my husband, then I pray for us to be happy together." After a few moments she added, "And I thank you for him, too. I guess. Amen."

She expected to spend another sleepless might, but fell asleep immediately. When she woke to the sound of the Call to Prayer she felt her usual energetic self. She joined her mom and dad in the prayer room and chatted cheerfully with them afterwards. Later, as the three black-clad women walked in single-file behind Mo as they did every morning, she joked to her mother, "Time for our little parade."

Aishah turned around to look at her and giggled. Then, looking straight ahead once again and keeping her head slightly bowed, she spoke just loudly enough for Hope to hear. "I hope you won't be making any of those kinds of comments to Adam tonight. I hear he is very observant of the law. You'll behave yourself, won't you, Hope?"

"Of course, Mom. I'll be a model of obedient womanhood this evening." When Hope turned back to glance at Natalie she saw anxiety clouding Natalie's usually calm grey eyes.

They're both worried about how tonight will turn out. And so am I.

CHAPTER TWENTY-TWO

Hope

Hope held the small jar of concealer as Aishah covered the last purple bruise on her face. She wished she could hide her feelings about this marriage as easily as the makeup hid her bruises. She wasn't sure she could pretend with this Adam guy.

Her mother seemed to read her thoughts. "Keep your feelings to yourself tonight, no matter what," she said. "Be like Natalie. You never know what's going on in her head."

"Be like Nana? Okay, Mom. I'll try."

Adam arrived promptly at eight o'clock. After sharing a few moments of awkward conversation with Mo and a heavily veiled Aishah who looked down at the floor and nodded silently, he was led into the living room to meet Hope. She sat ramrod straight on the living room couch. Mo suggested Adam sit opposite her in his easy chair.

"We'll just leave you two to get better acquainted," he said.

Hope knew her Mom and Dad would remain in the adjoining dining room listening to every word they said. She glanced at Adam and without speaking, reached up and removed her veil. Adam's eyes studied her face. He cleared his throat several times.

She realized he was as nervous as she was and somehow that made her feel more relaxed. She made an attempt to lean casually against the back of the sofa, trying to read the expression in his eyes. *Sadness, maybe?* Adam continued to gaze at her. She shifted her position on the couch.

She was quite sure the man should be the first one to speak, but after a few moments of uncomfortable silence, she couldn't endure the tension any longer. She surprised herself by blurting out, "Thank you for rescuing me the other day." Then she hesitated. "Well, maybe rescuing isn't the right word, but thank you for intervening."

"You're welcome," Adam responded, too politely, she thought.

She waited a moment for him to continue but when he did not, she decided if there was to be a conversation it was up to her to initiate it.

"I guess you'd like to know something about me. Just ask any questions and I'll answer them."

Adam smiled as he replied, "Okay. First question: What do you think of me?"

She hadn't expected *that* kind of question. She had thought he'd ask if she could cook and keep house—those kind of things. She had rehearsed her answers earlier in the day with Aishah and Natalie coaching her. His question caught her off guard.

"What do I think of you?" she repeated, and paused, asking herself the same question. "Well, I think you are kind, because you helped me, and I think you're strong and I admire you because you stood up to that gang of jerks."

Adam smiled. "And you think I'm bossy because I bawled you out for walking alone."

How did he know that? "Well…" Hope couldn't help but smile back at him, "Yeah, I do."

"I like your dimples," Adam complimented. "It's the first time I've seen you smile."

Hope's hands went up to her cheeks. Her face felt hot. To hide her embarrassment, she flung out the first thing that came into her head. "Nana says that when I'm an old lady they'll turn into wrinkles, like hers did."

"Well, we'll just have to wait and see, won't we?" Adam smiled again.

Her face grew hotter. She fixed her eyes on the floor in front of Adam's feet.

He continued to gaze at her and then suddenly said, "Look, Hope, I know you're not too thrilled about this marriage. Maybe not too thrilled about me, either. You're only fifteen. I know that's not too young for marriage these days, but it must seem too soon for you."

She didn't look at him. Instead, she glanced into the dining room where Aishah and Mo sat at the table, pretending to be having a conversation.

Adam followed her gaze, and then, dropping his voice he spoke so softly that Hope had to lean forward to hear his next words.

"You probably won't believe this, but it is important to me that I tell you." He paused a moment before continuing. "The other day when your veil came unfastened and I saw your face…" He cleared his throat. "I don't know. Something happened. I never thought I'd feel like this again. I never thought I'd love again."

Hope looked away, but she could feel his eyes on her. She knew she should be responding in some way, but she was so surprised she couldn't think of anything to say.

After a long silence, Adam continued.

"You know my wife died three years ago. I loved her very much. And I just never thought I'd feel like that ever again. But, I do. I love you, Hope, from that first glance. Something happened. I want to spend the rest of my life with you."

Hope still didn't look at him. *This is weird. It's like in Mom's book. Love at first sight, they called it.*

"I will do everything in my power to make you happy." Adam hurried on. "And there will never, ever, be anyone else but you. I need to tell you that. No second or third or fourth wife. I promise you."

In spite of her best efforts, tears filled Hope's eyes, threatening at any moment to overflow.

"That's very nice," she managed to say past the lump in her throat. "I'm sorry... I wish I could say—"

Adam interrupted her. "I know you don't love me now. I'm okay with that. Let's just get to know each other. We can be friends, can't we? We'll just be friends until you decide otherwise."

Hope head jerked up and she met his eyes. "You mean...?"

"Exactly what you think I mean. We'll get married soon. We both know the reasons for that. Your mom and dad say we can live here until we find a house of our own. We'll have a nice wedding celebration if you like, whatever you want, Hope. But you'll decide when you really become my wife."

Hope sat silently. She swiped at her tears with the back of her hand.

"Okay," she finally whispered, unable to meet his gaze.

"Just one condition," Adam said.

She looked up, her green eyes holding her question.

"Don't tell anyone. This is our secret. Just yours and mine, okay?"

"Okay," she whispered again, feeling relieved.

"Good," Adam said. He rose from his chair to sit down beside her, taking her hand in his two hands.

"Don't worry, Hope. We will have a long and happy life together."

"Inshallah," Hope murmured.

After a slight pause, Adam answered softly, "Inshallah."

They sat for a moment in silence. Then Adam rose to his feet. Looking toward the dining room, he spoke in a louder voice. "Whenever we can, let's spend time together before the wedding."

"Of course you should!" Aishah jumped from her chair. "Come for dinner tomorrow night. You probably need a good home-cooked meal."

"I'd love that." Adam said.

Hope glanced at her mom. *A good home-cooked meal? Since when? Mom does not usually make that claim-to-fame as Nana calls it.*

Aishah glanced at her daughter and said, "We'll barbeque. Hope will make a salad and Natalie will make dessert."

Mo laughed. "Better get ready for females planning your life, Adam. I'll be glad to have you in the household. It's been hard being out-numbered three to one—now it's just three to two. But we can hold our own, can't we?"

Adam grinned. "I hope so. I'm not so sure."

They all laughed, except Hope. When Adam smiled down at her, she saw in his eyes what she knew was love.

"Come and meet Nana," she said quickly, walking ahead of him to the casita in the front yard. Hope knocked gently. A veiled Natalie opened the door immediately.

Hope realized Nana had probably been waiting for them to arrive. *And she has probably been praying the whole time we talked.*

Natalie took one quick glance at Adam before lowering her eyes, and saying softly, "Welcome to the family, Adam."

"I'm happy to meet you, Natalie," he responded formally.

Although their exchange was brief, Hope had a warm feeling, "Like a bond between the three of us," she explained to Natalie afterwards.

"Funny. I felt the same way," Natalie said.

"Good!" Hope exclaimed, giving her a hug. "I don't know how I could handle this if you didn't like him. I'm not sure yet that I do."

"It'll all work out, honey. I'm certain of it."

* * *

Aishah and Mo decided on an April wedding. Hope tried to convince them that there was no hurry.

"Let's wait until fall."

But Mo had said, quite sternly, she felt, "We can't wait. The sooner you're married, the better. Something could happen to Adam."

"Like what?"

"Like an accident of some sort."

"Do you really think Brian would do something like that, Dad?" Hope couldn't believe what she was hearing.

"Well, we can't be sure. Do you want to take that chance? Your mom and I sure don't."

"Does Adam know all this?" asked Hope.

"I'm afraid so. In fact, he's already turned down another offer from Brian to break the engagement."

"Good grief, Dad!" Hope made a face. "Like I'm something he can buy. This is disgusting!"

"Of course Adam turned him down," Aishah jumped into the conversation. "But all the same… We don't want to take any chances, do we, Hope?"

Hope's heart skipped a beat. Her mind raced as she recalled all the things her Mom and Nana had told her about Brian. She hadn't really believed he wanted to marry her so badly. But now…

She remembered the conversation she had with Aishah the night before the official engagement was to be announced. It seemed to Hope that her mother was worried she would still somehow back out of the marriage. *As if that was possible!* Aishah had come into her bedroom and sat on the edge of Hope's bed. She looked embarrassed and Hope thought it was going to be *The Talk* as her girlfriends had laughingly called it.

"Honey," her mom said, "Your dad insisted I tell you some things you maybe don't know about marriage."

Hope took one look at her mom's red face and sought to rescue her from what she could tell was an uncomfortable topic for Aishah. "I think I know enough, Mom. It's okay."

"I don't think you do, sweetheart. Nobody talks about these things anymore. Do you realize that all brides have to go to a doctor and have an examination to make sure they are a virgin— that they've never been with a man?"

The colour drained from her face as Hope stared at her mother. "How…?" she managed and then paused. "Oh, Mom, that's awful. I can't do that."

"Well, you won't have to if you marry Adam. He doesn't want you to have the exam."

"Did Dad ask him? Did they talk about me like that? Good grief, Mom!"

"These things have to be talked about, Hope. But, no, your Dad didn't ask him. Adam actually brought it up himself when they were discussing the marriage. Adam said he trusts us… you, absolutely, he said."

"I guess so!" Hope felt her chest tighten with rage.

"And another thing," Aishah continued.

"There's more?" Hope could hardly speak. She noticed her Mom's face had turned even a darker red. *If that was possible.*

Aishah stammered. "Some men prefer… they prefer the bride to have been cut. Well, you know…"

"No, I don't," Hope said. but from the look on her mother's face she knew it must be something terrible.

"Well, honey, lots of parents have it done to their little girls, usually when they're around five or so… Cutting, down here… between your legs, you know?"

Hope stared at her mother. No words would come.

"We never did that with you," Aishah hurried on. "Your dad and I couldn't do that to you. He lied to the authorities here about you. He told them we had it done in L.A."

Hot tears rolled down Hope's cheeks. *Dad lied! For me! What if he would have been caught?* Aishah sat beside her, cradling her in her arms.

"No, no, honey, don't you worry about that happening to you. Adam definitely doesn't believe in that. He says it's a barbaric practice. But some other man might want it."

"You mean Brian, don't you?" Hope reached for another tissue.

Aishah nodded.

"It seems there's a lot of stuff going on that I didn't know about," Hope said, her voice ragged, "and a lot of stuff that nobody talks about... this is really gross."

"Yes, there's always been a lot of stuff going on that people don't talk about. In the old days it was considered 'politically incorrect' to talk about this, so most people, even the infidels, just tried to ignore it. My parents tried to do something about it... Well, never mind that. I'm only telling you because someday you might have a little girl of your own and you need to know these things."

Hope's eyes stared at the wall opposite her.

Aishah continued, "Your dad and I just wanted you to know how lucky you are to have a good man like Adam wanting to marry you, not wanting all that stuff." She paused. "But he's a good Muslim, Hope, don't ever doubt that. He even speaks Arabic. He's regular at prayers, keeps the laws. Everything."

Hope didn't know what to say. Finally, she murmured, "That's nice, Mom."

The conversation with her mother that night succeeded in convincing Hope that she must marry Adam. As she sat discussing the date of the wedding with her mom and dad, even the memory of what her mother had told her made Hope's cheeks redden. With an effort she pulled her thoughts back to the wedding date.

"Okay," she tried to sound enthusiastic. "Great!" April it is. Adam can pick the day. It doesn't matter to me anyway."

Aishah looked at her and sighed.

"He already has. He said as early as possible. We decided on the first Saturday in April. Okay?

"Okay."

The wedding plans went smoothly, Hope thought. Adam and Hope spent most evenings together in the living room talking. Aishah and Mo decided to stay in the kitchen out of hearing distance, so Hope felt freer in her conversations. She learned Adam was orphaned in his late teens and had no relatives.

"So there's no one on my side of the family to complicate our wedding plans," he grinned.

"Lots on mine, though," Hope said. "My Dad's family in L.A. is humongous. He has lots of brothers and sisters and they all have a zillion kids running around. I've had the best times with my cousins at family gatherings over the years. Not as much fun after I started wearing the veil and hanging out with only the women, though." She noticed Adam give her a questioning look, so she hurried on. "Anyway, Dad says Grandpa wants to give me a big celebration dinner at one of his restaurants in L.A. What do you want, Adam?"

"I just want to marry you, so whatever you decide is fine with me. The legal ceremony won't take long, but we could have a big celebration afterwards if your family wants that."

"Okay. There don't seem to be any rules about how to do it, Nana says—and she somehow seems to know all this stuff—she says there are so many different customs in America—so many different Muslim countries represented here—that we can pick and choose from lots of traditions for our celebration." She paused a moment before adding, "Almost." She was thinking of Nana's description of Christian marriage vows. *Marriage is a symbol of Christ's love for the Church where the bride and groom give their lives to each other as Christ gave His life for us.*

"Adam," Hope spoke rapidly, "Let's not have a lot of talk about what marriage means at the celebration dinner. Let's just enjoy ourselves. We should let Grandpa throw a big party for all his family and friends and we can invite a few people we want to come from here. It's only a couple hours drive."

Adam had readily agreed.

Natalie and Aishah used every available downtime at the bistro and warm March evenings around the barbeque to plan the celebration, dragging Hope reluctantly into the discussions. Adam usually joined them for dinner which meant the women were required to wear their abayas and veils. Hope was surprised her mother never complained about it. *Guess she's so happy I'm marrying Adam that even having to wear a veil at home doesn't dampen her spirits.* Natalie had told her that she didn't mind—it was a small price to pay for finding such a good husband.

Mo and Adam usually sat quietly, side by side, occasionally glancing at each other and rolling their eyes at some of the suggestions the women made.

"There has to be a cake," Aishah told Hope, her brown eyes sparkling above her veil. "Natalie says she'll make it and decorate it. She's made one before. We discussed what I have in mind: a heavy dark fruitcake—round—three layers high," she gestured with her hands. "One big cake on the bottom, smaller one in the middle, really small one on the top, with white icing."

Hope smiled as she recognized the description of the English fruitcake from her mother's novel. In the book there had been a miniature figure of a bride and groom on the top. Hope wondered what her mother would suggest for the top of the cake—*not human figures, that's for sure.*

"And we can have some Arabic symbols on top, to express the bride and groom's obedience to Allah, or something like that," Aishah eyes danced.

"Good for you, Mom. You are very creative."

"Well, I just heard about that somewhere, I guess," Aishah smiled back. "And you and Adam can stand together and cut the cake."

Hope grinned as she recognized more details from the novel.

Aishah continued talking. "Your dad is checking everything out with the imam, just to be sure."

Mo spoke up. "He's a good man, Hope. He's already told me as long as there's no law against it, we are to go ahead and enjoy our celebration."

"So he said 'yes' to the cake?" asked Natalie.

"He did. And 'yes' to the dress you're sewing for Hope."

Hope thought about the dress. *I'm as bad as Mom. I've given Nana ideas for my wedding dress from the novel, too. Maybe we should have just handed her the book and told her to do the cake and the dress exactly like that.* She smiled at Natalie and her Mom. *They're both so happy for me. Well, maybe not Nana, but she's as happy as she can be under the circumstances, as we all say these days. And she likes Adam.*

Aishah focussed her comments on Adam and Hope who were toasting marshmallows together. "So then, our plan is this: After the legal stuff, we will meet the guests at Grandpa's restaurant. You two will walk in last. Everyone will stand and cheer. You will stand together and cut the cake, just put the knife in with both of you holding onto it."

Hope thought again of the novel. *That's when lots of pictures were taken. Well, there won't be any pictures allowed now, that's for sure.*

Aishah was deep into instruction mode: "Then Natalie and I will cut the cake into little squares, put each piece in a fancy paper napkin and you and Adam will circulate around all of the tables, giving everyone a small piece of the wedding cake."

"We can do that, for sure, can't we Hope?" Adam managed to move closer to Hope.

She nodded. *I guess Mom's going to leave out the part where the guests are instructed to put the piece of cake underneath their pillow and dream of finding the one man or woman perfect for them.*

"Then for the actual dinner," Aishah continued, "The women and children will go into their section of the restaurant for their celebration. We can remove our veils and abayas there, everyone can admire your wedding dress, Hope, and the rest of us can show off our fancy clothes, too."

"I thought you women dressed to please your husbands," teased Mo.

"Well, of course. We do. But we like to show each other our finery, too," Aishah added hurriedly.

Everyone laughed.

"Of course." Mo said, smiling.

"And then we eat!" contributed Hope.

"Everybody eats lots, for sure," Mo said. "You know the kinds of celebrations your grandpa hosts. Adam, you're going to be blown away by his food."

Adam grinned.

Hope glanced sideways at Adam. *He's tall and slender, like me. Food is probably not a big thing with him, not like it is with Dad. He's starting to get a little pot belly. And Mom's rounding out.* She looked across at Natalie. *She always stays the same.*

"And then," Aishah continued, "After all the guests have gone, just our immediate family can gather together and say goodbye to the married couple."

"And then," Mo added, "You two can go to the hotel we've reserved for your wedding night."

Much to her disgust, Hope felt herself blush. She was glad she was wearing her veil.

"This fire's too hot," she said, moving back from the barbeque.

Everyone but Adam laughed.

He reached over and touched her arm gently. She stood up, almost knocking over her lemonade.

"Well, that's that," she said. "I'm going to bed. I'll help you make the cake, Nana."

"No, you won't," Natalie replied, a note of finality in her voice. "It's to be my gift and I want it to be a surprise."

"Good grief!" Hope said. "Everyone's making such a big deal out of this wedding. Goodnight, everybody. Good night, Adam."

He jumped up from his chair. "I'll walk you to the door." Hope tromped ahead of him.

She was surprised when he reached the door first and opened it for her.

"It'll be okay, Hope," he leaned over and whispered. "Trust me."

"Goodnight, Adam," she said as she closed the door firmly behind her.

Once she was in bed, she regretted her actions. *He's really nice. Why do I always treat him like that?*

Slipping to her knees beside her bed, she whispered, "Dear God, help me to be nicer to Adam. I don't love him, but help me to be kinder to him... I don't know why I'm acting this way. Please, God, just get me through this wedding junk. Amen."

* * *

The days passed quickly, and much to Hope's surprise, she did get through the *wedding junk*. Sometimes she got caught up in all the excitement, just like everyone else.

The wedding went as planned. After the signing of the legal papers, Adam and Hope joined their guests for the celebration. After cutting the cake, they circulated around the large banquet room, handing out small pieces of wedding cake. Hope was happy that a few of her childhood girlfriends had come to L.A. for her wedding. One of them whispered to her from behind her veil, "Adam is very handsome."

Hope looked up at Adam. "He is," she agreed. *Especially tonight. Maybe it's just because I've never seen him all suited up.* She patted her friend's shoulder. *Poor Elaine. Married to a man so much older than she is. And she's a fourth wife! I should be thankful that's not me.*

Even though Adam could not see her face, Hope smiled up at him, hoping he could read the expression in her eyes. He smiled back at her. They were separated for the rest of the evening as the women and men held separate celebrations.

Hope had to admit she had a good time. When the women finally got to take off their black outer garments, Hope was overwhelmed by the colour, the sparkles and jewellery the women were wearing. Aishah wore her usual carrot red, Natalie was in a deep turquoise gown, and they both wore fancy high heels, instead of the regulation black shoes.

Hope was the centre of attention, though, in her pure white empire-waist gown, with seed pearls sewn on by hand. She wore her dark hair swept up, with tendrils escaping around her face. Natalie had fashioned tiny pearl and rhinestone clips which sparkled in her hair. Her green eyes shone.

Earlier in the day when Natalie and Aishah had helped her get dressed, Aishah stood back and exclaimed, "You look elegantly beautiful, honey. Doesn't she, Natalie?"

Tears glistened in Natalie's eyes. "She does," she said, as she turned away and started rearranging combs and brushes on the vanity table.

* * *

The wedding night went well, too, in Hope's opinion. It was very late by the time the couple got to their hotel room.

"I'm exhausted," Hope said, as Adam locked the door behind them.

"Me, too," he said. He looked at her for a long moment. "Do you have any idea what a beautiful bride you are?"

Hope blushed.

"I'll change in the bathroom." Adam said. "You can change in here."

When he returned she had taken the sparkles from her hair, braided it into one thick braid and put on the ugliest nightgown she could find in Palm Springs—heavy navy flannel with purple geometric designs, a high neck and long sleeves. Adam looked at her and she saw his lips twitch in a crooked smile.

"Here's the plan," he said as he tossed the cushions from the couch and chair onto the bed. "We'll build a barricade of pillows to protect you from me, okay?"

Hope's face turned red. "I'm just teasing, Hope. But we will make a divider down the middle. It's a king bed, so there's lots of room. Okay? We can rig up something more permanent at home. I don't want you to worry."

"I'm not worried," Hope said as her face turned a darker shade of red.

"Well, it's just that I might reach over to you in my sleep—or something."

Hope picked up the largest pillow and in silence they built their wall down the centre of the bed. As they stood back to survey their handiwork, Adam noticed a large white envelope on the night table.

"Looks like another card." He handed the envelope to Hope. "It's from all of the family."

As she took it from him, she realized the significance of what he had just done.

"How did you know I could read?" she asked, looking up from the unopened envelope.

"Your dad told me. He thought I should know. He thought I might have concerns about it, since most girls can't read."

"And *do* you?"

"Of course not. You can help out with our business." Hope noticed he said *our business*. "Maybe you can design a new brochure. I'm not good at that. I think it's great that you can read and write."

"And I'm good at math, too," added Hope. Even as she said it, she wondered why she was telling him her accomplishments. *Mom says some men don't like a smart wife. Stop bragging about yourself.*

"Even better," Adam smiled at her. "You are a woman of many talents, I'm sure."

"I'm not a great cook, though." Hope didn't know why she was now confessing her short-comings. "Except for soups and stews. Anything that goes into one pot and cooks all day. I've started making those at the bistro to expand our menu. I'm really good at those."

"Don't worry about cooking. I doubt you'll need to do much of that with Natalie around—and your dad can make us his *delights*. And your mom, too, of course," Adam hastily added.

Hope laughed. "It's okay. Neither Mom nor me considers our claim-to-fame to be our cooking."

"So what is your claim-to-fame, as you call it, Hope?"

Hope thought for a moment before answering. *I certainly can't tell him that being a Christian is the most important thing in my life.* She wasn't at all sure that anything in her life came even close to that.

"I guess I have no claim-to-fame," she finally said. "But if you mean what means the most to me, I'd have to say my parents and Nana. I never want to be separated from them." Hope realized she should have said Adam was important to her. But it was too late now.

"Well, you'll probably never be separated," Adam said. "Although someday we should get a home of our own. We can't live with your parents forever."

"But it helps us save for our own place, doesn't it?" insisted Hope.

"Sure does," Adam answered cheerfully. "So what's in the envelope, anyway?"

Hope's eyes scanned the handwritten message. "Oh, Adam. You'll never believe this."

"Try me."

"It's from all my family—Grandpa and Grandma, all my uncles and aunts and cousins, and Mom and Dad, and Nana, too."

"What's it say?"

"They've gone together and bought us a house for a wedding present. I should have known they'd do something like this. Grandpa has kind of started the tradition with all his grandkids."

"Wow! Must be nice to have that kind of money."

"And it's the little house next door. I mentioned to Dad that I liked it. It's been empty for as long as I can remember. Probably a Chris—" Hope stopped herself. "Probably a bargain." She glanced at Adam. "It's quite run-down on the outside, so we can't expect much on the inside. I used to sneak into the yard when I was little. There's a gate through our side garden wall. It's a mess in there. But it's a nice little house."

She stopped short when she saw the grin on Adam's face. "You knew about this, didn't you?"

"Yeah, your dad and I went through it. It needs some work alright, but we can do it together. We don't want to live with your mom and dad forever, do we?"

"Well…"

"I'm sure you want your own house. Maybe your claim-to-fame will be as a decorator, Hope."

Hope laughed. "It's obvious you haven't seen my messy bedroom yet." She blushed again. "Everyone will help us, though. Nana will help us get the yard into shape, for sure. She loves gardening. Oh, I forgot, I love gardening, too, Adam, and animals and birds."

"So do I, Hope. We've got a lot to find out about each other, haven't we?"

Hope nodded. She read the note aloud this time. "I just can't believe it," she said. "I'll never be able to go to sleep now. I'm too excited."

"But we do have to drive back in the morning," Adam said, "So let's give it a try. Goodnight, Hope."

He climbed into his side of the bed.

"Goodnight, Adam," Hope said over the barricade of pillows.

It seemed to her that he fell asleep in mere minutes. She listened to his gentle, regular breathing as she stared at the ceiling of the dimly lit hotel room. She wondered what the little house was like inside. She had peeked through the windows one day, but she couldn't see anything through the years of accumulated dust. She thought of all the gifts her friends had given her. She had planned on storing them in her parent's garage until they had a home of their own one day.

But now I can use them really soon! Dishes, pots and pans, sheets and towels. All we need is furniture. I sound like an old married lady. She smiled. And then her smile faded. She stiffened.

She had gone through the legal requirements and the long wedding celebration as if in a dream. But in an instant, it came to her: *This isn't a dream—it's real.* She was a wife now. What kind of a man had she married? She remembered some of the women in the bistro saying they had to beg their husband for permission to go out for a cup of coffee—and beg some more for a ride.

Dad is never like that with Mom. And he's a good Muslim... But he's from the old days. Adam's been raised under Unity's rule. That's different. He's been nice, in fact more than nice, so far, but will things change now that he has complete control of my life? What if he says I have to stay home all day? Can I be the kind of wife he expects me to be? And if not, then what?

She had heard snippets of conversations while waiting on tables in the bistro. She knew bad things could happen. She thought of Veeda—the many times she had shown up at the bistro with bruises.

She propped herself up onto her elbow and looked at her husband sleeping on the other side of the pillows. She breathed in deeply and exhaled slowly several times as Nana had taught her. *Breathe in God's love, breathe out your fears.* Eventually she fell asleep.

CHAPTER TWENTY-THREE

Hope

After the first few weeks back in Palm Springs, Hope's doubts about her husband faded away. She felt that nothing much in her life had changed—except she was sharing her bedroom with Adam, there was a row of pillows down the middle of her double bed each night and she didn't have as much space as she was used to.

They woke to the call to prayer each morning, joining Mo and Aishah in the family prayer room. Hope's days had begun this way as far back as she could remember. She found comfort in the familiar family ritual, even though she knew everyone would be shocked if they found out she ended her silent prayers *"In the Name of Jesus"*.

After prayers, Adam left to pick up tourists and she walked to the bistro, Mo leading what Aishah laughingly called their *grand procession*.

"It's all working out okay—this marriage thing," Hope told Natalie one evening when they were alone. "Everything is the same."

Natalie raised an eyebrow.

"Well, almost the same." Hope shifted in her chair. "We'll just go on as we always have. Nothing is ever going to change."

She was almost right.

One hot morning near the end of June, Hope's comfortable world fell apart. Adam announced it was time they moved out of her parent's house and into their own home.

She managed to hide her anxiety with a smile as he explained that there wouldn't be many tourists in the hot weather, so they would have all summer to work on their new home together.

They had gone through the side gate many times to have another look at their small house. Hope had to admit, if only to herself, that she often day-dreamed about how the house would look if they actually carried out the plans they discussed. Swallowing her anxiety about living alone with Adam, she began working side by side with him in the dilapidated house.

The air conditioner was their first priority. After it was repaired, they began ripping out the old carpets. Hope was ecstatic when they uncovered hardwood throughout the house.

"Look, Adam. It's just like new. Don't you just love it?"

"I love that you're getting so excited about it, honey."

They usually quit working by mid-afternoon for a swim in Aishah and Mo's pool—just the two of them. They would race ten laps and the winner got to toss the loser into the water. Adam usually won.

One afternoon as they lay on the pool deck, recovering their breath and laughing together, Adam suggested they take the next day off.

"Really?" asked Hope. "We're never going to get finished at this rate."

"Carpé diem," he responded.

"Carpé what?"

"Seize the day. Do it now."

"Okay, I'm game."

"I'm going to take you on one of my tours. A private tour, though. Just you and me and our red jeep. I'll do everything, just like you're a paying client—even bring the lunch—so you can be a lady of leisure."

They set out immediately after prayers the next morning. When they left the highway and turned down a narrow gravel road Hope soon realized that even though she had lived her entire life surrounded by the desert, she knew almost nothing about it. Adam stopped the jeep frequently so that they could get out for a closer look at plants Hope had never known existed.

"Nana never taught me anything about all this—I guess because she's from one of the northern states."

"Yeah. She's probably just driven through the desert as you have, honey. Most people do. But you'll never really experience the desert if you don't at least get out of your vehicle. I know you're a city girl, but this is your country, so you should be familiar with it. There's no place else on earth quite like this desert. I'll take you to see the Joshua trees sometime. They're really weird."

"Okay. Look over there, Adam. It looks like a river once ran through here. See the high banks on either side? But it's dry as a bone. That's odd."

"That's called a 'wash', Hope. It can become a raging river when it rains in those mountains." He pointed to the east. "A wash may look harmless, but it's not. You never know when water might suddenly gush through, even though it's not raining right here where we're standing. It's very dangerous. We never go hiking in it, even though it looks like an easier route than some of the other paths we take."

"That's the lecture you give your tourists, isn't it?"

"It is. End of lecture. See that short, fat cactus? That's a barrel cactus. See how it's leaning?"

"Yeah, it's almost ready to fall over."

"Barrel cacti always lean to the south. If you're ever lost in the desert, you can always find your directions if you can find a barrel cactus. Some people call it a 'compass' cactus."

Hope looked at the miles of wasteland surrounding them. The distant mountains shimmered smoky-blue in the haze of morning heat. Even though it was warm, just for an instant she felt a cold shiver of fear. *Don't be silly. You'll never be lost out here.*

As if reading her thoughts, Adam said, "I know my way around, though, so you won't get lost if you're with me." He paused and looked at her for a long moment. "Hope, there's nobody for miles and miles. You don't have to stay covered up. Your jeans and t-shirt are more appropriate desert wear. Nobody's going to see you."

It took her five seconds to peel off her outer garments and toss them in the back seat. As they climbed back into the jeep, Adam said, "This is where the morality squad guys come to race their jeeps. Those idiots. It's not a good idea to wreck the desert floor like that—but since they've already done it… hang on."

The jeep careened across a vast stretch of flat sand devoid of plants or rocks. Hope had never before felt such freedom. She abandoned herself to uncontrolled laughter as the wind caressed her unveiled face and her long hair blew wildly in all directions. All too soon, Adam brought the jeep to a screeching halt.

"Your turn," he said, jumping out and running around the jeep to open Hope's door.

"You're kidding me! I don't know how to drive." *And it's against the law. Is he crazy?*

"I'll teach you. Just don't tell anyone, okay?"

"Okay!" Hope was euphoric. After a few tentative starts, she was soon speeding over the desert sand. "I can drive, I can drive! Look out for me!"

When Adam finally convinced her she had practiced enough, he drove to a large outcropping of rock and they climbed on top of a huge smooth boulder. He spread out a blue and white checked tablecloth and the lunch he had packed: roast beef sandwiches, a huge dill pickle for each of them, potato chips, a cola each and chocolate chip cookies.

"I made the sandwiches, but the cookies are from the bistro," he confessed.

"It's really nice, Adam. This is a great day off. Imagine! I drove the jeep! I wish I could tell someone." Just then a lizard darted out from behind a bush.

"That's a chuckwalla," Adam said.

"Okay, I'll tell that lizard." She leaned toward it, "Hey, chuckwalla, I can drive."

They both laughed as the lizard scurried back to safety. "He's getting out of the way." Hope turned to meet Adam's smiling eyes. "Thanks, Adam. This is one of the happiest days of my life. Let's come again."

Adam nodded. "We'll get away as much as we can. This has been one of the happiest days of my life, too. I wish we could stay all afternoon, but unfortunately we have to go back now. We'll bake out here if we stay any longer." He started packing up the picnic things. "What goes into the desert, goes out of the desert. I always remind my tour guests. There are no litter cans out here."

"You're a good teacher, Adam."

"I was a school teacher for a few years. Then things got complicated. So I started working for a tour company. I'll tell you about it someday."

"Sounds mysterious," she said. *I really don't know much about this man I married.*

* * *

For the next several weeks they sweated together as they worked in their bungalow. Their jeans and T-shirts were soon splattered with paint. It became an evening ritual for Adam to comb through Hope's dark curls, using turpentine to remove as much paint as possible.

"I am one sloppy painter," Hope admitted.

"Sloppy, but beautiful," Adam said.

Hope wished he would quit saying things like that. It always embarrassed her and made her feel guilty, somehow.

Aishah kept them supplied with cold lemonade and on the hottest days Mo closed the bistro early so that the whole family could join together to wash windows, scrub floors and cupboards. After a swim and a shower, they would all gather in Mo and Aishah's back yard to enjoy a late evening meal together, finishing off the day with their evening prayers.

Hope had never thought she'd enjoy working so hard, but she did. *Adam makes work fun somehow.* She noticed he laughed more often now, and the hint of sadness had disappeared from his eyes. She wondered why she cared about that.

By the end of the summer every room in the house had been painted, except for the tiny pink room next to the master bedroom. Adam thought it should be their prayer room.

"Like your mom and dad have. You grew up with a prayer room, so it's important that you have one here, too."

"Sure, okay, if that's what you want." Hope pried the lid from a gallon of pale green paint. *If he only knew who I pray to.* Her heart sank. *I'll never be able to tell him the truth. He spends so much time at the mosque, even more than Dad. And Dad looks so happy. I guess Adam is the son he never had.* She sighed as she stirred the paint. *At least he doesn't expect me to go with him.*

She had never forgotten the day her mother had explained the Unity Party's rules about attending the mosque for Friday prayers. Her mother was rolling cookie dough and Hope was standing on a low stool so that she could reach the counter top. Her job was to sprinkle the sugar on the cookies.

"How come Daddy goes to the mosque without us, Mommy?"

"Women don't have to attend, but men must be there, unless they have a really good reason. Otherwise, they can be made to pay a heavy fine—or sometimes if they find a man at home during Friday prayers, the morality squad gives him a beating."

That night the nightmares started—men bursting into her house and beating her daddy. Mo always came into her bedroom when she cried out and he had stayed with her, cuddling her in his arms until she went back to sleep. Although it had been years ago, she still remembered those dreams and the night she heard her dad scold her mother:

"Why did you tell her that?"

"Because she will find out someday some of the awful stuff that happens and it is better that she find out from us. I know. I had to find out the hard way." Her mother had stomped out of the room, slamming the door behind her.

"Is Mommy mad at me?" Hope had asked.

"No sweetheart. She's just mad at something that happened a long time ago. We have to let her get mad once and a while, okay?"

"Okay," Hope had murmured drowsily.

Adam's voice interrupted her thoughts. "That paint is going to turn into whipped cream if you stir it much longer." He laughed.

She laughed with him. "I'm just stalling," she said as she filled the roller tray with paint. Adam started the window trim and Hope began painting the pink wall in front of her.

"Such a pretty colour," she said. "This must have been a little girl's room. Oh, look! She wrote something on the wall with her crayons."

They bent down together to read the words, then straightened simultaneously as they deciphered the large childish scrawl: *Jesus loves me.* They turned in silence to meet each other's eyes. Adam was the first to speak.

"Just scrub it off and we'll give this wall an extra coat of paint." His voice cracked.

Hope nodded, swallowing hard. *But I'll always know it was here and I'll think about it every time we are praying in this room.* With each stroke of the paint roller Hope breathed a silent prayer for the unknown family. She wondered how Adam felt about this. She thought his voice had sounded funny afterward, but she wasn't sure.

They worked together in an uncomfortable silence, finishing the room by noon. Adam stood back to admire their work.

"We don't need any furniture for this room, just the prayer mats and some curtains, so it's the first room we have completely finished—and that's as it should be."

Hope nodded. After a moment, she said, "I can hardly wait to get all of our wedding gifts out of Dad's garage."

Adam grinned. "I'll bet he can hardly wait, either. He can barely squeeze the car in there."

Hope agreed. Her feelings confused her. *I never thought I'd be happy to move out of Mom and Dad's house, but I am. And yet, I'm scared, too.*

Moving day was a family affair. Everyone carried things through the side gate between the two houses.

"We can buy the rest of what you need at used furniture stores, just like your dad and I did," Aishah said. "It'll be fun. That is, if you don't mind us all tagging along with you."

"Not at all," Adam said. "We can't afford new stuff—except for our bed. We want a brand new bed—and king size."

Hope blushed and everyone pretended not to notice.

After scouring the city's second-hand stores for furniture and purchasing a bed from a department store, the couple moved in. They held their celebration dinner in Mo and Aishah's back yard as theirs was still a tangle of overgrown bougainvillea, cacti and weeds.

"Thanks, Mom, for letting us use your place so often," Hope said.

Aishah gave her a hug. "This will always be your home, too, Hope."

Hope found that she enjoyed living in her own house. She liked the coziness of it, she explained to Adam, as they somehow found space for all of their possessions.

Natalie sewed heavy coverings for all of the windows and as the three women hung the curtains one afternoon, Aishah joked,

"I'm guessing drapery sales people made up these privacy laws. What do you two think?"

Hope laughed. "I feel closed in when the windows are covered," she said, "so I'm not keeping the curtains at the back of the house closed, Mom, like here in the kitchen. Nobody can see into our back yard over those walls."

"But you need them anyway, just in case. Don't you think so, too, Natalie?"

"They do keep the house cooler," Natalie said.

Hope rolled her eyes. "Always so diplomatic, Nana."

"Remember when we could have pictures on the walls?" Aishah turned suddenly to Natalie. "When I was a little girl our house was full of paintings. My mom and dad used to collect works of art from all over the world."

"Did they, Mom?" Hope asked. *Maybe this time she'll tell me more about my other grandparents.*

"Yeah, they did." Aishah turned away to straighten a curtain. "Well, that was then, and this is now, as we always say."

Natalie changed the subject. "Everything looks really nice, Hope. You've done a good job." She pulled a chair up to the glass table Hope had brought from the bistro. "When's lunch?"

"It's all in the fridge," Hope said. *Guess that's that. Again. I'm never going to know anything about Mom's side of the family.*

* * *

By the time the cooler fall weather had arrived, the house was completely finished and Hope resumed her work at the bistro alongside the others. Occasionally, Adam joined Mo in the men's section if no one had reserved a tour, but sometimes Hope was sure no tourists had booked, and yet he was gone the entire day, often returning too late for their evening prayers together. He never explained and Hope felt it wasn't a wife's place to question her husband.

She wondered, too, about his monthly trips to Phoenix and why he never asked her to go with him. Sometimes he was gone for two or three days. *Why is he so secretive about this?* She hoped it wasn't anything to do with Unity, but she never mentioned it to her parents or Natalie. She knew her mom and dad were already worried that Natalie's brother might be working with the government in some way. They seldom saw Mike, except when he came to pick up Natalie for Ramadan or to take her to L.A. for a weekend. It seemed to Hope that her parents breathed a sigh of relief when he left. If they suspected Adam also was involved with Unity, they would feel they were living with a spy in their midst.

Nana has made it clear she doesn't want to talk about Mike's work, so I'm sure she doesn't want to talk about Adam's work, either—I'll just keep this to myself, just in case...

But she couldn't stop worrying about it. *Was he leading tours or was he doing something entirely different?* She decided that if she was involved in the tour company she would be in a better position to find out if any of her suspicions were true. *Does that mean I'm spying on my husband?*

"I can make the lunches at the bistro early each morning," she said to Adam one evening. "That'll save us some money, rather than you paying a caterer. Just tell me the number of people you have signed up for each tour the night before."

"Thanks, Hope," Adam said. "That will be a big help to our business."

When Hope told her mother he had said *our business*, Aishah said, "Just like your dad. I'm so happy he shares everything with you, sweetheart."

Hope turned away "Yeah," she said.

* * *

The pleasant temperatures of the winter months were welcome, as business picked up for both the bistro and Adam's tour company. Most evenings found the family gathered together, either around Mo's barbeque, or on cooler nights, at Aishah's kitchen table. To Hope's surprise, Adam turned out to be a good cook. He even surprised her by baking a cake for the family celebration of her sixteenth birthday. Aishah cooked a turkey as she always did on Hope's birthday and reminded everyone to be thankful for each other. Often during those times of family togetherness, a grey cloak of sadness would descend on Hope, threatening to overwhelm her. She longed to tell her parents the truth—she was no longer a Muslim.

When she talked with Natalie about it, Natalie said she felt those same guilt feelings and that they just had to leave that burden with the Lord. "Which is easier said, than done, I know," she added. "But to your parents it is shirk and they would be shamed. We all know the penalty is death. I know your folks wouldn't do that, Hope. But Adam is your husband now, so it would be his decision. What do you think he would do?"

Hope sighed. "I'm not sure. He says he loves me. But you know how well he keeps the law." She had a sudden memory of driving the jeep in the desert. "Well, most of the time, anyway."

"I believe he does love you, Hope. And because he loves you…
Well, we just have to count on that, don't we? But maybe no one
will ever find out."

"That's what I pray for the most, Nana."

She also prayed for Adam, especially when he was out of
town. And she prayed that if he ever found out she was deceiving
him, he would forgive her. After her prayers, she would go to
her clothes closet, pull out the box containing her white satin
wedding shoes, reach under the tissue, and retrieve the small red
book hidden there.

She read with a pen in her hand, jotting down comments or
exclamation marks in the margins. The most frequent comment
was simply: *Ask Nana*. When she had finished reading, she
stuffed the book back under the tissue, placed the shoes on top,
and pushed the box back into the furthest corner of her closet.

Sometimes she went over to the casita to read the Old
Testament Scriptures hidden in the quilt. If Natalie was home,
they would discuss passages together. Natalie said she missed the
Bible discussion group she used to belong to up north.

"That must have been nice, Nana. To be able to discuss the
Bible with a bunch of people like that. What happened if you
didn't all agree?"

Natalie laughed, "It made for some pretty lively discussions.
Hot and heavy, you might say. Sometimes we just had to agree to
disagree."

* * *

One spring afternoon, as Hope waited for Adam to return—
from where, Lord?—she busied herself setting the patio table. It
was to be dinner for just the two of them tonight. Hope listened

to the birds singing in their backyard and remembered the conversation she had with Natalie and Aishah as they cleaned up the bistro the previous day. Hope had told them she wanted to know about music. What did it sound like? Aishah and Natalie had glanced around the empty bistro before speaking.

Aishah said it was something like the birds' songs, but different. Both Natalie and Aishah tried to imitate the sounds of different musical instruments, and Hope had laughed at their efforts.

"Maybe I'm not missing much."

"No, no—we just don't know how to make those sounds." Aishah said she had almost forgotten the sound of a symphony orchestra.

"The Call to Prayer is actually very musical and people singing sound something like that," Natalie said. "Arabic is a very beautiful language."

Aishah laughed. "Yes, even if they're saying something really nasty, it sounds nice." She then tried to hum a tune, but stopped after only a moment, saying she couldn't remember how the rest of it went. There were tears in her eyes.

As Hope sat waiting for Adam, she realized that she would probably never hear actual music, but she could listen to the birds singing. "Thank You, God, for this beautiful music," she whispered. A warm, comfortable feeling enveloped her. For some reason she couldn't explain, she suddenly found herself saying out loud, "And thank You for Adam."

Just then Adam called from the living room, "I'm home. Where are you?"

"Out here on the patio. Dinner's ready. I just need you to help me bring it out here."

Together they carried the coffee and food to the patio table.

"Mmmm… you make the best coffee," Adam complimented her.

"I know. It's the only thing I do well," she giggled, realizing she sounded just like her Mom.

"You are good at lots of stuff, Hope. Don't put yourself down. Plenty of others will do that for you." Adam looked across the table directly into her eyes. "Besides, you're my wife and I don't like to hear anyone belittle you, even you."

His stern voice surprised her. She gazed back at him. "Okay, I won't." She drummed her fingers on the table. After a few moments, she asked, "So what should we do this weekend? Got any clients booked for a tour?"

"I don't. But you know what? Since you like our day trips in the desert so much, I think it's time we did an overnight camping trip. You've never spent the night in the desert, have you?"

"No, and I'm not sure I want to."

"Well how do you know if you've never tried it? Let's go tomorrow morning. We can spend the day hiking and then we can sleep in the jeep. The seats fold into a bed. We can have a marshmallow roast and all that good stuff under the stars. And you can tell me in the morning if you enjoyed it or not. If not, we won't go again, I promise." He paused.

Hope raised her eyebrows and rolled her eyes.

Adam continued in a firm voice. "But I can almost guarantee you'll want to go again. It's like another world out there at night."

Hope hesitated. "Okay. I'm willing to try it if you're that convinced that I'll like it. I don't know…"

"Great! I love your enthusiasm." Adam smiled into her eyes.

For some reason Hope didn't understand, she found herself smiling back.

"I love you, Hope," he said softly, reaching across the table to take her hand in his.

"I know you do," Hope faltered. He said it so often. She wished she knew how to respond. She wished she could say she loved him, but in the early days of their engagement he had told her not to say it unless she meant it. And so she never had.

"And someday, you will love me. I know that for sure," he had said back then. She had wondered how he could know that, but she didn't want to continue the conversation, so she hadn't asked.

Removing her hand from his gentle grasp, Hope jumped from her chair and with a clatter gathered their empty plates. "You bring the cups and we'll start getting ready."

"Okay," Adam imitated her quick movements, grabbing the coffee cups and pushing back his chair. "Race you to the sink!"

He won, as usual. They packed up the jeep that evening.

"See, two sleeping bags. One for you, one for me." Adam tossed them into the back of the jeep. "Unless, of course, we decide to zip them into one. Easily done, no problem."

Hope looked away, her face flushing as it always did when Adam even mentioned the possibility of sleeping together. *Maybe I shouldn't have agreed to this. But it's too late now.*

CHAPTER TWENTY-FOUR

Hope

They started their trip immediately after early morning prayers the next day. As they pulled up to the shack that served as a highway checkpoint at the outskirts of the city, a stocky black-clad security guard sauntered out of the small building. It was Adam's friend, Omar.

"Taking the little woman out for the day?" he asked lifting his dark aviator sunglasses to glance briefly at Adam's travel permits. When he leaned past Adam to look at Hope, she turned her veiled face away from his gaze and stared out the window on her side of the jeep.

"This time we're going to camp out overnight," Adam said. "First time we've done that together."

"Sounds like a good time to me. Have a nice day. And an even better night." Omar snickered. Hope felt her face grow hot and was glad of her veil.

"Thanks, we will," Adam said.

They had barely pulled away from the security booth when Hope spoke. "He gets more obnoxious each time we pass through. And I don't like the way he looks at me with his squinty eyes."

Adam laughed "Hope, I'm aware that you don't like him. But you know you can't see his eyes behind his dark glasses. How do you know what his eyes are like? Or that he is looking at you?"

"I just know. Women feel these things. And another thing—why does he always call me *the little woman*? I hate that."

"You are your mother's daughter, for sure." Adam grinned. "That sounds just like something she would say." He glanced sideways at Hope. She turned to look at him. Her emerald eyes stared coldly through the narrow space above her face covering.

"I'm almost as tall as he is, Adam."

"I know, I know," Adam said. "He can be a pain. But just ignore him. He means well. He always lets me through without checking out the jeep or asking a lot of questions. So don't sweat these few harmless quirks he has."

"Why do you care whether he checks out the jeep or not?" Hope was still cranky from the encounter. "You haven't got anything to hide."

"Well… Of course not. But it makes my tours easier if we don't have to stop and go through a search. Usually, I just slow down and when he sees it's my jeep, he waves me through. Much more convenient that way. Some of the other patrol guys make me unload stuff and search the jeep—just to demonstrate their authority over us mere mortals."

"Yeah, he does let us go through on our day trips without any hassle. So I guess you're right, Adam. He's an okay guy, as far as guys go."

Adam sighed. "Sorry your experience with men hasn't been that great."

"I like my dad, though, and Grandpa." After an awkward silence Hope added, "And I like you." She felt her face flush again.

"Well, that's a good start. There are lots of good guys out there. I think as you get older you will find that out for yourself."

"I guess so." Hope hesitated. "At least, I hope so. But how am I ever going to know what men are like? It's not like we can sit down together and have a conversation."

"That is a problem. Guess you'll just have to trust me on this one. Here's our turn-off."

Adam steered the jeep off the paved highway onto the gravel road they had taken many times before on their trips into the desert. Hope flung her veil and head covering into the back seat. She ran her fingers through her long hair, letting it blow in the breeze.

"Nobody out here in the desert except you and me." As usual, she was experiencing a feeling of freedom she seldom felt in the city, even in her own home. When she had told Adam about that one day, he said he felt the same way and that they should spend more time in the desert, alone together. She had readily agreed. But she hadn't realized he meant spending a night.

Adam followed the rough road to its end and then they bounced onto the faint tracks the jeep had made in the sand on their previous trips.

"This is as far as I take my tourists," he said as he slowed the jeep to a crawl.

Hope noticed that now even the faint tire marks had disappeared. The jeep zig-zagged around boulders, bushes and cacti as Adam found his way across the rugged terrain. After stopping for a quick lunch, they drove most of the afternoon with the pastel shades of the desert landscape stretched out before them. The spring flowers were in full bloom. Mauves, yellows, vivid pinks, and the occasional brilliant red of a cactus blossom broke the usual monotony of beige sand.

Hope turned to look in all directions. Rocks, scraggy bushes, cacti of various types, stretched as far as she could see. Far off in the distance, the muted earth shades of the desert gave way to the shadowy blues of the encircling mountains. Hope realized Adam was taking them into back-country she had never seen before. As he navigated the jeep around a particularly large outcropping of rock, she marvelled at the size of the boulders.

"Look, Adam. They're as big as our house—and yet it looks like some giant hand just tossed them randomly across the desert."

"Yeah. It always makes me feel pretty small and powerless when I come out here."

A coyote appeared out of nowhere. The lean grey animal trotted alongside them, turning its head to look curiously as the jeep bumped and crawled its way over rocks and potholes. As it loped along, not five feet from Hope's side of the jeep, she felt its slanting amber eyes pierce her own. She blinked to break the spell.

"Wild and free. It's not at all afraid of us, is it?" she asked.

"Not a bit, nor should it be. This is its home. It knows it has an advantage on us. It's just checking us out."

As if it understood what Adam was saying, the coyote suddenly veered to its right and trotted off across the desert. Hope sat sideways, watching it until it disappeared in the shimmering heatwaves dancing across the sand.

"It must be nice to be that free," she said dreamily.

Adam glanced at her. "I think so, too. I always admire the coyotes. They can adapt to any environment, hunt their own food or scramble for ours as they do in the city."

Hope smiled at Adam's enthusiasm as he launched into a detailed description of the coyotes' teeth, their close relationship with the family pack and their hunting techniques.

"You must know everything there is to know about coyotes," she finally said.

"Sorry. I got carried away. Just part of the talk I give to the tourists. Coyotes fascinate me. No one has ever figured out why they howl at night, but they seem to be calling to each other for some reason, You'll hear them tonight, no doubt. But don't be afraid, they won't be hunting you. Just small prey."

"I've heard them in the city, too," Hope said. "They seem to have taken over the vacant yards around us. They sound kind of spooky. I like to know I am snuggled safely in my own bed."

"Well, you'll be safe in the jeep tonight." Adam reached across the seat to squeeze her hand. "Don't worry. They're not out hunting for humans, in spite of the wild stories you may have heard."

"If you say so, Adam. But I'll still sleep in the jeep. Thank you very much."

Adam grinned. "No problem."

They bumped along in silence. After a few moments Hope said, "I'm not much for snakes, either—just so you know."

"Yeah, I know that. "I've noticed you looking around even in our backyard. No worries. I'll make sure there are no rattlers in our campsite. Besides, they're more afraid of you than you are of them."

"I doubt that, Adam."

He laughed. "Well, maybe not, but they'll leave us alone if we leave them alone."

"Deal. But I'm still glad we're sleeping in the jeep."

"Here we are," Adam announced a few minutes later as he pulled the jeep into the shade of a gigantic boulder. He jumped out and opened Hope's door. "Come and take a look."

Hope took his hand. "Thank you." She smiled at him as she stepped down into the sand.

"Close your eyes. I have a surprise for you."

Hope obeyed. She felt him lead her on a zig-zag course and knew he was guiding her around rocks and the sharp spines of cacti. She estimated they had gone about twenty steps when he said, "Okay, you can open your eyes now."

Hope gasped and took a step backward. They were standing at the edge of a steep canyon wall with a sheer drop to the desert floor. Far below, the beige sand was magically transformed into a vast tapestry of mauves, yellows, pinks—shades of colour she had never before seen. *This must be something like the Monet paintings Nana described to me.* She wished she could share her thoughts with Adam, but she doubted he would approve of paintings of any sort.

"The desert is in bloom," Adam spoke softly. "Just for you, Hope."

For once, Hope was speechless. She finally managed to wrap her tongue around a few words "This is incredible. I have never seen anything like this in my whole life. Thank you,"

He was still holding her hand and he squeezed it gently.

"You have to be here at just the right time to see this. Everything seems to bloom at once. Depends when the spring rains come. I've never brought any tours here and I've never told anyone else about this spot. I'm glad you like it." He put his arm around her. "I know I can't give you much, but I thought maybe

I could give you this view as a gift. It's our first anniversary today, you know."

"Oh…" Hope was surprised she felt a sudden ache around her heart. *How could I have forgotten?*

He raised her hand to his mouth and kissed it. One by one he uncurled her fingers and kissed her palm. "Hope, you know that I love you." He looked into her eyes.

Hope's face felt hot. She could feel her eyes fill with tears. And try as she might she couldn't stop one from splashing down her cheek.

"It's okay." Adam brushed the tear away with a gentle touch of his hand. "It's okay," he repeated. He cleared his throat. "Let's hike over to my private oasis—our private oasis, now. It's just over there" He pointed to a green blur in the distance. "We can cool off for a while—dip our feet in the spring water, and then drive to our campsite."

"I'll bring the water bottle," Hope said.

When they returned to the jeep, the sun was low in the western sky. After driving a few miles further, Adam parked their vehicle beside some large smooth rocks.

"It gets cold out here as soon as the sun goes down," he said. "And it goes down really fast. Let's get our campfire ready so we can watch the sunset."

Together they scoured the area for sticks of deadwood, bleached gray by the sun. Adam produced several small logs from the back of the jeep. He laughed.

"I always send the tourists out looking for firewood, but I bring some of my own along—just in case we can't find enough. Always be prepared, like the old Boy Scout motto."

"What's a Boy Scout?"

Adam looked at Hope for a moment. "Oh… in the old days boys used to belong to an organization that taught them about camping and stuff. I heard about it in my school teaching days. But it's long gone now. Let's get this fire built."

They chatted comfortably as they roasted their hot dogs and toasted marshmallows.

"Fit for a king," Adam pronounced.

"You sound just like Dad," Hope said.

"That's fine with me. I admire your dad."

"I do, too."

They sat side by side on their folding camp stools. Hope felt Adam's hand take hers and for the first time, she didn't snatch it back. It felt good to sit close to him.

She loved the feeling of being comfortable with no veil to limit her view and no abaya to weigh her down. Blue jeans and a T-shirt suited her fine. And she knew that they flattered her slim figure. Several times in the past year she had noticed Adam staring at her, especially when she climbed out of the pool and the bathing suit Natalie had sewn for her clung to her body.

That bathing suit is nothing like the one described in Mom's novel, that's for sure. But still, he likes to look at me. Now why does that make me feel good?

Adam took a blanket from the jeep and wrapped it over their shoulders. As he tucked it more closely around them, he leaned in toward her and she felt his lips lightly brush against hers. She recoiled as if from an electric shock. This was something she had never experienced before, but she felt she would like to have happen again. She couldn't decide what she should do. Should she kiss him back? *And where would that lead?*

She felt the warmth of his body close beside her as Adam pointed wordlessly to the sunset colours of red and gold, vibrant above the shadowed mountains in the west. She nodded. Neither of them spoke. The sunset seemed to last forever, slowly losing its brilliance, fading into soft pinks and buttery yellows until it finally dissolved into darkness. Hope lost track of time as they held hands and stared wordlessly into the dying embers of the campfire.

When only a few glowing coals remained, Adam said, "I guess it's time to go to bed. You're getting cold, aren't you?"

Hope shivered. "I am."

"Just keep your clothes on in your sleeping bag. You'll be glad you did. It's going to be cold tonight, but I'd like to keep the top down on the jeep so that we can look up at the stars."

They climbed into their separate sleeping bags. Hope expected Adam to kiss her again. When he didn't she felt a pang of disappointment. *And why didn't he suggest we would be warmer in one bag? Would I have agreed?* She gazed up at the stars, trying to sort out her feelings.

"Good night, sweetheart," Adam said. And then he *did* kiss her once more, again just barely touching her lips. She felt the same feeling of delight and surprise.

"Wake me if you need anything," Adam said.

Hope found her voice to whisper hoarsely, "Okay."

"Sleep well." He turned away.

"I will, thank you," Hope answered, rather formally, she thought.

She lay ramrod straight. After a few moments she could tell by Adam's steady breathing that he was asleep. She tossed and turned in the snug confines of her sleeping bag—sticking out her arms until they got cold in the chill desert air—curling up in a tight ball and then straightening out—tossing from one side to another. She prayed, asking God to look after her loved ones and to tell her what to do about Adam. She suddenly realized he hadn't observed prayer times that day and wondered why, but she was too tired to think about it.

The last thing she remembered before finally falling asleep was trying to count the stars in the inky black sky above her, "Too many, too many..." she muttered softly. She dreamed that she and Adam were travelling through space, dodging the stars which had become massive balls of fire. Adam was holding her hand and saying, "Don't be afraid. Just hold my hand, I'll get us safely through."

She awoke with a start. The coyotes were howling. Perhaps they had encircled the jeep. A frissom of fear ran up her spine as the sound echoed off the rocks surrounding them.

There must be dozens of them.

She heard a rustling sound. Sitting up hurriedly, she thought she saw a shadow moving—something slithering around the circle of rocks where their fire had been.

Snakes! She looked up at the canopy of stars spread above her and she remembered what Nana had said in those first days after she had become a Christian: *Don't be afraid. Wherever you are, God is.*

Hope whispered into the darkness, "Keep me safe, Lord."

Silence reigned as the coyotes ceased their calling. Only the black desert sky pierced by ice-blue stars met Hope's gaze. She realized she was cold—very cold. She felt her teeth chattering and was surprised Adam didn't hear and wake up. On a sudden impulse she reached out to touch his cheek.

"I love you, too, Adam. I'm sorry it took me so long to realize it." A sudden thought raced through her mind and she raised herself on her elbow to peer down at him in the darkness.

"Adam, did you plan this?"

"Of course not, sweetheart." He paused. "Well… maybe some of it."

CHAPTER TWENTY-FIVE

Hope

Hope woke as the first rays of the sun fanned upward behind the eastern ridge of mountains. She had never before witnessed the sunrise unaccompanied by the Call to Prayer. It seemed odd. Like something was missing. She snuggled closer to a sleeping Adam. Was it only a few hours ago that her life had changed?

I feel like I am in another world now… Please God, help me to figure this all out. Is what I have done wrong?

Adam snored softly as Hope unzipped her side of the sleeping bag and crawled out. The air was chilly. Shivering, she pulled on her clothes and grabbed her jacket from the front of the jeep. As she sat on a rock and stared at the charred remains of their campfire she could feel the coldness of the rock through her jeans. She looked out across the vast expanse of desert, broken in the distance by the ever-present shadowed mountain peaks.

The eerie shriek of an eagle broke the silence. She looked up. She could barely glimpse the black outline of the large bird as it circled high above her in the azure sky.

Nana says the Bible teaches that God is like a mother eagle, always watching out for its young, carrying them on its wings if they get into trouble. Whenever she sees an eagle it reminds her that God

*is taking care of her. Is God taking care of me now, I wonder? A
Christian sleeping with a Muslim man?*

She remembered the time Nana had talked with her about
how God answers prayer. It was shortly after she had become a
Christian.

"It's not always something miraculous, Hope," she said, "We
can pray for a miracle and that's not impossible with God. But I
have found that usually God answers my prayers through human
agency."

"Human agency?" Hope asked. "What's that mean?"

"That means often God will use another person, or perhaps
many people, to come to help us with our problem."

Hope shifted on the hard rock. *It really could be that Adam is
the answer to my prayers. I needed to be protected from Brian. I'll
have to talk to Nana. She'll help me figure this out.*

Hope got up to peek into the jeep. Adam was still asleep. She
whispered softly, "I love you. Thank You, God."

Adam stirred. He opened his eyes.

Good morning, sweetheart." He yawned. "I guess you have
breakfast ready?"

Hope laughed. "Not a chance. But if you teach me how, I'll
make it next time." She thought she would feel self-conscious
with Adam after last night, but she didn't.

Together they built a fire and put the coffee pot on to boil.
Adam taught her how to roast bannock dough on the willow
sticks he had brought: first, peeling the bark from the thick end
of the stick, and then forming the dough around it, like a hot dog
bun. He coached her how to turn the stick slowly over the glowing
coals until the dough baked golden brown on all sides, then how
to pull it off the stick and fill the long round cavity of hot bread

with butter and strawberry jam. They sat side by side, carrying on an easy banter, laughing at each other as they bit into the crusty bannock and the melted butter ran down Adam's beard.

"Our first breakfast together in the desert," Hope said. "Messy, but I like it."

"Our first breakfast together as a real married couple," Adam replied. "I like it a lot."

Hope leaned closer to him.

"Adam, I feel badly that I was so mean to you. Please forgive me. I love you, and I'm really, really, sorry. I wish I could undo a lot of what happened this past year."

"It's okay, Hope. I understand how you must have felt. You were basically forced to marry me. I didn't expect you would love me right away."

"But you said you knew I would love you some day, remember? How did you know that?"

"Oh, I just knew. Guess I thought you wouldn't be able to resist my many charms forever," Adam kissed her—a sticky strawberry jam kiss.

"Mmmm, nice." Hope licked her lips. "Strawberry kisses. If only I had known sooner…"

They were still laughing as they packed up the jeep for the trip home.

Once they had started on their way, Hope's mixed feelings about loving Adam crept back. She gazed silently out her side window. Adam didn't seem to be very talkative either. As they approached civilization, Adam pulled over. Hope got out to put her abaya on over her jeans. As she climbed back into the front seat and fastened her veil, Adam reached across to squeeze her hand.

"I'm sorry you have to do that, Hope. If I could change things for you, I would."

"It's not your fault, Adam. Besides, I'm used to this now. There's other stuff I hate more than wearing this veil."

"Like what?"

"It's hard to describe. I guess like just not being myself. Little things that add up to big things. Nana always taught me that I should think for myself, make my own choices. I don't have many opportunities to do that. And not being able to disagree with the law really bugs me," she stopped herself. *Don't talk like that to him. He's so observant of all the laws.* She thought she saw Adam glance briefly at her, raising his eyebrows. She quickly turned away. The highway patrol guard house was just ahead. "Oh, look, Omar's on guard duty again. Isn't that great!"

"I thought you didn't like him."

"His sneaky smile grows on a person."

Adam grinned.

After they had returned home and unpacked the jeep, Adam said he'd be going to the mosque for evening prayers.

"I'll just pop over to see Nana," Hope said.

As soon as she sat down at the casita's small table, Natalie asked if she had enjoyed the weekend.

To Hope's chagrin, her eyes filled with tears. She told Natalie everything that happened in one long emotional rush, finishing off with a tearful, "And now I don't know what to do, Nana."

"About what?"

"About sleeping with Adam, of course." Hope couldn't believe Nana didn't get the point of all this.

"Hope, you're his wife. You *should* be sleeping with him. I'm surprised you waited so long."

"Nana! Are you saying I'm wrong in this?"

"Not wrong, Hope. I can understand you not wanting to sleep with him if you don't love him. And obviously he's honoured that. But now you say you *do* love him, and you're married, so what's the problem?"

Hope spoke slowly as if explaining to a young child. "The problem is, Nana, and you should know this... that he is a Muslim and I am a Christian. That's a big problem.

"What choice do you have in this, Hope? Have you thought of anything you can do about the situation?"

"No, I can't come up with any ideas. I thought you would be able to help me."

Hope heard Natalie take a deep breath and let it out slowly. "Sometimes we don't have an answer. We just have to get used to that. Remember the time you said Christianity doesn't have laws about everything like you were used to in Islam?"

"Yeah. And you said we have the law of love. And that was a lot harder than learning a bunch of laws. You said to try to figure out what would be the loving thing to do in the circumstance." Hope fingered the bracelet on her arm. She and Nana had made it together a few days after she first told Nana she believed in Jesus. Just a simple weaving together of three coloured pieces of yarn.

"Like the Trinity, three in one, right?" Hope had asked. Natalie had nodded.

"It's called a WWJD bracelet, honey. It stands for *What Would Jesus Do?* Every time you have trouble making a decision, just ask yourself, WWJD? A bracelet like this helped me when I was your age. It's probably really out of style with Christians now—but nobody here will know what it is, so it's safe for you to wear it."

"What would Jesus do?" Hope repeated slowly, looking down at the bracelet on her wrist. She was silent for several moments.

"Well?" asked Nana.

"The kind and loving thing. I think Jesus would tell me to do the best I can. That I can't change the fact that I am married to a Muslim and that I should be grateful Adam loves me and that I should be the best wife I can be. And I should pray for my husband."

"Good for you, Hope. I agree. I think He'd say something like that, too."

Hope sighed. "I guess it's time for me to grow up, isn't it? My life is getting complicated. Good grief!"

Nana laughed. "It's not boring, that's for sure." She went over to her small bed, opened a patch on the quilt and handed a few pages to Hope.

"Here. Read these."

"Song of Solomon," Hope read. She could feel herself blush as she read through the few pages. "What does it all mean, Nana?"

"I don't know." Natalie giggled, surprising Hope. "Nobody knows for sure what it means. But it is interesting, don't you think?"

"It's all about sex, isn't it, Nana?"

"It's about lovers, that's for sure," she replied.

Hope silently scanned the pages once more. *How about that? This kind of stuff is in the Bible!* She handed the pages back to Natalie. "Guess I should go home now. Adam will be back soon." She gave Nana a warm hug.

"Have a good night, sweetheart." Natalie's grey eyes smiled at her.

"Thanks, I will."

* * *

But Hope didn't have a good night. She and Adam had no sooner finished their evening meal when she became violently ill. She barely made it to the bathroom before losing her dinner. Adam helped her into bed. Her nausea accompanied by alternating bouts of fever and chills kept both of them awake most of the night.

"What could it be?" she asked Adam between bouts of throwing up, as he held a basin with one hand and with the other held back her long hair.

"I don't know, sweetheart. Hopefully, just some bug you picked up from someone. Was anyone sick at the bistro last week?"

"Yeah, come to think of it Maria went home saying she was feeling nauseous. Guess I caught it from her."

Hope finally fell asleep. She woke to find the sun streaming into their bedroom and a fully clothed Adam sprawled beside her, snoring gently. They had slept through the dawn Call to Prayer. Hope climbed out of bed and slowly made her way to the bathroom, placing one foot carefully in front of the other. She hung on to the doorframe for support. After splashing cold water on her face she attempted to comb her matted and tangled hair.

"You look terrible," she whispered to the pale image staring back at her from the mirror.

Slipping her housecoat on, she walked gingerly to the kitchen. As she sat sipping a glass of water, she went over the night's events... Adam holding back her hair with one hand and the basin she was throwing up in with the other, wiping her face with a cool cloth... *And then the nightmare when I finally did fall asleep. I heard the late night Call to Prayer... I think... and then...*

The images rose fresh in her mind. She was walking out in the desert. Alone. The sun was comfortably warm at first, so she removed her hijab and veil. She saw a field of the most beautiful flowers ahead of her. She began to run toward them, picking up the hem of her black garments so that she could run faster. But somehow the firm sand beneath her feet had turned to quicksand. She struggled to pull her feet out, but each effort meant she was sinking even deeper. Sucked under... into what? The more frantically she struggled, the deeper she sank. Now the sun had become blood red and yet the air had turned icy cold. She screamed as her mouth began to fill with sand. She called out something, but she couldn't remember what she said. She woke to find Adam cradling her in his arms.

"Shush, shush, it's okay. It's only a bad dream. You're okay, sweetheart."

She had looked up at him, and managed a feeble "Thank you." Adam held her close but she was afraid to close her eyes. The dream might come back again.

But it hadn't and she had slept for a few hours.

She was drinking another glass of water when Adam joined her in the kitchen.

"You look like somebody beat you up," Hope said.

Adam ran a hand through his tousled hair. "So do you. This reminds me of the night we became engaged and we compared bruises. We couldn't decide who looked worse."

"I looked worse," she said. "You looked handsome. You do now, too."

Adam bent to kiss the top of her head. "Feeling better?"

"Yeah, I think so. I'm sorry I caused you so much trouble last night."

"Don't worry about it, Hope. That's what marriage is all about. It's good times and bad times. We're going to have worse times than this, I bet. And I'm counting on you to be here for me in my bad times. Deal?"

"It's a deal," she clasped his hand. Adam pulled his chair close to her.

"So, what was your dream about? Sounded bad."

Hope described her dream to him. "I think I called out loud just before I woke up."

"You did. Sure scared me."

"What did I say?"

"Oh, you called for help... something like that, anyway." Adam pushed his chair away and stood up. "Do you think you could keep something down? Toast maybe? And tea?"

"I'd like that."

As he made the toast, Hope wondered about the expression on his face. *He's looking at me differently this morning. No wonder! After last night. Oh well, I've got enough to worry about without trying to interpret every look my husband gives me.*

"I'm going to call your mom and see if she can come over to be with you, Hope. I don't want to leave you alone all day, but I have to meet someone and it's an appointment I can't cancel."

"That's okay," Hope said. "I'm feeling much better. I'll just lie around and read some..." She caught herself in time. "I'll just read the Koran," she smiled up at him.

Another appointment he can't cancel. I've lost track of how many times he's said he has appointments—not tours, but appointments. What if he's part of the morality squad? The smile froze on her face. The secret part that decides about stoning and prison and who knows what else? He wouldn't be involved in that. Or would he? Please God, don't let it be that.

A voice inside Hope nagged, "How well do you know him, anyway?"

I know him! I know he wouldn't do that kind of thing. It must be something else, but what?

She thought about it all day long, between naps and cups of tea with Aishah. Hope wished she could talk to her mom about it. *But what if he IS involved in the squad? I don't want her to know. She would hate him.*

Hope wanted to be alone, but Aishah wouldn't leave until early afternoon when Hope finally convinced her she would be fine on her own.

"Adam will be back soon, Mom. I'll just lie down until he gets home."

After her mother had left, Hope lay in her bed staring at the ceiling. She felt herself drifting back into her nightmare once again. *What did I call out? Adam said I scared him and he looked funny when he told me what I said.*

With a sudden sense of horror it all came back to her—the sound of her own voice shouting, "Lord Jesus, help me!"

Hope lay perfectly still, feeling the thud of her heart beat. She found it hard to breathe.

What will Adam do? He must have figured it out and that's why he left for the day. He's probably deciding what to do right now. What if he spent the day discussing this with the imam? Or the morality squad?

Hope wiped at the cold beads of sweat forming on her forehead.

She heard the front door open and Adam's voice.

"Hi honey, I'm home."

"I'm in here," she managed to call.

"Feeling sick again?" Adam asked.

"Kind of." Hope turned over so that he couldn't see her face.

"I'll just lie down beside you. I'm tired too," Adam said. "Wish I could make you feel better."

"Me, too," Hope murmured, keeping her back turned toward him.

They lay close together in a spooning position, Hope's tense back to Adam, as he snuggled closely against her, his arm around her. Neither spoke. She could feel his breath on the back of her neck.

He must know. What can I do? He's going to say something now. Oh God, help me.

She stared at the wall beside her, hardly daring to breathe. Several moments passed. And then she felt his fingertip on the nape of her neck. Slowly he drew a straight line down her spine to her waist. She tensed. *What is he doing?* Then firmly and deliberately, he placed his fingertip on her left shoulder and traced a horizontal line to her right shoulder.

Hope froze.

The Sign of the Cross! What does he mean? Can I risk finding out?

She hesitated, and then, not turning to face him, she dared to speak the first words of the secret Christian code Nana had taught her years ago.

"I am thirsty," she whispered.

"I have living water for you to drink," Adam said softly.

"O God, thank You, thank You." Hope turned toward Adam, unable to hold back her sobs. He cuddled her in his arms, brushing away her tears.

"Shh, shh. It's okay now. I would have done this sooner, but I didn't know until you called out in your dream last night. I couldn't let you know about me. I had to be sure of you."

"And I had to be sure of you, too," she sobbed.

Hope didn't know it was possible to laugh and cry at the same time, but they both seemed to be doing it.

After several moments, Hope was the first to speak.

"I thought... I thought you were part of the secret morality squad... all those appointments you had. Never telling me where you were going."

"I'm sorry, honey. I couldn't tell you. I'm not even sure I should tell you now."

"Well, it can't be worse than what I thought," Hope leaned on one elbow looking at him, their eyes mere inches apart.

"The thing is..." Adam hesitated, then began again. "The thing is, you were right. I am involved in a secret group, Hope, but it's a Christian group."

"So that's it. What a relief!"

"It's dangerous, though, for both of us. I even thought maybe I shouldn't marry you because of what I'm involved in, putting you at risk, too. But I believed that God meant for us to find each other... "

"The day of the beating?"

"Yes. When I saw your face, I fell in love with you right then."

"Even though you thought I was a Muslim?"

"Yeah," Adam answered huskily. "I was so surprised. I never thought I'd find love again."

Hope snuggled closer.

"So what are you involved in exactly that is so scary?" Hope's index finger felt through his beard for the cleft in his chin.

"I smuggle Bibles into Palm Springs."

Hope sat up. She stared at him. "Bibles? How?"

"Mexican Christians get them across their border—somehow and I pick them up in the desert at a prearranged drop point. Sometimes I go over to Phoenix to pick up a load. We've rigged up some spaces under the floorboards of the jeep. I drop them off at a few spots around Palm Springs."

"Adam, they'd kill you for this."

"I know."

When Hope spoke again, her voice was almost a whisper. "Who picks them up in town?"

"I don't know. None of us gets to know each other. It's safer that way."

"So where do the Bibles end up?"

"They're not the complete Bible, they're just the New Testament, so they're smaller, easier to smuggle in. Different people pick them up from the drop off points and just leave them all over the city for people to find. Everyone is desperate to have something to read so the books disappear quickly."

"Like where?" Hope felt a flutter of excitement rising in her chest. "Like where do you leave them?"

"Oh, like The Date Farm, for instance. Lots of people just wandering around there, lots of places to put the Bibles where someone will accidentally come across them."

"Maybe they leave them in the tomb?"

"Sure, that's probably a good place. People who find the book can slip it into their pocket."

"Or loot bag," said Hope.

"Loot bag?" Adam raised an eyebrow.

"Adam, that's how I became a Christian!" Hope couldn't believe it. She told him the story of how she had found the New Testament in the tomb. "I was only twelve. I couldn't resist that small red book."

Adam stared at her.

"What?" asked Hope. "Is that so hard to believe?"

"No, honey. It's not that." His eyes filled with tears. "It's just that I've been dropping off Bibles for a few years now and I've never met anyone who found one. I believed that what I was doing was right, that people would come to believe in Christ because of what I was doing—but I never knew, really, what happened to those books in the end. I know it sounds silly but I wanted to meet somebody that had found one. I prayed that I would meet someone. But I never did. I just had to believe…"

"It's not silly, Adam. You just wanted to know for sure that what you were risking your life for was important." Hope kissed him gently. "Well, I'm your proof. Without you, I wouldn't have become a Christian." Hope told him about reading the red book and finally getting up the courage to talk to Natalie.

"I'm not surprised to learn she's a believer," Adam said. "The first time you introduced me to her and she actually looked me in the eye… I don't know, I just saw something. I'd guess by her age she was a Christian before Unity took over?"

"Yeah." Hope paused for a moment as she considered her next words. "Adam, Nana asked me to never tell anyone, not even Mom and Dad, but I can tell you her secret, I think. If you promise to tell no one."

"I promise."

"Nana came to Palm Springs to find her daughter who had gone missing. She was a Christian, too. Nana never found her. You know what that means."

"Yeah."

They sat silently for a few moments.

"So anyway," Hope continued, "somehow Nana connected with Mom at the bistro shortly after I was born and she stayed here as my nanny. She's not from around here, though. Further north. She doesn't talk about her life before, so it's kind of a mystery. Don't ever mention it to her, please."

"I won't."

"But can you believe it? You and me?" Hope couldn't keep her excitement out of her voice.

"We have to believe it, honey. It's a miracle, I think. Such a weird set of circumstances."

"But how did you become a Christian, Adam? You were raised Muslim like I was. You can even read Arabic."

"Yeah, my parents gave me a good education, at least in terms of our religion. I'll always be grateful to them for taking me in as their foster child. They sent me to a boarding school in Phoenix when I was thirteen, and I guess in a way that saved me, because they were killed in a car accident a couple of years later. If I had been with them I probably wouldn't be alive today. Anyway, after I finished school I trained as a teacher and taught teen boys for a few years, got married, and as you know, my wife died of cancer."

"I'm sorry, sweetheart. I know you loved her very much."

"Yeah. She was all I had left. So I was in a pretty sorry state. Depression hit, big time. Plus, I was beginning to question some of the stuff in Unity's school curriculum. That's when I met José. He sat down beside me on a park bench one day and just started talking. To make a long story short, he risked his life to tell me about Jesus and then he gave me a red New Testament like yours and told me to read it and let him know what I thought." Adam shrugged. "We met in that park every week, and here I am today, smuggling those same small red books."

"What made you decide to be a Christian?"

"I was blown away by the fact that God loved humanity so much... That God would come to live with us, as one of us, and even die for us. And that God would love me no matter what. Even if I didn't do everything right. How about you?"

"The same," Hope said. "I was really scared, though. Were you scared to become a Christian?"

"Yeah, I was. I thought Christians believed in more than one God—that's shirk and I was scared of that. José tried to explain about the Trinity one day when we were eating lunch. He showed me his hard-boiled egg, peeled the shell away and then showed me the white and then the yolk and explained it was all one egg, but three in one. It's still a mystery to me, though."

"Yeah. Me, too. Nana had me take an ice cube, put it in a pan on the stove and watch the ice melt into water and then boil into steam. So I could see that it was the same, only in three different forms. I was pretty young to understand, but I caught her meaning."

Adam nodded. "I still see José when I go to Phoenix. He's involved in the Bible smuggling, too. I have a lot of questions about my faith and José says that's fine, we'll never know all of

God this side of time. I figure my experience of God is like one grain of sand, but God is like the vast desert."

"That's a good explanation, Adam. See—you are a born teacher. Maybe you'll teach again someday."

"Well, not here. That's for sure. Anyway, should we call Natalie and pop over to tell her our news? Do you feel up to it?"

"Do I feel up to it? I feel up to anything now. I could probably just float over our garden wall."

"I think you should put your shoes on anyway, sweetheart, and walk with me. I'll call Nana to warn her we're coming."

Natalie welcomed them with open arms and a wide smile. It was the first time Adam had seen her unveiled face. He stared. Then he looked at Hope and then back to Natalie again. "You two look—" he began.

"Happy." Natalie finished his sentence for him. "Yes, we are. Words cannot express our thankfulness to God for how things have turned out for all of us" She continued looking directly into Adam's eyes as she spoke. "Some things are way beyond our understanding, Adam, so we'll just leave them there, won't we?"

Adam took a breath as if to speak. "Won't we?" she repeated. He nodded numbly.

"Well, let's tell Nana your story, Adam," Hope urged.

The locked door and heavily draped windows of the tiny casita shielded them as they talked late into the night. Natalie covered the small kitchen table with a white cloth, and they obeyed Christ's command to remember Him as they shared bread and drank from a glass of grape juice.

They whispered the Lord's Prayer together before Adam and Hope prepared to leave.

Adam turned back just before opening the door. "How would you like to come to church with us next week, Natalie? It's just a small group, but you can meet some of the other Christians in Palm Springs."

"I'd love that."

"And can you believe it, Nana?" Hope said, "Adam says there will be music."

Natalie burst into tears.

CHAPTER TWENTY-SIX

Natalie

Natalie leaned against the closed door of the casita. She found all of it hard to believe.

Adam is a Christian! There's a church—here in Palm Springs! Just two more days and I will hear music again. Even when she spent the month of Ramadan with Mike each year, they had never been with more than one other Christian at a time. But this would be a real church gathering, her first in more than sixteen years. This was another of those times she wished she could talk to Mike— share her joy—but she would have to wait until he called her.

From where, I wonder?

Finally, Tuesday night arrived. They drove through the city just after evening prayers and began their steep ascent into the mountains. Natalie sat in the back of the jeep, looking out the side window as the lights of the city twinkled warmly far below them. Both she and Hope removed their veils to get a clearer view. Adam steered onto a side road and they wound their way higher. The city lights disappeared and except for the beam of their headlights bouncing off the white gravel road, they found themselves enclosed by velvety darkness.

"There used to be a huge illuminated cross on one of these slopes," Natalie said. "It belonged to the church nearby. At night you could see it from almost anywhere in the city."

"It's still there. Except it's been knocked down and all of the light bulbs have been smashed," Adam said. "Actually, the church is still there, too, but it's been converted into a mosque."

They drove in silence for the next several miles.

As they rounded yet another sharp corner, Natalie's eyes widened. *Could this be the right place?* She couldn't believe what she saw. A white ornate iron gate blocked their way and through the gate she could plainly see the outline of what could only be called *a mansion*. The owners had made no attempt to hide the sprawling residence. It was lit from the outside by numerous floodlights.

Adam stopped the jeep, rolled down his window and gave a low whistle. It was answered immediately from deep in the shrubbery beside the road. The gate swung open and they drove down a long paved driveway lined by tall palm trees, their trunks encircled by sparkling white lights. Adam was the first to break the silence.

"They're wealthy. They deliberately entertain a lot so that when we meet here as a church it just looks like one more social gathering, but we still take precautions. Don't expect a lot of people tonight. Just twenty, or so. Each cell group is limited to twenty people, just in case the Squad finds us... Well, only our group would be affected. We split off into another church if we get larger than twenty."

"Have you ever done that? Split off?" Hope asked.

"Yeah, twice. It's a hard time for us. Especially the last worship service with the entire group. We're sad because we know we won't be able to meet with them ever again. But we're happy because obviously more people have become Christians. So we split into two groups and we start again to build."

"Who organizes all this?" Natalie spoke through her gathering astonishment.

"We take turns. We don't have any pastors or ministers or priests, so we just have to do everything ourselves. We find that God has always provided us with the right people for the right tasks—preachers—even musicians. We have a guitarist right now and he leads the music." Adam parked the jeep and turned to look at Natalie. "I know this isn't what you have been used to in the *old days*, but it's the best we can do under the circumstances."

"I'd say it's working very well," she said. "People are risking their lives to join you."

"Well, I don't know anything about how it used to be," Hope said, "but I can't wait to get inside. Let's go."

The front door opened before they reached it as several women and men rushed to meet them with the ancient Christian greeting:

"The Peace of Christ be with you."

Adam and Natalie answered together, "And also with you."

Hope and Natalie left their outside clothes in the hallway closet and joined the group in the large living room. None of the women wore veils or abayas. Everyone was laughing and chatting together. Adam introduced Hope and Natalie. Natalie was so overwhelmed by it all that she promptly forgot everyone's name. In the corner of the room a woman was playing the flute and a man was strumming a guitar.

Natalie stared. "How did they hide their instruments all these years?"

Adam shrugged. "Don't know. But that violin is new. It must have been smuggled in since we last met."

Natalie followed his gaze to watch as a white-bearded man gently picked up the instrument and began tuning it. There were tears in his eyes.

Hope took Adam's arm. "Let's move closer. I want to hear this."

Natalie chose to sit in a corner by herself. Soon the room quieted when someone announced in a clear voice, "The Lord be with you."

Everyone responded, "And also with you."

The worship service began with everyone singing. Natalie knew none of the songs. Adam told her that much of their music had been written since Unity took over. She listened to the lyrics carefully.

> *Next time, we'll tell the world about You*
> *Next time, we'll show them that we care.*
> *We'll spread your message everywhere.*
> *Next time.*

She wept.

A man sat down beside her. "Can I help you?"

"No, thank you. I can't sing tonight. I'm okay just listening,"

"Next time you'll sing. I felt the same way the first time I came here."

And the next month Natalie *did* sing, and they sang *Amazing Grace*, her favourite, and she helped serve the bread and grape juice and she read one of the Scripture readings, and she cried when Hope was baptized, and then she ate far too much of the banquet their hosts provided afterward. And the month after that she made no attempt to stop her tears as Hope and Adam exchanged traditional Christian wedding vows.

Sorry, Mom and Dad. This stiff upper lip thing just isn't working. I am definitely wearing my emotions on my sleeve tonight.

* * *

Three months had passed and no one guessed the secret that bound Natalie, Hope and Adam closely together. Natalie was happy. Occasionally she wondered what their lives would be like in the future. Things couldn't go on like this forever. Could they? The question didn't consume her thoughts as it once had. She felt comfortable living day to day, and as Adam put it, "Just walking one step at a time in the light of the Lord."

One Friday afternoon, after Mo had gone to the mosque and Hope and Adam had left for a camping trip, Natalie set her sewing machine on the casita's small table and smiled. *Aishah is probably taking advantage of this time alone to read her novel. She must know it by heart by now.*

The sewing machine whirred as Natalie looked dreamily down at the sheer fabric beneath her hands, a surprise for Hope when she returned: an emerald green nightie. Natalie stopped the machine as she remembered the marriage ceremony with each one of the small gathering leading part of the service.

Much to everyone's surprise, an elderly man had presented two gold rings to Adam and Hope, saying, "Remember that the circle is a symbol of eternity and God's eternal love for us. Let these rings be a symbol of your love for each other."

Natalie later learned that the rings had belonged to the man and his deceased wife. He had kept them hidden ever since Unity took over, just as Adam and Hope would now have to hide them.

Natalie smiled. *They look so happy together, I'm surprised that Mo and Aishah haven't noticed anything different. Well, they're off on another camp-out now. I've only got two days to finish this nightie.*

She began sewing again.

With a crash the unlocked door of the casita burst open. Natalie turned to find a red-faced Aishah standing in the doorway.

"What... ?" Natalie began, but her voice trailed off into silence as her eyes met Aishah's cold glare. A sick feeling rose in the pit of Natalie's stomach.

She knows.

Natalie fought to keep her fear from showing.

"What's wrong?" she began again, in what she hoped was her normal voice.

"You know what's wrong!" Aishah advanced toward Natalie until their faces were mere inches apart. "How dare you? How could you come into my home, my family? How could you steal my daughter? What did you do to change her? A Christian!" Aishah spat out the words.

Natalie took a step backward, but the kitchen table blocked any further retreat.

"She's a Christian. And I know you're responsible." Aishah threw Hope's small red book across the room. It landed on top of Natalie's quilt.

Natalie opened her mouth to speak but no sound came.

Aishah railed on, her voice rising in shrillness and volume. "Don't try to deny it. I found this book in Hope's closet—"

"What were you—?"

"I was just going to help her out by vacuuming while they're away. Don't think you're going to make me feel guilty about this,

Natalie. You're the guilty one here. Do you know what Hope has written on many of the pages?"

"What?" Natalie answered weakly.

"Ask Nana," Aishah shouted. "How could you, Natalie? How could you? You have destroyed her. She has dishonoured our family."

Aishah collapsed on the small bed, trembling and gulping for air.

Natalie reached over to place her hand on Aishah's shaking shoulder. Aishah slapped her hand away.

"Don't touch me. Don't ever come near me again."

"Aishah," began Natalie, "I didn't force Hope to become a Christian. She made that choice for herself. No one can force you to believe something. You choose for yourself."

"Don't you tell me that! You're an infidel. Hope is a Muslim. You must have tricked her. I'm shocked and offended that you would have the nerve to say she chose Christianity. I am offended! Do you hear me?"

In that instant something inside Natalie snapped. The long years of keeping silent and measuring each word carefully when she *did* speak, came to an abrupt end. Words she had never imagined herself saying poured from her mouth.

"*You* are offended, you say? I'll tell you what is offensive." She was almost screaming at Aishah. "I find it offensive that in the name of God hands and feet and heads are chopped off—in public displays in packed stadiums, no less. I find it offensive that little girls' genitals are mutilated to please a future husband— "

Aishah interrupted her, "The majority of us don't believe in that, Natalie, you know that."

"Yes, I know that. But the majority is irrelevant. Where was the majority when your parents went missing? Where were the majority of you when Unity brought in all these laws? The majority said nothing, the majority did nothing."

"We were afraid—"

Natalie put her hand up to silence Aishah. "Don't you dare interrupt me. I've heard enough over the years about what offends *you*. Now I'm telling you what offends *me*. I find it offensive that women are forced to cover their faces, that girls aren't taught how to read. I find it offensive that my granddaughter was forced to marry far too young…"

Natalie put her hand over her mouth as she realized what she had just said.

Aishah's red face turned pale. Her eyes opened wide.

Only a couple of feet separated the two women as they stared at each other. Natalie was shaking with anger.

Mo's voice broke the silence: "Lower your voices. I could hear you from outside." Both women turned to find him standing in the open doorway.

"How long have you been here?" Aishah's voice trembled.

"Long enough. Too long," Mo's shoulders slumped as he continued in a shaking voice. "Come into the house. We'll talk about this inside our house."

The two women silently followed Mo out of the casita and into Aishah's kitchen.

Mo closed the door behind them. "Sit down and calm down—both of you. We've got to figure out what to do. This could mean death for Hope—dishonour for our family—and that's worse than death. Do you realize that, Natalie?"

"I realize that you believe that," Natalie said. She had used the brief walk to the larger house to pray for self-control. She found that she could answer Mo with calmness, almost in her normal voice. "I realize that," she repeated again, after clearing her throat. "I'd like to explain how this happened, if you'll hear me out. Could I have a glass of water, please?" She cleared her throat again.

"Always so polite. Get it yourself." Aishah tossed her head. "You know where everything is." She moved her chair to sit closer to Mo.

Natalie filled a pitcher of water, added ice cubes and placed a glass in front of each of them. Aishah pushed her glass away.

"Not from you," she said.

Mo shook his head as he placed his glass beside his wife's.

Natalie studied their faces in silence. She took a drink of water. "Okay. I'll begin at the beginning. Yes, Hope is my grand-daughter. My daughter's child. After her husband was executed by Unity she had only one chance to get word to me. Her note arrived too late for me to save her—if I ever could have." Natalie's voice broke and she swallowed hard. "But," she continued, "she told me where to find the baby if I didn't get here in time to rescue her. I came down to Palm Springs from Canada—"

"Canada? You never told us that," Mo interrupted.

"I told you I was from up north. I couldn't tell you I was from Canada. You wouldn't have trusted me."

"That's for sure—a Canadian!" Mo said.

"You said your brother brought you," Aishah's voice dripped with sarcasm.

Natalie made a split second decision not to tell them she and Mike were married. "Yes, my brother in Christ, willing to risk his life to save my daughter and my grandchild. That's what Christians are called to do."

"Spare me the propaganda," Mo said. "How did you convince our daughter to become a Christian?"

"I didn't. I prayed for her, every day, but I never said anything to her. She found a New Testament in the tomb at The Date Farm, at that birthday party."

"Good grief!" Mo turned to Aishah. "That's at least four years ago."

"You're telling us she's been a Christian all that time?" Aishah's voice shook.

Natalie nodded. "She'd never owned a book, of course. She just wanted to have her own little book—like you do, Aishah—so she brought it home and read it, under the covers at night. She decided she believed what it said was true."

Mo turned to Aishah. "I knew that book of yours would bring us trouble. And teaching her to read was a bad idea, too. If she hadn't learned how to read this never would have happened."

"You agreed it was a good idea, at the time, Mo," Aishah argued with him. "You even helped us teach her."

"It would have happened, somehow, even if she couldn't read," Natalie said. "I firmly believe that." Even though she knew she was feeding the flames of Mo and Aishah's anger, she couldn't stop herself.

Aishah glared at her. "Well, why didn't she tell us what she was doing? Why did she come to you?"

"She tried to tell you—asked you questions about people converting to Christianity, and you said they deserved to be killed."

Aishah looked down at the table.

"So she came to me," Natalie said gently. "I've always taught her to figure things out for herself—to ask questions—so I was the one she came to. She said she knew you would be mad and she wasn't sure of me, either, but she thought maybe I'd help her decide what to do."

"So you encouraged her to become a Christian," Mo said flatly.

"She had already decided." Natalie looked from one angry face to another. "You may find this hard to understand, but becoming a Christian is more than just saying 'I believe in Jesus'. It's asking Jesus Christ—God—to come into your life. No one can force you to make that decision."

"You're telling us she chose to believe in Jesus on her own?" Aishah was biting her bottom lip.

"Yes."

"Does she know what it could cost her?" Mo asked. "Does she know she is bringing dishonour to her family? The worst kind of shame possible?"

"Yes, she knows that. And she cries about it, even now." Natalie knew Mo was thinking of his parents in Los Angeles. *That large family. So closely knit. So observant of the law. What will they do if they find out?*

"Well, what about Adam?" asked Mo. "Surely he can talk some sense into her. He's her husband. He can demand she believe only in Allah. We'll talk to Adam and straighten this out."

Aishah's eyes lit up. "Of course. That's it! She'll listen to Adam. So there you have it, Natalie. So much for your scheming."

Natalie shook her head. "No". She watched silently as she saw the hope in their eyes slowly die away when they realized the truth.

"Oh, no. I can't believe this," Mo groaned. He buried his face in his hands, but not before Natalie saw the tears glistening in his eyes.

"He was a Christian before she married him, Mo," Natalie said gently. Aishah sat crumpled in her chair. Tears ran unheeded down her cheeks.

"Did you know that?" Mo whispered hoarsely.

"No, and neither did Hope. They found out about each other on their first anniversary, after that overnight camping trip."

Aishah had wrapped her arms around her chest, as if holding her body together. She rocked back and forth, speaking so softly Natalie had to strain to hear her words. "Oh, no. Oh, no," she kept repeating. "Not my little girl. Not my little girl."

Mo and Natalie exchanged anxious looks. Leaving his chair, Mo knelt beside Aishah.

"Honey, we'll get through this. We'll figure something out."

Aishah jumped up, a wild look in her eyes.

"We're telling no one, do you hear me? We're telling no one. I don't want anything to happen to her. Nothing will happen if we just don't say anything, will it, Mo?" she pleaded. She turned to glare at Natalie. "Have you told anyone about this? Who else knows?"

Natalie remained calm as she met Aishah's blazing eyes.

"First of all, I have told no one that Hope is my grand-daughter. I haven't even told Hope. And I won't. Ever. No one needs to know that you broke the law by claiming her as your own. I wish you could have saved my daughter—somehow—but I am grateful that you saved my grandchild. So don't worry about that part." She gazed into Aishah's tear-filled eyes. "I can't say I know exactly how you are feeling right now, Aishah, because I don't share your belief in what brings shame on a family, but I think I know something of the heartbreak you are feeling. I lost my daughter and I have never been able to tell Hope that I am her grandmother."

Mo nodded. Aishah continued chewing on her bottom lip.

"Anyway," Natalie continued, "If Hope is ever to know, it will have to come from you and Mo. I would advise against telling her right now. She has had too much trauma in her short life. Living with secrets from her parents—being beaten and then forced to marry a man she didn't love—afraid of Unity all the time. She doesn't need to know. What purpose would it serve? She is your daughter and she always will be. Unless, of course, you choose to disown her because she is a Christian."

"We can never do that," Mo said.

Natalie's eyes filled with tears as she heard the weariness and heartbreak in his voice. "I never believed you would," she said softly.

"So who knows Hope is a Christian?" Aishah asked again.

"Some of the Christians in Palm Springs know. We meet with a group once a month."

Mo sat up straight. "Where?"

"I can't tell you that. Adam was already part of the group, so Hope and I joined it. Before that there was only Hope and me. We used to read the Bible and pray together."

"I still think she might change her mind," Aishah said, "if we sit her down and talk to her—explain the consequences for everyone."

"Aishah," Natalie said patiently, "She will not change her mind. She chose to be baptized. She is a Christian now. And Adam, and me. That's just how it is."

"Well, we have to think of a way to handle this," Mo's lips were pressed together and his eyes above his bushy beard narrowed in thought.

The two women stared at their water glasses, avoiding eye contact.

Finally Mo continued. "First off, Aishah, don't you say anything or do anything to let Hope or Adam know you are aware of the situation. Natalie, don't you say anything either. We need to buy some time to figure out what to do. They're not back for a couple of days. We have time to sort this out."

"What are you thinking?" Aishah asked.

"I don't know… It's only a matter of time until someone finds out. Then Hope and Adam and you, too, Natalie—you know what will happen. And as for Aishah and me… if people find out that we knew and did nothing about it… "

"But we can't report them!" The words burst from Aishah's mouth.

"I know we can't. So what we're probably going to have to do is leave."

"Leave our home? My women's bistro? Everything we've worked so hard to build here? I can't do it." Aishah looked pleadingly at Mo.

"Honey, it isn't safe for any of us here. We'll have to get as far away as possible. The east coast, maybe."

"What about your folks? What are we going to tell them?"

"We'll tell them we're trying something new. They'll probably sense something is wrong and they'll find out eventually, but by then they won't know where we are, so they won't be responsible for anything our family does."

"We are losing our entire family," Aishah moaned.

"I am truly sorry," Natalie said.

Mo turned to her. "I suppose you can get out of Palm Springs with your Christian connections?"

Sadness swelled deep in Natalie's chest as she heard the sarcasm in Mo's voice. "Yes, I can."

"Fine. We'll find a way for the rest of us to leave. But I don't think we can do it as a family." Mo turned to Aishah. "Hope and Adam will have to choose where to go. They'll have to make their way somewhere else. We can't be associated with them."

"Of course, they wouldn't want to endanger you," Natalie said hurriedly. "It's risky, but it's possible for them to get out of the country."

"With the help of your Christian friends?" asked Mo.

Natalie saw the anger and hate in their eyes. Her throat had gone dry again.

"I think we should pray about this," she finally managed to say.

"I do, too," agreed Aishah. "But not with you. You go home now, Natalie, and pray to this Jesus of yours. We'll see what happens."

Natalie pushed her chair away from the table. "Okay," she whispered. "I know you are angry and heartbroken. I can only imagine how you feel."

"No, you can't," Aishah retorted. "We've lost our daughter."

"I lost my daughter, too, Aishah. In a way much more horrible than this. I had no choice. You do. You've only lost Hope if you choose to. She loves you both very much. I believe the Lord will work this out for the best for all of us."

Aishah looked away, but not before Natalie saw the look of disbelief in her eyes.

"I know you can't hear this now," Natalie said, "But I hope in the next few days you will remember how much we have meant to each other. I'm really sorry I can't fix this. And I'm sorry for my angry words earlier." Natalie's tears blinded her as she stumbled out of the kitchen.

CHAPTER TWENTY-SEVEN

Aishah

The bitterness that had filled Aishah's mouth when she first discovered Hope's small red book had taken up permanent residence in her stomach.

She and Mo went to bed as soon as Natalie left. But they couldn't sleep. Their discussion continued into the small hours of the night.

What would Allah have them do?

They knew what some parents had done in similar circumstances: simply bought a plane ticket, sent the offending family member to relatives in some far off country, and sometimes never heard from their child again. It was rumoured that they were put into asylums for the insane. Honour killings were another option spoken about in hushed tones. No one was ever prosecuted. It was not considered a crime under strict Unity rule. In fact, as Mo pointed out to Aishah, it was Hope who had committed a crime by converting to Christianity.

"It's treason, Aishah," Mo said. "Against Allah and against the whole country—and you know the punishment…"

"But you're not even thinking of that, are you? How could you!"

Mo answered quickly. "Of course not. I'm just saying what other people will be thinking if it all comes out. And it will all come out. You know it will. Sooner or later someone will find out. And then what? We know what will happen to Hope and Adam. Probably Natalie, too, even though she was never Muslim."

"Well, she'd probably tell them she was a Christian right away—and preach a sermon—or something." Aishah could hear the harshness ringing in her voice, so she was not surprised when Mo protested.

"That's not fair, honey." He took her hand as they lay side by side in bed. "She's protected us all these years by not attempting to take Hope away. You know she must have considered taking Hope out of the country many times, but she didn't do that to us. She stayed here—"

"Maybe she's done something worse," Aishah interrupted. "Maybe it would have been better if she'd taken her. Now what are we going to do? At least if she'd taken her we wouldn't be forced with such terrible decisions."

"We're not forced with such terrible decisions, as you call it." Mo squeezed her hand gently. "We will not even consider any terrible decisions, so get those out of your head. We will plan a way out of this. A way that involves no violence. We love Hope and let's be honest, Aishah, we love Natalie, too. Just like she was part of our own family."

"But she's a Christian," sniffed Aishah.

"She is, but we love her."

Aishah made no response.

"Don't we? Aishah, don't you?"

"Of course I do," wailed Aishah. "That's the problem. How could she do this to us?"

Mo put his arm around Aishah, drawing her close.

"She didn't do this to us. Remember? Hope made up her own mind to believe in Jesus." Mo abruptly stopped speaking. "I can't believe we are having this discussion in our house." He sighed heavily. "Anyway, we have to remember that Natalie honoured our belief. Could we have done the same if the situation were reversed? Could you have kept quiet if someone was raising Hope to be a Christian and you were her Muslim grandmother?"

"She says she had faith her God would work it all out," sniffed Aishah.

"Well, you have to admire her for that even if you don't agree with it," Mo said.

"No, I don't have to admire her. She deceived us."

Mo was silent for a moment. "It's late. Go to sleep. We've got a couple of days to think about this before Hope and Adam get back. We'll just keep it under our hats for now. Okay?" He kissed her gently. "Just go to sleep now, honey."

In only a few minutes, Mo was snoring gently. Aishah removed his arm from around her. He didn't waken.

Indignation mixed with the bitterness churning in her chest. *How dare he sleep at a time like this?* Aishah moved to her side of the bed, unable to stop the thoughts whirling in her head.

Hope's mother loved her baby so much that she was willing to give Hope to me in order to save her life. A sudden image of that day in the tomb flashed before Aishah's eyes: Looking down at the baby, but catching a fleeting glimpse of someone standing at the entrance to the cave. Over sixteen years had passed, but she now admitted to herself what she knew to be true: *It was The Man in White.*

She looked at Mo sleeping beside her. *Maybe I'll tell him when we have reached safety somewhere.* She shook her head, trying to banish her memories. *I can't think about that right now. I have to think of what Allah would have us do. Maybe it's okay to let Hope go into freedom because I love her so much.*

She stared at the ceiling for several long moments.

No, Allah would never ask us to go against the law and the law says she should die—because she is guilty—the worst kind of guilt—shirk. She thought back over her life. How many times had she broken the law?

Many, many times. I am not a good Muslim. Taking an infidel's child and telling no one. That was the worst thing I ever did. Now, not reporting Hope and Adam—and Natalie—those are major, major violations of Unity's law.

Mo told me once that if we are truly sorry for things we have done and intend not to do them again, Allah is merciful and could choose to forgive us. But I am not sorry for taking Hope as my own child and I will not turn her in to the authorities. So now what?

Maybe I've done enough good things in my life to make up for those bad things… If I can just do more good things in the future, perhaps I can escape eternal punishment when I die. I'll try harder. I promise to try harder.

But whatever it costs me, I have to do this one last thing—let Hope go into safety. Because I love her.

CHAPTER 28

Hope

Hope and Adam arrived home late Sunday afternoon.

"Let's make it a real celebration," Hope said to Adam. "We'll tell them our surprise during dinner tonight."

"Your mom will be thrilled."

"I know. And Dad, too, and Nana. I can hardly wait to see the look on their faces. I'll call Dad now and let him know we picked up steaks."

Hope ended her call with a puzzled look on her face.

"Dad sounded a little odd. When I told him to ask Nana to bring dessert tonight, he didn't answer for the longest while. Finally, he said he would ask, but I was beginning to wonder if he'd even heard what I said."

"Maybe he was just thinking about something else," Adam said.

When Hope and Adam came through the side gate carrying the steaks for the barbeque, Aishah and Mo were sitting around the pool.

"Where's Nana?" asked Hope. "She's usually the first one to arrive for dinner."

Aishah looked away, leaving Mo to answer.

"She said she'd be here later," he said.

Just then Natalie arrived, carrying a plate of her famous squares.

"Hi, Nana. Mmm... those look good. Nanaimo bars, my favourite. Where did you get that recipe? Nobody around here has ever heard of them." Hope noticed her mom look quickly at Natalie with what she could only interpret as an angry expression.

"I think I know where she got the recipe," Aishah said, looking away. Natalie ignored Aishah's comment.

"I'll tell you someday, honey. How was your camping trip?"

Aishah stood up abruptly. "I'll just get the potatoes from the kitchen."

"Great, Mom. I brought the salad." Hope sensed something was wrong, but she couldn't figure out what it could be. *Nana and Mom are not talking to each other!* All through the meal both she and Adam tried to lighten the heavy atmosphere enveloping them. Adam finally succeeded in getting them all to laugh as he told them about the odd question someone on his last desert tour had asked. *Are all of the animals out here wild?* Hope felt a warm glow as she looked around the table at the smiling circle of faces, ending with Adam. She squeezed his hand.

"Now?" she asked him.

"Now would be a good time," he smiled.

Natalie, Aishah and Mo looked at Hope.

"A good time for what?" Aishah raised her eyebrows.

"For our announcement." Hope's voice was high with excitement. "I'm pregnant. We're going to have a baby."

Mo's hand paused in midair as he reached for another Nanaimo bar.

Aishah let out a shriek of delight.

"Oh, Hope, that's wonderful!"

Hope noticed Natalie and Mo glance at each other.

"What?" she asked, looking from one to the other. "What's that look all about?"

"No 'look', sweetheart. We're surprised, that's all," Mo said.

"And pleased," added Natalie. "That's great news, honey."

"Well, I hope so," pouted Hope. "You don't look very happy."

"Of course they're happy," interjected Aishah. "It just takes a minute with those two for good news to sink in."

Through the glass top of the patio table, Hope saw Aishah kick Mo's ankle.

Mo got up from his chair. He hugged Hope tightly and shook Adam's hand, pumping it up and down.

"Great news, great news. So I'm going to be a grandfather!"

"And me a grandmother," Aishah bubbled.

"You'll be the great grandmother, Nana," Hope said. *Now why are they looking at each other like that? There's something weird going on here.*

She prattled on to hide her confusion: "Me, a mom. This is so exciting. Can you believe it?"

Aishah's eyes were welling up with tears.

"What's wrong, Mom?"

"You're only a baby yourself," wailed Aishah. "You're too young."

"I'm not too young," Hope protested. "Lots of girls much younger than me are having babies. You're just being old-fashioned. Nana, tell Mom she's just being old-fashioned."

Natalie smiled. "Us old folks… I guess we are old-fashioned, as you say. In our day women usually didn't have babies in their teens. But, Hope, we are all happy for you and Adam."

Adam rose and spoke directly to Mo who had resumed his seat.

"Mo and Aishah, I want to assure you that I will take very good care of your daughter and your grandchild. You have nothing to fear. You know Hope will be my only wife. I love her very much. We will give this baby a good home, with parents who will do anything and everything to provide the very best upbringing."

"Oh, Adam," Hope said, her eyes shining as she looked into his face. "You always express yourself so well." No one else said anything. Hope looked at the faces surrounding her.

"What's wrong?" she finally asked. "Something is wrong. I knew as soon as we came over."

Mo cleared his throat before he spoke.

"We can't talk out here. Let's go inside."

"Sounds serious, Dad. I'll bring the coffee." *What now? Probably some high drama involving Mom.*

They took their usual places around the kitchen table, Adam sitting between Hope and Natalie, Aishah and Mo across the table from them.

Mo looked at Aishah. "Should I tell them, or do you want to?"

"You tell them." Aishah's voice was almost inaudible.

All eyes were on Mo as he looked down at his coffee, stirring it slowly. Finally he said, "We know." He did not look up to meet anyone's eyes.

"We know," Aishah repeated, looking down, also.

Mo raised his eyes to meet Hope's wide-eyed stare. It seemed to Hope that an eternity went by before she could summon up the courage to speak. Her mouth was dry and her voice sounded hoarse as she forced her words past the lump in her throat. Mo had bent his head, covering his face with his hands so she couldn't see his expression.

But I know. I don't need to see his face. I know how hurt and disappointed in me he must be. "How long? How long have you known, Dad?"

When he didn't speak, Aishah answered for him. "Just since Friday night. I thought I'd tidy up your house for you and I found the Bible."

Adam put his arm around Hope. "Have you said anything to anyone?" he asked through tight lips.

Hope heard the fear in his voice and she held her breath as she waited for her dad to respond.

"We didn't say anything to anyone."

"Well, one person," Aishah corrected him.

"Who?" Hope and Adam asked together.

"Natalie," Aishah said. Hope and Adam switched their gaze to Natalie. She was staring down at the tablecloth. "I guess you know what happened then," Aishah's voice broke.

Natalie raised her head to look at Hope. "I told them the whole story," she said.

Adam put his other arm around Natalie's shoulders.

Aishah glared at them. "Look at the three of you! This is such a mess. Mo and I promised Allah we would raise our little girl to be a faithful Muslim. What did we do wrong?"

"You didn't do anything wrong," Natalie said. "You did everything right. You raised your little girl to be curious and smart. She is a kind and loving and generous person. She believes in one God... a God of love, revealed to us in Jesus Christ. She has to be true to what she believes."

Hope finally found her voice to interrupt, "Mom, Dad, I can't explain it now. I'm too upset, but I know God loves everyone around this table. Enough to die for us. I hope I can learn how to explain it better someday."

"I don't know where we went wrong, either," Mo said, ignoring Hope's comment. "We taught you the law as best we could. But we've gone over this with Natalie all weekend and we know we can't convince you two to change your mind."

Adam and Hope shook their heads silently.

"Here's the thing, though," Mo continued, "We all know what this can mean for the three of you, and maybe Aishah and myself, too. We have to decide what to do."

"I thought this would be a night for good news," Hope wailed, "and look how it's turned out."

"It's still good news, honey," Mo said. "It is a miracle to have a baby. Nobody knows that better than your mom and me." He looked at Natalie and then at Hope. "It was a miracle when we got you. Actually, it is a miracle that all five of us can sit around this table and cry together. Our love is a miracle. In spite of our differences, and yes, our anger and disappointment..."

"I'm sorry, Dad, but I can't help it..."

"I won't deny we are very angry and hurt. We feel betrayed by all of you. In fact, betrayed is too mild a word for how your mother and I feel. But we will all get our heads together around this—figure out what to do. We will all pray together."

Aishah stared down at the tablecloth.

"Yes, we will all pray. Your mom and me here, you three alone or together—whatever it is you people do. Let's ask Allah for guidance and protection for all of us. And His mercy on all of us."

The call for late evening prayer sounded as Hope, Adam and Natalie left the house. They hugged each other. No one seemed to know what to say. Natalie began speaking softly and the young couple joined her in the parting words spoken by Christians for over two thousand years:

The grace of our Lord Jesus Christ, and the love of God, and the fellowship of the Holy Spirit, be with us all, evermore. Amen.

For the next several days they all tried to act normally at the bistro. Natalie and Hope left Aishah and Mo alone in the kitchen to do the baking while they cleaned together in the women's section. When the three women worked together in the bistro, each of them made an effort to chat with the customers more than usual so that no one would suspect anything was wrong.

Hope told Adam she found the whole day exhausting. "I feel like throwing up and I'm not sure if it's the baby or just all this tension."

"I know what you mean. It's not easy working with your Dad either."

Each evening the family met around Aishah's kitchen table. Natalie had quit wearing her veil and abaya for the meetings, which meant Aishah was the only black-garbed woman in the room. There were late nights, loud angry voices, stony silences, and hard looks. Several times Aishah stormed out of the room in tears and Mo had to talk her into returning. They had gone over what their choices were for the future so many times, they had exhausted any new ideas.

Finally, Natalie said what they were all feeling: "I'm sick of all this."

They agreed they would each make an effort to discuss things more calmly. Hope told Adam it was probably because they were all simply too tired to argue anymore.

Somehow, despite their differences, they began to regain the family bond they had lost. Each evening's meeting now began in the same way: Adam would place in the centre of the table a piece of paper on which he had written in large letters: *OUR SHARED GOAL IS FOR EACH OF US TO REACH SAFETY.*

When the conversation veered off track, one of them would simply point to the piece of paper to bring them back to why they were meeting.

Possible solutions had been proposed. Adam wrote each one on a separate piece of paper. The pros and cons of each plan were discussed. Natalie said very little. One night Mo confronted Natalie about her silence. She looked around the table at the four pairs of questioning eyes and took a deep breath.

"Well, here's the thing," she said. "I'm not sure how to put this, but I will be staying in America."

Silence reigned as everyone stared at her.

Hope was the first to speak. "In Palm Springs, Nana? You can't do that! That would mean your life, for sure."

"No, not Palm Springs, the San Francisco area. I heard from Mike a few weeks ago. Remember, Aishah, I told you he had called me at the bistro?"

"I do. You said it was nothing important."

"Well, it was. I know this will come as a shock to all of you, especially you, Hope. Your parents already know that I came from Canada, that Mike is not my brother and that he is involved in Missions to Muslims, an American organization based in Canada."

Hope and Adam sat wide-eyed.

"What all of you don't know is that Mike and I are married. We got married when you were five, Hope, but I stayed here to be with you."

Hope couldn't take her eyes from Natalie's face.

"I can't believe this," Mo said. "How many other things have you kept hidden from us, Natalie?"

"I think that's about it," Natalie managed a weak grin. "I couldn't tell you any of this before without jeopardizing Mike's security, but circumstances have changed, haven't they?"

"And whose fault is that, I wonder?" Aishah asked.

"Aishah, let's not go down that road again," Natalie said. "The past is past. We're discussing our future, our very lives, for goodness sake."

Hope was surprised by the impatience she heard in Natalie's voice.

No one spoke.

"Anyway, Mike said if I ever wanted to leave Palm Springs his organization could shelter me somewhere in northern California. I can't tell you exactly where, but he's there now. He said they could probably get me a position as nanny in someone's family."

"In another Muslim family?" Mo asked.

Natalie nodded.

Aishah snorted. "Good grief!"

"Is that what you want to do, Nana? Leave us?" Hope fought back her tears."

"No, of course I don't want to leave you. I told Mike that at the time. But things have changed now and I really think it's the best choice for me, and for everyone. That's one less person to worry about. No one at the bistro will be surprised when I leave. After all, you are long past needing a nanny, Hope."

Everyone started talking at once, protesting Natalie's decision. Natalie interrupted in a loud voice Hope had never heard her use before.

"And there's more: Mike says if anyone wants to cross the border—south—they have information on how to do that. It's risky, but possible. So if any of you want to do that, it is another option."

"Mexico?" Mo asked. "Why would we want to go there?"

"Because we'd be free there," Aishah looked sternly at him.

"I wouldn't want to live there. There's no jobs. What would we do for a living?"

"Mexico is just a stepping stone to Canada, Mo," Natalie said gently. "If you can get across the border into Mexico, ships pick up people and take them north up the west coast to Canada."

"Canada?" exclaimed Mo. "Canada's not a Muslim country."

"That's the point, Dad," Hope said excitedly. "We could all go… and live there together. Nana, you could come, too."

"Honey, I think God wants me here. I think my place is in—" She stopped herself. "Well, northern California. Somewhere."

"With Mike?" Mo raised his eyebrows.

"Yes. But also with the people in this country. I care for them and I want to help them."

Aishah sniffed. "You see yourself as a missionary to Muslims, don't you?"

"Yes, I do."

"But Nana, you'd choose to live under all these laws when you could be free. You wouldn't even have to wear a veil in Canada. You know you hate your veil— "

Adam interrupted Hope, "Honey, we all promised we wouldn't argue with anyone's choice. If Natalie has made up her mind, that's her decision. Your mom and dad will make their decision. You and I will make our decision."

"We're going to Canada, for sure," exclaimed Hope. "That won't be a hard decision to make. I want to raise our baby in freedom."

Adam placed his arm around his wife's shoulder. "We'll discuss this together, honey, at home. And Mo and Aishah will discuss their plans alone, too. Then we can get together tomorrow night and see what everyone has decided."

"Well, I know we're going to Canada." Hope felt excitement rising in her chest. "And Mom and Dad should come with us. We can't miss this chance."

"There's some risk involved, Hope." Natalie said. "There is an underground network that will meet you once you're safely across the Mexican border, but you have to get down there on your own. Things could go wrong."

"Oh, things won't go wrong for us," Hope bubbled. "We'll be just fine. Adam knows the desert, no problem there." She turned to Aishah, "Mom, make Dad realize you have to come with us," she pleaded.

"We'll talk about it," Mo said, but Hope heard disinterest in his voice and her heart sank.

"What else can you do?" she said. "You have to come."

"No, I don't. Your mother and I do not have to leave America. We can sell this bistro, move to another city and start over. I've been thinking of New York City. Lots of opportunities there. It's harder for Unity to keep track of people in a big city like that."

"But... So far away..." Aishah protested.

"We have to protect my parents, all my family in Los Angeles, Aishah. It's best if we live apart from them. I'll explain it all later." He began to gather up the coffee cups, signalling an end to the evening's discussion. Adam, Hope and Natalie left in silence.

Anyone looking at the darkened houses that night would have assumed their inhabitants were sleeping. But no one slept.

* * *

The next morning the whole family walked to the bistro in silence. They had agreed they would not discuss their plans, even when they were alone in the bistro kitchen. At closing time they walked home. Again, no one spoke. It seemed to Hope this had been the longest day of her life, but finally they gathered that evening in Aishah's kitchen.

As soon as they were all seated, Hope reached to the centre of the table. Grabbing a piece of white paper and the black felt pen, she printed in large letters: *CANADA!* She placed the paper in the centre of the table, beaming at the circle of faces surrounding her. In spite of the tense atmosphere, the others laughed.

"Well, that's no surprise," Aishah said. She managed a tremulous smile at Hope.

"I may as well follow Hope's method," Natalie reached for another sheet of paper and wrote: *N. CALIFORNIA!*, squeezing the last few letters onto the page.

"That's no surprise, either," Aishah said. "So here's ours." She took a piece of paper and wrote: *N.Y!*

"Oh Mom!" wailed Hope. "Why? Why not come with Adam and me?"

"Because this is our country and as bad as it is, this is our way of life… and we aren't as young as you are. We're Muslim. This is who we are. We can't change who we are. And we don't want to adjust to life in a Christian country."

"You'd be free to practice your religion there," Natalie said. "Christianity may be the majority religion, but the government is not a Christian government. It's a secular government. All kinds of other religions and people of no religion at all live there. It's true that most of the Canadian Muslims moved down here when America became a Muslim country—"

Aishah interrupted her. "That's because they didn't know who was taking over. They were fooled like the rest of us."

Natalie nodded. "But some weren't fooled, as you say, and they stayed in Canada. You could join them. There is no Shariah law up there, of course. You'd have to obey Canadian law just like everyone else and abide by Canada's Charter of Rights and Freedoms."

"What's that mean?" Mo asked.

"Something like the Constitution the United States used to have."

"I remember learning that in school before Unity took over," Aishah said.

Natalie nodded. "Well, everyone in Canada is protected by a Bill of Rights: The right to health care, education, freedom of speech, freedom of religion, equality for everyone—regardless of gender, race, sexuality—things like that. You'd have to live among people whose life choices you perhaps didn't agree with. It would be different, I know. Not at all like Unity." She turned to Aishah. "You would find a reformed type of Islam there. From what you've told me, I think it would be closer to what your parents believed. Wouldn't you like that, Aishah?"

Aishah's eyes filled with tears.

"Yes, I would," she whispered. "But my place is with Mo. I couldn't imagine life without him. He once took a big chance on marrying me, because he loved me, he said." Her eyes turned toward Hope. "And later on he went along with choices I made in our marriage that were against the law—because he loved me. Now, it's my turn to agree to his choice, because I love him. We are making this choice as a couple. And you can't talk us out of it. We'll start again and we will share our life as we always have, together, through thick and through thin."

"For better or for worse," Hope said softly. "I can understand that, Mom. I feel that way about Adam."

Mo cleared his throat, before saying gruffly, "I hear rumours that millions of Americans who left the United States for Canada, are now sneaking back down here, infiltrating our system and they're planning a take-over of the government as soon as they can manage it. Is that true, Natalie?"

"Yes, it is."

"Well, I can't live there. I can't live with people who are planning to attack Islam. Not if that's Canada's plan."

"That's not Canada's plan, Mo. It's the plan of the Americans living up there. And they're not attacking Islam. They're attacking Unity. They want to liberate their country. They believe a majority of the people living down here now would join them if they organized a coup. And they're probably right. You know that Unity forced everyone to convert to Islam. How many of the people around you are truly Muslim? How loyal do you think those people will be to this government, if given a choice? The older Muslims who remember life as it was before Unity might even join them. Don't blame Canada if it happens."

Hope looked at Natalie, wide-eyed. She had never heard her argue with her father before.

Mo's face reddened. "But Canada supports them, let's them live there. Like taking in Adam and Hope—'Just come on up' Canada seems to be saying."

"Well, yes. Because they believe people should be free. Canada has always opposed the Unity government."

"Why did they do that? Unity never took over Canada. They could have just stayed out of it."

"Mo, we are not only responsible for what we *do,* but also for what we do *not* do. How could we stand by and do nothing? That's like saying we are in favour of what is happening—or else we just don't care."

"Well, that's that, then," Mo slapped his hand on the table. "Canada is our enemy. Anyone against our system is our enemy."

"Dad, just because someone isn't Muslim doesn't mean they are your enemy," Hope shouted. "I'm not your enemy. I'm your daughter. How can you think I am your enemy? Because I choose freedom? Mom, are you going to choose this way of life? You're a free person. You don't have to choose this." Hope burst into sobs.

Adam put his arms around Hope.

"Calm down, honey. I know this hurts you, but everyone has the right to choose what they believe. We may not agree, but we cannot force people to change if they don't want to."

"I hate this. I hate Unity. They've changed my dad. He didn't used to think like this," screamed Hope. "It isn't right that our family has to split up."

"Honey, it's the best we can do. Maybe we'll all be together again someday."

"Where? Certainly not here," Hope raged.

"You never know how things will end, sweetheart." Adam looked at the shocked faces around the table. "She doesn't really mean this, you know." He turned to Hope again. "Look, honey, we only have a few weeks left with your family. You want these last days to be as good as they can be, don't you?"

"Yeah," sniffed Hope.

"Okay then. Can we each agree to make the most of the remaining time we have with each other? No more arguing or yelling." He looked at Aishah and then at Hope.

Everyone nodded.

"Let's make a pact that we will be praying for each other, not just for the next while, but for as long as we're apart. Always. Agreed?"

"Agreed," everyone murmured.

"Okay," Hope said loudly, striving to put her normal enthusiasm back into her voice. She grabbed Adam's hand in hers and placed it in the centre of the table. Natalie put her hand on top of theirs. Aishah hesitated a moment, then placed her hand on top of Natalie's. Mo looked around at the circle of eyes focussed on him. He reached out and placed his hand on top of the pile.

Later, as they walked back to their house, Hope said to Adam, "Well, that's the best I could do. The hand thing. Kind of corny, but we weren't exactly up for a group hug."

In spite of the gravity of the situation, they both burst into nervous laughter.

"Oh, Hope." Adam gave her a squeeze. "You always make me laugh."

CHAPTER TWENTY-NINE

Hope

For the next few weeks, Hope didn't make anyone laugh. She could hardly keep herself from crying.

It seemed to her that everything happened too quickly. Word got around that Mo was putting the bistro up for sale, but before he had even hired a real estate agent, Brian came over to their house, *in person,* Aishah later told Hope. "He offered far more than we expected to get. And he'll take the house, too. So what could we do? It probably means the end of my women's place, but we had to accept. It means more money for us to buy a place in New York."

Hope and Adam met with Natalie several evenings as they planned their escape to Mexico. They gathered around the casita's kitchen table and Natalie spread out the rough map Mike had once sketched for her.

"He thought I should have it, in case we ever needed it," she said. "When he called last night, he said you should be sure to plan for the worst. Take lots of water and wear protective clothing. But I guess you know all that desert survival stuff, don't you, Adam?"

"He does," Hope answered, beaming at him. "We'll be fine, Nana. Don't you worry. Mom and Dad are doing enough worrying for all of us."

"We'll do everything we can to be safe," Adam assured her. "We'll pick a good time to go, wait a few more weeks for the cooler fall weather and we'll pack carefully. Don't worry about that part. Let's see that map again."

Adam traced his finger along the route. "Looks like there are some back roads we can take. That's great. We should be able to drive to within a few miles of the border."

Natalie nodded. "There's a chain link fence in that section, Mike says. It's the easiest place to get through. Some of the other sections are a solid wall, twenty feet high. They were built a long time ago to prevent Mexican people from illegally entering the United States. Now Unity uses the wall to keep Americans from escaping. Don't even attempt to cross at the walled sections."

"Okay," Adam said. "But how will we know exactly where to get through the chain link fence?"

"Mike's group has marked the crossing place by weaving a fish symbol into the wire. Like the early Christians used. It's about a foot wide and near the bottom of the fence. The wire is newer and so it's shinier there. You should be able to find it easily. Mike says to push it back and crawl under it. He says to be sure to replace it the same way you found it."

"I'll carry my own wire cutters, just in case we don't find the spot, so no problem, we'll get through," Adam said.

"Okay." Natalie handed Adam the map. "That's about it. Just one more thing: once you get through the border fence you'll have to avoid being caught and robbed. Unfortunately, a few thugs prowl around on the Mexican side of the border, just waiting to catch someone crossing. They're mainly after money. But, be careful, especially with Hope…"

Adam and Hope looked quickly at each other.

"It'll probably be okay. The Mexican Christians hang out around there, too and they'll get you to the coast. You should meet up with them, sooner or later, if you just keep an eye out for them."

"How will we know who they are?" Hope asked.

"You won't. But they've got the same code we use here. If you think you're talking to one of them, you just say: *'I'm thirsty'*. If it's them, they'll answer: *'I have Living Water for you to drink'*."

"Well, we know that one, for sure," Hope said. "We'll be fine, Nana. How are you doing with your plans?"

"I'm okay, sweetheart. Your dad says when they leave for their last visit with the family they'll give me a ride. Maybe I can patch things up a bit with your mom during the trip. Mike will meet me in L.A. and we'll drive north. We'll have a few days together before I start my job as nanny, but I'll be seeing a lot more of him up there. I don't have much to do to get ready. All I'm taking is my suitcase, my sewing machine and my quilt, of course."

"The dreaded quilt," Hope teased. "Of course you'll be taking that! You haven't told them what's in it, have you?"

Natalie shook her head. "I don't think they would let me take it and it's really important to me, it holds so many memories." She looked at Adam and his eyes met her calm gaze.

He nodded. "I know exactly what those memories mean to you," he said, placing his arm around Hope. "I guess none of us would have ever predicted how things would turn out, would we, Natalie?"

Natalie smiled as she looked at both of them.

"Well, I still think it's a shame you never found your daughter," Hope said. "Maybe she's okay somewhere." She gave Nana a warm hug. Natalie's eyes had filled with tears. "You know that you will always be part of my family, Nana. I don't know what would have become of me if you hadn't been here for me."

"I don't know what would have become of me if you hadn't been here for me, too, Hope." Natalie brushed at her tears as she glanced at Adam again.

"This is so bad," Hope struggled to keep from crying.

"It could be a lot worse," Natalie said, straightening her shoulders as she dabbed at her wet cheeks. "Actually, I think God has worked things out quite well for us."

"Under the circumstances?" Hope grinned.

Natalie smiled. "We've had a month to pack up. The business and the house sold easily. Your dad has a chance to visit with his family before heading east. He's pouring over roadmaps all the time. Aishah says they're going to make it a holiday. They've never really travelled before."

"It's really hard for them, though, Nana. Dad's going to try hard to hide the truth about why we're all leaving. He says he doesn't want them to be shamed." Hope's voice broke. Adam put his arm around her.

"We can't fix that for them, honey. It'll work out okay. We'll leave at least a month after the rest have gone. No one will think it's strange when we go. They'll just think we're joining your folks in New York. It's the best we can do."

"We sure say that a lot, don't we?" Hope said. "Will we be saying that up in Canada, too, Nana?"

"Maybe, but not as much as we say it down here,"

In spite of themselves, they managed a weak attempt at laughter.

* * *

The day of Aishah and Mo's and Natalie's departure had come and gone. That night Hope and Adam ate dinner indoors because of the heat.

"It seems so quiet, just the two of us," Hope said.

"This must be one of the hottest days so far this summer," Adam said.

Hope agreed. "I tried to help Mom pack up the car this morning and we almost burned our hands opening the car doors. We finally resorted to using oven mitts. This heat is making me so sick I wasn't much help. Had to run and throw up every twenty minutes or so."

"I wish I could do something to make it easier for you, honey. Nana said not to worry, though, she was like that with her pregnancy too. Anyway, we have a few weeks now for you to rest up. You'll probably be over your nausea by then. And the weather will be cooler for us to travel."

"I don't feel as bad about leaving as I thought I would," Hope said. "Now that the others are gone, there's not much to stay for. Except our house, of course. I love my little home." She looked around the cozy kitchen. "Well, no point in wallowing in sad thoughts, Nana always says. I think I'll get started on our food list now. That way I'll be super-organized by the time we go."

Adam looked over her shoulder as she wrote down the items they usually packed for their weekend campouts.

Coffee, make some bannock dough, strawberry jam, wieners and buns.

"Honey," he said carefully, "I'm not sure we'll be able to have a fire—so maybe we'd better not count on having coffee or cooking bannock or hotdogs."

"No campfire?" Hope turned to look up at him. "Why not?"

"Well, it's too easy to spot a fire at night in the desert. We can't risk it."

"Oh." Hope fought the fear rising in her chest. "I should have known that. Sorry. So just peanut butter sandwiches then?"

"Well, sure, honey. But you're creative with food. Canned beans are good cold. Canned peaches... and other stuff. Just remember the can opener, though." His laughter sounded brittle and Hope realized he was as worried as she was.

"Anything, as long as it doesn't need heating up," he continued. "We've got lots of room in the jeep. Bring the cooler full of stuff. We'll leave what we don't need once we start walking. So think about some light food we can carry in our backpacks, too."

With each word Adam spoke, Hope realized this was not just another normal camping trip. She had pushed her growing feelings of panic into the back of her mind, but now that their departure was certain those repressed feelings crept steadily forward. She finally had to admit to herself the nature of this trip: They had to get out and they had to get out before anyone found out about them. They needed to make sure they took every precaution for their safety.

If we are caught... I won't think about that right now.

She managed to smile at Adam as she said, "I've decided to figure out the food tomorrow morning. I'm just too hot and tired to do it now. I still don't think they should call it 'morning sickness' when it lasts all day."

"You go to bed, honey. I'm going to gas up the jeep tonight. I'll try not to wake you when I get back." He gathered Hope into his arms and kissed her damp forehead.

"I'm kind of clammy, aren't I?" she said. "I feel crumby. I must look awful."

"You always look beautiful. You are my beautiful wife and I love you very much." He grabbed the keys to the jeep from the hook beside the kitchen door. "I won't wake you when I get back."

Hope undressed. Feeling too ill to shower, she crawled into bed. It seemed she had laid her head on the pillow for only a moment when she felt Adam gently shaking her shoulder.

"What's wrong? What's wrong?" she muttered groggily.

"Honey, I've got some bad news. We have to leave right away."

Hope struggled to make sense of what Adam was saying. She sat up in bed, shaking her head to think clearly.

"Bad news? What bad news?"

"Now, don't panic, sweetheart. But…" Adam seemed to be struggling to find the right words.

"What? What's the problem?"

"We've run into kind of glitch, honey. Well, more than a glitch. When I got back from the gas station… When I drove past the front of the house…" His next words tumbled out in a rush. "Sweetheart, someone has painted the 'N' sign on our front wall."

Hope looked up at Adam. Cold terror filled her chest. Her voice shaking, she repeated, "The 'N' sign?"

"You know what that means." Adam's voice sounded higher than usual.

"Oh." She stared at him. She could think of nothing to say. When she reached out her arms and held him, she felt his chest trembling.

"Yes, of course. I know what that means. Someone has discovered that we are Christians. They will be coming for us."

CHAPTER THIRTY

Hope

Hope insisted on going out in her housecoat to look at the jagged '*N*' scrawled across the front wall of the yard. Under the streetlight's dim glow the red paint dripped like blood down the sun-bleached wall. Hope stood on the sidewalk in her bare feet, staring.

"The paint is still wet. They must have just done this. But who?"

Adam shook his head slowly. "I don't know." He glanced up and down the empty street. "Let's go inside. Someone will see us."

As they walked back into the house, Hope made no attempt to hide her anger. "It's Brian. I know it is. He's always had it in for us, ever since we got married. It's one of his gang."

"But how would he have found out?" Adam collapsed into a chair at the kitchen table, his head in his hands.

Hope took a long look at him. "I'll make some coffee. We need to think."

As they drank their coffee, they tried to figure out who could have discovered their secret. *They must have accidentally revealed their faith to someone. But who?* Hope glanced at the kitchen clock.

"Adam, we're just wasting time. It doesn't matter who did this or how they found out. We've got to leave. We were leaving anyhow. We'll just have to go sooner."

"We'll have to go right away." Adam said. "As soon as we get packed up, we're going."

"You mean right now?" Hope's eyes were wide with fear.

Adam nodded. "They'll come for us in the middle of the night so that no one will see them. We've still got a few hours. But the sooner we're out of here, the better."

"Okay," she whispered. "I'll get dressed and get stuff ready as fast as I can."

Adam stood up. "There's some left-over beige paint in the garage. I'll go paint over the 'N' now. With luck, no one else has seen it…" His voice trailed off.

"You go," Hope said. "I can get everything packed up."

Adam hurried out to the garage.

Hope pulled on a pair of beige jeans and a matching T shirt. *So that I blend into the desert.*

She glanced at her unfinished grocery list. "Water first of all," she muttered to herself. She grabbed a case of bottled water from the pantry and placed it at the back door. She opened the fridge. *Carrots, cheese, some fruit.* She tossed them into the open camp cooler. An orange rolled across the floor and under the table. *Just calm down, calm down.*

Hope stood in the middle of the kitchen, taking several deep breaths and exhaling each one slowly. Then she filled a grocery bag with canned food.

"The can opener," she reminded herself aloud and tossed it into one of the bags. *Nothing that needs cooking…* she could hear Adam's words: *"Some lighter stuff for the backpacks when we have to start walking."*

"So—bread, peanut butter, nuts, dates. I guess that'll keep us alive," she spoke into the empty kitchen. She stopped packing, abruptly straightening up.

"Keep us alive? What am I thinking? Of course we'll be okay. But it's so hot… Please, God, let us be okay," she prayed aloud as she lugged several bags of groceries out to the garage and stacked them on top of the sleeping bags in the back of the jeep. As she turned around, she almost bumped into Adam as he came out of the kitchen carrying the case of water. He removed the bags of groceries.

"Heavy stuff goes on the bottom, honey." He smiled a taut smile as he handed Hope a couple of bottles of water for the front seat and placed the remainder of the case on the floor in the back. He piled the groceries on top.

"Sorry. I'm not much of a packer at the best of times." She paused. "And this sure isn't the best of times."

"It's okay, honey. We'll be okay. It's natural for us to be scared." They stood together, hugging.

Finally Adam said, "Got your clothes?"

"I'll get them."

"Just an extra pair of jeans and the camping stuff," Adam called out after her. "That's all we can take."

"I know," Hope flung over her shoulder. "I won't pack any of my finery." She managed a crooked grin.

As she stuffed jeans, a T shirt and a heavy jacket into the duffle bag on the bed, Hope looked around the small bedroom. She turned to find Adam standing in the doorway.

"I know how you feel, honey. I hate to leave all this, too." He grabbed a few of his clothes, placing them on top of Hope's in the duffle bag. He talked as he worked. Hope was glad to see he was back to his usual efficient self.

"I've thought of where we can spend the night," he said, as he added his heavy jacket and zipped the bag closed. "We'd attract too much attention at highway security if we tried to leave at this late hour. But we can't stay at a hotel in the city—someone would spot our red jeep. We'll have to hide it somewhere. We can get out of the city limits to Thousand Palms Park without going through any checkpoints. And nobody will be in the park this late. We can spend the night there."

"I remember the day we visited the park," Hope said. "The palms were so old and so tall. I asked you if there really were a thousand of them and you said I could count them if I wanted to."

Adam smiled. "Yeah. Well, remember how the palms had never been trimmed and the dead branches hung to the ground? They'll be perfect to hide under. We'll just park the jeep under those palms and then in the morning we'll backtrack through the city again so that we go through Omar's check stop to the highway. I think he's our best bet. He will just think we're heading out on another camping trip."

Hope nodded numbly.

"It'll be okay, sweetheart," Adam said as he held her close.

She nodded. "I put a thermos of hot soup in the jeep. We can have that later. That will be our last hot food for a while, I guess. Let's go, Adam."

She put on her abaya and veil and joined Adam at the back door. They paused together at the doorway, looking back at the kitchen.

"I learned to cook here," Hope whispered. "You ate some funny meals."

Adam gave her a hug. "I'll pray," he said. Together they bowed their heads. "Dear Lord Jesus, we ask you to bless whoever comes to live here after us as You have blessed us."

"Amen," they said together.

"We have to leave just like the Christians who owned this house before us had to leave," Hope said, as she climbed into the jeep. "Do you suppose they prayed for whoever came after them, like we did?"

Adam reached across to take her hand. "I think they probably did. And I believe their prayers were answered, don't you?"

"Yeah." Hope's cheeks were wet under her veil.

"Honey, we'll have another home, and we will love it just like we loved this one. We'll build a new life together and it will be better than this one. I promise you."

"I know." She sniffed back her tears. "God willing."

Adam backed the jeep out of the driveway. Hope twisted in her seat, looking back until they had turned the corner. She suddenly remembered she had forgotten her red New Testament in the bottom of her closet. *It's okay. There will be plenty of Bibles where we're going.*

They spent a mostly sleepless night huddled together in their sleeping bags in the front seat of the jeep. They left Thousand Palms before dawn. As Adam backed the jeep from under the overhanging palm branches, Hope reached into the back seat for the box of crackers she had tossed on top of the jumble of supplies.

"For my morning sickness," she said, noticing Adam's raised eyebrows.

"If I could take some of it from you, you know I would." he said.

"Guess you don't know what you would be taking on." She chewed on a cracker. "Sorry, don't pay any attention to me. I'm just tired and crabby. I'll be okay. It would help if you didn't hit too many bumps today."

"Hah!" Adam snorted, "Honey, I'm a tour guide, not a magician." When Hope remained silent, he added, "I'll do my very best. And we'll stop whenever we can, okay?"

Hope nodded.

The early morning air was cold. Hope grabbed her jacket from the back seat. They drove back through the sleeping city in silence, reaching the outskirts just as the first rays of the sun glowed pink behind the mountains and the Call to Prayer sounded. They both jumped, then turned to each other, laughing nervously. The few cars that were on the road pulled over. Men were laying their prayer mats on the ground beside their cars.

"We have to stop," Adam said. "They'll notice if we don't."

"I know. Just think—this will be the last time you do this, Adam."

"Yeah." He pulled over and after rummaging in the back of the jeep, finally located his rolled-up prayer mat. Placing it on the shoulder of the road, he knelt and with forehead touching the ground, he joined the rest of the valley in prayer. Hope remained in the front seat, fidgeting and glancing at her watch several times.

"Finally!" she said, as Adam climbed back into the jeep. "What did you pray about?"

"I prayed that the border patrol wouldn't be anywhere near where we want to cross. And I prayed for help with this map. It's rather vague when we get close to the border."

"We'll be fine," Hope's voice sounded strained even to her own ears.

They drove on in silence.

"Just the check stop left now," Adam said, as they reached the city limits. "I hope Omar is on duty."

"Me, too. I never thought I'd see the day I'd be praying he would be on duty, but I am."

As they approached the large stop sign, they saw the familiar bulky figure of Omar slouched against the guard house.

Hope silently mouthed her *Thank You, Jesus* prayer as she and Adam exchanged glances. They pulled over to the kiosk. Omar leaned against the jeep on the driver's side, bending down, and looking past Adam to leer at Hope.

"Well, if it isn't the two lovebirds. Going out for a hot time in the desert? But it's going to be too hot for even you two, today, Adam. Haven't you heard the forecast? A record high. And a storm expected tonight. Not a good time to go camping."

Hope felt the same wave of revulsion she always experienced when she encountered Omar. She looked down at the floor, as she usually did, glad that her veil hid her expression.

"We'll give it a go, anyway," Adam responded.

Omar peered into the back seat piled high with the jumble of sleeping bags and supplies. "Looks like you're going to be gone longer this time."

"Yeah. We expect to be gone for a few days. Inshallah." Adam replied. "Not sure exactly when we will be seeing you again, but don't get concerned if we don't check back for a while."

Hope wondered why Omar was being extra chatty this morning. *Just let us pass,* she fumed. Her anger turned to alarm as Omar placed his hand on the roof of the jeep.

"I won't get concerned," Omar said. "You know the desert better than anyone around here." Suddenly Omar moved his hand from the roof and placed it on Adam's shoulder.

"Good luck, Adam. It's been an honour to know you."

Hope jerked her head sideways to look at Omar and for the first time their eyes met.

"You, too, little lady," he smiled.

Hope nodded. Omar stepped back from the jeep, gave two sharp slaps on the canvas roof, and motioned the car behind them to move forward.

Adam pulled away slowly. Neither of them spoke until the guard house was out of sight.

Hope turned to Adam. "He knows."

Adam nodded. "Yeah, he knows. But he won't say anything. At least not until the morality squad asks him if we passed through here. Then he'll have to tell them. But he would have stopped us now if he wanted to turn us in. I wonder how he found out? I guess that means other people know, too."

"I'm just so amazed he'd let us go," Hope said. "Do you suppose he's a Christian?"

"I don't think so," Adam replied. "But he's a good man. You never know about people, do you?"

"I guess you were right when you told me he was a good guy."

"Well, let's just hope the others who know will keep quiet, too—at least give us time to get closer to the border. This means I can't take the road I'd planned. It's the most direct way, but they will be looking for us there. We'll have to take a different route south. It will take us much longer."

"I still can't believe it." Hope hardly heard what Adam had said. "Omar let us go."

"Well, believe it. Most people will be kind if given a chance."

Hope spoke slowly. "Yes, if they are only given a chance. I think Nana is right—there are a lot of people who don't agree with some of Unity's laws."

They drove on in silence, following the highway for only a short distance before Adam made a sharp turn onto a narrow gravel road. Hope took one look ahead and reached for her package of candied ginger. They bumped and jounced their way for a few more miles. Adam slowed the jeep to almost a crawl as the trail grew more rutted, until finally they were following just two faint tire tracks in the sand. Soon even those marks disappeared. Adam stopped the jeep. Reaching into his jean pocket, he unfolded the crumpled map.

"We're taking a roundabout route, but I think we'll get to the same locations marked on the map, if Nana and Mike knew what they were doing," he muttered, half to himself.

"I heard that." Hope sat up straight. "Of course they knew what they were doing. They got directions from reliable sources. We're not the first ones who have followed that map."

"And did they all make it safely to the border?"

"How would I know?" Hope immediately regretted her cranky tone. She could feel nausea climbing in her chest. She paused to look earnestly into Adam's eyes. "Oh Adam, let's not argue at a time like this. I'm getting out to throw up. You study the map some more."

When she climbed back into the jeep a few moments later, she had removed her black garments. "What should I do with these? Take them with us or leave them here?"

"Keep them with us. We don't want to leave any clues about which way we've headed."

Hope tossed the garments into the back of the jeep. "Nana would say today will be a scorcher. Mmmm… This is much cooler. Besides, I blend into the desert better in these clothes."

They gazed at the expanse of wilderness spread before them. Except for a hawk circling in the cloudless sky, there was no sign of life. Muted shades of beige, grey, and occasional swatches of gray-green scrub brush met their eyes.

Adam turned to look at her. "You've dressed perfectly for the desert. You blend right in. Except for your dark hair."

"I almost forgot," Hope said. "Nana left us a farewell gift. She said to open the packages once we were on our way." Hope reached for a large paper bag she had placed at her feet. She handed Adam a gift-wrapped parcel, keeping a smaller one for herself. "One for you and one for me."

They unwrapped the packages together.

Inside each package was a light tan hat with a wide brim.

"That's it? That's our gift?" Hope stared at the hat in her hand.

"Well, they're nice hats," Adam said cheerfully. "Never saw anything like them before. Look, the label says, "Indestructible, guaranteed for life and floats on water."

"Yeah, that's just what we need in the desert, a floating hat." Hope was examining the label inside of the hat. "Made in Canada," she read out loud. "How on earth did Nana get these for us? From Mike, probably." Her voice grew more excited. "Look, there's a secret pocket inside. Something's in it. I'll bet she put a message in it."

Adam watched as Hope unfolded a scrap of paper.

"Oh," she said, disappointment ringing in her voice. "Just two words, *God bless.*"

"Well, there's money in mine," Adam said. "Must be Canadian bills—each one is a different colour. Pink, blue, green, brown."

Hope was busy sorting out the bills she found in her hat. "Mine's Mexican money. We're going to need this. We didn't even think of it, did we? Nana is so practical." Hope took the Canadian bills from Adam's hand and stuffed them into the pocket of her hat. "Once we reach Canada we'll use this."

"*If* we ever reach Canada," Adam said in a low voice.

"Of course we will. Don't be so pessimistic." Somehow Nana's gift of the hats had cheered her up. "We'll be fine." Hope clamped Adam's hat on his head before putting on her own. "See, we're Canadian already. We have the hats and the money. Now all we have to do is speak the language, eh?" She laughed. "Drive on, eh?"

"Did you ever hear Nana say 'eh'?" Adam asked.

"No, not before we all knew she was Canadian, then I heard her say it a couple of times. Guess she thought she could finally relax in front of us."

Adam grinned and they resumed their slow journey through the trackless terrain.

After several moments had passed, Adam suddenly said, "I will always be American, you know."

"Of course you will, silly. So will I. No one expects us to change. Nana says Canadians will always shelter Americans—like they did in their embassy in Iran and then when 9/11 happened. Did your folks ever tell you about that—the terrorist attack at the World Trade Centre in New York—and other places in America?"

"I did hear something about that happening a long time ago," Adam said. "But when I asked questions, nobody wanted to talk about it."

"Nana told me about it a few days ago when I was wondering if we were really welcome in Canada. She was only in kindergarten, but she remembers 9/11. It was a big deal in Canada. They were all watching television as the planes crashed into the towers and they thought some sort of war had begun. All the planes in America were grounded and no planes were allowed to land from overseas. So Canada took in all those planes, Adam, even though they didn't know what was happening—or if more terrorists were on the planes, or what. All the runways of their airports were full of parked airplanes. People took everyone right into their homes for several days. Nana says Canadians always remember it. They even made a musical play about it."

"I know they took in runaway slaves from the southern States, before the Civil War," Adam said. "Found that in an old history book. Well, they're still taking us in today, aren't they? North still means freedom."

"Yeah. Nana says they've had to tighten up their borders now, though, to make sure people coming in really are seeking freedom and not trying to take over their country like they did America. Then she said something funny, Adam. She said when they get mad at Americans they call us their noisy neighbours who live downstairs."

"Are they quieter than we are?"

"Nana says they are—and I guess she's a good example of that, isn't she?"

"She certainly moved mountains, though," Adam said, "for such a quiet person. Maybe we should be worried about those Canadians up there." He laughed.

"Nana says we'll like living there. But we can come back whenever we like. Some people do come back even today, as missionaries, like Mike. Nobody knows how many are living down here."

Adam turned to look at her. "That's really risky."

"Well, no more risky than you smuggling Bibles."

"I guess so. Do you want to come back? If we make it, that is."

"When we make it, you mean. Sure, I do. But we have to see what God has in store for us. Maybe we'll come back, maybe we won't. We'll just have to trust the Lord. I don't want to raise a child—or children—under Unity's rule, though. Maybe when our family is grown up and it's just you and me we could come back, as missionaries. Or maybe America will be free by that time and we could all come back."

"I hope so," Adam spoke softly.

"Well, that's my name," she said brightly. "So we will hope and pray, eh?"

"Right. Hope and pray. I've figured out the map. I think if we go in this direction we'll be okay."

Hope wondered if he knew she could hear the uncertainty in his voice.

The jeep bounced over rocks and around boulders on the flat expanse of desert as the sun climbed higher in the sky.

Hope fought to stay awake but she felt drowsiness overtaking her in the stifling heat. Several times her chin fell on her chest and she jerked herself to attention, feeling she should be awake to keep Adam company. In spite of her best efforts she finally fell asleep, her head lolling on her shoulders with each jolting movement of the jeep. She dreamed she was watching airplanes land on a crowded runway—plane after plane touched down. *But why are they making such an odd humming sound?* She woke up, but the humming sound continued.

She straightened up in her seat and looked over at Adam. "What's that odd noise?"

"A plane." he said. His voice sounded strained.

"Is it coming our way?" Hope whispered.

Adam stopped the jeep and they both listened as the faint hum grew to a rhythmic throbbing.

"Yeah, it's coming our way," Adam said. "It's probably Jim in the air patrol. It's our unlucky day. They don't have the money to fly every day. I was hoping this would be one of the days they didn't patrol."

A small yellow plane approached them. Looking up, they could clearly see the familiar black markings of Unity's security unit. Hope ducked her head as the plane dropped altitude and whizzed over the jeep.

"That was close," she said.

"Not that close, but it's a natural reflex to duck. He's just buzzing us."

The plane climbed higher to circle over them again. Then it buzzed them a second time. Again, Hope ducked. The pilot dipped the wings before the plane climbed higher to finally become only a dot in the cloudless sky.

Adam breathed a sigh of relief. "Jim always does that. Comes in really low, buzzes the jeep, then does the wing-wag thing. The tourists love it. He'll think we're just out for a drive today. No problem." He glanced over at Hope.

She sat stiffly in her seat.

"No problem, honey," he repeated. "It's okay."

Hope was breathing heavily. "You mean he won't report us?"

"He won't report us right away, anyway. But when he hears we are missing—which he will—sooner or later—he'll report where he last saw us. I hope not, but probably."

Hope's eyes widened with fear. "When will he find out, do you think?"

"I don't know. Maybe not till he gets back to the airport. Or maybe right away on his radio." He paused. "We have to assume he will find out soon and that he'll report seeing us. So we're going to have to change our route. Again. Right now. It's probably best if we get away from this area entirely and hide out for the day. It's getting too hot to travel further, anyway."

"What about Nana's map?"

"We can't follow that now. This changes everything. We have to take a longer way to the border, not as easy for us, but somewhere they would never think to look." Adam was silent for a few moments. "Probably our best bet is the hills. They won't look there."

"Why not?"

"No roads, no path, it's too dangerous."

Hope stared at him. "Okay. Whatever you say."

"I'm sorry honey. This is our best chance. We'll take the jeep a few miles further, put our tarp over it and cover it with some scrub brush. That'll make it hard to spot from the air. We'll have to leave it there, carry our food and water in our backpacks."

Hope nodded, swallowing hard on the lump of fear forming in her throat.

They had driven only a couple of miles when Hope commented on a high mound of earth off to their right. Adam slowed the jeep to a crawl.

"Look at that, Adam. It looks like somebody was here with a bulldozer and made that mountain of sand. Why would anybody do that way out here in the middle of the desert?"

Adam didn't answer.

"Have you ever seen this before, Adam?"

"Nope, never been out this way before."

"Drive closer and let's stop for a minute. I want to take a look. Maybe it's something to do with the native people's religion or something."

Adam didn't think they had time to stop, but Hope insisted.

They stood for several moments staring silently at the high pile of earth.

"It's been here for a long time," Adam finally said. "You can tell by the bushes growing on it."

Hope turned to Adam as he spoke, but he didn't meet her eyes. He was staring into the distance. Her hand flew to her mouth as she realized what the mound of earth was.

"There are bodies in there, aren't there?"

He nodded, still not meeting her eyes.

"Christians?" she asked.

"Some, I'm sure."

"Nobody knows they're here," Hope said.

"God knows." Adam finally met her gaze.

"And *we* know. Adam, we have to do something."

"Like what? There's nothing we can do."

"We can leave a marker." Hope stooped and began gathering stones. "Let's make a cross for them. I'm just glad I don't know any Christians who might be buried here."

Adam looked away again. "I'm glad you don't, too, honey. Let's get this cross done and get out of here."

Several minutes later they were on their way again. They drove in silence until Adam stopped the jeep beside a dry wash overgrown with desert scrub. They rummaged through the bags of groceries, choosing food and bottled water for their backpacks and piling it all on the banks of the deep gorge past floods had carved in the desert floor.

"We ought to manage fine with this," Adam said. "You stay up on the bank. I'll drive the jeep into the wash and get a few more things we need. Then we'll cover it up with branches."

Hope sat on a rock, watching Adam manoeuvre the jeep on an angle down the steep banks of the wash. She heard a low rumbling sound. *That's odd. Sounds just like a freight train coming toward us.* And then she remembered Adam's words on a camping trip last year.

"Adam," she screamed. "Get out, get out."

He had heard the sound, too and was already half way up the bank.

She reached her hand out for him and hauled him to safety just as a torrent of muddy water swept through the wash, carrying with it small boulders, shrubs, cacti and what Hope was sure was a snake. In the next moment their jeep became part of the raging river. They watched as it tumbled end over end, eventually disappearing from sight. The rush of water slowed to a trickle. They stared into the gorge as an eerie silence surrounded them.

Hope was the first to speak. "Well, I guess we don't have to camouflage the jeep now." When Adam didn't answer, she said, "I'm just trying to make the best of it, honey. We were going to walk anyway. Things could have been worse, you know. *You* could have been in that jeep."

"You know what was still in that jeep, Hope? Our GPS and the map. We needed those things."

Hope took a deep breath. "We will just have to trust God that we can get through without them. I am thankful you are alive. Aren't you?"

"Yes, I'm thankful to God. Sure, we'll just trust God that we make it. That's the best we can do."

Hope thought of how often she had heard that phrase in the last few weeks. "If I hear someone say *'that's the best we can do'* one more time, I think I'll throw up," she said. And then she did. "See, I told you."

Adam put his arm around her. "When we find some shade we can stop for the day. I think I see some big boulders over there." He pointed into the distance. Hope could just make out some blue-gray lumps on the horizon. "Maybe there will be a place to crawl in out of this heat."

They pulled on their backpacks and started walking. Adam glanced at Hope trudging along beside him. "Make sure you drink lots of water, honey. We don't want to get dehydrated."

"Do you know where we are?" Hope asked.

"Not a clue. I've never been here before. We could be in Arizona for all I know. But here's a barrel cactus. Remember what I told you?"

"Yeah. A barrel cactus always leans south. So we'll just follow the cacti all the way to the Mexican border?"

"Well, more or less. We'll make it, don't worry."

They spent the better part of the afternoon walking toward the far-off boulders, resting several times, but only for a few minutes.

"It's better not to stay out here in this mid-day heat," Adam explained.

"Yeah. Mad dogs and Englishmen go out in the noon day sun," Hope said.

"Where did you hear that?"

"Nana used to say it to me when I was little and wanted to sit around the pool when it was too hot. Her family came from England and I think it was a favourite English saying, came from the days the English were in India."

"You are a treasure trove of knowledge, did you know that? Even if you never went to school."

"Well, thank Nana for that. She was a really good teacher. She has two university degrees, you know.

"No kidding? What did she study?"

"The psychology of the different world religions."

"That figures."

They finally reached their destination—a huge outcropping of rocks.

"It looks like there's a cave over there," Adam pointed. "We can crawl in there until it cools off."

"You check for snakes." Hope stood outside the cave's small opening.

"Everything's good," Adam announced a few minutes later. "Come on in. We can rest for a while and then eat something."

She crawled into the coolness of the cave. Inside, there was room to stand up. Hope stood for only a moment as her eyes adjusted to the semi-darkness. Then she lay down on the sandy floor. The last thing she remembered was Adam tucking her backpack under her head as a pillow.

She woke some time later. At first she thought she might be dreaming. *Strange noises? Again?* She had never heard anything like this. She leaned on one elbow to listen. *Singing? Howling? Was someone moaning?* She exhaled a sigh of relief when she realized what it was. "It's only the wind," she said out loud.

Adam woke and sat up.

"It's only the wind," Hope said again, noting the frown on his face.

"Must be the storm Omar warned us about. That's kind of a mixed blessing."

"What do you mean?"

"It's good because our tracks will be covered by the sand and also nobody will come out looking for us in a sand storm. But it's bad because we can't go any further. We'll just have to wait it out." He stepped to the mouth of the cave, bending to look outside. "Fortunately, the wind is coming from the other side of these rocks. Otherwise, we'd be breathing sand right now."

Even so, sand had sifted over their backpacks and Hope felt grit between her teeth.

Adam searched in their packs. "Let's eat now, while we still have some light, then we can move as far back into the cave as possible. Might as well catch a good night's sleep while we can," He opened a can of beans and found a spoon for each of them. "Canned peaches for dessert."

"Yum. I tucked in a couple of candy bars, too," Hope said.

Adam held up two dripping packages. "Looks like they didn't survive the heat."

Hope looked down at the pool of melted chocolate forming in the sand at his feet. "Will *we* survive the heat, Adam?" Her chin quivered.

"Sure, we will. We just have to keep going. We'll keep heading south as soon as this storm passes. We'll make it. Not to worry."

"Okay, if you say so. At least it's cool in here. Let's snuggle. We've got a long night ahead of us."

They curled up together and slept until the faint light of daybreak entered the cave.

They stood outside the cave, surveying the vast expanse of desert stretching into the distance before them. The wind had stopped sometime during the night, but not before it had obliterated their footprints. Sand had sifted over the sharp rocks and scraggy shrubs, creating rounded mounds which softened the desert landscape. In the pale dawn light, the desert glowed pink.

"Wow," Hope said. "It's really beautiful, isn't it?"

"Beautiful, but dangerous," Adam said. "Let's eat and get going before it gets too hot to travel. If we don't make it today, we'll have to find some shelter to spend another night."

* * *

They didn't make it to the border that day. As it grew darker and the stars began to appear, they found themselves hunkered down behind the only shelter they could find—a few rocks, not more than two or three feet high. As it turned out, the cave had been a luxury.

"Oh, no," Adam said, as they heard the low moans of the wind begin again. They ate their food in silence. Overnight the wind picked up strength and by morning the blowing sand had penetrated their clothing. Adam scratched his chest under his shirt. Hope gave up trying to shake the sand out of her long hair. She emptied sand from her boots before she put them on.

The wind was still blowing as they set out to walk again, but as Adam said, "It's not as bad. At least we can see where we are going."

They tied their extra T-shirt over their mouth and nose, pulled their hats down low on their foreheads, adjusted their sunglasses and plodded onward. As they picked their way around the scrub brush and cactus, their eyes on the ground at their feet, Hope's backpack grew heavier with each step.

They stopped around noon. Hope plunked down on the hot sand and peeled an orange. She handed it to Adam and started peeling a second one. She wasn't sure how much food they had left.

"I'm not even sure I care, anymore," she said.

"Of course you care. You have the baby to think about."

"I'm not forgetting about the baby. I think about it every time I throw up."

Adam sat beside her in the sand. "Hope, remember when you told me about Nana's experience of being somehow safe in God, in Christ?"

Hope nodded. Her tears washed clean furrows through the sand caking her cheeks. "Yeah. She told me I should see myself where I really am—in Christ, no matter where I might find myself in the future."

"So, here we are. And here Christ is. We're almost there. I can feel it. Have some water and let's get going again."

We're almost there. Hope kept repeating Adam's words to herself as she placed one foot in front of the other.

They stumbled resolutely on through the bleak landscape. Not a sound could be heard. Suddenly a shadow passed overhead. In alarm they looked up. An eagle soared low above their heads.

It lazily circled above them. Then it flew straight south until it was lost to sight. Hope and Adam exchanged glances, too exhausted to speak their thoughts.

"That's Nana's sign," Adam finally said.

Hope nodded.

Energized by the sighting, they resumed their journey.

Hope saw it first—sunlight reflecting off something in the distance. She gestured to Adam.

"There," she said, pointing. Her voice sounded loud and harsh in the silence.

"It's the border fence." Adam nodded. "Thank goodness it's not the wall. It's the wire section we've been looking for."

The fence seemed to shimmer and disappear and then reappear again in the hazy distance.

They plodded on, conscious only of their laboured breathing and the oppressive heat. Sweat ran down their foreheads and into their eyes. As they came closer, they could plainly see the fence— chain link steel—with five rows of razor wire coiled on top.

They stood staring at the barrier in front of them. "It must be more than twenty feet high," Hope whispered into the strange silence surrounding them.

"There's got to be a way through," Adam said.

"Just use the wire cutters. We'll worry about crossing at the right place once we're on the other side."

"The wire cutters were in the jeep, Hope."

"Oh."

Hope's bloodshot eyes looked up and down the fence. "Nana said to look for the sign of a fish woven into the chain links. You go that way and I'll follow along the fence this way. We'll find it." Adam didn't move. His head hung down. "We'll find it, Adam.

You go that way." She gave him a gentle push and started trudging along the barrier, looking carefully at the silver steel links close to the bottom of the fence.

She had gone only a few yards when she called out, her voice seeming unnaturally loud in the still desert air. "Here! Here it is!"

Adam ran to her. They stood side by side, staring at the clear outline of the ancient Christian symbol. The new wire outline of the fish sparkled silver, but otherwise blended in perfectly.

"You'd have to know what you're looking for to find that." Adam's face held a look of wonder. "Now, how do we get through?"

"Nana said pull on the wire at the bottom."

He bent down and pulled at the coil connecting the fence to the steel pole. The wire mesh easily pulled away from the pole. "Look at that! It's not connected here! We can crawl underneath. I'll hold it up for you."

Hope fell to the ground. Not bothering to check for thorns or sharp stones, she scrambled through the opening. She stood up and held the fence as Adam pushed their backpacks through the opening and then crawled through himself.

"Come on, come on," she said impatiently.

Adam replaced the steel coil so that the fence appeared to be attached to the pole again. They joined scratched and bleeding hands as they trudged toward a small building barely visible in the distance.

"Please, God, let us be safe." Hope spoke the words out loud.

As they drew closer they could see a man and a woman standing on the crumbling porch of a weather-beaten shack. The man held a rifle.

"Maybe we should go back now," Adam said.

"We can't go back. They've seen us. Just pray we've come to the right place."

Hope called out in her loudest voice, "We are thirsty."

It seemed like an eternity passed before the woman on the porch called back,

"Tenemos agua viva para que beba." And then in heavily accented English, "You two look terrible."

Hope's heart sank.

"Well, come on in," the woman said. "We have Living Water for you to drink."

Together Adam and Hope staggered to freedom.

Epilogue

Banff, Alberta, Canada
In The Canadian Rocky Mountains
Christmas Eve

Baby Aishah Natalie's emerald eyes blinked at the bright lights on the Christmas tree. Hope had insisted Adam buy a real tree—not an artificial one.

"The biggest tree we can fit into the living room," she had called after him as he trudged down their front sidewalk pulling a toboggan through the deep snow. They both laughed when he returned with a tree so tall they had to saw a couple of feet off the bottom.

"It looked a lot smaller in the tree lot," Adam said, as they struggled to pull the tree through the front door and into their living room.

The people at their church had made it their Christmas project to provide Hope and Adam with decorations for their first Canadian Christmas. "Thank you, thank you. We'll use all of them," Hope had promised, teary-eyed as she surveyed the piles of tinsel, holly garlands, sparkling baubles, angels, stars, and even a sprig of mistletoe.

"And one large star for the top of the tree, just like in Mom's novel," she said to Adam as they unpacked box after box of decorations.

"Hope, I know you told them you'd use all of these, but you can't possibly use all this stuff in our small house."

"Yes, I can," Hope insisted.

And she had.

When she had decorated the tree to the point that it threatened to topple over, she proceeded to adorn every object in sight with greenery or brightly coloured ornaments. The fireplace mantle, each picture frame and available surface in every room of the cozy house held some sort of decoration.

She placed the Nativity scene figures on the coffee table. Each time she passed by it, she bent to re-arrange an animal or a shepherd or one of the wise men. Finally, she decided to leave the arrangement details to Adam when he came home from his skiing lesson.

When Hope heard him on the front step, stomping the snow from his boots, she ran to open the door, eager to show off her decorating skill.

"What a transformation," he said. "The wreath on the outside of the door, and those bells you hung there—a nice touch." He sniffed deeply. "Mmmm... smells like a pine forest in here. It's amazing what one tree will do."

"And I hung up the mistletoe, so you have to kiss me," Hope said, standing on tiptoe, eyes closed, waiting for his kiss.

A beardless Adam bent to kiss her.

"Wow, that's some cold kiss," she said, "but such a gorgeous cleft chin even if it is a bit chilly." They both laughed.

"Maybe I should grow back my beard?"

"Naw, I prefer your cold kisses."

After dinner they stood at the living room window, watching feathery snowflakes float lazily downward. Adam held their sleeping baby in one arm. His other arm was around Hope.

"Listen," she whispered. The sound of church bells echoed faintly, muffled by the falling snow. "Did you ever think you'd hear bells?"

"No, I never did," Adam said softly. "Let's open the door so we can hear them better."

Hope grabbed a comforter from the couch on her way to join Adam at the door. Adam wrapped it around the three of them, making sure baby Aishah Natalie was warmly covered. The family stood in the open doorway.

Their new life in Canada had brought many never-before experienced sights and sounds, but tonight seemed to eclipse them all.

"It looks like the Christmas cards people are sending us," Hope said, as she gazed at the scene in front of her.

Adam looked up at the whirling flakes. "Did you know, of the billions and billions of snowflakes that are falling, no two are exactly alike?"

Hope nodded. "Nana said when she was a little girl she used to stick out her tongue and catch a flake. Let's try."

They laughed as the snow melted on their tongues.

"If anyone sees us, they'll think we're crazy," Adam said.

"We are. Crazy in love with this place."

The falling snowflakes had erased Adam's earlier footprints, creating a front yard that was now an unbroken patch of silver-white with an occasional mound where the snow had covered a bush. Soft snow had settled on the top of each post of their white picket fence, and then, as if unwilling to fall to the ground, it continued to gather there, forming a large rounded dome. Hope told Adam it looked like their front yard was now guarded by a row of giant white mushrooms.

"Now I know why Nana called the frosting she covered her cakes with *White Mountain Icing,*" she said.

The couple looked down the street as red, green, blue, and yellow lights decorating the houses blinked back at them.

They could hear the bells more clearly now.

"It's Silent Night," Hope and Adam said at the same time, turning to smile at each other.

> *Silent Night, Holy Night, All is calm, all is bright.*
> *Round yon virgin mother and child,*
> *Holy Infant so tender and mild.*
> *Sleep in heavenly peace, sleep in heavenly peace.*

As the last peal of the bells sounded, they gazed down at their sleeping baby.

"Let's go inside," Hope finally said, shivering slightly. "I'll make hot chocolate."

Snuggling together in front of the fireplace, the baby sleeping beside them on the sofa, they talked softly of their hopes and dreams for their new life.

"We told the immigration people we wanted someplace with mountains and a lot of sunshine, didn't we?" Hope said. "We sure got the mountains."

"We got the sunshine, too," Adam said. "Most days we have clear blue skies with lots of sun. We still have to wear our sunglasses. Just like at home."

"Only colder, eh?" Hope laughed. "But it was warmer when we arrived here last fall and once spring comes it will be warm again." Adam raised an eyebrow. "Well, not hot, maybe," she said. "But warmer. Anyway, I'm looking forward to next winter—all the stuff I'll do. I'm going to learn to ski. And skate, too. I love to watch everyone skating—the little kids with hockey sticks, even the girls. Do you think Aishah will play hockey?"

"If she wants to, she can," Adam said. "What if she wants to figure skate, or snowboard or ski?"

"She'll do them all," Hope said.

"I'll teach you to ski next winter," Adam said. "I'm learning really fast. It's not that hard—kind of like sliding on butter. And snowboarding and cross country skiing is great, too. William says I'll be ready to lead hiking trips by early spring. He says it's not that much different from being a tour guide in the desert."

"Really?" Hope raised an eyebrow.

Adam laughed. "Well, anyway, I'll be bringing in some money."

"We're okay for this first year. The church made sure of that. Don't worry, everything will be fine." Hope looked down as Aishah Natalie squirmed beside her. "Her first Christmas. She'll never know a time when life wasn't peaceful, will she?"

"I hope not. We'll have to do everything in our power to make sure she lives in freedom and peace."

Both of them were silent, staring into the crackling logs of the fireplace.

"Do you think by next Christmas Mom and Dad will have joined us?" Hope said.

"Maybe, honey. We'll just keep praying they'll make that choice." He grinned. "Your mom is pretty persuasive with your dad. Remember that."

"But they've only called Mike three times and he can't tell us much—just that they got a bistro. They haven't seen their grandchild. I can't even send them a picture. That's no way to be a family." Hope's eyes filled with tears. "I can't believe I'll never see them again. They *have* to come here."

"I know, honey, but it's up to them. They know we could sponsor them and they could live with us."

"They'd want to start up a coffee shop here, for sure," Hope said. "And I could help."

"You could," Adam said slowly. "But I think you should take advantage of the education you're being offered. Your friends here are going to school and probably they'll go on to university. You've got to catch up to them. And you want to be an educated mom for Aishah."

"You're right. Nana would have a fit if I didn't at least graduate from high school. I wonder how she's doing as a nanny—seven little girls!"

"I think we know how she's doing," Adam smiled. "That rich guy and his four wives are no match for her. He wanted his girls educated—and bless his heart for that—but I doubt he knew what Natalie would be teaching them."

"She'll be teaching them to think for themselves, just like she did with me. Ever since I can remember, no matter what we were doing—playing, or whatever, she always told me that it was all about freedom to choose. But it's not really her teaching," Hope said. "It's her praying. She never taught me a thing about Christ, and yet look what happened. When Nana prays impossible things happen."

"That's for sure," Adam cuddled Hope more closely.

Both of them were silent.

"Why did she do it?" Hope suddenly burst out. "Why did she leave Canada and risk her life to come down to Palm Springs?"

When Adam didn't answer for a long time, Hope turned and looked at him. "Adam?"

"Because she loved…" He began and then he stopped. He looked at Aishah Natalie sleeping peacefully beside them on the couch. "Because she loved someone so much she was willing to risk her life for them."

"You mean her daughter?"

"Well, yeah, her daughter… and other people."

"And now, she says she'll probably never leave because she loves them all," Hope said. "It's like the Christmas story—loving people so much that you want to live with them, even if it might cost you your life."

Adam nodded.

"Still… Do you think we will have the courage she had—to go back down there—if that is God's plan for us in the future?"

"I think we will," Adam said. "After all, Nana is praying for us." He smiled. "I think we'll probably return some day."

"Because we love?"

"Because we love."

Acknowledgements

I have been inspired by American authors who have risked their lives to publish their memoirs about the choices they have made in their faith journeys. Among them are:

Rifka Barry "Hiding in the Light"

Nabeel Qureshi, "Seeking Allah, Finding Jesus"

Ergun Mehmet Caner and Emir Fethi Caner, "Unveiling Islam"

Esther Ahmad with Craig Borlase, "Defying Jihad"

Ayaan Hirsi Ali, "Infidel" and "Nomad"

And by women's personal accounts of life in Iran following the Revolution:

Azar Nafisi, "Reading Lolita in Tehran"

Betty Mahmood, "Not Without My Daughter" (Also a movie)

And from Saudi Arabia: "Breaking Free: Rahaf Mohammed's Escape to Canada. CBC.ca

Because of space constraints, a full discussion of several interesting concepts mentioned in this novel was not possible. (N for Nazarene, Adoption in Shariah law, Honour killings, Vacation cutting, shirk, ISIS and crucifixion, Abrogation in Islam, WWJD

What Would Jesus Do, and any unfamiliar terms can be easily researched using the internet.)

As always, a heartfelt "Thank You" to my husband, Mike, for his love and support throughout the writing of this novel. I know you must have grown tired of dealing with my angst and insecurities, but you were always there for me. Thank you also to my "First Readers"—Nora, Leslie, Zetta, Nicola, Joan, Donna and Linda. Your comments were invaluable. Thank you to my writing group who listened to excerpts and ideas as the novel progressed. Thank you to my editor, Jim Zang, to Ronda for her computer skills, to John for legal assistance, to José for retrieving the novel from a crashed hard drive.

Please visit my website (www.camalakhayes.ca) for stories of faith and hope, recipes from Aishah's bistro and Natalie's Canadian kitchen, and much more.

Blessings always,
Camala Hayes.

Readers Guide

1. What role does running the bistro play in Aishah's life? What do you think she would have done if Mo had not agreed to divide the bistro into male and female sections?

2. Why did Mo struggle more than Aishah with the decision to take the baby?

3. Forgiving the people responsible for taking her parents and brother was not easy for Aishah. Why did she do it? Are forgiving and forgetting the same thing?

4. Would you have done what Natalie did when she received Karyn's note? Why or why not?

5. Why does Natalie never reveal to Hope that she is Hope's grandmother? Do you think she should have told her? Adam suspects, but does not tell Hope. Aishah and Mo do not tell her. Should any of these people have told Hope the truth?

6. Hope is a spoiled "only child" when she is forced to marry Adam. What do you think is the major reason she finally agreed to the marriage?

7. Who do you think was the biggest influence in Hope's life?

8. Walls are a recurring symbol in this novel: high garden walls, tiny casita walls, the dividing wall in the bistro, heavily curtained walls, walls with no pictures. Discuss the positive and negative role of walls in the lives of Aishah, Natalie and Hope.

9. Natalie explained to Hope how the female eagle carries her young on her wings and shared the mother eagle metaphor for God with Hope when she became a Christian. (The King James Version of the Bible, Deuteronomy 32:11.) Why do you think this metaphor is so important to Natalie? What is your favourite metaphor (or metaphors) for God? Why?

10. Everyone in this novel (with the exception of Brian) either lies or hides the truth in some way. Discuss how and why each character lies.

11. This story is told from the point of view of three women. How would it have been different if it had been told from only one woman's point of view?

12. Who is your favourite female character in this novel? Your favourite male character? Why?

13. When Natalie is arguing with Mo about whether Canada should support the Americans fleeing Unity, she tells him, "We are not only responsible for what we *do*, but also for what we do *not* do." (Martin Luther said, "You are not

only responsible for what you say, but also for what you do not say.") Do you agree or disagree?

14. Discuss how Hope was influenced by the three books available to her: Aishah's novel, The Koran, The Bible. Do you agree with the saying, "The pen is mightier than the sword"?

15. Were you surprised by the choices Aishah, Natalie and Hope make in the end? Why or why not? Do you think Mo and Aishah will someday join Hope and Adam in Canada? Why or why not?

www.camalakhayes.ca

To order more copies of this book, find books by other
Canadian authors, or make inquiries about publishing
your own book, contact PageMaster at:

PageMaster Publication Services Inc.
11340-120 Street, Edmonton, AB T5G 0W5
books@pagemaster.ca
780-425-9303

catalogue and e-commerce store
PageMasterPublishing.ca/Shop

About the Author

Camala Hayes in the pen name of the author who makes her home in Calgary, Alberta, Canada. She and her husband enjoy short stays in the Palm Springs area of California when the snow flies. She holds a Bachelor of Arts and a Master of Arts degree in the Psychology and Philosophy of World Religions, and a Master of Divinity degree.

Visit her at her website: camalakhayes.ca